Bounty Hunter

Copyright © 2024 Kaylee Jarvis

Contact Info: kaylee@kayleejarvis.com

Book Cover Design : GRAPHICSOULART
Map Design: GRAPHICSOULART
Editor : Whitney Morsillo of Whitney's Book Works
Author Photo : Lisa Jerald Photography
1st Edition 2024

BOUNTY HUNTER

THE BLACK TULIP CHRONICLES

1

KAYLEE JARVIS

Dedication

To my husband.
Thank you for believing in me, for imagining with me, and
encouraging me to make my dreams reality.

KINGDOM OF MONEYRE
THE BLACK TULIP CHRONICLES

OF

SHIFT FOREST

FAE
LOW KINGDOM

OBSID
DES

LUCENT

KIVAN

SHIFT CITY

NESTBUSH VILLAGE

BLACK CANYON DESERT

MERCENARY CAMP

ABYSMAL DESERT

FARLOW
LOW KINGDOM

OCEAN OF
ROGUES

LUCENT
DEEP

FARMLAND

MONEYRE
HIGH KINGDOM

HARBOR OF
MONEYRE

AN
T
VER

LUCENT
MOUNTAINS
NYMPHS

ORLET
LOW KINGDOM

MIDON
LOW KINGDOM

Prologue

Four hundred years ago...

The young king surveys the immense field of black tulips spread before him beneath the light of the three moons—Queens of the Night, Lucentia's favored flowers and named after Lucentia herself. Each flower stands sentinel—still and stoic—within the thick stand of fir trees surrounding them. Their color is pitch black, and when the moonlight hits the petals just so, a hint of deep purple rises from their depths. Some sort of fluffy, tiny bird settles on the pommel of his saddle, quirking its head, an intelligent eye appearing to stare into his soul. It appears to nod and then takes flight with a flutter of wings and feathers. He swallows and slides from the saddle, leaving the reins of his horse with his men.

His best soldiers sit astride their horses around him, all weary from the long and rigorous journey, but prepared to defend him, if need be.

"I go alone," he says, holding a hand out to stop those who move to join him.

He makes his way through the field, noticing the white

birds humming from their nests in the trees, flying and swooping all around him. Tulips appear to bend to either side slightly, creating a small path toward the sheer mountainside ahead. He stares with a furrowed brow at their unnatural movement. *Magic.* He pulls back his shoulders against the unease stirring at the foreign power and continues along the path. What he is looking for, he doesn't know.

After a time, the path of dark flowers guides him to a cliffside with an intricate engraving depicting a woman, the same white birds... and the tulips that surround him, framed as if he simply has to walk through a doorway to greet her. He places a hand on the wall. Nothing.

"Lucentia," he says.

Only the soft flutter of the birds overhead breaks the silence.

He searches the engraving, scanning its details. The path led here, but how to reach Lucentia, the goddess of lucent magic?

Far across the field, he sees his men, waiting. Everything depends on his securing Lucentia's help. The thoughts of his brother-turned-enemy, and the large part of his army that followed him, weighs his shoulders down with sorrow. This is their only recourse. With the continual battles, so many of his people dying... If he does not gain Lucentia's aid, his kingdom will fall.

He clenches and releases his fists, stretching his fingers as he gazes around, trying to decipher what to do next. Moments later, one of the small birds coasts through the air with a freshly picked tulip in its tiny beak. He holds out a large hand and cradles both gently. With intelligent eyes, the bird gives a jerky nod toward the mountainside picture.

He turns toward the engraved, sealed doorway, uncertain.

Never has he taken instruction from a bird. He reaches out a hand and presses against the engraving once more. "Lucentia," he says, unsure if what he's done is correct, but the engraving in the doorway begins to take on color and depth until it's no longer a picture in solid rock, but an opening. Dripping vines obscure what lay beyond, and he looks back once more at the soldiers waiting for him before using a shoulder to push aside the greenery and step through.

He breathes a sigh of relief when he finds a woman in a dress of deepest black that matches the petals of the black tulips standing guard in the field he just crossed. The small, fluffy, white birds surround her and settle on her shoulders in small blobs of stark contrast. He releases the one in his hand, and it joins the flock of others, roosting around their mistress. Black tulips are woven within the almost-white gold of her tresses, and more tulips at her feet spread before him. The greenery and trees, even the stars spattering the dark night sky, seem somehow more vibrant in her presence. Power emanates from her, almost tangible.

"Lucentia, Queen of the Night." The youthful High King kneels before her.

"Rise, King. You are worthy." She considers him with a knowing gaze. "You have a request."

The handsome, battle-hardened king squares his shoulders. "You are known as the goddess of lucent magic, the magic that combats darkness... I am the rightful heir to the throne of Moneyre, but my twin brother does not agree. I exiled him when he attempted to take my life and many of my people left with him. He has led formidable attacks on my kingdom these past years and we tire of warring. Our people are dying needlessly in battle. I would abdicate the throne but—"

"He is not worthy." She finishes his sentence. "I also have a brother who craves the fight." She says it so quietly the king barely hears it. A sad smile pulls at her lips.

She twists the stem of a black tulip between her fingers. The woman contemplates for a moment, her face pale, granite beauty. After what seems an eternity, she finally speaks.

"I am bound with the lucent magic of this world, it, bound with me. I am lucent magic, lucent magic is me. My magic protects and shields from darkness. I *am* the Queen of the Night. The light in the dark." Her voice, both powerful and smooth, pauses as she eyes the king with a shrewd look. "To maintain balance and order I allow humans to work things out amongst themselves, even if it leads to kingdoms destroying one another—a natural course is usually best." She looks at him pointedly.

The king opens his mouth to speak, but Lucentia continues.

"*But* your heart is worthy and your desires noble, which inclines me to offer aid. A gift that requires much from you." She tilts her head to the side and looks at the king. "Are you married, worthy King?"

It seems she already knows the answer, but he shakes his head, confused. "No, Your Majesty."

A serene smile lights her lips. "I will share my magic with you and your kingdom on two conditions, both which will ensure my power is not abused and used for selfish gain."

The king nods his agreement, and she continues.

"First, your soul and those of your heirs, and all kings hereafter, will be bound to your kingdom, and with it, your magic. If your people suffer, *you* will suffer. If your people thrive, *you* will also thrive."

The king considers carefully before nodding. "That is fair. My fate is tied with those of my people."

Now her gray eyes light like liquid silver, and a power he's never felt before rises heavily in their midst.

"Second, you and every heir hereafter must marry and bridge your magic with a Queen of the Night, a Black Tulip, a woman chosen by my magic to maintain the lucent magic your kingdom will require. Your souls together will be inextricably bonded with the kingdom itself. You cannot do it on your own. *Only* a Black Tulip is capable of this."

The king nods, listening carefully.

"With more power comes more responsibility—and risk. If you, or your heirs, fail to do as I have said, gloam will slowly overtake lucent, until, eventually, the lucent will be overcome by gloam entirely, and you will lose the protection my magic, and my Tulips, have offered, leaving your kingdom vulnerable to past and future enemies... and I will not help you. Your kingdom, people, and heirs will perish—engulfed in inescapable darkness." She lets her words sink in for a prolonged moment before she continues.

"As specially chosen conductors of my magic, and chosen by me, my Tulips deserve the deepest of respect and adoration and will be treated as such. If they aren't, I will not send one strong enough to bridge, until a king worthy of her takes the throne. By then, it may be too late. Ensure that you, and your future heirs, do not fail in this." She caresses the soft petals of a tulip in her hand.

The king carefully runs the words through his mind. "Every heir must simply marry and bridge with a Black Tulip, a Queen of the Night. Care for her and protect her. That's your price?" He stares, bewildered that so simple a thing be asked in return for so great protection.

Lucentia nods. "Yes. But beware the jealousies and passions of mortals."

The king lifts a confused brow. "Is that a prophecy?"

"Take it as you will, but let neither you nor your heirs forget it."

"I agree."

"Magic is presented in many forms, different for every person. All born with magic will be marked according to their strongest gifts to show that all are equal and chosen by magic. But you and your heirs will have a different mark, one that will grow with every generation and indicates your direct bond with your kingdom." She stands. "Bare your chest, King."

He does so, his movements sure and unwavering even as the weight of what he's doing settles on his shoulders.

Lucentia's eyes glow silver once again as she places a pale, delicate hand against his heart. The black behind his lids is replaced with warm light, all he can see is light, and behind that light, the width and breadth of his kingdom and people flow through his mind and find a place in his soul. His soul tugs and knots, woven and made as one with the very fabric of his kingdom. It fills his chest, his vision, his blood. Then, curling warmth travels down his upper left arm, down the top of his shoulder blade, and down to his collarbone. Lucentia removes her hand, and the light fades from his vision, but his gaze is drawn to where the still lucent mark now rests, one with the skin of his shoulder, arm, and chest. Wonder lights his eyes as he feels the magic running freely through his veins. His vision sharpens and clears, his hearing amplifies, his senses of touch and smell increase, and his muscles fill with easy power and strength like never before.

Lucentia smiles. "You are a hunter, as will all your heirs be. You will learn to control it, to use it to help your people."

She gestures to the tulip the king still holds in his grasp, its petals tightly hugged together. "You'll need this to bridge your magic with my Black Tulip. Every bridging must take place with a black tulip, not yet in full bloom. Already a woman has been chosen and marked, her magic complimentary to yours in every way. Your soul calls to her, the heat of your magic yearns for her cool—and hers to yours. Go, King, *have care*, and have magic."

"Thank you, Queen of the Night."

Chapter 1

Vera

Present Day

I smack an errant branch out of my face as I stomp through the forest. An unrelenting drizzle has my boots soggy. My contract was canceled last minute, and instead of moving on to the next job—or heading to Mr. Eddieren, who usually hires me between jobs—I have to take what Tatania, the leader of the Tulips, calls a happy *break* to attend the 'yearly required meeting of the Tulips.' I hear it in her sweet, motherly voice, but she doesn't know what a stomach so empty it's collapsing on itself feels like. She's an elf, a rich one. I'm half-fae, half-human, all-orphan, and I'm poor. I'm a Tulip by blood, part of the exclusive group of women nicknamed for the black tulip emblazoned by magic at the base of our necks. A mark that designates us as protectors and strengtheners of kingdoms. It used to be an honor. A mark that tells the world that we can bridge with a king and combine our powers to protect the kingdoms. Except, no one knows if we can anymore. Even if we could, if people knew we still existed, we would be hated and hunted, just like we were before.

What once was a beautiful stone building covered in green,

reaching vines and surrounded by well-kept beds of black tulips appears before me. A long-forgotten building that the forest has decided to overtake and claim as its own. The somewhat majestic entrance still commands, and a now uneven cobbled path leads up to a grand set of stairs that ushers visitors to the pillared doorway. Trees, bushes, and grass now grow where flowerbeds once lay, and invasive tendrils of long, vining plants have attached to the outside of the brick and claimed over half the front wall. The large wood doors are faded, the windows that line the front of the building foggy. A visual representation of the state of the Tulips, unfortunately. I sidestep a stone that sticks up more than the others on my way to the doors. There's no way this place is still safe, but maybe no one cares since the Tulips are supposed to be obsolete. Before I reach the entrance, a soggy white blur soars toward me through the rain, and I smile, even though I know she's going to plaster her wet little body to the side of my neck to get warm in the next few seconds. Rupi lands with a flustered flap of soaked wings and a pitiful sounding *cheep* as she nestles up to my neck.

"You can come," I tell her, "but stay hidden. No shenanigans."

Her responding chirp sounds a little saucy.

The handle at the entrance jiggles loosely beneath my grip, and I hope it doesn't fall off in my hand as I open the resistant door. I step inside a grand main hall with a staircase that splits into two, each curving away from the other and connecting to a landing above. A once-charmed chandelier above hangs dormant. If the door handle hasn't gotten the attention it needs, I highly doubt the chandelier has either, so I intentionally skirt the hall to make sure I'm not beneath it in case it comes crashing to the ground. The state of disrepair is somber, but I've never known it any other way. I pass the stairs, go beneath the landing, and enter the ballroom. I pull my cloak hood down and remove my hair from its messy braid, using it to conceal Rupi's presence. Tatania would never allow a bird to enter the building. Renna and I jokingly call her the dictator of the Tulips, but it's more truth than joke—she runs a tight ship.

The entire back wall is a series of floor-to-ceiling windows, two stories tall, that overlook a deep, green-filled canyon. I've always found it breathtaking. I imagine the deep green walls of the ballroom adorned with heavy curtains, music filling the empty silence, dimmed lights adding intimate warmth, and dancing couples twirling across the wood floor. It could be beautiful again. But the giant room sits empty except for the seven wood chairs placed in a neat semi circle near one of the back windows. To my left is a fragile-looking wood desk, and seated behind it is Tatania's ever-joyful assistant, Lillath. She's not a Tulip, but she's trusted.

"So glad you've made it, and *early*. If only everyone was as eager as us to be here." She smiles widely as she passes me a fancy envelope stamped with my name.

Yes, so eager. I put aside my work and am currently starving so I can sit amidst a group of women that pity me. I keep my mouth shut with my lips shaped into a firm sort of smile as I reach into my pack and pull out the money I've saved to pay the dues. Precious, hard-earned money. My stomach growls as I stuff it into the envelope and seal it with a somewhat messy blob of wax and my personal stamp. I slide it back across the desk and turn before I do something irrational, like snatch it back and head to the nearest tavern to spend it on a month's worth of hot meals. But a sated belly would be exchanged for the loss of anonymity that would come from my bracelet lapsing due to lack of payment. Can't have that.

Lillath busies herself writing something, so I step away to find a seat. Even though I try to step lightly, my boots make loud squishing noises as I cross the dull, wood floor. And unfortunately, as Lillath so happily stated, I'm early. I slump into a seat and try not to care about the puddle of water that is slowly forming beneath my boots as each drip seems to echo across the silent, empty room. I habitually hug the sleeves of the overlarge coat I wear down over my palms and grasp it with my fingers as I cross my arms and wait.

It's not long before a tall woman in a beautiful sea green gown just a shade lighter than the moody green of the walls around us enters the room, pushing a dainty cart full of tiny, feminine pastries, teacups, and a kettle. A large vase of fake, silky-looking black tulips adorns its center. Another Tulip in a gown just as fine walks beside her. Rupi's feathers begin to turn quill-like, scratching at my neck.

"Avenera," Tatania greets me with a smile.

It's strange to hear my given name—the only ones who use it are those who attend this meeting and Mr. Eddieren, the odd fae who's a master at potion making that will take my help whenever I offer. I sit up a little straighter in my chair, smile, and give an awkward half-wave. I never know how to be around these people. The woman beside her, Maven, smiles in a friendly way.

The two women wheel the cart to the middle of the semi circle as the rest of the Tulips begin to trickle in at random intervals. Each seals an envelope with the dues and gives it Lillath, as I did on arrival. I watch as Nova, another noble-born Tulip with a willowy frame, hair of spun gold, and clothed in a silky-looking day dress, takes a seat. Nessa, a mild-mannered woman with pale skin that contrasts starkly against her dark brown hair, sits beside her, and they dive into a conversation.

Those two have been close since I began attending the Tulip meetings as a young girl. One after another, two more enter, children of wealthy merchants and traders, Fina and Petra. Petra has a flawless, tawny-brown complexion and dresses in the latest fashions. Today is a sage green day dress that even *I* might wear.

Fina steps into the room with a look to die for. Her dark brown hair is separated into three, thick, intricate braids, and she flashes me a radiant white smile. Her tan skin glows with healthy, sun-kissed color. Leather, form fitting pants hug her long legs, encased in tall boots, and completed with a shirt that blouses out of a cinched waist piece, and which effortlessly emphasizes her bust *just* enough. I refuse to think of my worn trousers, soggy boots, and man's shirt that neither clings nor emphasizes anything in a complimentary way. In fact, I've been mistaken for a teenage boy on three occasions.

Finally, Renna enters, in a hurry now that she's late. I watch as she quickly stuffs her envelope and practically tosses it into Lillath's hands before she walks over with an apologetic look on her face and promptly takes a seat to my left. She's as poor as myself—I should know since we live together in another city. She's my closest friend, practically my sister. Before I can ask her how her last job went, Fina takes a seat beside me, graceful and ladylike, but with a touch of danger about her. Last I heard, she'd contracted with a second-born prince from one of the low kingdoms as a ship commander to head their exploration and exporting efforts. I can't help but feel small beside her.

Tatania stands before the tea cart, her beauty no more diminished than when I first met her fifteen years ago. As an elf, she ages much slower than the rest of us. I can't decide if that would be a blessing or a curse.

"Welcome to our annual tea, Tulips. I have so missed your presence over the last year. Let's begin with Nova and update everyone on our current accomplishments, shall we?" She gestures to the first woman to her left, and she begins.

Our magic seems to have a taste of all the factions within it, which means as Tulips, we can choose which faction to mask ourselves with. Most of them, like myself, act as Originators since they are our closest match, though all but Renna and I have permanent positions originating lucent magic for healers, weapon charmers, and builders. We're too poor to be chosen for permanent, prestigious positions such as those. Nova has chosen to work under the guise of a hunter, working with animals and training. They make good money since they're rare. All of them have perfectly respectable and appropriate work because they're nobles. And now it's my turn.

Every year I botch my work description, but I've been rehearsing a little, and I think I'm better prepared this time. "I am still working with all five kingdoms' government offices apprehending criminals for reward. Mostly Class B and C, rarely Class A. Class A is pretty dangerous, so I usually avoid assisting with those." I realize I'm saying too much and finish up quickly. "I work with healers sometimes, too." I laugh a little. There. That was professional. At least, I think it is until I see the other women's faces.

They blink at me, some look at me oddly, unable to comprehend what my jobs actually entail. Renna offers a supportive smile, but of course she would. I pretend to miss the flash of pity that crosses Nova's eyes because I hate it—the others have varying looks of distaste at the thought of my choice of work or open mouthed looks of genuine confusion over why I would ever choose to do what I do. I don't blame them—they don't understand. Not only are the majority of the Tulips not forced into the working class because of their upper class birth, but working with bounty hunters is a unique job choice for a woman who isn't of the hunter faction. Especially a woman of my small size and who is untrained in weapons. But they are all wealthy nobles, which makes it much easier to get a permanent position for respectable work with healers, builders, and weapons masters, if they so choose. Those like Renna and I, poor lower class citizens, are forced into contract work, usually in hunting positions, jumping from job to job to survive.

Fina looks at me thoughtfully, and I'm glad that at least there's no judgment in her eyes. I resist the urge to defend myself, knowing it will only worsen their opinion. So, I seal my lips shut and let Renna stumble through her own awkward update, mentioning how she's taken a contract position as an Originator for a Lucent River captain. I force my cheeks not to burn for her. It's the one Originator position most would never want. The Lucent River is more gloam than lucent and very dangerous to travel regularly anymore.

Tatania must sense the tense vibes and quickly invites us to taste the delicate pastries as she serves tea. I waste no time filling my plate, and soon, the awkwardness around Renna and I's choice of work has cooled, and Tatania begins again.

"As our leader, the eldest of our group, I recognize that it is my honor to protect you as best I can." Her eyes scan the seven of us still seated. "I have heard nothing of concern, but as always, please keep your marks hidden and your chosen status as a Tulip a secret. It is for the protection of us all."

Here begins the annual reminder. I honestly don't know why we have to go over this every time. Tulips are obsolete, and no one really knows about us anymore, or cares for that matter. Being a Tulip no longer brings honor and prestige. The last time a Tulip bridged was over two hundred years ago. And to top it all off, we pay for the protection and anonymity magic offers. The cost alone should save me from another torturous lecture, but it won't. So, I fill my plate again, force a pleasant look onto my face, and settle into my hard, edgy chair.

"Never trust the kings." Tatania's light blue eyes turn frosty. "Many, many years ago, the High King approached Lucentia, the gifter of magic. Such a worthy man was he that she allowed him to find her field of Tulips and even granted him entrance to her very presence. And here is where our account differs from the royals." Her voice lowers in a dramatic, ominous fashion. "Lucentia gifted that king and the kings thereafter the Tulips." Her gaze crosses the room, touching on each of ours in the silence. I stop chewing the buttery biscuit in my mouth momentarily. It just doesn't seem right to be eating biscuits and pastries with so solemn a mood. But I had to punch another hole in my belt and cinch it tighter two days ago. I can't afford to *not* eat when it's offered.

Her gaze moves on, and I continue chewing.

"For many years, the High Kings married and bridged with Tulips, ensuring the strength and balance of lucent magic across the kingdom. The kings connected to this very kingdom, and the Tulips ensuring that lucent magic stayed lucent. It was a happy, peaceful time." She smiles as if she were alive then, remembering it fondly. "Then the Originators became jealous, specifically one, Sorana. She claimed that a powerful seer had seen a Tulip bridging with an ancient enemy, resulting in the kingdom being overtaken with gloam and destroyed. What had always been seen as a benefit, our ability to bridge and offer more magic, became the basis of her turning the kings against us. She twisted history and manipulated their minds so thoroughly that soon the Tulips were hunted down and murdered, so dangerous they were said to be." Her voice turns light and wispy, "So detrimental. So useless." Tatania's eyes grow sorrowful. "Because the kings grew so unworthy, hunting us down instead of offering protection, magic no longer sent Tulips powerful enough to bridge. It was many, many years before another Tulip was born bearing the mark of Lucentia herself, the Black Tulip—it was, in fact, me. We assume there is still no king worthy enough and not one of us has shown signs of having the vast power needed to bridge."

She looks around the room. "Our power with lucent magic was more powerful than the most powerful Originators in the kingdom. To my knowledge, none of us bears that amount of magic." She looks around the group, and the other women shake their heads.

I continue chewing.

"So, though we bear Lucentia's mark, we do not appear to have the power our earlier Tulips had. While it would be quite miraculous if one of us was able to bridge at all, we still take precautions so we are not hunted and killed."

She continues, but I try with very little effort to keep my attention tuned to her lilting voice. I've heard the history of the Black Tulips at least fifty times. It's a tradition to share the story and all its warnings every year. Just in case one of us happens to forget not to bridge, I suppose. Or like they fear we might trip and find ourselves accidentally bridged with a king. I pick up a fluffy, scone-like pastry next. In addition to the bracelet we pay dearly for, Tatania says our magic isn't even strong enough to bridge. I trust her, so I continue to eat and think about my next contract.

Tatania is still talking, and I realize I've devoured a ridiculous amount of pastries and at least three cups of tea. A testament to my lack of concern over this issue and my ravenous appetite. In my entire twenty-six years, I've never met the High

King or seen him, and even if I did, he would never recognize me. *Thank you, magic bracelet.* And if he did see me, he'd probably think I was a boy. *Thank you, raggedy men's clothing.* I sip my tea tartly in my baggy shirt. I think the chances are pretty slim this is any sort of concern for us with the precautions we take and the apparent weakness of our magic anyway. Right now, food tops my list of priorities, but the other women sit uptight and still, concern creasing the corners of their eyes.

"In closing, we all wonder, and I'm sure you have observed, that magic has yet to add a truly magic-gifted, powerful Tulip to our group in many years. See it as a positive." She smiles comfortingly. "The only reason Tulips were so powerful before is because the kings were worthy of them and the close proximity and working partnership between kings and Tulips fostered strong magic. Until they change their ways, Lucentia, our wise gifter of magic, will not send one powerful enough to bridge."

A few of the women nod, nervous. This topic is always uncomfortable for them.

"I do encourage you to find a nice man and marry, as it will protect you from any future attempt by the king to force us into servitude again. They can't very well bridge with a married woman."

A great reason to marry. I drain another cup of tea.

"Now remember that Tulip dues are to be paid by the last day of the sixth and twelfth months, or the protections of your bracelet will lapse. I see you've all paid today, so your bracelets are in service and will continue to be. You are safe." She holds out her hands. "Let us finish with our precious oath. Stand with me, Tulips."

We all rise and begin at the same time, our voices echoing against the walls of the bare room as one.

"We will never remove the bracelet and will always pay our dues on time. We will never reveal our Tulip identity. We will never work with soldiers, armies, or kings in any way. We will always attend the annual meeting. We will never bridge with a king."

In the silence, Tatania's smile grows wide. "I will see you all next year. Stay safe, Tulips."

Chapter 2

Ikar

I look across the wasteland before me. What once were rolling hills scattered with neat farms and bounteous crops sit empty and naked. Dead. *It's my fault.* It has to be my fault. As the High King, it is my magic that is bound with our world. There's no one else to blame. It's as if someone washed the vibrant color from a landscape painting and left only the shadows and grays. If I were stronger, my kingdom would be stronger, so they say. But nothing I do stops the dark from spreading, sucking out the lucent magic that we require to survive and protect ourselves, leaving death in its wake. Miles and miles of nothing spread before my eyes, but it's mere illusion. It's not just *nothing.*

I feel its awareness. Drawn to our load of charmed weapons like a moth to flame. To our lucent magic, our energy. The gloam is never satisfied.

My soldiers toss the last of the tents atop a convoy of heavy-laden wagons, four in the middle are loaded with swords, axes, knives, bows, and arrows to bolster my army. The weapons are newly charmed by the weapon masters who created them, of the Maker form of magic and gifted in weaponry. They are the only ones who can charm them in a way that will harness lucent magic, and kill gloam. They come at a hefty price, one so high it feels as if we carry actual treasure straight through a thief-infested land. It's not *if* gloam and its creatures will come... it's when. We stay alert, and rather than the usual low rumble of conversation and comfortable camaraderie between my soldiers, it's quiet. We've been traveling for over a week, the going painfully slow. A journey so important I joined it myself to ensure its protection, but rather than thieves, our greatest enemies are the dark creatures birthed from gloam as we cross the deadened, lifeless land I used to be proud to call my own.

The outlying boundaries of my kingdom have taken the brunt of the darkness, just this year the gloam has moved in further than ever before, but still our Originators protect us, and I owe it to them. Unfortunately, some of our farmland is now desolate like the land we travel, and people are beginning to struggle, not just for lack of magic, but for food, as well.

With that heavy thought on my mind, as it always is, I mount my large war horse, Champion, and give the command to head out. We roll forward slowly, too slowly.

Nadiette takes her usual place beside me, astride a blindingly white horse that matches the armor fitted to her body. There's a confident set to her lips and a glitter of challenge in her green eyes. She craves the fight. She carries only a sword, her best weapon the power of her magic. She's one of the most powerful Originators I've ever met. Her power combined with her team have kept gloam at bay for years, as her mentors did before that. She was raised alongside me, and what once was friendship between young children turned to attraction and then more as we became adults. I couldn't have asked for a more perfect soon-to-be fiancé and future High Queen.

Though nothing has been made official in regard to our relationship, I plan to make it so soon.

I hear the rider coming before he shouts and turn in the saddle to gauge the situation.

"Your Majesty!" The man's face is slicked with sweat, his eyes wide with worry. "A shard beast at the rear of the convoy. The traps are giving out."

I immediately halt the lumbering convoy with a sharp command as I turn and gallop toward the fight, Darvy and Rhosse, my closest friends and two of my top commanders, right behind me.

Champion eats the ground before me with a speed so fast the dead grass blurs beneath us, and still, I push him harder.

I pull the reins up and jump from my horse before he's completely stopped, taking in the deteriorating scene before me as I pull my sword, enchanted and made specifically to fit my hand and height, to wield my magic. At least twenty of my men have combined their magic to create a trap, a sort of shield trapping the shard beast in their midst. It looks as if a giant crushed an obsidian vase and mashed the jagged shards together to create the monster. Gleaming tips of wicked-looking edges catch the light, filled with the gloam mist that pulses from its darkly beating heart at the lower left of its chest, giving it its smoky-black color. Its face is a mottled mess of edges, glass like a row of knives forms a sort of mane. Knives, all of it.

I eye the heart, a spot deeper black than the rest that pulses as the creature gives a roar to match its shard armor, the sound of breaking glass piercing my eardrums so painfully I wince. I hear shouts and cries of pain around me, and some of the men drop their parts of the trap, grasping their ears and panting, falling to the ground, exhausted. More move in to fill their places, deaf as we all might be by now. The creature rears up and charges, slamming its body against a portion of the shield, and I watch in horror as the men fly back with the force of it before more fill their places.

Three men lie unmoving within, warriors brave enough to confront the monster first, now dead. I recognize them, some of the most powerful hunters in my ranks. Dead. *Dead.* My jaw clenches in anger. I hear shouts as the men still standing yell to each other, one pulling more magic here while another takes a break there. But all of them struggle, and if I don't hurry, some will die just from the overexertion of pulling lucent magic where there's not enough. I run forward, ignoring Darvy's shouts from behind me.

"Let me through!" I shout and push past the men holding the shields in place. When they see it's me, their looks of refusal drop to submission, and they immediately release it enough to allow me entrance.

The shard creature turns its black gaze toward me with a swing of its great neck. One brush against it and my armor, my skin, will be shredded. I pull lucent magic through my veins, feel its warmth and power as my hearing and smell become more acute, my vision sharper and fuller. My body fills with strength beyond a mortal's, my muscles warm and prepare for battle. I keep my focus on its heart, my target. Confidence settles my mind. I've fought shard beasts and came out victorious. I know exactly what I need to do.

It charges forward, sounding like glass scraping against glass, and with my hearing heightened, it makes my ears ache. It lowers its head, pointing the row of knives toward my midsection. I move quickly, magic making my movements a blur to the normal eye, before it gets too close, attempting to keep it from hitting the trap shields and further injuring my already weakening forces.

I run toward its side while it searches for me, caught off guard by my speed. I thrust my sword expertly between the glass shards, but instead of reaching its black pulsing heart as it has in the past, it sticks halfway through its armor. Like I've hit a wall of impenetrable steel. My mind spins. I've fought these before, and that has always worked. I pull back on the handle, but it seems stuck as if it's now one with the beast. I curse, unwilling to release my sword.

The monster roars again, and I instinctively retract the magic to dull my hearing. Its head whips around in anger, and I duck while keeping my grip on my sword. *I can't lose my sword.* The edges along its head scrape along the bracers protecting my left forearm, shredding it in mere seconds like a hot knife through fresh butter. I feel the warmth of blood trailing down my arm, but as long as it functions, it doesn't matter right now. I'm yanked along with it as it sidesteps, attempting to get a better position to stab me with. I pull copious amounts of magic through my muscles, so much that dots begin to dance in my vision. Too many people using such a small amount of magic. My body rebels. I hope the strength I've pulled is enough, knowing my position is vulnerable and the shard beast is going to kill me if I don't take control of the situation. I grit my jaw and pull, and with the aid of magic, finally the sword slides free of the beast's clutches. I immediately jump back to avoid its wide, jagged feet.

We circle each other, and my mind scrambles for a way to get through its armor, since it appears brute force will no longer work. But it doesn't wait for me to figure it out. It runs forward again, and I dodge it, swiping at its side with a powerful stroke. A small piece of its armor cracks and chips. *Not enough.*

I dodge another charge, sweat dripping down my back. The day is cool, the sun on its way down, and the air crisp with the turn of seasons. But my magic runs hot, especially when I pull as much as I am now. I am as a furnace beneath a sweltering sun; it's borderline painful. And then an idea hits me. If it doesn't work, I and my troops may very well be killed this afternoon.

"Allow Nadiette through!" I shout, as I run and dodge the beast.

There's only a moment before I see her slip through a small break in the shield and then it closes up again.

"Stay behind me. I need magic. All you have."

She nods with a determined set to her mouth as she positions herself behind my back. I feel the power of her magic as we both fight to pull it. She pulls so much from around us I struggle to maintain my own high amounts, which shows how powerful she really is. We battle to keep what we've pulled and gather so much that the trap my men are holding begins to give out as we take everything they have. Out of the corner of my eye, I see several fall to the ground. No more magic can be pulled by those weaker than Nadiette and I in this small space, so instead our trap-made arena narrows as the men still able to maintain their traps shrink its size in order to fill the gaps. I hope those who have dropped have only passed out and aren't dead from overexertion with us practically forcing their magic from them. I grit my teeth and more dots dance before my eyes. Sweat drenches my clothing, making it one with my skin.

"Give it to me," I shout. And she does. Raw, hot magic pours into my body in a wave. I feel as if I have stepped into a blazing fire. The shard beast rears and charges once again as I force the hot, lucent magic through my hand and into my sword. The handle becomes so hot in my grip it feels as if blisters are forming. I push harder, more and more as I grit my teeth against the heat. The blade begins to glow brighter, my hand feeling as if it has grabbed hold of molten metal, and a war cry of determination and pain rips from my chest as I run toward the shard beast, ignoring the gleaming knives that are attempting to disembowel me.

I'm not as fast as I'd like to be, with the energy required to keep this much magic flowing through my blade, but I know it must be hot. Fiery. Molten. What I give up in speed, I make up in heat. I jump to the side, avoiding most of its knife mane and thrusting my sword up in an arc beneath its neck and hope my plan works.

What shapes glass? *Heat.*

With a shatter my sword crashes through and the pulsing light pauses, the shards seem to mold to my blade, then the heart flashes with a burst of darkness so dark and cold my sweat temporarily cools, and the beast crashes to the ground. I fall to my knees in exhaustion and then collapse. In mere seconds, Darvy drops to his knees beside me, his focus on the bloody wound spreading deep red blood across my torso I didn't realize I had. While he works, I look at the beast beside me, still and cold. As I may be soon. Its shards are no longer obsidian, the black pulse of its heart forever extinguished. Now it simply looks like a mountain of clear glass, its tips eerily lit by the orange of the three suns in the sky. I release the magic from my pull, and it flows from my body like a cooling river. I think maybe my life drains with it as darkness edges into my vision. A circle of people stand above me, and I spot Nadiette's concerned face. Is she crying? I've never seen her cry before.

"How many dead?" My voice is gravelly and rough and drifts at the end without my control.

"Don't worry about that now," Darvy says, as he continues to work.

I'm grateful I drift into oblivion before I feel the torturous burn of his healing magic.

By the time we arrive in the city several days later, word has spread of my victory over the shard beast and Nadiette's part in it. While my people have always harbored great respect for her as our most powerful Originator, protector of their High King, now she is a heroine. The story has grown to epic proportions, as stories passed ear-to-ear tend to do. While I'm uncomfortable with the exaggerations, I acknowledge that my people need this. *Hope.*

The people crowd around my guards, attempting to give their thanks to myself and Nadiette as we enter the High King-dom, to get closer to the powerful couple, 'the couple who will save the nation,' they shout. Nadiette rides beside me, graceful and calm on her white steed. She gives a serene smile and nods to the people surrounding us. The people practically beg me for the wedding. Traditional wedding flowers are tossed around us, and I realize the story is more than a hero and heroine, it has also become one of love. The people love Nadiette. They love the symbol of our power and the hope it instills. At least I can offer that... for now.

Amidst the crowd and their chanting, their begging, their honors and well-wishes, my mind flashes back to the battle. My body hot with magic, my hand blistering around the handle of my sword. I pulled more magic than I ever have in my life, and it was barely enough to beat the beast. I think of how close I was to overexertion—maybe even death. I can't stop thinking about the fight.

It didn't used to be that difficult to beat a shard beast, and this time it killed ten of my men and almost cost me my life. Never before has one had to heat a sword to almost melting point to defeat gloam creatures. The only one who is capable of that is me. What will happen when even *I* cannot defeat them? Either the dark creatures are getting stronger, or we are getting weaker. From the state of my mark, probably both. I nudge my horse forward, done with the crowds and the hope they so badly want from me. I feel as if I am an imposter, acting the hero when I am in the process of utterly failing my people.

Later that evening, I inspect my mark before a tall mirror in my room, wondering when more will turn black. An intricate, scrolling mark begins at the top of my shoulder, trailing down half my left bicep, down my collarbone, across one quarter of my chest, and a quarter of the way down my back. It is the mark of the High King, given by Lucentia, the goddess of lucent magic. Every king since it was given has been born with his own added portion, his lasting mark upon the kingdom carried on with each heir. The earliest parts of the mark are light, like the lucent magic we use. But the later parts, the generations just before me, are the coal-black of gloam.

When I was born, and even as a young boy, the small portion I added to the mark was light, shimmering like gold, and I hoped I would be a worthy king, such as those earlier ones who saved our kingdom and helped it prosper. As I grew, the burning began. I wasn't yet eighteen before the first parts of my mark began to blacken like soot and ash. The excruciating burning caught me off guard that first time—my shouts had healers rushing to my side, and rumors flying in just days. I was full of shame and embarrassment for months. People's pitying

29

looks and whispers behind my back were torture. I never allowed that to happen again. In the ten years since, it has only grown more black, though, and through sheer discipline, I show no reaction to the pain. No one needs know how unworthy I truly am, or I'll have mutiny on my hands on top of the other problems I face. I think of the King's Council I must attend in four months' time. The weight of their stares and silent judgements. I can almost tangibly feel the unrest between the low kings, kings that should be united under my leadership. Still more failure on my part. *Unworthy.*

My gaze catches once more on my portion of the mark and the black that fills the uppermost lines. Then I pull a loose shirt from my wardrobe and toss it over my head, eager to cover the mark and all the ugly truth it holds.

Chapter 3

Vera

Four months later...

T'm bumped and jostled as people press closer to the street, cheering and shouting. Rupi fluffs her feathers in irritation at the movements as she attempts to barricade herself between my long hair and the warmth of my neck. I wait for a tiny prick from the ends of her feathers, they turn quill-like when she's agitated, but gratefully, she settles in as I back further into the shadows of a shop entrance that's closed for the night. I'm grateful these celebrations always occur beneath a dark sky—it's a lot easier to hide.

I pull the hood of my over-large cloak a little lower until it covers my face in black shadow and watch carefully for anyone who might recognize me. If they see me, they'll wonder why I'm not also dressed in white garb fit for royalty and adding to the show of light and power soon to come. The conversation would be an awkward one if I were to tell them I don't actually belong.

Heads turn as the first sign of the Originators appear. A white glow surrounds the group who've formed a parade, like they carry literal sunlight. It grows brighter the closer they come until we see the first of the group of Originators appear a ways down the street. Small orbs of magic hover above some of their hands, others send great arcs of light in shapes of dragons, shooting stars, suns with sparkling rays, and magnificent shimmering sprinkles over the crowds, lighting the street ahead of them. The people go wild, reaching out their hands with teary *thank yous* as they walk by, others cheer and shout to the Originators, our kingdom's heroes. And of course, everyone soaks up as much of the free raw magic being thrown about as they can. It's as if they scatter breadcrumbs to starving people. And in a way, they are. In a world being slowly starved of lucent magic, these people need any extra they can get. But despite the nearly tangible joy expressed around me, I despise the entire situation.

Why do Tulips join Originators if they're the ones who hunted us down and murdered us all those years ago? Simply put, because our magic most closely matches theirs. We silently joined the Originators, and that is the faction most of us are known by, but if anyone did any digging, they'd know it's a lie the Black Tulips tell so we can live some semblance of a normal life. Originators are similar to us in many ways, but none of them have the magnitude of power necessary to bridge with a king and balance magic for entire kingdoms. Don't know how that works exactly, but that's what I've always been told. I've also been told none of us current Tulips are powerful enough to do so. Instead, lucent magic is dying, disappearing, however you want to describe it. That means that pulling magic takes more energy to use, and every single day it gets worse. Some people are no longer strong enough to use any magic at all. And that's where the Tulips come in. Similar to other Originators, some of us work with healers, some of us work with those of the Maker faction—people who craft and enchant weapons, fae potion makers, and builders, among others—and others work with hunters. We are their power source for assistance in pulling magic since it's so taxing and dangerous to do it on their own.

Rupi shuffles within the confines of my hood, getting antsy as the light show continues. I look down to find a skinny cat with ratty fur curling between my feet. I'm used to it. Animals love Tulips. When I travel through the forest, it's common to have small animals trailing behind me. That's how I adopted Rupi.

We are also natural healers, though that aspect is one we steer clear of. Healers of the Healing faction can heal even the most serious of wounds—if they have enough lucent—but I've heard it hurts like the sting of a thousand wasps for a bad injury. Tulips can heal others without pain, so none of us are allowed to act as Healers—it would give us away and bring attention to our abilities again. Not only that, bloody wounds disgust me. Funny, since my mother was a Healer and loved her work.

I had to choose which faction I would make my way in since advertising that I'm a Tulip is practically a death sentence. Most Tulips choose to join the Originators for practical reasons, but there are still risks. The biggest one? The fact that—as is being so brightly shared before us—Originators' lucent magic has a yellow-orange tint to it, and its temperature matches, like the warmth of the rays of the suns setting. Tulip magic, on the other hand, is cool and bright white. We've learned that if we're very careful in how much we share at a time, no one notices. Which is why no one will ever spot a Tulip in a parade such as this.

The Originators begin to pass by, the night sky no longer visible beyond the brightness of the lucent magic they carelessly display. They are dressed in varying styles of white, some with flowing dresses, some with brilliant white armor, some with fancy, pure-white, three-piece suits. I can see the design of their mark, a half-sun with straight lines shooting out of a half-circle shape, dots trailing outward to create additional rays between each line, cut out of their clothing and light magic shining through to light it up. All of it adds to the magnificent shining glow that surrounds them as they pass by. The people around me practically worship them, the only ones who have been able to beat back the darkness and maintain our world against dark magic for the past two hundred years. They continue to pull magic as they pass and put on a show of light strikes, bright sparks and patterned flashes, pleasing the crowds with their power while the people continue to pull it desperately.

A particularly bright streak of magic shoots over the crowd and light showers down like warm rain at sunset, meanwhile, I get a sharp poke in the tender skin of my neck as Rupi shifts up and down the ridge of my shoulder, once again aggravated. The people cheer, and Rupi chirps irritably, still shuffling around inside my hood and tickling my ear with her anxious movements. I begin to cringe away, knowing that her currently soft feathers will quill into the painful weapons they turn to when she feels threatened. Still, I reach up a calming hand to rest over her small body while I shrink back a little further. I can't wait for it to end, seems as if Rupi can't either. Every year, this celebration serves as a reminder that I don't belong, that these people, who so readily and easily love the Originators, will hate me if they ever know what I am. And I hate that I am considered one of them. I can't wait until I've saved enough money to never have to call myself an Originator again.

The celebration will last late into the night with dancing,

food, and copious amounts of drink. The Originators will continue to share raw magic, which usually costs so much that only the rich can afford to hire one. Sometimes, even kings will make their presence known at these celebratory events. Even more reason for me to skedaddle as soon as possible—wouldn't want to chance that. I shiver, imagining the cold, hard planes of the face of an older man sitting on a throne, his heavy, ornate crown atop his long hair, powerful with dreadfully hot magic.

I've never met a king in person, or seen one for that matter. That's how wide I steer clear. And I do a good job avoiding them apparently—a skill I intend to keep sharp. I touch the bracelet, reminding myself that the Tulips are safe from detection, our magic disguised by the charmed bracelet around our wrists. No need to worry. Normally, kings and Tulips are drawn to each other. It's instinctive and strong. It's a nightmarish thought, and I wonder why magic ever would have created something this way. Why would someone with magic as cold as mine ever want to bridge theirs with the warmer, even hot, magic of a king? Sounds like a lukewarm disaster waiting to happen. I'll never remove the protection of the bracelet. But if I ever meet Lucentia, the goddess of magic, in person, I'll definitely be putting in a complaint.

More-so than their love for the Originators, though, the need for raw magic is the true reason the crowds grow so large. But as soon as they pass, my obligation is complete. I quickly slip along the back of the crowds and hurry home. I leave the glow of their lucent magic behind, and soon, I can see the night sky again. I breathe in relief and feel Rupi relax the further away we get.

What does it say about me that I prefer the coolness of the dark sky over their warm light? My lips quirk in a self-deprecating smile.

The twinkling stars and the three moons glowing softly above are a blessed reprieve from the blinding Originators. I leave the upkept, clean area of town and make my way deep into the rundown, dirty, and dangerous side where I pay monthly for a small space with Renna. Spending my last teen years with Mama Tina, my wealthy fae adoptive aunt, made this part of town feel especially scary at first. But when Drade, my boyfriend at the time, suddenly became low king, I knew I had to leave. I had to make a life of my own, and here I am. A set of rickety wood stairs, the paint so faded I don't know what the original color was, wrap around the building and up to the fourth story, which is where we live. I ignore the slight sway as I climb up. They haven't collapsed yet, so I simply assume they won't today. But I make sure not to use the rail to avoid splinters. I insert the old key and give the door the usual solid kick as I turn the knob, and it swings open like a charm.

No light comes from inside, so I assume Renna is still out. I pass through the small apartment and head to my bedroom to ready for bed. Once I walk through the door Rupi immediately flaps her tiny wings a few times and coasts gently to the rough-hewn perch that stands beside my bed where she promptly ruffles up her fluff before settling herself and cleaning her feathers with her stubby beak. She appears as relieved as I to be home. I follow her over and pour a bit of birdseed in the tray nearby.

I remove my cloak and boots, but before I extinguish the orb of light I've held in my palm, too lazy to light candles, I lift my bedding and uncover a roughly-stitched seam of my lumpy mattress. I pull the string out, reach inside, and fumble around until I find the money I've stashed. I sit cross-legged on the rough wood floor, and my heart picks up its pace as I count it. I set the last coin down with a breathy exhale. I have two more jobs lined up, then I'll have enough. Enough to buy a little space for a shop where I can sell odd trinkets and never have to use my magic or care about what faction I'm in. It won't matter that I'm lower class. I'll live simply. My shop, my bracelet, and Rupi. Even Renna, if she wants to join me. But I'll never have to call myself an Originator again.

Chapter 4

Ikar

I settle my large frame carefully into the ancient, half-fossilized wood chair, cringing as it ominously creaks beneath my weight. The others, the four low kings, have already taken their seats, but I prolong the discomfort of the hard chairs as long as possible, knowing this will be lengthy. I lean back, putting on a relaxed air even though it feels as if I am in a den of snakes. These annual meetings of the kings are a tradition not easily broken, nor do I think they should be, but their length is absolutely criminal. It is a facade of unity and friendship between the low kings when in reality, each wants the best for his own kingdom without care for any other. And I think, beneath the surface, they'd all like to do away with the High King all together. Which is where I, the High King, come in.

"Welcome to the 1,712th semi-annual meeting of the kings," I begin, and the conversations immediately halt. "We'll begin with the oath. Everyone, rise."

We all stand, except for King Adrian Farlow, who's chin

has just met his chest in sleep. Odd, rumbling snores already sound from his nose. He's the oldest of us by far, crowned when my grandfather was still High King. For that reason, he remains undisturbed. I feel mildly jealous that he can get away with napping the entire council away as we continue with the oath and seat ourselves, and I proceed to listen for the next several hours. My mouth quirks as King Waylon Orlet's eyes fixate for the eighth time on the aged, sleeping king and frowns. It's amusing how much it bothers him. He always does enjoy the stuffy, ceremonial parts of the council.

I listen as disagreements between kingdoms are brought up, lengthy deliberations continue back and forth, at times some shouting, and there's even a heated exchange involving the drawing of swords that I had my guards step in to stop. Fortunately, I have nothing to contribute to this part of the conversation this time, other than preventing a sword fight. With time, the low kings come to fragile agreements, but I listen closely anyway, aware that everything that is discussed is under my rule. Their people are my people. Everything from new trading routes, raising and lowering all sorts of taxes, banning of illegal goods, the running of shipping ports, catching elusive and dangerous criminals to risky river travel. I jump in when needed, my focus solely on protecting the interests of all equally.

In the early morning hours of the next day, things finally wind down. With burning eyes, I place my hands on the table and begin to stand to end the council when the youngest of the low kings, King Rhomi Miden, suddenly speaks, looking uncomfortable but determined. I relax back in my seat, curious, and motion for him to continue.

"Though none of us want to admit there is a problem, we

know magic has been struggling. The gloam creatures are coming in larger and larger numbers. My low kingdom is literally shrinking, and it is difficult to pull magic at all. What should be done?"

The room is silent. Guilt tightens my jaw. The question of my life.

"Come, now. I know for a fact your kingdoms have been hit as well." He attempts to meet the eyes of every king around the table, but all look away.

While I am aware of the true state of each of the low kingdoms, thanks to my own trusted advisors with lofty positions in their courts, it is taboo to speak about weakness amongst the other low kings, and he has just spilled his to the entire council. It is unfortunate that the lack of trust between us goes this deep. But he isn't admitting to weakness that none of the rest of us have, so is it really any more vulnerable?

I speak up then. Done with the drama and this eternal meeting. "Waylon, your wood has tripled in price in the last two years. We all know the gloam has been infesting the forests."

He shifts uncomfortably.

My eyes slide to his right. "Drade, the fae's healing potions hardly hold their potency long enough to be effective anymore."

Drade, the fae low king, looks at me with wrath-filled dark eyes. "If you don't like them, don't buy them," he snarls.

I ignore him and look at Rhomi. "The gloam creatures have been coming out in larger numbers in *all* the kingdoms." Then I check to see if Adrian is awake. "Adrian?"

His eyes lift and his head jerks upward as he briefly wakes.

"We know the weapons are becoming weaker. Not the

steel. The enchantments. We know it's magic weakening." My hand burns at the memory of the molten metal of my enchanted sword in my grip. I lean back, not caring that I've just ruffled the feathers of every low king in the room. It's refreshing. "So, I second Rhomi's question. As protectors of the people, what will be the solution?" I wait. I hope more than I should that someone will come up with something that I haven't. From the heavy silence, it's not likely.

I hear another of the ancient chairs creak somewhere in the room, and a few seconds later, Waylon swallows with so much effort I can see the tightening of his throat with the motion. "We'll need to work together more than ever before," he spits out, trying to sound helpful but actually sounding like he hates the idea.

His answer is dodgy at best. I hold back a heavy sigh.

"Magic will decide our fate," Adrian mumbles, slow and ominous. The old man has practically passed back to the other side of magic already and seems to have given up.

Waylon speaks up again, and all of us swing our gazes back to him. "I agree with Adrian. Who are *we* to believe we can manipulate magic? It cannot be forced to our bidding, the only thing we can choose is how we react to its decline. We can lower some of the prices, try to invigorate trade."

Rhomi nods, thoughtful.

Drade speaks up. "Our healing potions still work well within our borders, so I can offer to make it easier for those in need to enter our kingdom."

I nod, actually impressed at the compromise on Drade's part. We all know the fae have the strictest crossing regulations of all the kingdoms.

Waylon speaks up again, "There have been times such as this that light magic has struggled beneath the weight of dark, but it has always pulled through. We are hopeful that your marriage to my niece, Nadiette, will bring more power to our world, in the form of an heir."

He smiles with pride shining in his eyes. There is nothing to indicate that my marriage to Nadiette will improve the condition of magic in our world, and I am highly aware that I need an heir. Especially after the shard beast incident.

"There is nothing to indicate that a marriage between myself and Nadiette will improve the state of magic," I say bluntly.

Waylon's eyes darken, but he doesn't disagree, and the conversation continues. I listen as the low kings continue to discuss, adding their opinions and comments, all in support of Waylon that we simply need to be patient with many congratulations on my coming engagement. I end the meeting with no true resolution and more pressure than ever to marry.

I knock once and enter my top advisor's private office. He's strange but knowledgeable and trustworthy, so I ignore most of his shenanigans. I call him my advisor, but he's more the mad-wizard type. If there are such things as wizards outside our storybooks. Highly intelligent, odd, powerful, but loyal and trustworthy.

I catch him with beakers and bottles of all sizes, filled with colorful liquids above boilers, tubes and ingredients scattered messily across a desk. A rancid and slightly fruity smell washes over me, and though it smells five times stronger to me with my hunter senses, I'm not sure how he can handle it. It's currently very close to inducing my gag reflex. I make my way around the room and slam open the windows along the outside wall of his tower office, gulping in fresh air and waving the rancid out.

"Good gracious, Jethonan," I growl.

He looks at me over his shoulder, like he's just noticed I'm here.

"My lord! How do you this day?" Pieces of his long, brown hair are plastered to his sweaty face.

"Better before I entered this room," I mumble beneath my breath. My eyes linger on the mess in front of him, and I itch to clean it up, but after eyeing what looks to be burn holes through his robes, I instead fold my arms across my chest and take a seat near one of the open windows—the sacrifices I make to keep a good advisor...

I let out an audible breath of air, gathering my patience. "What are you doing? This smell could kill everyone in my castle."

He chuckles like he thinks I'm joking. "I got a recipe from a fae healer. I'm trying my hand at a healing potion."

I frown. Fae healing potions are the best of the best, and they smell that way too. The last one I used smelled of sweet berries, another fresh citrus.

"Either, the recipe you got is fraudulent, or something has gone horribly wrong in the process," I say, feeling nauseous the longer I sit.

Jethonan spills something, and I hear him curse beneath his breath, then there's a sizzle and an audible *pop* before a beaker explodes. I think the hint of smoke actually improves the odor.

"Imagine how creating our very own healing potions will help our kingdom!" He speaks animatedly, his eyes bright.

He has a point. The fae potions have grown weaker with the lack of lucent magic. They are now only potent in the fae realm, making them very difficult to use when needed. I wonder when the charms the weapon enchanters weave into our weapons will begin to fade too, leaving us defenseless. Which reminds me why I'm here.

"Jethonan. I need you to create some type of conductor for my kingdom. We have to harness more magic. Five of my soldiers died on patrol last night, villagers are suffering, our food production is down, the weather, pulling magic... It's all falling apart."

He turns toward me finally, and I see that I've caught his attention. He nods as he thinks for a moment. He is well aware of the problems facing our kingdom and does everything he can to combat it, which is why I leave him to his creative hunches like the one currently happening. Jethonan has a brilliant mind —if anyone can do it, it's him.

"One of the low kings suggested something to do with marriage to a Nadiette, and the people are hoping it will help. It seems ridiculous to ask, but is there a way to harness Nadiette's power to spread further?" I feel like an idiot even asking. If there was a way, I'm sure we would already have been doing it generations ago.

A thoughtful look comes across his face, and he thinks quietly for a moment, his utter stillness as his mind works a high contrast to the busy and constantly moving Jethonan otherwise.

"I'll look into our options, Your Majesty."

Then he's moving again. Something behind him bubbles over, and he turns, his robes spinning around his ankles as he tinkers with whatever he's using to heat something that smells like rancid potion currently brewing on the table.

I stand, ready to escape the odor that is overwhelming my heightened sense of smell. "As soon as you find something, send for me."

"Of course, Your Majesty," he says, as his hands flutter around the table.

I can't help but grin a little. I close the door behind me and lean down to sniff the shoulder of my shirt. The smell has infiltrated its fibers, and I frown. I don't have time to change. I'll have to meet Nadiette the way I am.

Chapter 5

Ikar

Nadiette and I stroll slowly through the main city street, arm in arm, trailed by four guards. The streets are perfectly cobbled, the storefronts tidy and clean, windows shining and filled with goods to sell. The heady scent of flowers trailing from upper balconies hovers in the air around us as we stroll by. It's an almost unbelievable contrast to what I experienced on the last convoy, and so many other patrols just like it. I push down the nightmarish memories and nod and greet my people as we walk, and she does the same. They look at us with hope shining in their eyes, and Nadiette seems to glow beside me.

I admit we make an excellent couple, and I'm confident she will step into her role as queen smoothly. We've worked as a team, steady and unbeatable for years now, so it's only natural for us to marry. The people have grown to love her more and more, as I do. She is a classic beauty, her green eyes filled with a youthful joy, and her hair seems spun of auburn fire. A deep contrast to the white gowns she wears, specifically made to compliment her mark, as is customary for Originators. Today, she wears a gown with flowy skirts, a wide belt wraps around a fitted bodice, and a row of pearl buttons lead up to her neck. The white, silky fabric gathers elegantly at the tops of her shoulders and drops like the bow of a curtain to the bend of her low back, revealing fair skin blemished only by her mark. Her hair is braided intricately to the side, revealing the easily recognizable mark of the Originators—a half sun. My own wardrobe seems muted compared to her assortment of pure white ensembles since I prefer darker greens, blues, and browns. Beside me, she appears to shine all the more.

We stop at a favorite bakery of ours with small tables in a front garden area where tall bushes have grown and been pruned into a privacy wall for customers. I pull out a chair for Nadiette at our usual table.

"You seem distracted today." She rests her perfect chin on her small hand and waits.

I hesitate, unsure how much to reveal. "Another bad patrol last night," I say, as images of the five soldiers who were killed last night come to mind.

She purses her lips and calls me back to the present, "It must have been horrendous. I feel so terrible for their families." Compassion fills her eyes, and my defenses go up.

"I'd rather not discuss it." My voice is hard, hoping she'll change the subject. At times, though, she can be relentless, always going on about how we can figure this out, trying to be positive. Most of the time, I appreciate her positive outlook, but in regard to this, she has no idea the fault rests entirely with me. I wait for it and try not to clench my jaw when she begins exactly as I knew she would.

She places one of her hands over mine where it rests on the table and gives it a light squeeze, looking deeply at me with her vivid green eyes. "We'll figure this out together, my love. We are the two most powerful people in the kingdom. We will rule together, and with our power, we will protect our people. A perfect match. And who knows, maybe the combination of our power will produce an heir so powerful that the kingdom will be rid of gloam forever." She says it gently, but there's a sureness behind it.

I merely nod, a token to keep her happy and ease her worry. But she doesn't realize that the only person who can figure this out is *me*. Heir or no heir, the responsibility for my kingdom is mine.

A couple of sweetened drinks and fresh pastries are brought to our table, and the conversation switches to lighter, more comfortable topics. But I can't help but feel like the worst sort of person for enjoying a day out with a lovely woman after five of my men died the night before, their families currently in mourning. The pastry sits untouched on the table before me as Nadiette carries on with the one-sided conversation between us.

Soon enough, we return to the castle, and she walks with me to my office.

"Mind if I join you this afternoon?" She looks at me, a hint of worry creasing her brow. I feel a stab of guilt at how quiet I've been.

I smile wider than I want to, but I truly do welcome her presence. "Not at all. I have no meetings."

It's become common for us to spend occasional afternoons together when we are free from our regular responsibilities and meetings. Me, focused on the workings of my kingdom that only I can oversee, her supervising Originator rotations for patrols, reading a book, or writing letters. I take a seat behind my desk and watch with a smile as she sets aside decorum and curls her feet beneath her skirts, getting comfortable against the side of the sitting couch and opening a book she pulls from her fancy bag. I return to my work.

Today, I am reviewing the ledgers that our master of the treasury has submitted for my final review. I work through the numbers, not taking a break until my eyes burn. I look up when I hear a giggle from Nadiette on the couch. She's still immersed in her book, but I appreciate the companionship of one of my closest friends. Seems to make the tedious work lighter. I hear a knock at the door, and a guard looks in.

"Jethonan is here to see you, my lord."

It's not unusual for Jethonan to visit—he *is* my second in command in regard to the workings of the kingdom. I simply nod, and the door is opened wider for Jethonan as he walks through, straight to my desk with two thick books in his arms. I'm pleased to see that there are no burn holes through his robes this afternoon. Hopefully, that means he's given up on the healing potion concoction.

"My lord, I've found..."

As he passes her in a rush, Nadiette looks up from her book with a smile. "Jethonan. Good afternoon."

He startles slightly, pausing halfway to putting his books on my desk. When he realizes she's there, he gathers them back in his arms and stands, a fleeting look of concern crossing his face.

"I missed you in my hurry to speak with the king, forgive me." He bows slightly before he returns his attention to me.

"A word in private, Your Majesty?"

I nod. "Of course."

Nadiette places her feet back to the floor and slips her book back into her bag before standing gracefully. The layers of her gown slide perfectly back into place, and she glides across the floor.

"I'm meeting with my Originators soon anyway, so I'll

leave the two of you to your meeting." Then her gaze meets mine. "Tomorrow, Ikar?" Her eyes glint with a flirtatious eagerness.

"Yes, I'll meet you at the stables."

"Wonderful." She smiles and slips from the room, leaving Jethonan and I alone.

I wait until the door clicks closed and get straight to the point. I feel the thump of my heart grow hard with anxiety. "What have you found?"

He proceeds to set the books on my desk with a heavy *thump*. "I've found the conductor." I can hear the excitement thrumming in his voice. He slides the first book off the one beneath and flips it open.

He uses magic to find the correct page, and the pages whir by, creating a slight breeze before my face. The fact that he has enough power to pull magic for a task of convenience shows how powerful he really is. Most people are forced to carefully preserve their magic these days.

"Here it is." He taps a page filled with an artfully drawn flower. I'm not one to know the names of plants and flowers, but it looks like a tulip. A deep purple tulip, mid-bloom, almost black in color.

"A... purple flower... is our conductor?"

"It may look like a simple purple flower, but this is a *Black Tulip*."

I tilt my head and inspect it a little further. I can see how the name fits, I guess. The purple is so deep that in parts it does appear black. I'm still not sure why the name of this flower matters so much, and I'd rather get to the point.

"What do we do with the flower?" My mind is already spinning plans to get a search party together. Should be easy enough.

"I'm not finished yet." He flips a page with a snap. "Look at this."

This one depicts a woman dressed in a beautiful black gown. Both her hands are outstretched, in one hovers an orb of shining white light, which I assume is lucent magic. In the other rests a small white bird holding a black tulip in its beak. I have no idea how to interpret it. The book itself is written in the old language, and while I know some, I don't know enough to read the page in a reasonable amount of time. I'm growing frustrated with Jethonan's dramatic style of sharing the much awaited information.

"Get to the point," I growl.

"This is the point, my lord." He taps the picture. "You need a woman marked with a black tulip." His eyes are wide with excitement. "*They* are the conductors, the recyclers, the power-houses, whatever you want to call them."

Pieces begin to come together, and I wonder now if the women he's talking about are the same that my father and his before him warned us away from. If it was anyone but Jethonan, I'd have slammed the book shut and sent them away. But I trust him, and my kingdom is in such dire straits I force myself to stay silent and listen, instead of argue.

"According to these books, Black Tulips have the unique ability to bridge their magic with a king, which then connects them directly to the magic of the kingdom. Doing so allows their magic to provide an astronomical amount of lucent for your people and reduces the gloam, through *your* bond to your kingdom. It offers protection and improves... everything, it seems. In fact, through the immense power of his Tulip wife, your grandfather four hundred years ago was able to magically banish and imprison his brother who attempted to take the throne. Can you imagine that sort of power?" His eyes are bright with excitement.

My hope plummets. "What is their official name?" I ask, but I already know. So much for my search party plan to find a simple flower. Of course it's not that simple, and if I'm right, there will be no search party at all.

He frowns, appearing to be confused about why I need that random piece of information.

"A singular Tulip is also called a Queen of the Night, the group of them Queens of the Night. Have you heard of them?"

I slide my hand down my face, weary. This can't be right. This can't be his solution.

"My lord?" Jethonan asks, confused.

"I can never, never bridge with a *Tulip*, as you call them. They were killed for a reason."

He stands so still it's like I literally sucked the joyous air from his billowing sails.

I continue, "As I'm sure you've learned through your reading, kings used to bridge with Queens of the Night. It was common and encouraged. Then a seer saw a Black Tulip bridged with our enemy and our kingdom destroyed." I give him a pointed look.

"Ah, you speak of the seer vision, which unfortunately, triggered the hunt and murder of the Tulips. You are correct that the vision showed a Tulip bridging with an enemy, which led to the downfall of lucent magic and our kingdom." He says it all rather quickly and to the point. "But we all know that seer visions are quite subjective and are rarely accurately predictive of the future. And just a theory on my part, but I believe that enemy is still magically banished. Though for how long, I don't know, with the state of lucent and gloam."

He isn't wrong about seer visions not being accurate, but to completely disregard a seer vision is also unwise. Finally, I look up and say heavily, "There is a reason they are named after the night, is there not?" He stares at me blankly, so I continue in an overly patient voice, "Night... darkness... gloam creatures... evil...?"

He snorts and then he leans forward and laughs, his brown hair swinging with the motion. I'm not amused. I'm about to kick him out of my office when he finally stops and takes a deep breath.

"I'm sorry, but I can't believe that explanation is the reason our world is being overtaken by gloam magic. It's ridiculous." He waves a hand through the air like it's preposterous. "And unfortunate for those Tulips who were needlessly murdered. The past cannot be undone," he frowns and then lifts a finger, "but it can be prevented from happening again. Now, moving on."

He opens the second book, and the pages whir before my face again. These must have come from his personal library because I swear I get a hint of that rancid fruit healing potion he was working on last week, and I lean away. The pages settle, and he takes a second to find the right section, then he spins the book toward me and points.

"It says here that magic keeps at least five Tulips in existence at a time."

"Your point?"

"You, all of us, are in a desperate situation. You either take a calculated risk by bridging with a Tulip or the kingdom continues to decline beneath the weight of gloam while people continue to die. You and the Tulips were made to *bridge*. You, as king, were intended to be a protector to them, and in return, they keep lucent magic strong and gloam in check." My brows pull lower, not liking that what he says makes sense. Even with my darkening expression, he continues. And this is why I chose him as my advisor. "Now, may I be honest?"

"Aren't you always?" I narrow my eyes at him suspiciously.

"Only a figure of speech, my lord." He smiles tightly and quickly continues. "Magic chooses the Tulips, one or two out of thousands may stray from the duty instilled in their souls and turn evil. But if there is any sort of power struggle to worry about, I'd say it would more likely begin with the kings."

I ponder what he says for a moment. I don't like that it makes sense. If I allow it, it will pick at the strings of doubt freshly cut by Jethonan and quickly unravel the comfortable and familiar beliefs about the balance of power and magic I've been taught since I was a boy. I was raised to be the *king* of my kingdom. The one with absolute power, authority, and control. Things aren't perfect, we struggle at times, but the inner workings of my kingdom run like a well-oiled wagon wheel. Beside the fact that it's practically disintegrating at the edges from gloam. I clench my jaw. I admit that the reality that I can't control the strength of magic in my kingdom any more than I can manipulate the suns in the sky has me frustrated. After years of dedicated learning and effort, years of weapons training, and years of battle experience, according to Jethonan, I'm to completely rely on and trust some unknown woman to save my kingdom, simply because she's marked with a flower. I don't like it.

"I'll think about it."

Just saying so twists my chest into a knot. He nods and gathers his books, chattering about needing to get back to another project he's working on, but I don't really hear him as my thoughts spin and churn. Could I do it? Could I search out a Tulip, marry her, *bridge* with her? If what I've been told is a lie, what have *they* been told? What about Nadiette? And would the King's Council ever agree to a plan such as this?

Chapter 6

Vera

I get varying reactions when I tell people what I do for work. The Tulips give me looks of confusion bordering on horror. Some people take one look at me and think I'm full of it—don't believe me a bit. A very few seem impressed. Maybe it's my petite size, or maybe I have the face of one who looks too young. I dunno, but I kinda like the startle I get when I tell someone new.

I'm choosy about the criminals I help chase. I learned that the hard way when I first started out. Took a Class A bounty for the large reward offered. I was a dirt-poor newbie, and it was too tempting. I found out real quick to never take a Class A again. The hunter I contracted with ended up dead, the bounty escaped, and I was on the run with no money or food at just eighteen. Big fail, that one. Had to eat roots and leaves from the forest and the rare fish I was able to catch for over a month until I found my way back to civilization and picked another contract up. Let's just say, my talents don't lie in navigation or my sense of direction. Somehow, I survived, but if that happened now, I'd be dead four times over. Gloam has always been a problem, but now it's a formidable opponent.

So yeah, it's dangerous to wander the gloam-infested forests, but other than that first time, I've always had a hunter nearby for protection. I work smarter now than I did eight years ago. We've come upon gloam creatures and forest beasts that were here before gloam was even a problem, but both are dangerous. I simply lend the hunter a bit more magic—they can't tell mine is white and not the more yellow sunshine color of a true Originator unless I were to send a literal fountain of it —and he usually takes care of it quick. And at times when I'm on my own, I have my trusty short sword. I rub a hand down the worn pommel and aged leather grip. In all, bounty assisting is all about teamwork, and I like to think I'm rather good at it by now.

I lean back against a large tree and cross my legs as the last of the three suns sets. The thick fabric of my loose trousers is already worn and filthy, so I don't worry about sitting in the dirt. One of many benefits of drowning myself in men's clothing. Rupi hops from tree branch to tree branch above me, her happy chirps carrying softly in the breeze. I rip off a large piece of jerky that the burly hunter, Ravio, gave me. He's not a talker, but he sure likes to eat, and I'm not complaining. I'm never better fed than on bounty jobs, with fresh-caught meat cooked over the fire every night, and sometimes even fish. Their packs are always loaded with jerky, dried fruit, nuts, and sometimes even bread and cheese if we aren't gone too long. My loose clothing appreciates the extra food, and I chew it contentedly. Another benefit of working with hunters, most of them have a hearty appetite and almost never skip meals, unlike healers. My stomach cramps at the memory of working with Mardine, a woman so devoted to her work that I was woken at all hours of the night and skipped days of meals at a time as we traveled to help those in need. A worthy job, but a hungry one, one that my already willowy frame could barely afford. And so, besides Mr. Eddieren, I stick to bounty hunting for survival.

Across camp, the bounty we caught two days ago sits beside the fire where the hunter keeps a close eye on him. He's considered a Class C criminal, the lowest of the three grades. I'll only take a Class B contract if I'm feeling desperate, since the higher grade the criminal is, the better the pay. But I never take Class A grade bounty contracts, even though they pay more than any other contract of any other profession I could take. I prefer to live.

My part in this job has consisted of lending my raw magic for about two minutes, while Ravio cuffed the guy and I ensured he had plenty of magic to work with, if needed. Ravio's huge and powerful enough in his own right, but he's also smart and knows there are other things to avoid while we trek through the forest. He's basically traveled the forest his entire life, at least that's what I got from the few words he's spoken.

We'll be back to the city to turn the criminal in by tomorrow afternoon, and this time, even with the end of the good food, I can't wait. While I love the hunter appetite and hearty meals, this criminal is giving me the creeps. His green gaze meets mine, and while he's good looking enough, his eyes emanate something dark. His lip curls when my eyes snag on his, and I quickly avert my gaze. I've seen his type before, the ones whose eyes showcase the darkness of their souls while masking it with a handsome face. I've seen others who smell, and look, as if they rolled right out of a pig pen, some who've lost their sanity and laugh like madmen the entire trip to prison, and a rare few who seem to be perfectly innocent. Usually, those innocent looking ones are women, and they're a dangerous sort. Definite downside to bounty hunting—the criminals. I've met more than enough for my lifetime. Over the course of my adult years, I've taken more bounty contracts than I can remember, so none of this is new to me. But I'm done after this one. I have one more contract with Mr. Eddieren that I've already lined up, and then I'm *free*.

I think of the odd assortment of items I've gathered over the years of my travels. Unusual candlestick holders with shapes and bases forged into animals that I bought from a traveling shifter merchant. An assortment of spider silk clothing I've snagged from my wealthy fae aunt, Mama Tina. She always has a pile of clothes for me a mile high when I visit that I pack away since they are completely impractical for my line of work. I even have a pair of earrings shaped as tiny, intricate, *usable* knives that a weapon master enchanted for me. I would have claimed them as my own, but with no more than basic sword training, I worried I'd end up stabbing one of the minuscule blades into my own neck. Instead, they sit carefully wrapped and stored with all my other precious wares, waiting for a shop to be sold in. I currently carry a fancy comb engraved with flowering vines and small gems. I'll store it with the others at Mama Tina's when I get there.

And when I have the money, I'll no longer have to hide myself amongst people who hate me... Originators. I can even call myself an Absent, someone born without any magic at all, and no one will care. I can run my shop, travel to find more to fill it, and never worry that I'll happen upon a king or that anyone will care about what I am.

Hopefully, Renna will be able to find work nearby, or I'll be successful enough to hire her. We are sisters by magic, as much so as I'm a sister to the other Tulips. But Renna and I have a bond forged by the struggle to survive on top of it. That time I almost died taking that Class A criminal contract? Renna took me in and helped me be willing to try again. I don't intend to desert her now.

Chapter 7

Ikar

It's much too soon to revisit this uncomfortable seat, but I force myself to sit and watch the lower kings closely, waiting patiently for the ceremonial beginnings to finish before I bring up the topic of our meeting.

"I've called a meeting of the kings to discuss the issue of growing gloam. The Originators have worked well until now. Now, we need a solution."

Rhomi and Drade's expressions are neutral. Waylon's eyes turn hard, but a mocking smile begins to lift his lips. He's of the mind we wait. I disagree.

"What solution could there be? Didn't we *just* discuss this?" Waylon asks sourly.

I pause a moment, and when no one speaks up, I forge ahead. "The Queens of the Night. The Tulips." My tone dares any one of them to challenge me.

I hear the quill that Rhomi has been spinning around drop to the table. Drade's eyes widen, and a strangled sound escapes Waylon's throat.

Adrian curses. "They'll take over your kingdom in a fortnight," he growls, actually alert.

"But will they? *Can* they?" I look around the circle of powerful rulers. "Have any of you found an actual record showing that that has happened?" I hope no one brings up the seer vision. This fire doesn't need more fuel.

Waylon scowls at me across the oblong table. "You are young, Your Majesty, so you may have been saved the horror of the stories that have been passed down for generations. No record is required. All that matters is that it is *possible* for them to destroy our kingdom. I advise an immediate vote."

I sit back, giving off a relaxed air when inside my body is tense as a clenched fist. My brows raise at his powerful rejection. "You refuse to consider an idea that, according to historical records, preserved magic and maintained its powerful and balanced state?"

Everyone's eyes swing from me back to Waylon. A vein in his forehead throbs. "Is anything worth risking our kingdoms to those... manipulating thieves? The *Night Queens?*" He sounds truly disgusted. I decide not to correct him on their proper name right now, or the fact that they are *my* kingdoms.

"If one of us does it, we risk encouraging the dratted vixens and having more of them springing up." Then he looks at me hard. "Aside from that, you have committed to Nadiette."

"You forget your place, Waylon," I say coldly.

The room goes silent, and my guards step up behind me at my tone, waiting for my command. I could arrest him in a moment, raise his taxes, send more of my men to watch his courts—but I won't. I need the unity of the low kings, and I won't get it by force.

I allow a moment for the chastisement to sink in around the room. "My commitment above all is to my kingdom and it always will be," I state forcefully. He is her uncle, so I am not surprised at his reaction. Though I didn't realize it was possible for a frown to grow so dark, he brings to mind the face of a deathstalker with his brows so low. Not a good look for him, but I move on. I have more to say. "And they do not *spring up*. They are chosen by magic, as the rest of us are. All to play a purpose and combine our efforts to better our world."

Waylon's face is still flushed from my reprimand, but again, he pushes back. "Forgive me, Your Majesty." His voice is like a viper. "Truly, though, it is reckless and puts our entire kingdom at risk if we introduce one of them back into a ruling position."

Drade keeps his face expressionless, but I see the dark intensity in his eyes. Rhomi fidgets, looking indecisive. "It's possible for them to take over our minds, our kingdoms?"

Waylon nods solemnly.

I step in then, watching the actions before me with deepening anger. I direct a blazing glare at Waylon. "There is no proof of what you say." I'm a hair's width from setting my guards on the insubordinate leech.

I could offer a vote right here, right now. As High King, I have the ability to over-rule a vote if it doesn't end in my favor, but it can lead to rebellion and war, something I don't want. It could kill my people much faster than the growing gloam. Tensions are strung tight in the room.

"All in favor of the Tulips, raise your hand," I say.

Drade raises a hand. Rhomi's twitches on the table, my eyes practically willing it to join mine and Drade's, but it doesn't.

"All in favor of waiting, raise your hand."

Waylon, Adrian, and slowly, Rhomi's hands rise.

I inwardly scoff at the cowardly men who call themselves kings. The meeting is done. Nothing I say will budge the other kings at this point, and I have no choice but to agree to the useless plan. In reality, it's no plan. For now. I want to fight back, I want to stand up and tell them that as High King, I will find a Tulip and they can say nothing, but I can't. The teaching, drilled into my very soul from the time I was a child, was to do all that I can to keep relations between the low kings and myself in a careful balance, sometimes requiring compromise on my part. But this seems like too much. All I can hope is that my kingdom survives until I can convince them.

Chapter 8

Ikar

One month later...

I ride amidst the patrol, flanked on all sides by guards. Around my guards ride sixteen of my soldiers. The horses are anxious. Champion pulls at the reins and shakes his head, and I can tell he wants to be anywhere but here. I rub a hand down his dark gray neck, calming him. Darkness infests the forests, and for every bit that magic weakens, gloam hungrily fills the space. We've been pushed back by an enemy that seems impossible to battle, and I hate to see the kingdom that was entrusted into my hands after centuries of dedication and work by my forefathers dwindling due to my weakness. I employ Originators throughout all the kingdoms, and they have helped in some areas. They pull raw magic, sharing it with my people in the small amounts they are able wherever they go, but it's not enough. It's like a drop of water in an ocean. It is said that weak kings have weak kingdoms, and naturally, they die off early. I'm in my late twenties, but interestingly, I feel at more of a prime than I was even five years ago. Nothing adds up, but guilt is a constant companion.

We ride in silence, watching warily. The further the three

suns set, the more chance something will come forth in an attempt to claim even more of our land. Just a few miles away, a small farming village relies on the protection of these patrols, and the same goes for all the outlying villages. If we can't protect our food source and our kingdom's main source of income, mainly exporting wheat and other crops, the situation is hopeless. I battle the despair daily, because even if we protect our farms and our people, lucent magic is dying, and it has affected every part of our world. The weather is more sporadic, sometimes even violent. Our main river for travel is now inconsistent and dangerous, and the soil and plant life are struggling. And on top of it all, every day it seems harder and harder to pull magic for protection. Only the strongest can now do so without collapsing or dying within minutes.

Shadows reach longer and longer, and an eerie wind begins to blow from the darkness beyond. The warmth of the suns is replaced with a bitter cold that quickly reaches my core. A few minutes later, the head soldier signals us to stop. It means he sensed something, same as I, as my eyes search for something unseen. I place my hand around the grip of my enchanted sword as our horses prance uncomfortably, shying away from the black forest line several hundred yards away.

I want to remind them not to pull magic. It will drain us too quickly. We have only one Originator traveling with us as I don't have enough to send two with every patrol that is constantly protecting our borders. We've increased our training with enchanted weapons to counter the effects of the lack of lucent magic, but it's difficult to fight the instinctive ability to pull magic when in danger.

I see the silver tips of the curved stingers that rise unnaturally from their backs, their four powerful legs crouched and prepared to spring, and in the last of the dusky light, I see their black, fathomless eyes. Deathstalkers. I readjust my grip and pull my sword. Round heads lined with a halo of dark, pointed spikes step out of the shadows. Their dark eyes are magnetizing, and I intentionally avert my gaze so I don't get stunned. They pull their lips back, revealing razor sharp teeth as they stalk forward. A reptilian-like skin armors their bodies, thick and tough. They are the monsters of grown men's dreams.

One of my men stiffens, beginning to release his grip on his weapon. I watch in horror as the soldier next to him immediately jumps into action, catching his sword mid-air and snapping him out of the stun, but the Deathstalkers lunge, and we all race to battle.

I rest on a comfortable sitting chair in my room beside a hot fire, my armor and clothing stripped from my tired body long ago. I'm left in undergarments while one of the healers wraps a wide bandage around my lower thigh. Even with an Originator to assist, he wasn't able to pull enough magic to heal it in one sitting, but I'm grateful for the pain that's left. It grounds me in reality when it's so easy to get lost in the darkness and imaginings of what my kingdom is becoming.

"I'll remove the dressing tomorrow, Your Majesty."

I nod, but inside, I feel hollow. I stay sitting long after he leaves. Defeated. Over and over again, I see the way my soldiers were stunned, killed, ripped from their horses while their magic and then their souls were devoured by the Deathstalkers right before my eyes. I'm supposed to protect them.

My eyes burn with emotion that never truly shows itself. I realize my jaw is clenched when my head begins to ache. I've let my people down. I've let my soldiers down. Yet, why has magic kept me alive? Every morning, I wake, waiting to feel the call of death, feelings of weakness, anything to indicate that magic is displeased. And there's nothing. I have no heir, so now would be the perfect time for magic to choose a new, stronger king. It's not up to me, though, so I'll continue to honor my position and serve my people with everything I have.

There has to be a better way to deal with the gloam. In fact, Jethonan has already suggested a better way. I sit and think about everything he told me. The picture he showed me in the ancient book... I don't know what all the symbols mean, but I trust Jethonan. If he says it will work, I have to believe it will. Memories of my father and his advisor drilling me about how to handle the low kings battle with more recent memories of Jethonan urging me to find a Tulip.

My thoughts turn into a mixed haze of indecision until I take a breath and clear my mind. My father was a good man, a strong king. He taught me well, was a loving father, trained me in every way possible to prepare me to be king. I glance down at the mark on my left shoulder, eyeing the section of it that was created at his birth. Dark as gloam. Even he, my strong and peace-keeping father, wasn't able to keep lucent strong. I don't want war, I don't want the low kings to rise against me, but if ever there was a time to go against the decision of the council, against the advice of my father, it is now. If I do things the same as he, nothing will change. I sit in my chair, unmoving while the decision settles, wondering why something that feels so right seems to be so wrong. I only hope I have enough time to convince the low kings it's right before I have mutiny on my hands.

I dress as quickly as my leg will allow and make my way to where I hope Jethonan will be. I reluctantly step into my advisor's office, waiting for another stomach-flipping smell to assault me as I open the door. Instead of a smell, though, this time I feel mid-winter cold wash over my body, raising goosebumps along my arms.

I frown. "Jethonan?"

The dramatic-robe style he usually sports is covered beneath heavy furs and has him looking like a somewhat skinny bear. Strands of his long hair and even his eyelashes carry icy clumps, and his nose looks partially frostbitten. I rub my arms to warm up as I walk over to his work table. A large, oblong glass container sits in a metal stand, almost like an empty glass egg that's been stretched at both ends. A heating element beneath exudes a miniscule flame of blue and yellow. I lean closer to investigate the smoke-like, wispy threads circulating inside.

This looks very similar to the mist that comes before a murk attack. I look at Jethonan with a quirked brow.

He shoves some notes aside. "Not to worry, Your Majesty. It's only a sample."

I decide not to ask what he plans for it—or where he got it. I prefer not to know.

"We need to talk."

Jethonan's frozen brows raise. "Of course, my lord!"

He leads me through another door, and this time I find a messy room lined with over-stuffed bookshelves. More books are stacked in teetering piles throughout the room. So many, in fact, that there is no free place to sit. But it's warm, and I immediately begin to thaw.

"I need to know more about the Tulips. How do I find them?"

A pleased expression crosses his face. "I've prepared something for you."

He gathers a pile of books in his arms and balances it

precariously atop another smaller stack. I wait for it to tip, but the swaying stops and the tower stills. He gestures for me to take a seat.

"Because you were apparently taught incorrectly about this topic from your birth, I will start at the beginning."

I frown at him but ignore his antics as I wonder again where exactly Jethonan came from and how old he is.

"Tulips and kings are made for each other. Magic chooses Tulips, and they are automatically bonded with the raw power that holds our world together at birth. Raw power is where lucent magic comes from, as you know."

I nod, it all makes sense so far.

He stops for a moment, thinking with a finger and thumb stroking his chin in a manner far more mature than he looks. "How to word this?" He paces for a few seconds longer. "Your kingdom loves your magic, and you are bound to it. If it suffers, you suffer." I nod, thinking of the blackening mark on my shoulder. He continues, "Lucent magic, when used, turns gloam. For years now, there has been no Tulip to recycle the magic, and so naturally, gloam is growing as lucent has decreased. You need a Tulip to restore the gloam to lucent. Even a king can't do that." He clasps his hands behind his back and strides from one side of the small space to the other, almost in circles. "Lucentia placed within all the royal heirs and within her chosen Tulips a draw to each other. Which is the reason you will have a magnetism toward a Tulip."

"You mean like attraction?"

He shakes his head. "There can be that, too, but what I'm talking about is deeper, a magical magnetism." He repeats himself with a smile. "I like that. *Magical magnetism.* Has a nice ring to it, doesn't it? I do enjoy alliteration."

I pull him back to the conversation. "A natural draw to their magic. Continue."

"Yes, yes. That draw, it's how you'll know you've found one since they'll likely keep the mark on their neck hidden. Their reputation has suffered the last two hundred years, you know. Not to mention they were hunted down and murdered."

I nod, but this all sounds crazy. Maybe Jethonan drank that rancid potion, and it ruined his brilliance. I narrow my eyes at him, watching for oddities, but I realize that's useless—he's full of them on a normal day.

"What exactly are their abilities?"

"Ah, yes, another important point." He walks to his bookshelf and pulls out the book he used last week. He opens it back to the page showing the woman in the gown. "See the white bird here? That indicates peace. Black Tulips have only defensive magic. The black tulip flower is the ancient symbol of magic itself."

"A *black* tulip? Black symbolizes gloam." I lift a brow at him, still not completely sure if I believe they aren't evil incarnate as I've been taught.

"Not really. Magic is magic. Lucent. There's always a bit of gloam, and always will be—just as there is night and day in perfect balance. It's the unrecycled waste of used magic, and it's currently out of balance because we don't have a proper way to restore it. But when our kingdoms work with the Tulips and they fill our kingdoms with lucent magic, the gloam is naturally restored, and things come into balance, effectively drowning out the dark creatures naturally and quickly turning it back over to light." He looks up with a frown, thinking. "Though, I'm not sure how that balance will be repaired since it's been so long and gloam is thriving. Better find a mighty powerful Tulip." He chuckles off-handedly, like he's not talking about the survival of my kingdom. "Something we'll see, I guess."

He begins pacing slowly around his office with his hands behind his back. He's always had difficulty being still. "Anyway, where was I? Ah, yes. The black tulip is the ancient symbol of magic and indicates that they are *very* powerful. Where all others risk death if they pull too much magic, Tulips have no limit."

My brows raise, impressed. I know well the fine balance between pulling magic and the energy required to survive. It can be dangerous, more so with how much more energy is required now to pull even small amounts of magic. I experienced it firsthand while battling the shard beast. People have died just trying to use magic to accomplish simple tasks now that things have gotten so bad.

"They're peaceful and powerful. Got it. But what can they do with all that power if they don't use it to fight?"

Jethonan pats the book as he's passing by. "According to the book, they can share it with individuals on a case-by-case basis, but there are no details about how that works. Seems similar to an Originator, at first." He shrugs. "But they seem to have gifts of a variety of forms of magic." He lifts fingers as he lists. "Originators, Hunters, Healers... you get my point. Makes them very difficult to recognize without the magical draw between them and a king or a visual of their mark."

I list off a quick version of what I've learned so I remember it. "So, they can offer raw magic at will, heal, and have some hunter senses."

Jethonan nods. "It seems their magic is most similar to Originators, to me. Though from the sounds of it, their magic runs cool and is white, whereas Originators, as you know, have more of a yellow magic that runs hot when shared in great amounts.

Lucentia wanted her Tulips different, their magic made specially to complement the king. After all this time, though, they're likely very good at hiding it, and it may not be noticeable." He looks at me like that's a big deal when all I can think is that this search is like a needle in a haystack.

"Where do I find them?" I run a hand roughly through my hair.

He passes by again, his robes fluttering behind him while he gestures again to the book. "These books are ancient records, so it is impossible to verify their current-day accuracy. I'll tell you what I do know. They used to be a tight-knit group, even had a school where Tulips would live, a sort of boarding school to learn about their gifts and *how* to be a Tulip. Now? I don't know."

Right. I'm supposed to find a woman who has skills that could place her among any of the factions, without seeing a mark, and she could potentially take over our world by bridging with an enemy. That's going to go over well if this information is widely spread.

This is a lot to take in, and I'm still not sure *how* I'm supposed to find one. "Thank you for your help, I'm sure I'll be back with more questions." I nod to him and head for the door, but he stops me.

"One more thing, my lord!"

I turn slowly, not sure I want to know *one more thing*. "Yes?"

He laughs uncomfortably. "There's also a flower you'll need in order to bridge. The Tulips know where to find it, but..."

"I'll have to search for it," I say flatly. Of course no one knows. I curse under my breath and sigh. "Where can I find another one... more... of the flowers?"

"It can only be found in the Lucent Mountains. There lies the only field of black tulips. Only a worthy king can take one. I read that Lucentia ensures her Tulips are cared for only by the best."

I stare blankly at him. No one goes there. It's probably entirely engulfed by gloam at this point. And a worthy king? From the looks of my mark, that's not me.

He continues quickly, aware of my darkening mood and seeming as ready as I to be done with the conversation. "I would highly recommend taking an Originator to amplify your magic for the journey."

"The High Kingdom can't spare any of the Originators. I'll have to find one elsewhere." I can't leave my people completely unprotected and helpless while I'm away, though I only hire the best of the best Originators, and it's tempting to hire one of them for this important journey. "We'll discuss this more later."

As I stalk down the echoing hallway, the literal downpour of information I just endured seems too deep—as if I can't come up for air and the weight of it is going to crush me. And what about Nadiette?

Chapter 9

Vera

T almost giddily make the hour-long journey to Mr. Eddieren's healing potions shop. It lies in a neighboring city, over the fae border, one much larger than the city I call home. I intentionally travel a busy road filled with others heading to work—merchants with their large wagons full of wares, and farmers with carts filled with food to sell at market. I slip between wagons and horses, but I don't mind the traffic. Well-traveled roads such as these are safer for someone like me who's traveling alone.

Rupi flutters to my shoulder amidst the busyness and nestles into the warm spot against my neck. I greet her with a smile and a small pinch of birdseed I always keep in a pocket of my long coat as I walk. The gentle cracking of the seeds in her tiny beak as she eats is a comforting, familiar sound, and her delighted chirps every so often bring a smile to my face. She showed up just before my parents died, hopping around me in the forest one day. And the next, and the next. Until I started bringing her home every night. The rest is history. Somehow, I think she knows how much I've needed her.

I don't know much about birds, but I never thought she'd live this long, though she seems as young as ever. At first, I was just happy simply to have a pet, but I found out fast that Rupi is an excellent judge of character. And she's a weapon in her own right with the way her fluff can turn to sharp edged quills with a ruffle of her feathers. I consider her my guard bird. She's saved me from taking bad contracts, among other things. It seems silly to say, but I trust her judgement completely. I trail a finger down her tiny, smooth back, and she flicks her head to peck at my finger affectionately, then with a gentle flap of her small wings she takes off into the air and lands in the nearby trees. I don't worry. She often leaves and always finds me again.

Soon enough, I enter the small potion shop that I've called work for the last three weeks, but not before noticing the sulfuric-scented fumes billowing from the chimney in dark, fat clouds. My nose wrinkles, and I hurry inside. I've contracted with enough potion makers to know that a scent like that indicates that Mr. Eddieren is in need of magical support. I find it's even worse inside, the blend of smells coming from the back room are enough to drop a deathstalker. I quickly hang my coat and bag on a hook behind the counter and force myself to enter the awful-smelling back room to see sweat pouring from the potion master's brow, the strain pulling at his face, and shaking in his hands. All signs of pulling fatigue. I quickly pull magic, invigorated by the cool of it as it runs through my veins. It's difficult for me to comprehend the extreme energy it takes for others to pull magic when it seems so drawn to me that I have to be careful how much I pull and use in order to keep my true identity under wraps, not to speak of the way it's cool and people will notice if I send too much at a time. I push it toward the potion maker, and he turns, relief in his eyes.

"Perfect timing!" he calls, as he accepts the magic with

relief. He keeps his focus on bringing the boiling solution before him to an exact temperature, muttering to himself here and there, but mostly in his own potion-making world now that he has enough magic and can focus.

I'm content to let him be throughout the day. I help customers at the front counter, chat with a few of the regulars, but am always sure to keep the offered magic flowing at a medium trickle as he finishes at least twenty more batches of an assortment of potions. By the end of the day, with the help of my magic, he seems no worse for wear and is chipper as usual. That's what I'm paid for, after all, to pull raw magic and share it in a usable form so that those who aren't Originators don't die from the exertion of pulling, or lose their jobs from lack of magic. With gloam out of control and lucent diminished, it's exhausting for those of other magic types to pull any amount of magic. The resource is limited and takes so much energy to use that some are basically Absent, but for most people, magic is a vital part of their existence and many struggle. It gets worse every year.

Though I hold a somewhat prestigious title, that of Originator, I am unwilling to charge as much for my services as most. Those who contract with me are struggling as much as I am. No upper class noble is going to hire a lower class Originator on permanently, like my Tulip sisters, leaving Renna and I to forage for the odd contracts here and there to create some type of consistent income. For some odd reason, magic made me able to pull large amounts of magic without tiring, and I don't feel good about charging the poor people, who will actually hire me, their life's savings to pay for it.

Most everyone struggles, thanks to the terrible leadership in all five kingdoms. The kings don't care about the people I work with and care for—the poor and struggling. And if I'm honest,

I'm one of 'em. I've seen the kingdoms continue to diminish, heard the history from Tatania at the annual Tulip meetings, and seen firsthand the destitute state of too many people whose forefathers thrived. But aside from helping where I can, and offering less for my services than most, I'm just a Tulip pretending to be someone I hate, and I want to be done.

I grab a duster and begin cleaning, another of the duties I've taken on voluntarily. No sense in sitting around bored for days at a time. I've worked long hours for the last eight years to make enough to pay the semi-annual Black Tulip dues every six months and still build my savings to make a new start. To finally do something that doesn't require me to live under the guise of an Originator. Every cent I have is taken by the outrageous cost of the complete dump I pay to live in, and the rest goes to Tulip dues, my savings, and very little amounts of food. My loose clothing attests to that fact. I look down at the belt I had to poke another hole in to cinch a little tighter, the waistband now scrunches up oddly around the men's shirt I wear tucked into it. I shrug, they do the job. No one looks twice when I wear these clothes, which is helpful for a woman who travels alone, but I know I've gotta find something better to wear when I visit Mama Tina or she'll outfit me in a wardrobe of her choosing, and I can't have that. She always had decent suggestions when I was a teen, but I shiver when I think of the last outfit I saw her wearing—made her look like a genuine ostrich.

Instead of dreading how I'll have to spend valuable coin on clothing I don't care about, I spend a little time daydreaming about the perfect space I plan to purchase, where I'll sell my odd trinkets, and best of all, how it has nothing to do with Originators or even Tulips. I couldn't be happier at the thought. Of course, owning my own shop has its risks. If I don't make enough to pay the Tulip dues for the next six months, I'll be forced to return to bounty hunting, or worse, having to beg money off Mama Tina, which I have never done in my life and refuse to do. And, maybe, after I've gathered the dues, I'll finally have enough to buy food and fit in my clothes once again. It may not be a perfect, comfortable plan, but I can't wait to get started.

I happily whip the duster between an assortment of bottles on a shelf. But then an annoying thought pops into my head, reminding me that I'll miss many of the people I've contracted with over the years. I'll worry for them. Healers, hunters, potion makers, weapon enchanters—I've worked with all of them here and there. My duster droops in my hand for a moment. Then I remind myself again that I'm a hated and obsolete Tulip, the best thing I can do is hide away.

By the end of the day, the entire building blessedly begins to smell of fresh fruit, sunlight, and honey, and I know I've done my job. I watch as Mr. Eddieren carefully pours the completed potion into small vials, marks the date of their creation on the bottom, caps them, and carefully sets them out under his front counter to sell.

I throw my ratty long-coat around my shoulders while he shuffles to his safe and returns with a small wad of cash. It should be much larger, if I charged him the average going rate for an Originator, but I take the money with a smile and pocket it, happy I can help a fellow struggling citizen.

"You'll do great things, Avenera." He squeezes my hand in a strong, fatherly grip.

I'm not so sure I'm capable of great, but definitely good. Average, at least. I smile anyway. Then my eyes get teary, and I know it's time to leave. Though he's distant and distracted most of the time, and I've only contracted with him a few times, he's been kind and offered tidbits of wisdom here and there. And this is my last contract using my magic as I do. I give him a hug, smelling that sunshine and honey scent once again before I leave with a teary smile and one last wave. I take a moment to imprint the picture of his quaint shop, him standing at its door and smiling.

Then I turn and realize I'm a free woman, free to move on to the next chapter of my life, and joy rushes through my limbs. I will no longer need to call myself an Originator. I can call myself an Absent, if that's what I want to be. For the first time in my life, through sheer grit and discipline, I've gotten ahead. I resist punching the air—I don't like drawing attention to myself. Instead, I shove my hands deep into my coat pockets and tug it tight around me like a celebratory self-hug. I've struggled through soul-deep weariness and lack of food at times, worked long hours, taken semi-dangerous jobs, but I can feel the extra bounce in my step today. This last job has given me enough to pay my dues for another six months, and I've made enough to take my savings and buy the perfect spot. I run the entire way back to the city I call home. Rupi flies around beside me, sensing my joyous mood. I'm planning to splurge on tender meats, cheese, and homemade bread to share with Renna in celebration when she returns from the river job she's taken in a week. She's been there all along, my best friend, the one who understands the struggle of being a Tulip in a world where we are hated. Of being poor and the excitement of finally getting a little ahead. I smile again at the rush of joy that surges through my veins.

Chapter 10

Ikar

I excuse my personal servants, in no mood for any help with preparations for bed. It's not like I'll be sleeping anyway. I sit in my favorite leather chair, hunched forward with my forearms braced on my thighs. Simon crows from an enormous tree branch that seems to sprout directly from the wall. Arrow lays his head in my lap. I call him a wolf, but really, he appears to be a cross between a wolf and a bit of dog, with some hints of an armored creature, evidenced by the hard armor-like layer that covers his back, hidden beneath his wiry fur. His teeth and face have the appearance of a wolf, but his ears come to sharp silver points that split two ways, maybe another gift from his armored history. I don't know, but he's a loyal beast. I carefully scratch behind one of his ears as my mind drifts.

I leave tomorrow morning. I think Arrow can sense it. I have put off telling Nadiette. I have to say something before I leave, which means there are only hours until I have to tell her, the woman I've come to care for and the woman my people expect me to be with, that I can't marry her. If things were different, we could have the celebration I know she's already been planning. To be honest, that the entire kingdom has been planning. Talks of having the cathedral church decorated in the finest silks, the design of her dress, and the light blue flowers that would be in her bouquet...

We've been in the same circles for years. We grew up together, so it's only natural that we'd seek marriage with how we so easily get along and the attraction we share. We have an easy companionship, hours upon hours of conversation, and seem to balance each other in just the right ways as a future king and queen should. It would be too easy to simply go forward and marry her. My people would be happy, I would be happy in some respects, but it can't be. It seems our being together really was too good to be true. I don't worry about if she'll marry or not. She's a beautiful, cultured woman, and I have no doubt that once she's known to be free of me that many others will seek her attention. A hint of jealousy flares in my chest.

I rest my head against the back of my chair and stare up at the crisscrossing beams of the high ceiling. Hopefully by morning, I have the words to say. All I know is my heart must be locked before I see her, or she will be mine and my kingdom's undoing. If I marry her, I may have a short lived joy, but my kingdom and people will disintegrate beneath my fingertips. I groan and run a hand through my hair in frustration.

I have to remember *why*. The faces of the soldiers who've died from the gloam attacks flash through my mind in random order. Men with families, children, parents, siblings. All mourning. Funeral after funeral. And then the people who've died just trying to pull magic for every day, mundane things. Usually, children, the sick, or the elderly. More funerals. The continual sight of so many fresh graves, the mounds of dark dirt contrasted with the deep green of grass. Our crops grow smaller every year, the weather patterns are getting more unpredictable and further decimating our kingdom's food sources. It's like a horror story that never ends and only grows worse. I'm helpless to stop it if I continue my current path. I may not know where to start, how to find a strange flower or a Queen of the Night, but it's something I can *do*. I have a mission. I feel an infinitesimal drop of hope, made smaller by the knowledge of the feats I must accomplish, but it's hope, nonetheless.

"*A Black Tulip?*" Nadiette says, disdain lacing her voice. She can't stop the lethal mixture of anger and disbelief from rising in her frown. "Tulips are obsolete, nonexistent. Everyone knows that."

She reaches out and wraps her hand around my arm, and I clench my jaw, purposefully unresponsive to her familiarity.

She narrows her eyes. "You and I together, Ikar. We can overcome it all. We are the two most powerful people in the kingdom." She infuses hope into her tone, and I feel my expression instinctively soften as my guilt attempts to choke me. I've heard this so many times. She doesn't realize that what she's always believed is untrue, and now is not the time to argue with her. But she seems to misinterpret my expression and uses it to fuel her next words. "Originators are the modern Tulips. You know that. How is a Tulip better than I?" Her chin lifts in challenge with her words.

I clench my jaw again. This conversation is going as horribly as I assumed it would. "Not better, per se. Different. And different is what duty requires."

"I am not naive. I have seen firsthand the death and

destruction caused by magic untamed, but I refuse to believe there is no other way. You don't need a Tulip. You need *me*." Her eyes are as fiery as her hair now.

I find myself frowning at her response, unsure how to proceed.

Her hand still remains clasped around my bicep, but now she closes the last few steps, and in the next second, her lips find mine. We've kissed many times, and I respond instinctively, but just as quickly, I pull away.

The emotion in her eyes is so raw and clear as she searches my gaze that I have to look away. She needs to believe that I do want this duty or she will continue to hold out hope. I gently ease my arm from her grasp and place my hands on her shoulders, matching her gaze. "I will always need you as an Originator for my people, and I hope you will continue to serve them in your position. But in any other way, we can never be. As High King, my duty is to my people, and right now, that duty is to find a Tulip." I drop my hands from her shoulders, feeling like I've pressed a hot iron to my palms. Her magic must be building with her emotion. I watch as she takes a breath, clasps and unclasps her hands, and then when she looks back up at me, it is a look in contradiction to the hurt that only moments ago filled her eyes.

"So, I must be creative to make you mine," she says flirtatiously.

It falls flat when I refuse to respond as usual and the moment turns awkward. Before she can continue to attempt to persuade me otherwise, a servant hurries down the hall toward us.

"Your Majesty." He gives a light bow and hands me a rolled scroll, then the servant acknowledges her with a slight nod. I turn away slightly to read in privacy, and, after only seconds, allow it to roll up with a snap.

I look into her eyes. "I must go. I wish you the best, Nadiette. You will always be a cherished friend." With a final, stiff nod, I turn and stride away.

I walk toward Jethonan's work room. It was he who sent the message that I should meet him there, unknowingly rescuing me from the conversation with his impeccable timing. I'll make sure to thank him for it. That conversation has been a weight I've been dreading, and I feel a sense of relief now that it's done, though I can't say that she took it well. I hope with time she accepts it and we can maintain our friendship. The kingdom will still need her, even after I've bridged with a Tulip.

I knew it would be uncomfortable. I've had a few weeks to process the fact we can't be together, and she's had only moments. I hadn't planned on the kiss, but when she had leaned in, it felt natural to return it. It wasn't sensual or heated in any way, and I'd intentionally kept it short, bundling all the years of courtship into a final goodbye. It seemed appropriate at the time, but now I'm not so sure. I hope she feels the same closure I feel.

Soon enough, I'm at the door to his office. I knock once and enter. I never know what to expect when I enter Jethonan's work room, but it's not this. The absence of odd smells, fumes, extreme temperatures, and general mess is odd, and I'm not sure what to think. My hand instinctively goes for my sword as I turn, knowing the only way this room could be clean is if something terrible happened to my advisor. I don't sense an enemy, but oddly, I *do* sense an unseen mess around me. It's disconcerting, my vision and intuition at war. I shrug it off due to the fact that I've never seen this room clean since before I hired him. I cautiously glance around, then take an uneasy seat in my usual chair near the bookcases. But before I've fully sat back, Jethonan enters the room from a door to the left in a flurry of rushing robes. I release the handle of my sword finally, relieved that he appears alive and well.

He showcases the cleanliness of his office with a broad sweep of his hands. "Does it meet your satisfaction, my lord?" He smiles smugly, and I'm wondering what's gotten in to him.

"Thought you'd been murdered," I mumble. "Who did this?" I look around, suspicious.

"I did, of course." Jethonan's smile only grows more smug.

"Impossible."

"Your lack of faith in my ability to tidy up is astounding."

A grin twists my lips, but then my vision seemingly flickers, and I glimpse the usual mess that is Jethonan's work room beneath... *what?* It's gone before I can blink. But it's there, it's around me. I can sense it, but I can't see it. Now I understand why he wasn't more offended at my disbelief. I grip the arm of the chair and lean forward, narrowing my eyes. Born with hunter magic, my senses are naturally heightened, my vision more than excellent when I want it to be. I pull a bit of magic, testing whatever magic creation he's used here, but all looks neat and clean.

"What did you do to this room?" I ask, astounded. "Is it a shield?"

Now that satisfactory grin is back on his face. "It works!" He whispers a charm word, and whatever it is that masked his office disappears. I'm instantly assaulted by a smoky, burn-tinged aroma mixed with a strong floral-spicy scent and a lingering hint of the ever-present sour smell that I have come to believe has been baked into the castle walls.

I grimace. "Please tell me you haven't attempted the healing potion again."

"Ah, yes. I'm very close with that, but that's not what I've been working on." He turns to his table, and I hear clinking glass, a sizzling sound, and something hard rolls across the surface. Then there's a shuffle of papers before he turns back around with a vial between his fingers.

"The fae are masters of the glamour, naturally. They commonly use it to further their criminal activities, as you know."

I gather my patience, knowing how he enjoys drawing out these conversations.

"You'll be easily recognized on your journey, which could endanger you and possibly even prevent you from accomplishing the tasks. Your people love you so much you'll be accosted by well-wishers and be entirely unproductive. To combat that, I've created a perfect match for fae glamour." He hands me the vial, and I hesitantly take it, holding it up to look closer at the liquid inside. I've seen and even used fae glamour before, but it's always come directly from the fae.

"Have you tested this?" I ask doubtfully.

"Of course. Three times, to be exact." He sounds offended that I even asked. "Its only limitations are those that also apply to the fae and their natural glamours. No one will recognize you."

I clap him on the shoulder, "Thank you, Jethonan. This is just what I needed." I toss the bottle lightly in the air and then catch it as I stride across the room, eager to be away from the aroma assaulting my nostrils. I pause by the door and turn. "How long will it last?"

"Three weeks, at least. I'll send another with you, just in case."

"And it won't kill me or turn me into gloam, right?" I'm only slightly serious.

Jethonan's lips press flat, and he doesn't respond. I pull the door shut behind me with a chuckle. For the first time, I feel eager to leave. I head straight to my office and scrawl two messages, one to Darvy and one to Rhosse, each with only four words.

We leave at sunrise.

Chapter 11

Nadiette

I clip a flower here, a flower there, feeling all the feelings of a woman spurned. So much so, I've taken to a servant's job, grasping any distraction available. I've always thought Ikar achingly handsome. *Clip.* Kind, honorable, strong. We'd grown up together, laughed and planned together. *Clip.* Kisses stolen on horseback, wandering his lands on lazy, warm afternoons. The way he'd caressed my cheek just days ago. *Clip. Clip.* Our children would be beautiful, his rugged handsome features combined with my classic beauty. Add to that, his kingdom is enormous with bounteous crops and wealth. Now he tells he is forced to take a *Black Tulip* as a wife. *Clip. Clip. Clip.*

I look at the pile of mutilated flowers fallen across the moist soil and growl in a way that would have my mother red in the face as I pluck a mostly whole, light pink tulip head from the ground. Between two fingers, I spin it back and forth, and more petals fall, spinning toward the ground. An exclusive group of women that thought they were more entitled to royal marriages and power than other magic factions, leaving powerful Originators like *me* to search for the passable leftovers. The second and third sons or other nobles. I know the kingdom's history. I know of Queens of the Night. It didn't take much research to find the seer vision that tells of their danger. They are no secret and had disappeared as *awful* things should. In fact, they were so evil, they were hunted down and destroyed—by Originators, no less. And it seems it will have to happen again.

The mess of flowers before me will all be wilted by morning, just as the Queens of the Night soon will be. It seems that just as my strong Originator magic-ancestors were forced to hunt them down, I will also be forced to protect the kingdom by clipping them off until none are left for Ikar to choose from. I will save him from his honor, and when it is comfortably assuaged and his search futile, he will return to me. I will forgive him and we will marry in the marble cathedral church with a bouquet of the whitest flowers and have powerful, gorgeous children. The people need never know the difference, since nothing official has been announced about our impending marriage. My cheeks redden at the thought of him arriving home with another woman on his arm, supposedly more powerful than me. I drop the tulip head to the ground. Of course, no tulips will adorn my bouquet. No tulips will grow on our lands at all. I stand, leaving the mess of flowers on the ground, and when I pass the gardener, I pause.

"Remove every tulip. I don't want to see another," I say stiffly.

The gardener frowns at the seemingly odd request but nods as a dutiful servant does. "Yes, my lady."

I watch as he kneels by the first bed and begins weeding them out from among the other flowers.

I smile. *For you, Ikar.*

Chapter 12

Ikar

Darvy, Rhosse, and I intentionally pass the sleek royal boats docked at the side of a busy boardwalk along the river. The glamour Jethonan created must be working since no one has spared me a glance. Darvy and Rhosse have gotten a few salutes and head bows. Being two of my highest commanders, they are well-known amongst the royal crews and soldiers who patrol the dock. But we make our way forward otherwise unhindered. We come to a boat already half-filled, headed toward Kivan, a decent-sized city to the south that is a hub where we have decided to begin our search for a Queen of the Night. After a quick inspection of the steel-bottomed ship, we quickly pay the fare and board. We take our seats on hard, splintery benches planted around the deck of the ship and bolted to the wood floor. If I didn't know anything about enchanted river boats, I'd be worried by this one, but I don't care if the top is rotting through, it's the steel bottom that matters, and this one appears solid enough.

Moments after we take our seats, clouds roll in, dark and black, obscuring two of the three suns above us. I take a second look at the sturdiness of the ship we chose. The weather can be violent at times, and it grows worse with the ever-increasing gloam.

"What d'you wanna bet that this thing sinks before we dock in Kivan?" Darvy leans forward and speaks around me to Rhosse as he flicks his eyes toward the clouds speedily rolling our way.

Rhosse considers seriously for a moment, his arms crossed over his chest as he inspects the ship. "It'll make it, I think." He knocks his large knuckles against a piece of the deck railing. It makes a suspicious cracking sound but doesn't appear to break. "This trusty boat has made it this far. It'll make another trip."

Rhosse and he begin to banter back and forth about the wager while a middle-aged woman sitting nearby, who obviously overheard, begins to glance worriedly around and whisper with the teenage girl beside her.

I elbow Darvy in the ribs. "Stop it. You're scaring my citizens," I growl.

"Shush, Simon," Darvy says, happily forgoing my title as I instructed him.

"Do not call me Simon," I mutter. I refuse to take my hawk's name.

Rhosse pipes up next, "How is it we went over every detail of this plan *except* your name?" he asks low.

"My name is Ikar, no need to change it. Enough people named their kids after me after I was born that it won't be a problem. Common as any name, now."

The ship captain stomps up the plank, tugs it inside, and tosses it on the deck before he mumbles some warnings and instructions so incoherently that I have no idea what he said. Moments later, the ship takes off, sailing smoothly into the dark, gloam-infested river.

As I keep an eye on the roiling clouds moving in above us, my thoughts wander back to yesterday. My chest squeezes uncomfortably when I think of Nadiette's face when I told her I couldn't marry her. No matter what I do, I feel guilt. If I forgo my duty and marry Nadiette, my people suffer and possibly die. Yes, my people will be disappointed that their favored Originator will no longer be my queen, and I know Nadiette will also be embarrassed about the turn of events. And then I wonder, how will they receive a Black Tulip who I intend to marry instead? Hopefully, my people's loyalty will also come to include our future Queen of the Night. And maybe I can even hope, in time, that my people come to love her. But I won't. I will have to share my kingdom, my people, my rule, my bed, and even my magic with her. My heart will stay my own.

As much as I know about love, I can say that I love Nadiette. At least, I think I do. But it's over, and now I need to prepare myself to marry and bridge with a Tulip—if I can find one. There are not many records kept on the history, so all I have to go on are stories and personal journals. My great-great-grandfather and grandmother were a bridged marriage, and from what I read, they seemed to be happy. But the thought of sharing such an intimate bond with someone I don't know has me swinging from angry to fearful. A standard arranged marriage is intimate, yes, but my magic stays my own. It feels as if magic is forcing me to give access to one of my most cherished parts to another. It's strange and disconcerting and necessary all at once, and I struggle to maintain the motivation to continue the mission.

That leads me to my biggest question. Where do I find a Black Tulip? One of the biggest problems I face is the fact that the Tulips are no longer an organized group. They have dispersed and spread since being hunted down, they likely don't even receive any sort of training. I have to track one down and hope she's willing, before my glamour wears off, and my kingdom disintegrates. It's a monumental task.

We've been in Kivan for over a week, and I feel my patience diminishing like sand emptying from an hourglass in a steady stream. We've frequented every tavern, gambling establishment, and friendly bakery in this city. We've walked every street several times over, listening and watching, asking questions here and there, only to be given odd looks or completely ignored as people rush away. Half the people we've asked don't even know what a Black Tulip *is*.

Tonight, we sit in a tavern that has rooms we've paid for on its second level. But it's almost a waste of money, as I assume we'll be sitting amongst the drunken gambling crowds until well into the early morning hours if tonight is anything like the others. Here on the main floor is a large room full of scarred and chipped round tables, rough-cut wood chairs around each. A bar counter spans the width at the back, lined with stools of varying heights. It is our last night here before we move on to the next major city.

I look across the room and see Darvy immersed in a game of cards, a heavy pile of money sits at the center of the round table, surrounded by a rough-looking bunch of men. He says something, and the man beside him laughs until they set their cards down and then he frowns at Darvy's hand. I smirk. Darvy looks much more innocent than he truly is. A young face, that one, but his experience with weapons, and especially healing, are unsurpassed.

Rhosse, on the other hand, has the seasoned lines of a

mature warrior on his face, though that doesn't seem to detract from his appeal to women wherever we go. My smirk grows wider when I see him on a stool at the counter at the rear of the tavern, a drink nestled between his large hands while a blonde tavern girl appears to coyly be moving closer with a flirtatious air about her. For some reason, the heaviness of danger that accompanies a man who's seen as much as he seems to attract some women rather than chase them off. Where Darvy excels at the technical parts of sword fighting, Rhosse commands a sword with more lethality than anyone else I know, including myself. But he also has hunter magic as I do, his strongest gifts in tracking and working with animals. I've never met anyone or anything that can outrun Rhosse. I assume a Black Tulip won't, either. I chastise myself a bit for comparing my future queen to prey, but if I think of it more as a hunt it seems to settle better.

I stretch my shoulders back and shift in the uncomfortable wood chair. I've been watching a door at the back of the tavern, just past the bar counter. It's a door that most would assume leads out to a back alley, but I've noticed there's an unusual amount of traffic coming in and out. My hearing is sharp with magic that I've been pulling the entire time we've been here, in small amounts in order to keep it up for the duration of the night. The struggle is tuning out the heavy mix of conversation when all I'm searching for are words to do with Black Tulips. Like a needle in a haystack, this search. Along with the amount of people entering and exiting that door, though, it's noisy. Most wouldn't be able to hear the cheering I hear with the rumble of voices in the dining area, but it's clear something is going on back there.

I stand and casually make my way to the back when I see one of the brazen tavern girls hanging on the arm of a drunk man heading toward the door. I glance over my shoulder to see

Rhosse still pursued by the same blonde woman, but no matter. I slip in beside them on my own and find myself in a long, dark hallway. I've no choice but to follow it now. Seems more productive than sitting in a chair the rest of the night anyway.

I follow the unaware couple, who turn the handle of a door at the end of the hallway and enter another room. I follow them into a press of people, shouting and jeering and immediately jostling against me. I push my way forward, curious about what the focus of their excitement is. The heat of the crowded space presses on me, and I find myself sweating after just minutes. Swearing and jeers ring in my ears, and soon, I see why. From several rows of people back, I see the ropes of a fighting ring. A man in jet-black leather armor stands on the corners of the ropes, his long hair tied back, and with a strong arm jams a small piece of parchment in the air.

"Winner gets the list!" he shouts. "Last call!"

The crowd roars and pushes forward, and I watch as several large men move forward to sign their names on a parchment near the ring.

I look around, trying to figure out what is going on. What is the list about, and why would so many be willing to fight for it? Probably just a bunch of bored drunks out to have fun. I'm about to leave before I decide to ask a somewhat coherent-looking man what the deal is.

I raise my voice to be heard over the commotion, "What's the list?" I gesture toward the man still standing on the ropes and waving the list, tauntingly, urging fighters to sign up.

"A list o' Tulips to be found for reward and only one list to be had." He grins.

List of Tulips? My heartbeat picks up its pace. *It can't be this easy.* The man is about to begin weaving through the crowd again, but I stop him with a hand on his shoulder. "To be found? For what?"

The man is beginning to look annoyed, but answers me anyway. "Someone's set a reward on Tulips. Wants 'em dead. If you want it, better join the fight, or you won't know who to look for and who to go to for payment." He jerks his shoulder from my grip and disappears into the swarm of people. I don't stop to think about it. If that man is right, that list is exactly what I need. And also exactly what I need to keep from anyone willing to track Tulips down to kill them.

Without thinking any further, I roughly push my way to where the list of competitors sign up and reach for the quill, but a greedy-looking man with gaps of missing teeth in his smile opens up a large bag and taps the amount posted on a sign to join the fight. Above the price, it's clearly noted that this is a fight between mercenaries. Can a person decide he's a mercenary at any time? I don't know, but I just did. I pull out the money—it'll take everything I brought tonight—but I drop it anyway, knowing it will be well worth it if I can get that list. I grab the pen from him and scribble my name beneath the long list of competitors.

"What are the rules?" I ask.

The man laughs, and air whistles between the gaps of his teeth. "Aren't any."

I'm pushed aside by three more men and a woman who also pay and sign their names beneath mine. I clench my jaw. It's going to be a long night.

Chapter 13

Nadiette

I sit across from Tryn, my second in command and ever-faithful assistant. Plates of exquisitely-plated food are set before us, then the server gives a slight bow and moves to the next table. I pay the other diners no heed, still in knots about Ikar's decision. He left three days ago, and the days have been torturous.

Tryn takes a delicate bite and comments on the food, but I hear none of it. She keeps up the conversation, talking about the newest Originators and how their training is going until a server with a message on a small plate bows slightly before me.

"For you, my lady."

My eyes widen momentarily before I slip the message off the plate and nod my thanks. The server leaves, and I break the smudged wax seal, scanning the message quickly

Abruptly, I speak. "I need your help."

Tryn, a bite halfway to her mouth, slowly places the utensil back against her plate. "Of course." She wipes her mouth carefully with a white napkin that looks dull compared to the pure white of her gown.

"I spoke to you of Ikar's foolish plan to find and, not only *marry*, a Tulip, but bridge with her. Our ancestors protected the kingdom from them before, and we must do so now."

Tryn nods, concern in her eyes. "What do you plan to do?"

I hold the message up between two fingers and wiggle it with a smile. "Stop him, of course. I meet Rita's contact tonight. I asked for a list."

Tryn leans forward, eyes wide and speaks in a whisper. "A list of the Black Tulips?"

"Yes. But I need your help to figure out how to use it."

Tryn sits back, frowning. "Well, we could gather a search party and find them all—"

I shake my head. "No, it would attract too much attention. The less who know of Ikar's recklessness, the better."

Tryn ponders for a moment. "I've never known Ikar to be reckless." Doubt laces her voice.

I fist the linen napkin in my hand. "So, you believe that bringing the Tulips back to their former position of fame and power is safe?"

Tryn hesitates. "I... haven't had a chance to learn—"

"And hopefully, you don't. It would be the worst thing to happen to our kingdom in two hundred years."

Tryn presses her lips together.

I continue, "I need to act quickly. Think it through tonight."

Tryn whispers again. "It's really not safe for you to go to that place."

I laugh lightly. "You have no idea how many times I've been there. No need to worry."

Long after the suns have set, I shed my white apparel for a pair of somewhat ragged breeches, a dark shirt, and black jacket. The regular when I step out to meet with contacts of a special sort.

In positions such as Head Originator, it's important to have eyes and ears everywhere to better protect my Originators and the kingdom. How else am I supposed to do my job well? I throw a long cloak over my shoulders and pull the hood forward before disappearing into the night, sticking to the shadows as I cross into the side of Moneyre that most women are afraid to travel at night.

Among the street lined with leaning and shabby taverns, I enter the worst of them. The owner, a woman with fiery red-orange hair, meets my eyes and gives a small nod.

I slide into a seat and wait until the woman waves me toward the back. Then I stand and make my way around the unruly, boisterous crowds.

"Rita," I greet from within the shadows of my hood.

"Through here." She opens the door into a darkened, more private room at the back. As soon as I walk in, she pulls it shut behind her.

The only other person in the room is hunched over in a chair in the corner, as cloaked and hidden as I. Ignoring the twinge of fear, I stride across the room, pull out a chair, and confidently take a seat.

I sit across from the figure, who I sense returns my stare, for one minute, then two.

Done with the game, I stack three gold coins on the table. Enough to buy warm meals and lodging for two months.

"You want the Black Tulips?" The voice sounds intentionally raspy, hiding its true nature. Maybe even glamoured. But if I were to guess, I'd say it's a woman.

I nod and wait for her to continue.

She's silent for another moment. I place another coin on the stack.

Then another.

She pulls a tattered piece of parchment from the folds of her cloak and places it on the edge of the table nearest her.

I sigh and place two more coins on the already towering stack, getting annoyed.

The woman finally slides the paper across the table, and I snatch it before any more of my coins are forced atop the stack. I unfold it and find a hastily-written list of seven names. When I look up to ask where the information came from, she's already gone.

The next morning, I stand, turning my back on the list that lies flat on my desk, and walk to my window, my white gown trailing behind me. I look over the courtyard, servants busily crossing back and forth, soldiers, nobles, and others talking as they pass through the curated gardens and fountains. Rounding up the Tulips is a start, but Ikar is competent, strong, and smart. If anyone can find a Tulip, it'll be him, and that cannot happen.

I stare unseeing out the window now. Last night, I was ecstatic to have the list. Now, sobered by a long night of no sleep, I wonder how to slow him down without hurting him. The castle feels empty without Ikar here, and it only adds to my longing. He started the search for a cursed Tulip several days ago. If he happens to find one right away, he could be back any day. I press a fist to my lips as I hold back a sob, imagining a new woman on Ikar's arm who's wearing the crown meant for me. I fist my hands at my sides and blink rapidly to clear my eyes. Somehow, he must be stopped. He must have time to return to his senses.

Tryn speaks from a small settee at the opposite side of the room, "You could use the Royal Hunters to track down the seven women."

I shake my head, still looking out the window so Tryn doesn't spot the wetness in my eyes. I never show such weakness in front of my Originators. "Again, I don't want too much attention drawn to this. No one from the castle or any of his soldiers. We need someone relatively trustworthy but not too honorable, or they won't accept the job."

Tryn thinks for a moment. "The mercenaries?"

I nod slowly as the idea grows on me. The mercenaries are known to be a dangerous bunch. Some are ex-soldiers, and most just violent, well-trained criminals who'll take any job that pays well enough. *But should I care who captures the Black Tulips? I'm no murderer, but I certainly don't want one ruling by Ikar's side. What lengths am I willing to go to protect our kingdom?*

"Yes," I say with finality, rushing back to my desk with swirling skirts and pulling a new sheet of parchment from a stack before neatly and quickly scrawling the seven names of the women I paid for. I take a moment to consider the reward amount, knowing it must be large. I add the information to the bottom, fold it up, and then stand and walk to the window again.

"Nadiette?" Tryn asks.

"The plan is missing something," I say quietly. "I must think."

Someone will be tracking the Tulips with the list Tryn is about to sell. Still, Ikar will have to be delayed, as it would put him in danger if he happened to find a Tulip and then attempted to protect the evil woman from one of the mercenaries. Ikar will simply need to be re-routed for a time, protected from the mercenaries. Just in case. But how?

I begin pacing the room. Tryn watches silently. Riches are always the best motivator. I'm almost positive it will be a mercenary who ends up with the list—brutal and savage. They will take care of the Tulip problem efficiently, no doubt, but I don't want mercenaries after Ikar. They are loyal to none, so it's too risky. And he too valuable.

Honestly, if Ikar wasn't so noble and true, it would be much easier to get him home. In fact, he probably wouldn't have even left in the first place. *So true and noble.* I laugh gently, remembering when, as a child, he was accused of replacing his tutor's soap with a concoction that turned her skin purple for days. Of course, it hadn't been him. Even then his strength of character was straight as the finest arrow. And then I freeze. *Why not?* I pace faster now, matching the speed of my thoughts. What if he's accused of a crime? Temporarily, of course. He's under a glamour, so people won't know he's the king. He would be dreadfully annoyed, but I imagine far into the future, when we'll laugh over this ridiculous journey, happy that it brought us together like we always wanted. His laugh, deep and rich, near my ear as we sit beside the deep blue lake and watch the suns go down as we've done so many times before.

I sigh and return to the present, striding back to my writing desk and pulling out another crisp parchment and dipping my quill. I scrawl a lengthy note with a reward amount listed at the bottom. Then I touch the quill to the page and begin a rough sketch. After, I prepare to drop a bit of wax on the folded paper to seal it, then pause. Mind spinning, I lift the quill and look at its tip, considering the glamour Ikar is using. I'd heard him briefly mention it. With a bit of the same glamour applied to the tip, I could quickly go over the sketch once more and it should come to match the glamour.

With that thought in mind, I pocket the quill and make my way to Ikar's room. If luck of magic is with me, there'll still be an empty bottle I can steal a drop from that he left behind.

It doesn't take long to find a discarded vial, and with a bit of water on a dried bit stuck on the bottom, I dip the quill, hurry back to my office, and finish the sketch. I quickly jot out the reward amount for his arrest, drop a circle of hot wax, and press it firmly with a blank stamp I keep in my drawer.

"All ready now, I think," I say, holding the two folded parchments in my hands.

I hold the first parchment up. "Have this list sold to the highest bidder." I hold the second up, "And this one is for a legal bounty. My name is not to be associated, the funds for the reward are to be kept with the treasury in town. Make sure no trail leads back to either of us."

Tryn keeps her expression carefully neutral. I can tell she begs to ask about what I'm telling her to do, but I keep my expression blank and stern, unwilling to offer anything. These things are best kept close.

Tryn nods respectfully and leaves the room.

Chapter 14

Vera

I left Mr. Edierren's shop over a week ago now, and I've simply been waiting at home for Renna to return to celebrate the end of my Originator career before I leave to purchase the shop I've found. She should be back tonight. I'm already scheduled to sign a contract for the shop next week and the thought sets giddy butterflies fluttering in my stomach.

The evening sunlight shines warm on my skin, and I bask in it. I continue down the sidewalk toward my favorite tavern, and as soon as I enter, I catch a mouthwatering display of a variety of foods behind a wood counter. I wouldn't normally splurge on a meal like this for Renna and me, but I want to celebrate, and this is exactly what I need. She's no better off than I, so I know she'll appreciate it. I hurry in, highly aware of how empty my stomach feels now that I am surrounded by food.

"Vera!" Maurine greets me cheerfully, coming around the counter to fold me into her motherly arms. "You're skin and bones, m'girl. Let's get you set right."

Before I can ask for a bag of food to go, she bustles back

around the counter and proceeds to slice fresh bread, meat, and cheese while she jumps straight into the latest news. "The oldest Rismond twin married off last week," then under her breath she adds, "much faster than I thought she'd be."

I laugh, Maurine always fills me in on the news I've missed while I've been away. I let her continue, *mm-hmm*ing as needed.

"Jarne sold his carpentry shop to a new man in town, a good-looking one at that." She looks up and winks at me, then continues filling my plate. I smile, but I'm not interested. No one wants a magical misfit, I learned that a long time ago. Right now, all I'm interested in is the hefty plate she places in my hands.

"Go sit, m'dear. I'll get you some soup and some of the fresh cherry tart I just finished, and I'll be back."

Moments later, I'm sitting and trying my best to eat like a normal person, but it's hard when food is scarce. Maurine sits down in front of me, spots from her busy morning coloring her white apron.

"I also forgot to mention the latest drama." Her voice lowers as I sink my teeth into the delectable bread in a bite much too large to be considered ladylike, unconcerned about the usual *drama*.

She continues in a hushed voice, "Word has spread that mercenaries are tracking down a Tulip, maybe more than one. Who woulda thought? Tulips haven't been heard of in *years*. Thought they were gone."

The bread turns gluey in my mouth, and I gulp down the half-chewed, too-large mouthful with a choke and a swallow. "Excuse me?" I cough once more to clear my throat.

"It's true." Her brown eyes are wide.

"And what exactly are they doing with them... her?" I keep

my voice natural, but inside, I'm spinning. Why would someone be after us?

"No one knows, but they're about to start disappearin'. I hear it's for the reward money. Atrocious, isn't it?" Maurine purses her lips and shakes her head. "Just served a man that looked like one of those dastardly mercenaries the other day. I shoulda shooed him out."

"You couldn't know for sure," I mumble a half-hearted attempt at comfort, but my mind is elsewhere. Mercenaries after Tulips? A mercenary. *Here?*

"But on to happier topics..." Maurine continues chatting, filling the silence with her voice while I eat the rest of my meal, not in enjoyment now, but out of necessity. If a mercenary, the rough, blood-thirsty fighters, find out in any way who I am, and there's reward money attached, I'm dead. And what about *Renna?* If what Maurine said is true, we need to be more careful than ever.

Once I finish, I give Maurine a big hug, smile at her reminder to stop in more often, gratefully taking the full bag of food she shoves into my hand and simply shrugging my shoulders at her chastisement to take better care of myself and "fill out those cheeks."

I step out of the tavern, still waving to Maurine over my shoulder when I feel a shoulder bump mine and yelp in surprise. My heart calms when I see it's just Rhette standing there with a grin. "I've been looking for you. Before you race off, I have something I want to talk to you about."

My heart starts pumping faster for a different reason now. For all the flirtatious feelings I've been sensing the last several months, he has yet to ask me out. I've worked with Rhette, a hunter, often over the past several years. I use the term *help* loosely, as I really only carry a pack and offer magic.

This is it, though. I know he's going to ask me out. I've been waiting for this moment, and I find it might be just what I need to make this day better. I'm thinking a clean tavern with a nice dinner, but really, anything is romantic without a bounty between us. Whatever it is, I'll take it.

He looks around to ensure our privacy before he slides a folded piece of parchment from inside his jacket and says low, "A new bounty. I just got the information this morning." He smiles and leans in a bit, his breath brushing against my ear. "One of the highest reward offers we've ever had."

My smile grows tight. Not a date, then. Just work. Again. Sometimes I think I'm only wanted for my magic. In fact, I know it, another reason I can't wait to be rid of this title. I sigh, letting my smile drop and hold my hand out for the paper, all but snatching it from him in my irritation. The man is either not interested or completely oblivious, I have no idea which. I open the paper and my eyes widen. The sketch is roughly done, and hopefully, it's done by the hand of an awful artist or this poor man is greatly lacking in the looks department. If it's *accurate,* that is. These sketches are not overly helpful because of the inaccuracies.

My eyes skip to the bottom of the parchment, and I quickly read the description and pay. I am sure my brain misfires when I read the reward amount. Surely, my eyes see the numbers wrong. I blink a few times and pull the paper closer. We'll be competing with at least half the registered bounty hunters once they hear of this reward, which is a formidable challenge.

"Why so much?" My voice is an awed murmur, but I see exactly why the reward is so much. The criminal is a Class A.

"A noble really wants this guy."

I lower the paper and look suspiciously into his eyes. "Why's he Class A? Is he a maniac? A murderer?"

He laughs like he thinks I'm joking and leans a strong shoulder against the brick of the tavern I just exited. "Apparently, he refused to fulfill an agreement he made."

"So, again, why so much? And why Class A?"

He hesitates for a split second. "I assume it's because they want him caught quickly... or because he's a mercenary." He says the last part a little quiet and really fast.

I immediately shove the paper toward him. "I'm not taking this one." No way am I attempting to act as Originator to help arrest a mercenary, a Class A criminal, especially after what I just learned. I tried that once and failed, almost died, actually. This one's going to be a big *nope*. He simply pushes it back toward me.

"Think about it."

"I don't need to. This guy could kill me in half a second." And also, I'm a Tulip, which will only add fuel to the fire if what I've learned is true. But Rhette can't know about any of that.

"I won't disagree—mercenaries are known to be ruthless. We'll have to be smarter than him, but I know you need the money, and I can't do this one alone."

My cheeks heat. No hard working, independent woman wants to talk about the desperate state of her finances with her prospective love interest. I don't necessarily *need* the money, a little cushion would be nice, but it's not worth my life. Out of habit, I glance out the window toward the large board where all announcements, wanted ads, job offers, and scheduled events for this kingdom are posted. The wanted section sits pitifully bare.

Rhette sees me eyeing it. "There are no other wanted ads right now, this is it." And then he adds, "Maybe if you didn't discount your rate for every needy person you work with, you would make enough to survive." He quirks an eyebrow.

Judgy hunter. I glare at him. He's never had to tell an elderly healer that he can't help them when they can't pay your rate, or refuse a weapon enchanter who just lost a hand who's struggling to feed his family because he can't keep up the amount of work he used to. But I can't argue with him.

"Come on. It'll be fun."

I avoid looking at his eyes while I think. I have a soft heart, and he will take full advantage of it with some sort of sweet and sad combo expression that will convince me to take this job. But no, I don't *need* it. I have just enough for now. It's most definitely not worth the danger for me as a Tulip.

"Not this one. You shouldn't either." I firmly shake my head. This time I do take a peek at his face and see his letdown expression, but still, I stay firm. This one is just too dangerous for me, and I'm done being an Originator. In fact, I just ate my celebratory feast, and I'm not gonna let him ruin it.

"Let me know if you change your mind. I'll be leaving in two days."

"I'm not going to change my mind."

I quickly forget about Rhette and his ridiculous contract as I hurry across town and race up the wobbly and terrifying stairs to my home that sits two floors up from a dirty street in the outer parts of the city, the small bag of food swinging wildly from my hand. I give the usual twist and kick, and the door swings open.

"Renna! I did it!" I hold the bag of food up like a trophy. In the shadows of our home, Rupi worries a path along the back of a wood rocking chair.

The curtains are drawn, the space dark and quiet. That's definitely not how I left it. My expression morphs into concern as I step inside and close the door behind me.

"Renna?" I call. That's when I hear the sob. The hand holding the sack of food drops limply to my side, my shoulders following. Her jerk boyfriend probably said something again. I've told her to stay away from Originators, especially ones like him, but sobs don't belong on a day like today, especially not ones caused by Jerrit.

"Come on, Rupi." I'm not the best with these break up situations, and Rupi is a comfort, so I scoop her from the back of the chair and lift her to my shoulder, then head to Renna's room. I hesitantly push open her door to see her lying on her side, facing the wall, still and unmoving. Her clothing looks grungy, unusual for Renna, which means it must be bad. Even when the door squeaks open and she knows I'm here, she doesn't move. Rupi chirps. Still no acknowledgement.

"Renna, I've told you to break up with hi—"

"I don't have the money." She says it with a distinct lack of emotion. Like all of it was sucked out and she's just a fragile, empty shell now. She can't mean what I think she means. The dues have to be paid in just two weeks. My eyes move to the bracelet on her wrist.

I take a hesitant seat on the edge of her bed. I don't want to hear it, but I sit anyway because that's what best friends do. Inside though, all I really want is to pretend like this isn't happening, open this sack of fresh food and fill my belly full again while I revel in the knowledge that I am finally free. I box up that joy to be fully enjoyed later. Rupi hops from my shoulder down to Renna's, then bounces lightly in front of her. Her stubby beak affectionately pulls at a piece of her shirt, and she tilts her round head quizzically, as if she's truly trying to understand.

"My last contract... the river boat..." She gives a sob. "I didn't mean to... I was so tired from the last trip, and I fell asleep. Without the magic I was hired to offer—"

"What happened, Renna?"

"I had to pay... damages." She presses her face to her pillow and sobs.

She continues rambling, trying to sort through the situation, but it turns fuzzy in my ears. River boat jobs aren't easy, as the river is so violent. Any distraction on the Originator's or Tulip's part can lead to disaster. But what's done is done. If she doesn't have the money for the Tulips, her bracelet will lapse, and she will no longer be protected and anonymous. If this mercenary situation gains the interest of the kings, these bracelets really will matter. I can't let that happen.

"How much do you need?" I ask, resigned. If I have to pick up another small contract to make up the difference, I will. It's no big deal, right? Dues are paid six months at a time. We have two more weeks to gather the money, and that's enough time if she didn't give too much away. I hope.

"All of it," she whispers, still staring at the wall. "It's going to lapse." She lifts her bracelet enclosed wrist and then drops it lifelessly on the bed. "I'm going to be found. Killed."

My jaw drops, and my mind spins. I'll never let that happen. I don't mention that mercenaries are reportedly tracking us down, now's not the time. Instead, I aim for motivation.

"You still have two weeks! Get up, get dressed, and let's go find another job." I'm already thinking through options. There's always a plan. It just has to be made.

She shakes her head. "I contacted Tatania right away. If I don't have enough by the due date, she has agreed to allow me on as an indefinite servant to the charmer of the bracelets to pay the dues."

Nausea claws at my belly. Beautiful, sweet, caring Renna as a servant to the odd charmer with eyes so black they give me chills? That is no life for her.

"No. Don't give up." I set my jaw in painful decision. "I'll help you. Get another contract, do what you can, and give me two weeks. I'll have it."

Renna sits up, and Rupi tumbles a bit with the movement of the quilt. But Renna is too busy wiping her face with the bottom of her shirt, her voice muffled through the fabric, to notice. "That's not possible. There's not enough time."

I scoop Rupi off the bed and place her back on my shoulder. If I have to use up my savings, I will. But I'll do everything I can to get the money without giving up my dreams first. Either way, my Tulip sister won't be going anywhere.

I swallow, realization setting in. I will have to go to extreme measures to help her. I want to rant and scream and cry at the unfairness of it all, but it won't change the fact that she's my magic sister, my best friend. I was free for just over a week, but a blessed and joyous week it was. Enough to wet my tongue and leave me craving more. And I'll have that freedom back, just... not yet.

"I'm taking a big job, and I leave in two days. I'll meet you at Mama Tina's. I'm sure you can find work there until I get back. Don't sign any contracts with the charmer." It's a command, not a question. And hopefully, being with Mama Tina protects her from any mercenaries.

She frowns. "But I thought you were done?"

"One more job. You must have been confused." I grit my teeth to hold back tears. Rupi nestles into my neck.

She nods.

"We can do this. We're Tulips." I say, for her as much as myself.

I get the feeling she doesn't quite believe me, and I'm not sure I do, either. First stop, swallow the bitter pill containing my pride and find Rhette.

Chapter 15

Vera

I know right where to find him. He frequents a tavern in town with rooms above-stairs anytime he's in the area, and that's exactly where he is. I've never had a reason to track him down or enter this establishment before. He sits at a table, a scantily-clad woman upon his lap as he drinks and laughs with four other men, a forgotten game of cards lies strewn across the table. I frown. I shouldn't be surprised by what he does on his own time, but I ignore the pang of disappointment. I'm not here for a date anyway, if I was, I would be no longer. I'm here for a job. I set my resolve and straighten my shoulders, blatantly ignoring the woman who scowls at my approach, and stalk toward Rhette. When he spots me, he quickly sets the woman to the side and stands, his eyes guarded. Rupi's feathers ruffle sharply against my neck. She doesn't hate him, but she certainly doesn't like him. We're on the same page right now.

"I didn't expect to see you here."

Obviously. I choke down betrayal. He never indicated he wanted to be more than friends. I just misread all the relationship cues, as usual. I gesture toward the doors with a nod, and we leave the building, finding privacy in the alley beside it.

He begins to speak. "That girl and I..."

I cut him off, not wanting to hear it. I get straight to the point before I cry at how this day has turned. "I'll take the contract. Where was he last seen?"

His smile slowly grows, and I can practically *feel* the *I knew it* that is so clearly written in his expression but remains wisely unspoken. "With the mercenaries, of course." His eyes light with that hint of eagerness that I see in many hunters before tracking their prey.

"Of course," I mutter.

We head directly to a local official contract shop, and as I watch the parchment begin to be filled with the conditions, I begin to think about what I've agreed to do.

"What happens if either of us gets injured or dies?" I ask the contract writer.

The man stops writing for a moment to meet my eyes through his spectacles. "You are paid in relation to your work. If you die before he's arrested, or if you end up not helping in the arrest after all, you'll get nothing. In the case of death, whatever you've earned will be prorated and sent to next of kin."

I gulp. Every contract has asked about next of kin, but it's something I never think about. This time, I am. I give him Renna's name first and Mama Tina's as a second. Rupi sidesteps on my shoulder, either feeling my tension or disapproving. I hope it's not the latter because it's too late to turn back. Within the hour, I've committed my magic, and possibly even my life, to assisting Rhette in capturing a Class A criminal to save my Tulip sister.

Two days later, I'm still trying to convince myself this was my only option. Too late to change my mind anyway, since I signed the contract and all. But signed contracts don't stop thoughts. I admit it's dangerous to take a bounty hunting job, but oh, how well they pay. *For Renna.* I repeat for the hundredth time, steeling my resolve. We wait for an enchanted river boat to become available, sitting on a damp, warped, wooden bench several feet back from the churning waters with an assortment of other nervous travelers. Rupi sticks close to my neck, her tiny body unable to handle the colder weather, but I don't mind, her presence helps me.

I don't think people really get used to river travel. I roll my shoulders to combat tense muscles caused by a heavy dose of apprehension. The rushing of the river, its dark depths, freak me out to no end. My magic already picks up on the gloam that lingers in its depths—gloam creatures. I appreciate that warning aspect of my magic, but sometimes I wish it could be quiet.

"You've done this a hundred times, Vera. Relax," Rhette mutters.

Logically, I know that, but it doesn't help. If one of these boats capsizes, and you touch the water, you have no idea how many miles ahead, or behind, your intended destination you'll end up. You go where the river sends you. Or you'll get eaten alive by some atrocious river monster before you end up anywhere at all. The main river that twists through this land, the Lucent River, winds between the kingdoms and is full of magic. It used to be the most efficient, preferred way to travel and trade. A simple connection with magic would have you going in the direction you wanted, with the current or against, and did I mention *fast*? The water is said to have been so clear and bright that you could see every pebble and fish beneath its deep, shimmering surface. It went from beautiful, accurate, and fast... to inconsistent, muddy, and dangerous. Dangerous is the only way I've ever seen it. The enchanted steel crafted by weapon masters lines the bottoms of the boats, acting as a buffer against gloam and its monsters, but we still don't have the abilities to travel the river like people did before.

One of the larger boats dock, and a frail-looking plank is tossed across the expanse of water from boat to river bank. I stand back and watch warily as a few other people walk across the dangerously bowing board and pay their fare. The captain lifts a no-nonsense, bushy brow at me and asks if I'm coming. I nod and cringe as I walk ever so carefully up the plank as it bends beneath my weight, over the dark water, but I make it aboard and dump a handful of coins in the man's hand. I take a seat beside Rhette and press my back against the ratty, cushioned bench. At least this one has cushions. Most don't.

"The city of Kivan is near some of the mercenary camps. We'll start there," Rhette says as he rubs his arms to warm himself.

I nod. "Sure." Like I know what he's even talking about. I know my way well enough on the main thoroughfares between large kingdoms and villages. I travel those distances often and choose my contracts accordingly. I go off the beaten path occasionally, only with experienced hunters on bounty hunts that I was supposed to be done with. I blow a piece of stray hair from my face.

These bounty hunting contracts are an iffy sort. Sure, they pay great—there's got to be *something* that entices people to bounty hunt. Along with that excellent pay, though, comes danger and sometimes losing out on the money altogether, like if the bounty escapes or we can't find them, or worst case scenario, we die. I remind myself that all the hard stuff, the tracking, fighting, physical strength, and map reading are all the hunter's job—not mine. I simply need to share raw, lucent magic and stay alive. I can do that.

I repeat it to myself as the boat starts sailing, and I grip the edge of my seat tightly. I feel Rupi's gentle tremors, my generally calm bird hating the river as much as I do. It's a testament of her loyalty to me that she hasn't flown from my shoulder and left me to the consequences of choosing river travel. Rhette gets comfortable, sliding down a bit in his seat and folding his arms. I press my lips together and shake my head at his lack of concern, but I admit many hunters have the same disposition.

A nerve-wracking amount of time later, we dock right outside the city of Kivan. I've been through a few times. It's a major shipping and trading hub. The familiarity of this city is calming, and I allow myself to relax and browse the shops as we make our way along the cobbled streets. We visit several of the taverns, but it's tricky asking about a mercenary when so many people we ask have a good possibility of being one themselves. I don't know their culture, if there's some sort of *brother code* or if they all hate each other as much as they seem to hate everyone else. I mostly stand back and let Rhette do the asking, hanging in the shadows with my hood over my head, hands in my pockets, trying to be invisible. Any one of these honorless soldiers could be hunting Tulips. I don't know how they would recognize us, but I'm not intending to find out.

While I'm in the midst of perfecting the art of blending with shadows, Rhette comes out of the last tavern with a grin on his face. I'm apparently not very good because he spots me right away.

"Owner said the bounty won a big prize during a fight here a few nights ago." I can almost sense the hunt driving him forward. He gets like this when he knows we're getting somewhere, and I almost sigh. Means we'll continue tracking into the night. No cozy bed at a nice inn for me.

"What was the prize?" I ask out of boredom, as I follow him down the stairs and back onto the dusky streets.

"Some list of Tulips or something," Rhette says flippantly.

I jerk my head toward him in horror the same time Rupi's feathers burst into quill tips and stab the tender flesh of my neck. I wince, but he doesn't notice my reaction. He's tracking, instinctively still on the hunt. I wince and carefully touch the top of her head, the only place that won't draw blood, until she calms and I can rub the spots of blood from my neck. She rarely stabs me, so she sensed something, my own reaction or the information Rhette just shared. I know she's intelligent, but at times, I'm still caught off guard and wonder how much she truly understands.

"Why would a mercenary want a list of flowers? Strange if you ask me," he mumbles and shoves his hands in his pockets.

I am silently screaming in my head. Rhette has *no idea* that it's not simply a list of regular garden flowers. I want to wrap my arms around myself and rock back and forth to self-soothe, but instead, I force my hands into my coat pockets and pull it tight around myself. I still have my hood up so that Rhette doesn't see the expression on my face as I grapple with whirling panic. The mercenary we're after is a *Tulip killer,* and I have no choice but to keep my end of the contract.

Chapter 16

Ikar

We left Kivan quickly after I'd won the fight, knowing the same mercenaries I'd beat to win the list, plus more, would probably be after us for it. The list *and* all the money Darvy won last night. I scowl.

"I still can't believe you snuck off and joined an illegal mercenary fight without us," Darvy says sulkily.

Rhosse's face is like stone. Mine would be too if I'd been pursued by a persistent tavern girl for as many hours. I grimace in sympathy.

"In my defense, I didn't know it was illegal," I say.

"You also thought it was okay to say you're a mercenary?" Rhosse asked, a brow quirked. "They find out you did that, and they'll be after you."

"They already are," I say, unconcerned.

All that matters is I have the list of Tulips, and as long as it's in my hands, it means no one else can find them. At least, I hope not. It was worth the injuries I received from surprisingly worthy opponents in the ring last night. I hadn't had my enchanted sword, those types of weapons aren't generally allowed in taverns, which meant no one else did, either. And since I didn't want to kill anyone, the fights lasted longer than they otherwise would have.

"Overall, I'd consider the evening a success," I say, as we continue through the dark forest.

Darvy snorts a laugh. "Did you forget about your broken ribs and nose, the split lip, and everything else I had to take care of after?"

No, in fact, the pain is still quite fresh. Still, I respond, "The cost was worth it."

Darvy is the best healer I know, but it's a horribly painful process.

We walked for hours through the night and have finally come to a quaint village settled in the depths of the dark forest. Some are more run-down than others, but this one is tended and well-kept. Bits of light and sunshine find their way through the thick treetops as the suns rise. Thatched roofs of small cottages are covered in moss and pine needles from the fir trees that grow tall and straight. Some have gardens larger than the size of their home, and birds nesting in the trees twitter back and forth noisily. Most have neatly laid cobblestone paths that lead up to their doors, and as we get closer to the main street, the dirt path widens and also becomes paved in stone. Forest flowers and greenery grow at the base of thick tree trunks, between mossy boulders, and nestbushes and other flowering plants grow so thick I can hardly see the forest floor off the path.

The main street consists of only five small buildings—a falconry office for sending messages combined with what looks like one sheriff's office, a healer's house marked with a hanging sign, a small stable, and the largest building has a sign naming it the *Nestbush Inn.*

We enter the inn to find an assortment of tables scattered throughout the room, a variety of men and a few women occupying the seats. One table has a game of cards in play, and there's a low murmur as conversations carry around the room. The left of the room holds a staircase that leads to the second level, where I assume the rooms are. Darvy, Rhosse, and I take a seat at an empty table in an area where we have full view of the room and pull out the parchment. It's not likely we'll gain any useful information in a small village such as this, but I'm desperate enough I'll be asking everywhere. A young woman approaches our table and places rich smelling soup filled with plump dumplings and vegetables with a thick slice of nestberry pie on the side in front of us. My mouth waters. We haven't had fare like this in a week, but I put off food for a moment longer.

"Before you go," I ask the serving woman, "can you tell me if you know any of these names?" I hand her the slightly wrinkled list.

She frowns as she takes the list in her hand and scans it. "Can't say that I do. Sorry." She shakes her head and places it back on the table.

"How do we know if the list is even accurate?" Darvy ponders aloud after she's left.

"We don't," I admit.

Rhosse is quiet, but I sense the frustration behind his stoic gaze. He is the best tracker in the entire five kingdoms, but even he, without any sort of direction, can't say where to start—even with a list in hand. And so we will continue our mindless, directionless searching until we catch a scent.

"All we can do is keep searching." The thought of what that

means for me, mainly marriage, twists uncomfortably. I still feel an uncomfortable burden of guilt about how I told Nadiette we could no longer plan to marry. The worst part? The look of betrayal and hurt in her eyes.

Darvy and Rhosse waste no time getting started on their meals, but as I lift my spoon, the inn door opens, and a young woman walks in. At first glance, with her hood up, she could be taken for a teenage boy, the way she's dressed in decidedly masculine attire that drowns her frame. But as soon as she drops the hood, it's easy enough to see she's certainly a woman. Dark brown hair hangs over her shoulder in a messy braid. Her eyes are cool gray and framed by lashes so thick it's as if she's used coal to line them. Beneath her petite nose are a set of lips that could never be called boyish. Her well-worn, loose-fitting trousers are tucked into dirt-covered leather boots, and a long sleeve nondescript shirt sits beneath a vest, with a long, navy jacket tossed over her forearm. A short sword fits snugly against her hip, its hilt worn from pommel to guard, the leather wrapped around the grip looks so aged I'm surprised it hasn't fallen off. A pack over one shoulder completes her attire. Her gaze scans the room for a moment, meets mine, and holds for the shortest second with what seems a flash of recognition before she breaks the contact and makes her way to the counter to order.

Warning tingles. Why? I have no idea. I have never seen her before, and even if I had, the glamour Jethonan gave me should prevent anyone from identifying me. I push aside the worry, gauging her physical threat level at *maybe* a two on a scale of ten. Unless she happens to be some lethal warrior who is an expert in weapons while simultaneously appearing completely harmless. Which could be a possibility. A very unlikely possibility. I detail her just like I detail everyone else who comes into this inn, even though she doesn't look the part of the usual customers. Five foot six. Dark brown hair. Even with the large clothing, it's obvious she's thin, maybe too thin. Her face lacks the fullness that comes from regular meals. She strides confidently through the middle of the room, unaware of the attention she has grabbed from the current customers as they eye her. She doesn't fit in here, and my interest is piqued.

Darvy raises a brow in question when I stand, pausing momentarily with a heaping spoonful of fat dumplings halfway to his mouth.

Rhosse looks up. "Searching for another illegal fight to join?"

A grin lifts one side of my mouth as I push my chair in, but I don't respond to his good-natured ribbing. I know I'll never live that fight down.

He chuckles and returns to his meal.

They probably think I'm desperate as they watch me, and they'd be right, but something about this woman has caught my attention, and with the stakes what they are, I intend to find out why. I make my way to the counter beside her. I slide onto a stool two down from where she sits and rest an elbow on the counter in what is, hopefully, a friendly and non-aggressive manner. I also hope it covers the blood that has dried onto my jacket and shirt. Maybe I should wash up before continuing this search.

"New here?" I smile in an easy sort of way, not wanting to chase off a possible source of information.

She eyes me, then without any further attention goes back to the bowl of soup before her, as if I'm a fly she just waved from her space.

I slide the wrinkled paper toward her. "Are any of these names familiar?"

She looks at it while she slowly chews her bite of soup, then finally presses a slim fingertip against the parchment like she's disgusted by it and drags it closer. Her gray eyes skim the seven names, widening a bit before her face washes of emotion. Then she rereads it. I resist a triumphant smile. She knows something.

Chapter 17

Vera

I'm positive this man is the bounty we've been searching for. The moment I stepped into the inn and saw him, I knew. My mouth feels dry. *The sketch was inaccurate.* I take in his features with disdain. He is dreadfully handsome—unlike the artist's rendition shown on the parchment in my pocket shows him to be. Surprising. Most sketches, especially of the criminals I search for, give a little more in the looks department than is true. Doesn't matter. I do this for pay, not boyfriends. But this man is different in that I don't sense the... 'I'm a criminal' vibe about him. Doesn't mean it's not there, though.

Along with that, I get the sense he has a glamour. My magic enables me to see through glamour, which is probably the explanation for the large discrepancy between the bounty sketch and his actual appearance. But while they don't work on me, I wonder why he uses one. Can't be for anything good. I should know, I was raised with the fae, but my instincts have failed me before. I won't be one to be taken advantage of by his looks and charm, his blue eyes, and the roughness that a few days' scruff adds to his strong jawline. He has the list, which only confirms that he's a mercenary, and he's after *my kind*.

"Can't help you," I say to the man.

"Can't, or won't?" he challenges.

If he's asking me that, he already knows. I intentionally take a very loud and obnoxious slurp of soup as I consider what to do. The man looks at me oddly. Good, I don't want him looking at me any other way.

I know I should mind my business, let Rhette track him down later. I have enough information that I know he'd find him in a day or two, but what if he can't? I need the money, and he's *right here*. According to the rules, I am simply an Originator—that's all I signed up for. Rhette is the hunter. But still, I'm *this* close to guaranteeing this job. What if someone else snatches him before we do because I don't do anything? It's too bad Rupi stayed in the forest while I grabbed a bite to eat, or she may have reined in my impulsivity, but she's not here, and I make a split second decision as I eye the despicable list of names—women I know personally—and mine is included. *Can't have that.*

I know I shouldn't anger the man without Rhette's protection, but he won't need that list after we arrest him anyway, and it'll feel so good. I grab my glass, and with a quick flick of my wrist, a large splash of hot tea soaks the parchment through. Immediately, the ink begins to run and turn blotchy in parts, the man jumps up and attempts to salvage the dripping mess with a look of anger and surprise. I smirk with warm satisfaction, shovel another bite of food in my mouth, and take my exit from the inn without another word.

I feel genuine regret at leaving half a bowl of long-simmered, hearty soup behind. I shouldn't have provoked him, but my plan has satisfied two needs. One, the man is angry and will probably lead himself right to us. Second, even if it is the tiniest bit of ground, I've set a mercenary off course and destroyed a list that could identify myself and my Tulip sisters. If he's worth his hire as a mercenary, he'll find me soon enough. I cackle to myself as I leave the cobblestone street and make my way into the forest. I don't generally use myself as bait during contracts—haven't ever, actually. I don't get paid enough for that. But right now, I need the money and Rhette has my back... I hope. I just need to get back to camp and hope he's there by now.

I stride quickly in the direction I took into town, following the same spotty deer path I took on my way into the village. Rhette and I made camp about half a mile away, and I can only hope he's ready when I get there because I have a feeling that the criminal is already on my trail. I, of course, won't do the arresting. I am here solely for magical support, but from the previous bounties I've assisted with, it's best to do the arresting away from the public eye so no one interferes. And that's the case, especially with this guy, who can probably get whatever he wants with a quick blink of his blue eyes. Or his fists. I recall how he won several rounds of vicious fighting to get that list. I scoff. No, he wouldn't need violence to kill my Tulip sisters. If he finds them, he'll probably lead them to their deaths with a simple roguish smile.

My anger grows tight and hot while I walk in the direction of our camp, but I begin to realize the area looks unfamiliar, the deer path too well trodden at this point. My confidence goes from fiery to fizzling in moments. I slow my steps but continue forward, feeling a bit of panic stir in my chest. If I can't find my way back to Rhette, and that man finds me first... I swallow, but my throat is tight with anxiety, and it turns into an audible gulp. *Rules, Vera. There are rules for a reason.*

My eyes scan around me hurriedly, for something, any sort of new plan. I glimpse a perfect, large evergreen tree ahead and realize if I can climb that, I might be able to find the trail, or at least hide until the man passes through and let Rhette find him later. Feeling my confidence recover a bit, I hop over a couple of boulders and clamber through bushes and long grass to get there. My eyes are so busy concocting a plan that will have me waiting in the tree above that it's not until I smell a hint of the sourness that clings after goblins have passed through that I slow. It's too late, a rope cinches tightly around my right ankle and I let out a yelp as it yanks me into the air, my ankle popping uncomfortably. I awkwardly turn my head as I hear the pattering of soft dirt and the rustle of foliage around me. Dozens of the short, smelly goblins gather beneath me. My nostrils burn, and my eyes begin to water. These creatures could put a close-proximity encounter with a skunk to shame. I kick and buck until it feels like my foot is going to disconnect completely from my leg. It's no secret what the goblins do to their prisoners. *Never break the rules,* I mentally chastise myself. The rope is released without any warning. I hit the ground head-first, and everything goes black.

Chapter 18

Ikar

T he woman leaves with a maddening, careless smirk. I have no idea what I did to deserve that kind of treatment, but I don't have time to think about it. I return to our table and hold the ruined parchment above the scarred wooden surface, watching in horror as water drips steadily from its edge.

"Memorize as many as you can," I say, as my eyes scan quickly down the list of names, over and over while they continue to bleed and spread across the swollen page. A few are already too illegible, dark smears on paper stained a bruised color by the insufferable woman's tea. I have no parchment or writing instruments at hand, so memory will have to do until I find some. I repeat the names I've read to cement them in my mind while I quickly finish my now lukewarm meal in angry silence.

"I can track her," Rhosse suggests mildly from my left, as I take my last bite. I sit back and think about it for a moment. Our time is precious. If I'm tracking her to exact revenge, I don't have time, but I'd bet my enchanted sword she knows something. While I intended to use Rhosse to track a Tulip, this woman is the next best thing at this point.

I nod, not bothering to pick up the soggy parchment. "Let's go."

Darvy, Rhosse, and I make our way into the forest, Rhosse in the lead. Like me, he is of the hunter faction, but not all of one faction are exactly the same. As a king, I have more magical abilities among the hunter faction than usual—speed, strength, increased hearing and sense of smell—and one of my lesser gifts includes tracking. Most hunters have one or two magical abilities, and Rhosse's are tracking and working with animals. Naturally, he picks up the woman's trail quickly, guiding us along what can hardly be called a path and navigating through dusk shrouded trees, logs, and bushes covered in moss and climbing vines.

I allow my senses to attune to the sounds and feel of the forest as the suns go down. I hear the first of the evening insects begin their light chirps and buzzing, and the breeze cools as the suns set to the east. Shadows lengthen beneath the trees, and animals rustle into their forest homes for the night. It is the peaceful time between when the daytime creatures of the forest find their rest and the criminals and night creatures rise to reign until dawn. We venture deeper into the woods, though the path she traveled now turns to one more visible. I cringe at the faintest sour scent of goblin on the breeze.

"Goblins in the area." My magically heightened senses inform me before Rhosse and Darvy have any chance of smelling it.

It's a bit early for goblins to be venturing out of their nests, but not uncommon. We travel further, and the scent grows stronger, so strong that all our eyes water and I find myself wiping the corners and blinking rapidly to clear my vision, as do Darvy and Rhosse. I pull the magic back to reduce my heightened smell, but even without it, my senses are sharper than those of other factions, so I'm stuck receiving the brunt of the effects of the rancid odor.

Rhosse stops several feet ahead and inspects a wide area where the forest grasses and dropped pine needles have been scattered and pressed into the soft earth, probably a scuffle of some sort. He glances up and points to the disrupted bark of a large branch.

"Goblins caught someone today."

Probably some traveler or merchant, unaware of the danger. Unfortunate, but a well-known risk when traveling in this part of the forest.

Rhosse turns back to me, and my chest tightens as I realize what he's about to say as he lifts the old short sword I saw on the woman's hip at the inn.

"The goblins have her," he says. "On your orders."

I clench my fist. *Of course they do.* I run a hand through my hair and think. I, of course, don't want her dead—I wouldn't wish death by goblins on anyone. I also need the information I know she has, but I don't have time to track her for another day and possibly set up a rescue mission. Darvy and Rhosse wait for my decision. I can't, in good conscience, leave the woman to be skinned and killed by goblins, knowing she's likely still alive.

"Continue to track her," I growl.

It's not difficult to track them, their scent a far cry from mild, even for those who aren't experienced. They also leave a trail the size of a shard beast stampede wherever they go. We catch up to them easily and make use of the deepening shadows to cloak our presence while we gauge the situation. I immediately see the woman from earlier, fighting against the ropes restraining her, being hoisted high up a broad, giant tree on a flat board attached to ropes. I track its intended path up and notice an intricate mess of pulleys and lifts that lead to gigantic wasp-nest-looking huts attached to branches in the towering treetops above. I curse under my breath.

We could take on an entire tree of goblins and survive, but while towing a woman who may or may not have any fighting skills? I don't feel in the mood to shed my skin today. My mouth sets in a grim line. The woman bucks and fights, tilting the board every which way so violently I wonder if that will be her undoing rather than the goblins. Probably preferable. The goblins roughly pull the thick rope through the squeaking pulley, lifting her up in a jerky and uneven fashion to one of the creepy-looking nest huts before whisking her inside. I know we only have a few minutes to reach her before it's too late.

"I'll circle around to the other side and drop our packs, then I'll climb up and grab her. You guys take over the pulley for our exit, and we'll head out there, grabbing our packs on the way." I point to the opposite side of the goblin nest tree.

"That's a terrible plan," Darvy whispers.

"I second that," Rhosse grunts.

If they weren't my closest friends, they'd be in the stocks. "Have you got something better?" I snap. "We've got thirty seconds." After a few seconds of silence, I stand. "My plan it is. Hand me your packs. Wait until I get to the nest, then take over the pulley."

I circle around through the forest, stopping only once when a small group of goblins with trapping equipment draped over their shoulders leave the nest perimeter and head into the darkness of the forest, out for another capture. As soon as they pass, I continue my path around the perimeter until I reach my destination and drop our packs. Even with my heightened vision, I can't see Darvy and Rhosse in the shadows directly across from me, several hundred yards away, but I assume they are still there, waiting.

I wait until it seems likely I won't be seen, bend low, and run toward the tree, heading for the deepest shadows to begin my ascent. I dig my fingers into the thick, gnarly, half-rotted bark, ignoring the inky black bugs that skitter across my hands. What is not easy to ignore is the potent sour smell that seems to emanate from the bark itself, and I find myself holding back the contents of my stomach as I scale my way quickly up. I pause when a lift passes too close and press myself against the tree, remaining unnoticed. I finally reach the hut they've taken her to. I grab and hoist myself onto the top of the branch that the nest is dangling from and step carefully along its length. I've never seen a goblin nest this close before, and I notice how it's attached around the strong branch I walk along, its odd mate-rial connected to the bark of the tree like a continually growing, slimy glue. But unlike a liquid object, its texture is almost weaved... and disgustingly fuzzy. I've done a lot of dangerous, scary, awful things in the name of duty, but climbing into a goblins nest will be a first for me. The nests themselves are the size of small huts, oblong with narrow openings.

All is quiet at this particular nest, and I assume the goblins have left momentarily. Probably to gather their knives in order to skin the woman. Around me, lifts move up and down at dizzying speeds. It's only a matter of time until I'm noticed. I artfully swing down and through the opening into the nest and land on the soft floor in a crouch. The woman is before me, tied up, but rather than relief when she sees me, her eyes grow wide with alarm.

I hold up my hands in a peace offering gesture, trying to show her that she has no reason to fear me. "Look, I know we got off on the wrong foo—"

A goblin lurches wildly from the shadows with a strange high-pitched wheeze at my right, and I react instinctively, ripping my knife from its sheath with a speed only gained from experience and thrust it quickly into its neck. I push it back against the sloped wall where it slides into a smelly heap, coming to a slow stop only a few feet from us. I hear the commotion below and around us, and I know Darvy and Rhosse have made their move. It's time.

I wipe my knife off using the odd textured nest wall, then turn back toward the woman and hold a finger to my lips to indicate she should stay quiet. I untie the gag around her face and quickly cut the ropes around her wrists and ankles before sheathing my knife. She appears unharmed, so I move to the next part of the mission. Escape.

"How did you find me?" she whispers. I wrote off her previous look of fear as her warning me about the waiting goblin, but that look is still in her eyes, and the only way I can describe it is that she's fearful of *my* presence. The woman is off her rocker.

"Tracked you." I see her pack in a heap along the side of the nest and quickly toss it to her. "Put this on." I poke my head out of the opening, my mind on the mission. Conversation can wait.

My vision locks on Darvy and Rhosse, engaged in a fight with over twenty goblins with more heading their way. Swarms of them stream from the forest and the tree above us. The grunts and shrieks of the goblins are audible, even from our position hundreds of feet above. Pulleys and lifts are constantly moving around us, most now headed down and filled with groups of goblins ready to join the fight. I watch for the right moment. It's darker now, and I hope if we stay quiet, we can make it to one of the platforms unnoticed. I see an empty lift passing to the right, going down, but it passes too quickly. We need a better angle. I climb out of the nest, back on to the branch from which it hangs, and stretch my hand out to help the woman up. She stares at it for a moment, unwilling to take it, then knocks it aside with a shoulder as she haphazardly scrambles up next to me on her own, keeping to her knees and firmly grasping the thin branch. I'd laugh if I wasn't so irritated.

I track another lift on its way down, I can't see how many goblins are on it, since it's coming from above, but we have no choice. I reach for her hand again, and this time I snag it in my firm grasp even as she attempts to shake my hand from hers.

"We're jumping on that lift. Hang on tight, or you'll fall." I scowl at her—now is not the time for whatever this is. I still don't understand why she's averse to me. Would she rather I leave her to the goblins?

I count down quietly, but even with the warning, she lets out a surprised yelp as I yank her hard, and we jump toward the moving platform—knowing if we miss this, we fall to our deaths below. I miscalculate my angle a bit, what with my arm turned back to pull her with me awkwardly, causing my opposite shoulder to catch on one of the tightly strung ropes. I fall hard, the woman beside me, and find four delighted goblins hovering above us. We're like a couple of fish who jumped right into their net. They immediately come at us, brandishing some poor human's weapons they stole before they killed them.

A couple find their target and hit against my leather armor, one slices at my unprotected shoulder, and a blossom of red burgeons through my shirt. I quickly jump to my feet and pull my own weapon. For being so small, goblins are very strong and make formidable enemies. I shove the woman behind me and into a corner as I begin to pick them off. I grab one by its tunic before I realize it's made of human skin, instinctively tossing it away and off the side, its chittering fades below us until it hits the ground with a thud. Two more come forward with their swords, and I quickly dispose of them with a couple of well-placed stabs. I toss them off, as well. The only one left is running the pulley. We battle, our swords moving quickly, blocking, stabbing. This one is good, but I feint to the left when he thought I'd go right, and after a well-placed stab, I send him sailing over the side to join the others.

I sheathe my sword and immediately grab hold of the rope to send the lift down, but the rope begins jerking in my grip and I look up to see two goblins making quick work of sawing the thick ropes that hold us aloft. I curse beneath my breath and allow the lift to fall dangerously fast. Our hair and clothing whip around us, and I look down at the forest floor to see a swarm gathering in wait. The woman looks at me like I'm crazy but doesn't let go of the side of the lift. I glance down at the swarm again and hope they'll be enough to cushion our fall. I know we need to reach the ground before those ropes are cut, but not too fast or we could be injured—or die. I have no idea what that speed looks like, but hopefully, this is it. Rhosse and Darvy slowly make their way toward our intended landing spot, the swarm around them constantly growing, the smell stifling, even from our height above.

"Hang on!" I call to her. She clings with both hands as we fairly drop from the tree. Then we hit, and we both stumble to our knees and slide forward, our landing cushioned by at least ten goblins so that our platform is an awkwardly skewed ramp. I grab her hand tightly, and we slide off, jumping into the violent fray. I drag her through the melee, pulling lucent and sending it through my sword, making quick use of it to clear our way.

Immediately, Darvy and Rhosse are behind us, still fighting

off the goblins that are attempting to swarm and overtake us. I fight through a few layers of goblins until we get to the outside of the group. Then we run for it, hard. Without stopping, I swing by the stashed packs and throw mine over my shoulder. I hear Darvy and Rhosse behind us. They're fast, and I know they'll catch up. I'm more worried about the woman keeping pace the further we run.

But I realize that won't be a problem. The river lies ahead, and if we change course to attempt to bypass the river and circle around, we will lose precious ground. The goblins will be able to catch up. We're good at what we do, but I know this area is littered with their deceptive traps. If we get caught, there's a good chance they'll kill us on the spot. But the river is full of its own dangers. I have only seconds to decide.

"Everyone, grab hands!" I shout. It's the only way we'll stay together when we touch the water. I'll do everything I can to direct the river, but I know it's pointless. The Lucent River will send us where the Lucent River wants.

Rhosse grabs the woman's outstretched hand, and Darvy grabs his. Like a human chain, we run full speed toward the looming edge of a steep, pitch-black drop-off.

Chapter 19

Vera

I hadn't believed my eyes when I saw the Class A criminal Rhette was supposed to cuff, the Tulip-killing mercenary, drop into the goblin's nest. At first, I'd thought that somehow he'd discovered I'm a Tulip and he was here to capture me for the reward. But instead, apparently, he's only here to *rescue* me. And now I'm following him, more like being pulled, toward what looks very much like a steep drop-off. The edge looms quickly closer, but he isn't slowing, and neither are his friends, which means neither am I. My feet miss a step for every three with the way the large men are practically lifting me to run faster. The four of us are linked by hands, so I don't really have a choice. Even if I tried to stop them, I couldn't. And if I could, I wouldn't. Jump in the deadly river with the mercenary and his friends, or be skinned and killed by goblins? *Horrid options.* I keep pace with them the best I can.

Just before the drop off, the criminal shouts over his shoulder, "No matter what, don't let go!"

Then he and the others pull me off the edge. I'm not sure which is louder—the blood rushing in my ears or the river below. A panic-induced scream rips from my throat, but the two men holding my hands keep them wrapped tightly enclosed in theirs. A steep, short hill leads directly into the river —there is nowhere else to go. Images of dark, hungry river creatures flash through my mind. I can't believe I'm doing this, but I instinctively grasp their hands tighter, knowing that my best chance of survival is with these awful criminals, at least for now. They seem willing to rescue me at this point, so I'll go with that. Without them, I'll likely end up ripped apart and shared between river creatures as a midnight snack.

We slide through a steep mix of dirt and mud. I slide down on my back, hitting all sorts of rocks, sticks, and plant life that have found a way to grow out of the hill. My body aches, and I'm sure I'll have bruises and scratches, if I survive. Somehow, toward the bottom, my hands are still in theirs. And then we are free-falling, cool air rushing around my body before I hit breathtakingly cold water with a loud clap.

Heavy silence fills my ears, the pressure of our drop beneath the deep water pressing against my body, and it begins to ache as we sink lower and lower in the darkness. It's murky black, but it doesn't stop me from searching the depths for the reptilian, monstrous creatures who inhabit these waters. All I see are big blotches of darkness appearing and disappearing at random, and I feel the darkness of the magic that gives them life. My lungs feel pressed to my spine, and dots begin to dance in my eyes, then after what feels like too long, my arms are yanked above me, and I begin sluggishly kicking to help in reaching the surface. The added weight of my wet clothing and boots are like literal anchors at my feet as we kick our way up, but finally, we break the surface. I take in a single lungful of air before I'm drug beneath again. Once more, two hands are pulling mine to get me above the surface.

I hate water. I'm not a confident swimmer, and it shows. I feel the current of the river pulling us, and though it seems like we are moving in the same direction as the current, when we climb out, we could be hundreds of miles in the opposite direction with no explanation. The river has a mind of its own.

I look behind and see desperate goblins falling into the river behind us, screeching and flailing. They can't swim, so I know they can't hurt us in the water, but I watch in horror as they begin to disappear under the surface, snatched away too quickly for them to have drowned. A shiver of disgust runs down my spine, and I kick faster, hoping my flailing feet don't make contact with anything solid beneath the surface of this cursed river. Other goblins disappear, seemingly into thin air, and I assume the river decides to send them somewhere else. It's disconcerting, to say the least.

My attention returns to the men at my sides, the criminal still grasps my left hand, his dark-haired friend my right. The friend with light brown hair, who looks more innocent than he can possibly be, is on the end, to the right of the dark-haired man. It's difficult to stay above the surface with the awkward swimming I'm forced to endure while hand holding, but I know if we let go, we'll probably be separated. I certainly can't have my bounty escaping now that he's so conveniently in my hands. Quite literally.

Suddenly, the man on the end shouts and struggles. He pulls his sword from its sheath and stabs it into the water with a grunt. I see darkness bloom beneath the water and stare with wide eyes. Nothing happens for a moment, and just as I think it's safe to assume he's killed whatever attempted to attack, he's yanked beneath the surface. The dark-haired man jerks and strains to keep hold of his friend and stay above the surface, but in his effort, he, I, and the criminal begin to struggle and slip beneath, as well. The first man's head bobs above the surface with a strangled gasp and then disappears, dragging us beneath once again.

This is the beginning of what it feels like to die in the depths of the river. I know it. I'm screaming, choking, kicking frantically. I almost don't hear the dark-haired friend next to me when he speaks.

He spits out a mouthful of water as he gains the surface again. "We'll find you." He gasps out as he struggles to stay above. And then I know he's going to let go, sacrificing himself to help their friend, so the criminal and I have a better chance of survival.

The panic and fear, and the strange camaraderie that's only built during situations such as these between strangers has me feeling a sudden wave of compassion toward these supposedly evil mercenaries who decided to rescue me, and who will probably die in this river tonight.

"Moneyre." I shout. "Meet us in Moneyre!" It's where Rhette was meant to deliver Ikar—the criminal—to the officials. They can find him there. Reducing their need to search for each other is the least I can do for their aid in rescuing me. I hope I don't come to regret it, but we all know it's not likely they'll be meeting us anywhere. I don't even know if he heard me, but he lets go of my hand and immediately disappears beneath the surface.

"Rhosse! Darvy!" Ikar shouts, his voice strangled. "No!"

He scans the river in every direction, searching, but we never see them rise again. I don't know if the river took us away, took *them* away, or if they died.

Besides our splashing and heavy breathing, and my teeth beginning to chatter, Ikar and I are silent. I feel numb inside and out. Two men, likely dead. Ikar pulls me along, fighting the current and heading toward the opposite shore from where we entered. I'm content to let him lead—for now. I wait for a bump against my leg, a bite that will dig in to my soft flesh and drag me under the dark surface, something the likes of what Darvy and Rhosse experienced. But besides my blood seemingly freezing to ice in my veins and my chest tight with shock and sorrow, nothing happens. After what seems like hours, we make our way out of the river and onto a gradual incline, still muddy, but not so steep it's difficult to climb. Ikar doesn't let go of my hand until we're both completely out of the water and several feet away from the river's edge. Then he sits down heavily in some patchy grass, rests his arms on his knees, and lets his head hang. I fall flat on my back, breathing hard and shivering a couple feet away.

A light breeze blows over my chilled body, and my shivering increases. And while all I want to do is close my eyes, sink into the dark blackness of sleep, and pretend this night never happened, I'm forced to face reality. I can't help but feel sorrow, and a hefty dose of guilt, for the two men who died in the river tonight while rescuing *me*. I feel strangely empty at the thought. They can't truly be gone, can they? But I saw them go down and never come up. I try not to imagine what they suffered. More guilt spreads through my body. All this because I broke the rules and didn't wait for Rhette. Not only that, but I don't know if Rupi will be able to find me now that the river has carried us who-knows-how-far-away. I hope she can find her way home without me. I take a deep breath, trying to relieve the tight worry in my chest. It doesn't help much.

I turn my head to the side and look at the criminal that sits beside me. He carries a commanding presence around like it radiates from his core, but his shoulders have dropped, and he presses a thumb and finger to his eyes like he might be stopping

—No. Mercenaries are heartless and violent. They don't cry, or mourn, or have friends. He probably just has silt and river creature blood in his eyes and is simply clearing his vision so he can continue with his dishonorable life.

Even with that explanation filling in the cracks of my guilt and sorrow, it feels like the ultimate lack of gratitude to now place a cuff on him, the criminal who has become my rescuer. I scramble to sort through all the rules I've been taught, but none of them shed light on this bizarre situation. Law says he should be captured, but it feels so wrong. Then I remember that he's not just any man. He's a mercenary, and if he knew that I'm a Tulip, he'd capture me in a heartbeat and kill me. I feel the resolution building. I already tipped his supposed *friends* off to his future destination, in a weak-hearted act of compassion, so if they survive, they can find each other that way. That's as far as my gratitude goes. My heart hardens further. He's the one who broke an agreement with a noble and hunts Tulips. And on top of all that, the reward money is staggering, and I need it badly. Hence, why I'm here on this dreadful river bank in the first place.

He speaks and snaps me out of my thoughts.

"You okay?" His voice is smooth and deep.

"Yeah." My voice is raspy from screaming earlier, and I swallow to try to moisten it, all while telling myself it's not true concern I hear in his voice.

The cuff that I've never had to use before practically burns my chest through the fabric of my shirt. It's supposed to be for emergencies. I think this counts. I realize that it's now or never, and right now, he isn't expecting anything besides gratitude and weakness from me. I shift to pull the cuff bead from my vest pocket, then reach over like I'm going to lay my hand on his in a thankful or comforting sort of way. Instead, I touch the bead to his bare skin, and it sizes itself to his wrist like an inky, slithering snake. It glows a bit before it turns a matte black of interconnected chain links.

He lifts his wrist and takes in the presence of the cuff. "What the he—"

Faster than I can blink, he has secured both my hands above my head with one hand and straddles me, my throat at the mercy of his other large hand. He looms over me, all concern and kindness now eerily absent. His face is a handsome mask of dark ice, and I can almost tangibly feel the magic behind the cuff pushing against its brand new lock. I tremble, and I want to blame it on my cold, drenched state, but I'm terrified. Here is the Class A criminal in all his glory.

I find very quickly that it is quite difficult to speak while half-strangled, but I force the words out before he finishes the job. I have never actually made an arrest, but I've seen Rhette and others do it, so I do my best to copy them.

"You are under arrest." I suck in air with an attractive wheeze. "Letter. In my pocket." My voice is a hoarse whisper. He gives me a prolonged, murderous look before he removes his hand from my throat, and I breathe in lungfuls of air. As much as I can with his weight still atop me.

"Which one?"

"Left side of my coat."

He is careful to touch me as little as possible. I'm not sure if that implies he's a gentleman to a point or that I'm so disgusting right now even a loose-moraled mercenary doesn't want to touch me. I assume it's the latter. He pulls the remains of a document from my pocket, now heavy and dripping with river water. His lips flatten. He does a quick pat down to check for weapons within my reach before he releases my arms. Treating me as though *I* am the criminal. The nerve. His weight effectively holds me prisoner while he carefully pries open the sopping parchment. I can only hope it's still readable. His brow furrows as he scans the page in the moonlight. Then he stands, his intimidating figure towering above me in a way that has me scrambling quickly to my feet to decrease the difference in our height. Not that it does much—he still stands almost a foot taller than me.

"This is a misunderstanding," he growls.

"You don't need to explain anything to me." I fold my arms across my chest and try to stop my teeth from chattering. Chattering teeth aren't professional.

"I'm not explaining anything." His eyes darken. "Remove the cuff."

There is something so forceful in his command that I actually feel the urge to obey, but I won't. He is a criminal, and I need to protect the Tulips... and I need the money for Renna.

"You are under arrest," I repeat. "If you hurt me, kill me, or run off, your magic is gone." I surprise myself by making a poofing gesture for good measure, and his face drops to a handsome scowl. Having him under my cuff has me feeling all sorts of powerful tonight. I begin to see why bounty hunters do what they do.

"I am familiar with charmed cuffs," he says, frustrated.

I raise my brows at him. "That comment doesn't improve my opinion."

He's got the dark and broody look down pat. I swallow.

I'm left wondering how many times this man has been arrested. Nothing has gone as I expected with this contract. In fact, that original contract is now void. I'm on my own. In addition to that, I expected some drunk, filthy, half-starved ex-soldier of some sort. Like I said, the bounty sketches usually give a lot in the looks department. In his case, it didn't give nearly enough. I purse my lips.

I refuse to admit he is handsome even as my eyes linger on the planes of his face, accentuated by the shadow of night and the full moon's light. His nose has a bit of a bump, but somehow it's still perfect, and that has me frowning. To complete the combo are a set of dark brows and a strong jaw. I can't see his eyes in the dim light, but I know from our conversation yesterday that they are a stormy blue. His hair is a medium length on top, short on the sides, and is currently drying in a messy sort of way that I find highly attractive. Strangely, it only adds to his dangerous air, whereas I am positive I look like a half-drowned kitten. Add to all that his tall frame and what I assume—from his skill and strength—to be muscle beneath his long coat, along with some sort of leather armor and an assortment of weapons I've glimpsed.

I do not feel prepared to handle this man or his heavy, commanding presence for days. Even hours. I'm simply a Tulip masquerading as an Originator, bounty hunting for the first time. I only ever *assist* people in these sorts of jobs.

"I assume you already know my name, so I will skip my introduction and ask for yours." His voice is cultured, smooth, and ice-cold.

"Vera." I blurt out without thinking. I cringe inside, knowing he had that list with my full name, hopefully he doesn't make the connection.

"I can't say that I'm pleased to meet you, but I'll make you a deal."

"I'm not interested," I say quickly, before he can say anything further. I'll adopt a deathstalker before I make a shady deal with a Class A criminal. Something splashes loudly, and I decide it's time we get some distance between us and that cursed river. I turn and stride away, stopping only to use two hands to climb up and over a very large boulder. He hops over one handed right behind me. And once again, his long strides have him easily keeping pace beside me while I'm still out of breath from the river fiasco.

"My friends and I have already rescued you from being skinned alive by goblins, and they possibly died because of it." His voice is so sharp it could slice through the steel of an enchanted sword. "In addition to their sacrifice, I will offer you the same amount as the reward money for my immediate release."

The hinges of my jaw seem to lose all control, and my mouth sags for a second before I snap it back and give him what I think is my most bounty-hunter-tough *don't mess with me* look. I don't want his murder money, no matter how much it is. Though I do feel guilty about the rescue part and possible death of his friends. I didn't want anyone to die. But still...

"I don't make deals with criminals."

"Even lucrative ones?"

"No. Because I am not a *criminal*." I grind out and start walking.

"Neither am I," he states angrily, easily matching my stride.

"You're acting like one." I give him a pointed look.

He lets out a frustrated breath. "I'm looking for something. It's urgent."

"What? A Tulip to kill?" I almost slap a hand over my mouth. I shouldn't know anything about that, but in my anger and weariness, the words slipped out without thinking.

He stills, and a sardonic smile lifts one side of his handsome mouth. "I knew you knew something."

And cue the Tulip killer. He doesn't even have the sense to sound ashamed. *Dirtbag.* "Yes, I know *about that*," I reply saucily, casting a glare in his direction for good measure. I may not be able to help my magic sisters right now, but I can scold the heck out of this mercenary while I keep him from finding any of them.

"You've got me all wrong." His deep voice comes from behind me now, the path too narrow for us to walk side-by-side. He must not realize that literally every criminal tries that line, but it makes my skin crawl to think that if he finds out who I am, he won't be making small talk. He's a dangerous package, this one. Too handsome. Too strong. Too tall. Too good of a liar. I know if I'd seen him passing on the street, I woulda looked twice—maybe even three times—and my body reacts accordingly. I don't usually have this problem. Most criminals I help capture are dirty, smelly, raggedy, or handsome with a heavy dose of evil in their eyes, making them easy to place in the *criminal* category in my brain. This guy doesn't fit the molds, and I don't like it.

I turn from him with a huff and continue my march through thick forest that gradually turns into what appears to be wasteland desert. I realize after several minutes of walking that I headed off without any sort of direction in my moment of powerful confidence brought on by my first arrest. That flame of confidence is quickly doused. Again. I have no idea what direction we should be heading, nor do I know how to find out. I admit I always intended to learn, but it's easy to put aside when the *hunters* who contract me are supposed to take care of all that. I'm basically there to power their magic and help them survive, getting a cut of the bounty as payment. And when I'm not with a hunter on a contract, I travel the main thoroughfares as a matter of personal protection since I don't have much skill with weapons. Never any need for map reading.

I shove all the doubts down. What's done is done, and

hopefully it pays off. I don't want to show any weakness, including the fact that I don't know where we are, but I smother my pride and take a moment to kneel down and dig through my pack for my never-before-used map. He stops a few feet away, and I feel his gaze on me. It makes me feel clumsy and hyperaware, and I fumble with the folded parchment in my attempt to get it open. Doesn't help that it's sopping wet. I finally pry it open, grateful to see that the map markings are all intact. I scan the page in the weak light of dawn and see the main river we just escaped, but the river is *long*, and the amount of land where we could have ended up is incredibly vast, including no less than three different desert-looking areas. I have no idea how to pinpoint our location.

Chapter 20

Ikar

S he has no idea how to read that map. She's an interesting conundrum, claiming to be a bounty hunter but lacking many of the skills necessary to make money in such a competitive, dangerous job choice. That, and I never sensed any hunter magic about her.

I know exactly where we are. Raised to be the High King, I spent hours with tutors learning all subjects. My study of geography was particularly intense and difficult, and when I grew old enough, I traveled and trained with soldiers of all the low kingdoms within my own—one of my main reasons for needing a glamour to hide my identity. I'm still curious how the artist of the bounty picture got some of my glamour, it's the only way that bounty sketch could've been made. I saw the picture myself. I know for a fact Jethonan would never have been involved, but who? Apparently, someone close to me at the castle who can't be trusted. Something to consider.

Right now, we're wasting time while she pretends to read the map and will likely get us further from our destination if I don't help. But I don't want to help her. Anger tempts me to make this the most miserable, impossible job she's ever taken. I want to be so awful that she gives up and releases me so I can get on with my mission to save the kingdom of people that I'm responsible for, including her. But my mother raised me better than that, and I don't have time to play games. Though I find it irritating that even after her shady arrest, my protective instincts are triggered, and I want to smooth the wrinkle of concern that shows between her brows as her eyes scan the map. I lean over her shoulder, taking mercy.

I place my finger on the map. "We are here in this area somewhere," I say tersely, circling a large desert portion of the kingdom.

She stiffens beside me.

"And we're heading to the High Kingdom, Moneyre." I state, scanning the map and locating the city far to the north.

"No. First, the fae," she says.

I jerk my gaze to hers. "I don't have time for errands." Barely contained anger laces my voice.

She steps away, shooting me a dirty look. "Keep your distance." She goes back to studying the map after she decides she's a decent distance from me and frowns. "I'm in charge, and we'll be visiting the fae first." She gives me a pointed look, then looks at the map again. "We are much, much further than we were in Kivan. The river did a number on our travel days."

There's nothing to say to that. It's frustrating, but the river was the only option to escape the goblins, so I can't regret it. I fiddle with the strap of one of my scabbards while she continues to look over the map. I'm about to begin breathing exercises to extend my patience.

Finally, she seems to make a decision and folds up the map decisively. I have zero confidence that she has chosen the best route. So, naturally, I begin to suggest one.

"It would be fastest if we—"

"I don't need your opinion." She throws her pack over her shoulders and starts walking.

My instinctive response, drilled into me for over twenty years, is to reprimand her for her disrespect, like she's one of my soldiers, but she's not. I hold my tongue, barely. The problem is, if she doesn't accept my help, it's very likely that I'm going to end up forever cuffed to this stubborn woman.

It's been almost an entire day since we left the riverside. We made camp a few miles from the river and attempted to get a few hours of sleep, then continued our journey early this morning. Before long, we found the deep black canyons that this desert is known for. Maze-like, tiny paths wind through its narrow crevices. Some of them are wide enough to travel side-by-side, but most aren't, and some I even have to turn sideways to get through. Others are pitch black, enclosed, tube-like tunnels we're forced to scramble through. A claustrophobic's nightmare. Even with the suns high in the sky, the canyons are so deep and narrow that the light that reaches the bottom where we travel is dim and dusty. Occasional winds kick up the loose sand beneath our feet and send it flying around and over us, so much so that my clothing and skin feel gritty. I keep my mouth pressed shut. Don't need sand there as well.

She glances every so often at me, cool gray eyes full of distrust and hate. I keep my face wiped of all expression. I don't want her to know how irritated I am. According to the document she showed me, I have been classified as a Class A criminal. I don't want to be proud of that, but it does help ease the sting of being cuffed by an obviously inexperienced hunter. I try not to show that I care too much about the cuff, but whenever I catch a glimpse of it on my wrist, I have to tamp down a frown. It's a literal, portable prison. My magic is stopped like water behind a solid dam. I force the pressure of my magic against the cuff, testing and attempting to pull and manipulate it, but it doesn't work. I'm basically an Absent. I hope my skill and strength with weapons and fighting are enough to fend off anything we come up against during this journey, but my hope is lacking. I've relied on my magic heavily these last few years to win the bigger gloam battles. Without my magic, if I can't protect her, and she dies, this cuff is stuck forever and my kingdom is doomed. And to top it all off, the small woman walking ahead of me is infuriating. Nothing like a charmed cuff and an arrest to thank someone for rescuing you, and an attitude much larger than her small frame to top it all off. It doesn't help that I feel like an idiot for dropping my guard after I rescued her. I'd made an easy catch.

"How long have you been a hunter?"

"I started working with hunters five years ago," she says evasively.

So, not even a hunter. The shame surrounding my arrest deepens, and I want to punch the nearest canyon wall, but I'd probably end up with busted knuckles for the duration of this eternal journey, and I no longer have Darvy as a healer. The vulnerability is real, and I don't like it.

"If not a hunter, what faction are you?"

"Why do you care?" She raises a brow with another heavy dose of attitude for such an innocent-looking woman.

"Just wondering who arrested me."

"You don't need to know anything about me."

"So we just walk in silence, and I trust that you are who you say you are and that you know where you're going?"

"That would be preferable." She smiles sweetly, but there's venom in her words. The sandy winds have pulled strands of her dark brown hair from her braid, and they float around her face in a wispy dance. At first glance in that tavern, I thought she was too skinny, boyish even, in her oversized clothing. But right now, with her hair messy and loose, her gray eyes framed by dark lashes, and the lightest sign of freckles across her nose, I could never mistake her for a boy. Up close, she's all fragile beauty.

I pull myself from whatever mesmerizing trick she's playing. Defiance rises in my chest. I am the High King. I have an entire army at my command. I have a high kingdom and four low kingdoms of people to care for, who depend on me, and an important mission to complete to keep them safe. But right now, I'm labeled a prisoner and criminal and am under complete control by a wannabe bounty hunter. I can tell her I'm a king—I have my seal and my mark—but will she even know what it is? Do I risk more by revealing my identity to someone I don't trust while I have no magic and no backup or keep my mouth shut?

I'll have to make the journey back either way, and I decide it's best to keep my anonymity. Seven days. Give or take a few. I've done worse for that length of time. Like the time when I assisted my soldiers with a rescue in the mountains, and we were stranded for a week in a shard beast and scorpion-infested cave in blizzard conditions. Strange mix, that. An awful battle ensued as we fought for shelter. I can still feel the depth of the cold in my soul. Or the time we hauled a large convoy of weapons through dead, gloam-filled forest in a sand storm so thick I couldn't see my hand in front of my face. Didn't like breathing dirt much.

I eye the small woman ahead of me, practically drowning in

the men's clothing she wears. Her braid continues to be pulled from its twists by the gusts of wind. She seems harmless enough. I can do this for seven days. It will undoubtedly be easier than many of the missions I've commanded.

In the silence between us, I spend the hours watching for dark creatures hiding in the crevices and shadowed canyon walls and wondering *who* would set a bounty on me and how this happened. Those who know me know I am king, and those who don't know me have no reason to do so. Most would recognize me on the spot, and since Vera doesn't know who I am, I have to believe the glamour is still working. So, at least there's that. I know without a doubt that Jethonan didn't betray me. One of the servants maybe? They've all worked for me for years, so it doesn't make sense that all of a sudden one would develop a grudge.

I continue to think on it, picturing the servants that frequent my rooms and office as our current, narrow crevice path opens into a wide open space. The ground is covered in weeds and plants with sharp, poky leaves. Three other paths lead out at the other side, two narrow crevices such as this one, the other a cave-like entrance. Vera stops suddenly, jarring me from my thoughts. I freeze and listen, instinctively attempting to pull magic, but it doesn't come. My hearing and vision, my strength, all stay the same. They aren't what they should be, and I clench my jaw in frustration.

"There's a gloam creature nearby," she whispers.

Another thing I should be able to sense with my magic.

I pull my sword, crafted and enchanted by a renowned weapons master, from its scabbard at my side. I may not be able to power it with magic like I did to beat the shard beast, but its enchantments will still help defeat most gloam creatures. Even a magic cuff won't stop the enchantments crafted into my weapon. I grin at the thought.

"What direction?" I ask, my voice low.

"Coming down the path to the right, I think."

I watch closely, scanning the tall canyon walls and down each of the other paths as well. But instead of a creature bounding out and attacking violently, a dark, thick mist begins to fill in the space around us, and the canyon becomes heavy with an ominous silence. I know exactly what it is and immediately try to slow and limit my breaths, knowing that if the mist thickens enough and I stand in it for too long, it will eventually kill me. Vera, as well.

"A murk. Try not to breathe it in."

The woman seems inexperienced, but I hope she knows what a murk is. Gloam creatures with no definitive form, who use hallucinogenic mist as their offensive weapon to confuse, paralyze, and kill their prey. An enchanted weapon will kill them, but finding them in their half-solid state in time is the problem. That, and protecting the wannabe bounty hunter that I can no longer see. I turn, scanning, listening. My magic strains against the cuff, and I clench my jaw at the vulnerability and weakness I feel with the lack of it. The space that had once been wide open and full of weeds is now pitch black.

The back of my neck tingles with awareness, and I quickly spin to my left just as mist forms into a darker shadow and lunges from my left. Its shapeless, gaping mouth angles for my chest with a skin-crawling rasp in its attempt to suck the lucent magic from my soul for its own survival. I thrust my sword where it should be, but it's gone, and I only slice through mist so thick that now I can't even see my hands in front of my face. I have no idea where Vera is. I take slow steps to where I think she was last, hoping that lack of a struggle means the murk hasn't found her yet.

"Vera?" I ask, my voice low, as I turn in all directions.

My brain begins to turn foggy, my thoughts churning like thick mud. I see Darvy and Rhosse in front of me. They're here. I smile in relief before I remember that the three of us are in a battle of some sort. *What battle?* My gaze swerves back and forth as I search. My friends end up in a different spot than they were when I spin around again. That's okay—they're here and alive. I stride toward them and watch as they pull magic to prepare for the fight, and I feel a rush of relief and camaraderie that was missing just moments ago. Why? I pull magic, and just when I begin to wonder why it's not working, they fall dead and gloam overtakes their forms like a rabid dog, twisting and snapping. I shout and rush to their aid. But just as I swing my sword at the gloam, it's gone. Steel strikes dirt with a thud.

I turn. *Where is it? Where is... what?* I cover my eyes with a hand as I try to pull my thoughts from the mud they've been immersed in. *What am I fighting?* But my muscles burn with fatigue even just lifting my arm, and the hand grasping my sword is slick with sweat. I hear a feminine voice shouting, but it's muffled and difficult to discern. I recover one word from the string of others. *Hallucination.* It's enough. I lift my gaze and search. I see the dim shimmer of light through the mist and blink several times to make sure it's not another hallucination created by the murk.

The mist gets thinner, and my thoughts clearer, the closer I get until I realize it's Vera, holding a ball of lucent in her hand. Shock erupts through me. She's an Originator. And she must be powerful in her own right to hold off a murk attack like this on her own with that tiny lucent orb. The mist isn't as quickly condensing around her, due to her lucent magic, but it's slowly filling in. Her comments from yesterday make more sense now, but I don't have time to think over it. I blink, and she's gone. I hear her scream, but it sounds like it's coming from all directions at once. I begin to turn, then stop and try to gain my bearings again, but my eyes burn, and my movements begin to feel increasingly sluggish once more. The murk mist is so dense now that it feels difficult to inhale, like I'm breathing in pudding.

Then like the beginnings of a tornado, the fog begins to pull and spin in thick clouds around me. My hair and clothing begin to forcefully whip around my body. I grip my sword firmly, holding it tightly as the murk attempts to rip it from my grasp with its powerful, gale-force winds. My eyes struggle to blink, tears streaming from their corners, and then the funnel tightens. The wind has gathered loose debris from the forest floor, and I lift my arms to protect myself from the loose rocks, sticks, sharp leaves, and thorns that seem to be attacking me. I feel the sting of cuts on my face, neck, and hands. I feel the hit of larger rocks battering my body and know there will be bruises if I survive.

Tighter and tighter, the wind narrows, sucking the last precious bits of oxygen from my grasp, bit by precious bit, until it stops and instantaneously gathers into the dark oxygen-stealing blanket that is murk. It's all over me, suffocating. All I see is black. I shout as I feel it pulling my magic to the surface of my soul through my chest—it feels like death. My breathing sounds like a sharp wheeze, and my blindness is accentuated with bright dots due to my lack of air. I hear Vera shouting but can't make out what she's saying. My body burns with murk-induced fatigue, and it takes all my will power to lift my arm. With a wild swing that my weapons trainer would balk at, I slice through part of it with my sword, and it temporarily falls away, gives a long, drawn out rasp, and comes at me again. Blackness once again enshrouds me, and I pull my magic so hard against the cuff I'm surprised it holds.

Of all the struggles I've had in my life, being absent of my magic has never been one of them, and I think it might be the worst. I see Vera's light press through its form on the opposite side, and immediately, with her lucent magic, the murk's power weakens enough that my vision clears. I lift my sword before the murk can dissipate again and stab straight through it. The charm around my weapon practically sizzles as it comes in contact with the murk's physical gloam form, neutralizing it into a wisp of air that rises and disappears in seconds. I stand there panting and wipe a smear of blood across my face with my sleeve, taking great gulps of air and feeling relief as the burn and fog leaves my body.

"Enchanted sword? Those are pricey." Vera lifts a shapely brow and looks pointedly at it while her orb snuffs out as if it was never there.

I sheathe my sword, more grateful for it than I've ever been. It's my only lifeline at this point. "And you're an Originator."

She shrugs like it's no big deal, brushes past me, and continues in the direction we were headed before the murk appeared. I follow, but my mind is turning as it continues to clear. Originators, especially those who can share raw magic like those I employ, are sought after by all factions of magic. It makes sense now, why she would be working with bounty hunters. Their ability to increase another person's magic, like a magical conductor of sorts, is extremely valuable and has only become more so as magic has begun to decay at a steady pace. The energy required to pull and use magic has become almost unsustainable, but having an Originator changes everything. Healers, hunters, even other types of Originators, need more magic. She's exactly what I need to find the flower since I was forced to leave my personal Originators with my kingdom, and it wouldn't have been right to ask Nadiette to help me with this mission. I feel a stab of guilt again at the way I had to end things, but there's nothing for it.

I push the thoughts away and refocus on the woman ahead of me. Suddenly, I find I'm not quite as angry toward her as I was a few minutes ago. I've found a powerful Originator, now I just need to hire her. I could find another Originator if she says no, but another Originator doesn't also carry knowledge about the Tulips. I want this one. I want her.

There's just the small fact that she doesn't currently view us on equal grounds, me being her prisoner and all. I frown and lift the cuff to see its links around my wrist. With my current state of luck, as soon as she delivers me to the officials, my glamour will still be working so well they'll lock me up and leave me there until it wears off or Darvy and Rhosse show up —if they ever do. A deep sorrow stabs through my chest. The hallucination caused by the murk felt too real, seeing them torn apart by gloam as if I was watching them die a second time. I force the image out of my head, unwilling to mourn. There's a chance they are alive, and I'm not giving up hope. My two closest friends aren't dead. They can't be.

Back to the matter at hand—I don't have time to rot in prison. And I don't intend to end up there. Better by far, is convincing her of my character and my law-abiding reputation. She doesn't need to know I'm king, but I need her to trust me. I've got a week to sway her opinion. In the meantime, I need to put together the offer of a lifetime to get her help.

Chapter 21

Ikar

A day later, we're still making our way through what is called the Black Canyons. We've kept a quick pace, our only real stop the murk attack, and half a night's sleep. Seems that the wannabe hunter doesn't like these canyons much. I would laugh, but I admit that their twists and turns and tight spaces seem never-ending, and maybe they are, if you don't choose the right path. The first sun sets, and I would have grown even more concerned with the lack of a forthcoming exit, except I notice that the canyon walls aren't quite as steep, the crevices wider. Soon, evidence of green shrubs overtaking the prickly, stick-like weeds adds to my optimism. The second sun sets, but we continue. It's not until the third sun is on its way down that Vera finally stops.

We stand in a small flat field of grass, the shadowy tree line several yards distant on all sides. Canyon walls are miles apart by this point, and I grudgingly admit she seems to know how to survive. I look over my shoulder at the Black Canyon far behind us in the distance. Grown, experienced men have lost their way between those narrow walls time and time again. If she has luck, it must be a hefty amount. I shrug, no complaints from me. I'll not be questioning anything that speeds this journey up.

"We'll stop here," Vera says, as she removes her pack. She's hardly looked in my direction today, and now is no different. I'm not sure if she's scared of me, disgusted by my presence, or both. I've experienced neither of those directed toward me as the king. The opposite, in fact. People bowing so extravagantly they nearly fold in half, simpering women with their eyes on the throne beside me, and others planning ways in which to get ahead of another in my court—it's all quite exhausting. I watch for a moment as she busies herself preparing a place for a small fire, continuing to ignore me. At least I know where she stands.

I gather wood while I wrestle with the fact that she's in charge here. I'm not used to taking orders from anyone—it's been years since I've had to. But while I press my lips shut and force myself not to say anything I think about the last person who truly had the power to give me an order—my father. What would he say about my current situation? For a moment on this journey, I was two steps ahead, but now I feel as if I'm five behind. I try to imagine what he'd say. How to get out of this? He was a peacemaking king, a uniter of the low kings and the people, and he was loved for it more than anything else he accomplished. He'd tell me to be humble and win her over with kindness and respect, which I already know I need to do in order to win her trust as I've planned, but those are the last things I want to offer right now.

I see Vera startle from the corner of my eye as I place the wood for a fire and follow her line of sight. All I see is the Black Canyon in the distance and the sparse beginnings of forest trees at the edges of this large field. Maybe she senses something I can't see, but I'm magically helpless, so I don't know.

The gloam creatures normally lurk in shadow, but here, at least the moon shines brightly. Light won't keep them away, but it helps. I warily eye the trees at the edge of the field, but all is still.

Earlier in the evening, I used my bow to shoot a rabbit that appeared to be following us. Odd behavior for a rabbit, but I've seen stranger. I now cook it over our small fire while Vera settles and watches, quietly perched on a rough log she tipped on its side. A small bird, that looks more like a wad of fluffy, fresh cotton than anything that can fly, glides through camp and lands on her shoulder with a happy chirp. I watch, intrigued, as her face visibly softens and her eyes widen with pleasure.

"Rupi," Vera whisper-greets the bird with a tender smile.

She lifts a finger, and the bird hops onto it, wrapping its tiny feet around securely. It turns its head and looks at me with a judgmental, tiny, black eye encircled with a small gray ring, and lets out another chirp from its black beak that can be no longer than the tip of a flat quill. It's fluffy white all over. The fuzz around its face gives it a soft, friendly look that's at odds with the black eye directing a glare my way. The body of the bird is, at most, two inches long. Its tail another two inches. It's tiny. And somehow, oddly familiar, though I don't recall ever seeing a bird of this variety before.

"Is this your... pet?" I ask, as I turn the rabbit over the fire, waiting for Vera to snap at me for asking a question again.

Instead, she smiles affectionately at it, and I'm caught off guard by the soft tone of her voice. "Yeah, her name is Rupi."

Vera pulls a small bag from her pack and pours out a tiny pile of seed in her hand, the fluffy bird eagerly hops on her palm and begins pecking. It pauses with a seed in its beak and jerks its head toward the forest, seeming to listen. Then when nothing jumps out, continues cracking the seed and pecking for more. Vera watches quietly. Then the bird hops back to her shoulder where she promptly ruffles up her feathers and nestles into the warm crook between her shoulder and neck, cushioned by her cloak, looking like something so round and fluffy it belongs in a children's book.

"And what about the squirrel from earlier?" I'm positive it followed us for at least twelve miles.

A hint of wariness enters her eyes, but she laughs. "Just a friendly squirrel." She shrugs her shoulders.

A friendly squirrel? Right. I'm beginning to think she's some sort of animal whisperer. I decide not to mention the rabbit, since my questioning appears to be making her uncomfortable and I fear she'll quit talking altogether. Animal whisperers are a subset of the hunter faction, as Rhosse is, but she can't possibly be of the hunter faction because I saw with my own eyes her ability to pull raw lucent magic. She's an Originator, isn't she? I look a little closer at her, expecting the explanation to reveal itself. It doesn't seem to add up, so I decide I've made more of the friendly animal situation than I need to. There are bigger things to be worried about, like survival.

"How do you usually protect yourself on these bounty hunts?" I ask, as I continue to turn the meat. "I would think maybe you would have adopted something... bigger, for protection." I eye the bird.

She pours the leftover seeds in her hand back into the small leather pouch, still not looking at me. "Rupi is the perfect companion." Her voice is borderline defensive.

The bird turns its head slightly, like it understood my comment, and seems to give me a side eye of disdain, but the effect falls flat with the fluff surrounding its face.

She continues. "I accept contracts for work." She pulls two

strings, and the bag cinches up, then she wraps her hands around the bag and looks up, her forearms resting on her knees and her eyes meeting mine for the first time since this afternoon. "I work *with* bounty hunters, but am not officially one of them. As part of the contract, it is their job to offer me protection for the duration of the job, and in return, I offer them lucent magic. It's always worked well enough—until now." The emotion in her eyes is a mixture of guilt and independent attitude. I realize then that maybe she avoids making eye contact because her eyes reveal more than she likes.

"Why did you arrest me without a hunter?"

"I suppose I owe you that much, since I've put you in a bit of danger." She bites the edge of her lip, and there's that guilty flash in her eyes again before she directs her gaze to her fingers fiddling with the strings that tie the pouch of birdseed.

So, the woman *does* have a heart.

"I was supposed to go back to meet him. I was correct in assuming you'd follow me, and I thought I'd lead you right to him, but I didn't account for the trap. You know the story from there." Her nose wrinkles like she can still smell the sour of the goblins. I know *I* can.

"So, you're a rule breaker." I state the fact with a smug smirk. I can't help it, the way she's labeled me a criminal still irks.

Her eyes shoot up to meet mine, her brows rising in surprised denial and her mouth opening as if she's about to defend herself. Then she realizes I'm right, and her lips press together with a frown. I cast her a knowing glance with an accusatory brow raise, but find myself enjoying the open emotion I see in her gaze and immediately shut down the desire to find more ways to initiate eye contact. This isn't a game or a friendship.

"That's not fair," she says quietly.

"There's a good chance we'll both die out here if you keep me cuffed," I say bluntly. She knows it as well as I.

"Almost done?" She gestures toward the rabbit with a jerk of her chin.

I decide to let the cuff situation drop for now. I know if I push her too hard, it'll make it worse, so I simply nod. "What other types of contracts do you take?"

She fiddles with the small strings of her bag. "Healers and hunters, usually. Sometimes potion makers."

"You don't work with other Originators?" I ask, more curious than I should be about the woman across the fire.

Her eyes turn guarded. "No."

I can tell she will not divulge anything further along that line of questioning. Why would an Originator not want to work with other Originators? I tuck the question away for later.

I decide to test the waters without directly inquiring. Now isn't the time for me to offer her a contract, but I can still gather information.

"What about official kingdom contracts or permanent positions? Or working with armies, small missions, that type of thing?" I keep an innocent expression on my face. She has no need to know my position at this point.

Her gray eyes fill with ice, and the tense muscles that must have tightened in her shoulders have Rupi readjusting against the warmth of her neck. "I would never accept contracts for any official capacity. And I'm not *noble*, so it's impossible to find a permanent position anyway."

Now, it's *my* brows rising. What is the source of her disgust for official capacity jobs? They pay well. Many Originators compete for them, though I can understand her frustration about the limitations for lower class Originators. I'm not sure when that started, years before my time, but something about being here with her has me wanting to look into it when I return.

"Why would you, who apparently loves to live life by the rules, have an issue with officials?" I ask lightly, like her answer won't affect me, but my chest grows tight. If she refuses to work with me, I have to spend precious time finding another Originator. Time I don't have, especially after being cuffed and lost for days. I don't care if she's noble or not. She appears to be powerful no matter her class.

She raises her gaze to mine. "You're a mercenary, so I assume you don't like officials—or shall we be clear and say it's the *kings*—either, or you'd be working as an honorable soldier in one of the low or high royal armies. Right?" She looks at me, waiting. It smarts, but I choose not to be offended that she views me as less-than-honorable.

I lift my shoulders noncommittally, unwilling to outright lie. I'm not so sure now that I am prepared for her opinion when I see the ice in her eyes melt and fill with flames of fire.

"High Kings and almost all low kings are violent, selfish, wealthy, entitled, spoiled men who take and take from their people and are in constant search for more power. They allow needless murder and the poor to be mistreated and ignored. Look at the suffering of the kingdoms. What is there to like? Tell me one place that is thriving." She hardly pauses for a breath before she continues, "Why should nobility refuse to take on a low-class Originator for a permanent position? It's not just Originators, either. The lower class suffers across all forms of magic, and the kings have done nothing to help them or change it."

I feel like she punched me in the chest. I want to argue with her. Many parts of the kingdom are doing relatively well, considering the circumstances of lucent and gloam, but can I say they are thriving? Probably not. The one thing I can't argue at all is the fact that the suffering of the kingdom *is* my fault.

"I believe most kings are doing their best," I respond carefully.

"Have you worked for one?" She sounds doubtful.

"I've been around a few," I say vaguely. She doesn't need to know that I know the other four kings personally. Or that I am, in fact, the High King she hates. "Have you met one, seen one, even?"

"I've been around a low king, but I haven't met or seen any of the others, that I know of." She looks uncomfortable. "I find it odd that you, as a criminal, have such a glowing opinion of our leadership." She looks at me with a mix of thoughtfulness and confusion.

"I told you from the start this was all a misunderstanding. I'm not a criminal." I meet her gray gaze with mine, challenge in my eyes.

She looks away first. I want to ask her more. I understand her anger over the treatment of the lower class. I admit that I should consider how to approach such large cultural treatment of a class, but unfortunately, changes such as those take time and patience. In the meantime, I want to find out where those other beliefs come from, about kings, but I think I've pushed the limits of this conversation. I only nod as I pull the now-cooked rabbit from the fire and hand Vera her portion. We eat in silence, the fire crackling warmly between us. I have roughly six more days to convince this woman to accept an official contract. Six days to change an opinion that, from the fire in her eyes, has deep roots. Six days to figure out what she knows about the Tulips. I tear off a large bite of perfectly-cooked meat. This adventure just got a lot more interesting.

Chapter 22

Vera

I relay our conversation in my mind and internally cringe. *Why did I share so much?* Something about this man puts me dangerously at ease, even has me removing cemented bricks from my fortified, emotional walls. It feels a lot like we've developed a neutrality of some sort, and I only just arrested him two nights ago. It's hard because he is surprisingly... normal. I remind myself I didn't share anything overly personal, nothing that would give me away, but if this continues, I know it's not *if* I will, it's *when*. And that's the problem.

It's not often I find someone I can vent about my dislike of kings and classes to, and who better than a mercenary? He says he's not a criminal, but that's to be expected from a criminal. It felt good to say it to someone who understands, to get it off my chest, but it's also dangerous. I can't forget that he and his friends are after the Tulips. *They're after me.* I finish chewing and force the bite of meat down my throat. Though it's delicious, it sticks in my throat like I just ate a hunk of old, moldy bread. I am a naive fool to forget who this man is. Just hours ago, I watched him kill a murk without any magic, aside from his enchanted sword. I've never seen any hunter defeat a gloam creature without magic, but I made sure not to make too big of a deal out of it. The confidence nearly radiates off him, and I don't think he needs any extra. Besides, I don't want him knowing how much it shook me. I swallow tightly. Instead of feeling safer with the knowledge of what he can do, I feel even more scared of the danger he inherently is.

I lift my gaze to look at him across the heat rising from the fire, and his eyes meet mine for a moment that seems long. All steely blue intensity. Hard and focused. Calculating, even. I thought all his magic was securely locked behind that handy cuff, but I begin to doubt it. Aside from magic, there's no other way to explain the way his eyes hold mine and draw me in, and it's not all terror that's holding me there. I'll be the first to admit that my criminal is attractive. There's a pull about him that makes me feel a little panicky. Like I'm tied to a rope he's slowly but surely winding closer. He's intense. I can almost tangibly feel a drive within him that is entirely too intimidating. All day long I felt that presence behind my back, as if his over-confident self was just waiting for me to mess up so he could step into control and I would thank him for it. *No way, mister.* I narrow my eyes at him. He simply quirks a seemingly innocent, questioning brow at my glare, like he's wondering what in the world he could have done to warrant it. I've chosen the worst criminal.

I shake my head and turn my attention to Rupi, who's perched on my shoulder. She spent the last few minutes cleaning her feathers with her small beak, and now I stroke her fluffy softness. She pecks softly at my earlobe before she tucks her head down and sleeps. Which leaves me with nothing to do but watch the muscles of my criminal's forearms move as he stokes the fire. He'd rolled his sleeves to his elbows to clean the rabbit earlier and left them that way—to my detriment or plea-sure, I can't say. I press my lips together unhappily. Why can't he be filthy and gross? His voice nasally instead of rich and smooth? His hair matted or dirty instead of shiny and artfully mussed? I mean, we just walked out of a canyon pit full of sand winds and prickly bushes. Pretty sure it shows for me.

Just to show how much I don't care what he thinks or how attractive he is, I wipe my mouth with the back of my hand in a very drawn out, unladylike fashion. If he thinks I'm gross, then good. Maybe he'll stop talking to me. Then I stand so quickly that Rupi gives a surprised *cheep* and her feathers begin to quill at the abrupt movement. Ikar watches me like he doesn't know quite what to think, but says nothing. At least he won't be able to figure me out. I can't even do that myself. I laugh a little sharply to confuse us both even more as I stalk grumpily to my pack and prepare my bedroll. The *one* time I arrest a criminal on my own and he has to be like *this*. I huff a breath out as I adjust my blankets in an angry fashion, then fold my arms atop them and stare at the sky. There must be something wrong with me. Maybe I swallowed too much dark, disgusting river water, and now I'm attracted to hardened criminals for the rest of my life. I lay flat on my back and frown at the stars in the sky while I wait for sleep that refuses to come, Rupi's tiny body pressed up against the warmth of my neck and nested in my hair.

I'm still awake when Ikar rises to prepare his own bedroll. He tosses it out, then digs through his pack for a moment. In his efforts to find whatever he's looking for a small glass bottle drops out, rolls a few inches away, and settles comfortably against a patch of coarse field grass and dirt. Not sure if he noticed, and more curious than I should be, I scoop Rupi from the confines of my hair to the warmth of my blankets and climb out of my bedroll. I pluck the vial from the ground. *Fae potion?*

I know from personal experience working with the makers that these are quite expensive.

I hand it back to him, and after a mumbled *thank you*, he nonchalantly tucks it into an inner pocket, and proceeds to arrange his pack again just so. He's a tidy criminal, then.

"What kind of potion is it?" I ask, curious. Glamour or healing is the question.

"Healing, but it's no longer potent."

"Are you sure? How long ago did you buy it?"

When fae potions, which have always been the holy grail for healing elixirs, cross the fae borders, within hours they have lost half their power. And within a week or two, they will no longer heal at all. Part of the whole *magic dying* thing.

"I'm sure," he says in the darkness, "it's over a week old."

Most people buy fae potions for specific reasons, or even travel to the fae to use them to ensure they aren't wasted because their prices are so high. I've never known mercenaries to have so much money to spend... and waste. His enchanted sword looks like the best quality, custom type. And he purchases fae potions just to... keep on hand and forget about? But it's none of my business. He *is* a criminal, I remind myself. He probably lifted it off someone he killed or used dirty money to purchase it. Those reminders have me quickly settling back into my bedroll several feet away and feeling grateful for that lock around his wrist.

With the help of the map, we left the Black Canyons and its deserts and entered into a forest that is much like the rest that fills the majority of the kingdoms. The trees are tall and thick, and dark green needles fill long branches and dust the ground beneath. Moss grows along the trunks of the trees, covers rocks with its green cushion, and carpets the forest floor. Small flowers sprout amongst forest grass here and there, but the shadows prevent anything too tall from growing within these depths. We pick our way through, and I'm trying not to compulsively check the map, but it's hard.

I open it again and hope he doesn't comment on the fact that I just opened it a few minutes ago, but I can't help it. Everything in this dratted forest looks the same, and I only catch glimpses of the suns when there happens to be a gap in the tight weave of branches above. How am I to determine if we've been traveling in the right direction?

I squint a little to see it better. My criminal pointed out the Black Canyon Desert, which seems obvious to me now that I'm looking at it on the map, and we still need to get through the Shift Forest. Problem is, I can't tell one forest from another on here. I turn the map a bit, trying to see if I can match it up with our direction, and I just *know* he's watching me with that hard gaze of his. Judging my lack of map reading talent, I'm sure. I should just ask him. He's as motivated as I to get to Moneyre, so I can trust him at least this much, right? My pride, though, stings like a flame spider's bite.

Without allowing myself a second more to think about it, I stop in my tracks and angle the map toward him. He jerks to a stop, like I caught him off guard. *Good.* Keep things weird. Rupi takes this moment to coast on a light breeze and land gently on my forearm as I hold the map out, quirking her head between the map and Ikar. If I didn't know better, I'd think she knows how to read my map as well. It's a ridiculous thought. I would laugh, but I still have to ask Ikar for help. Best get it over with.

"Where do you think we are?" I keep my voice unemotional and flat, but inside, I'm hoping he doesn't comment on the fact that I'm asking.

He looks at the map, turns it the opposite way I had it, and then points to a spot in the middle of an unmarked forest.

"Here, but we should probably shift a bit to the north to get to the city that leads into the Shift Forest."

Rupi *cheeps* and hops to his still-extended wrist. Is this supposed to mean she *agrees* with him? My cheeks itch to turn red, but I quickly fold the map up. "Great, exactly what I was thinking, too." Never mind I had the map upside down. And what's up with Rupi? She looks even tinier perched on him than on me. I frown at her as she happily accepts a gentle stroke from Ikar's forefinger, who looks afraid he may break her with his touch. It could be endearing if the man wasn't a Tulip killer.

I grow a bit concerned about Rupi, wondering if she may have eaten something odd and it's affecting her behavior. Rupi in her right mind would never accept affection like that from a criminal—she never has in the eight years I've worked with bounty hunters. I wait a second longer for her to return to my wrist, but she appears content to stay where she is. Instead of waiting for her I scoop her into my hands and carefully snatch her back from the mercenary, now truly worried she's unwell. I decide I'll keep a close eye on her the rest of the day, so I deposit her on my shoulder.

"You need to stop eating strange things. It's not safe," I scold her, quietly. But when I twist my neck to see her on my shoulder, she angles one eye at me. And for some reason, I feel like if she could manage an eye roll, I would have seen one. "Stay close," I tell her, ignoring her attitude.

I start walking and look over my shoulder at him, but I shouldn't have. All I see is that smile he does that's annoyingly confident and calm, but this time it seems a bit smug. I whip my head back around. That's the last time I'm asking him for help.

I tell myself that I have to wait to open the map again for at least an hour as I try to head in a more *northernly* direction to find Shift City. I wrap my hands around the straps of my pack over my shoulders to ensure I don't grab the map in the next two minutes and prepare to trudge silently on through this dark piece of the kingdom.

Rather than continue silently, Ikar speaks from behind me. I brace myself to hear that I've gone in the wrong direction, but instead he asks, "You know I was serious about the deal, right?"

"What deal?" I feign innocence.

"I mentioned that if you released me, I'd pay you as much as the bounty reward, but I'd like to make one *minor* change to my offer since it hasn't been accepted yet."

"Make as many changes as you like, I won't be accepting." I glance at him, expecting to see a sign of frustration, but instead I still see the remnants of that grin on his face.

"I should clarify. I want to offer you a *contract*." He gives me a pointed look. "In exchange for you assisting me on my search, I will pay you double the reward amount that was listed on the warrant."

It is similar to what he suggested that first night I'd cuffed him when I immediately shut him down, and it's a jaw-dropping amount of money. It's an offer that can change my life. There has to be a drawback. I hate to act interested, but he's ignited my curiosity.

"What exactly do you need help finding?" I narrow my eyes at him.

"A flower with magical properties. I believe it can be found high in the Lucent Mountains," he says in his deep, rich voice that has me wanting to say yes just from the sound of it.

But I knew there was a drawback, and this is a huge one. The only thing I know about the Lucent Mountains is that no kingdom or realm has specific claim on them. They are, literally, owned and protected by magic. Lucent has weakened considerably. The entire mountain range may be engulfed in gloam by now.

"People don't go there," I say flatly.

He shakes his head in disagreement. "People have been there."

"They haven't returned!" I whisper-yell, my eyes wide at the insane idea he's presented.

"I'm sure they've returned. They just don't brag about it."

"The logic there is surprisingly lacking." He's a smart man. He's shown me that. Is he in denial?

"Doesn't matter if it's logical or not. It's the only place I can find the flower I need."

"You're sure about that?"

"I trust the king's advisor. So, yes. But I need an Originator to do it."

"Well, good luck finding anyone willing."

"Just think about it."

"Don't need to. I don't work with criminals," I say.

I look back at him after an extended moment, wondering why he didn't respond. I barely catch the way his eyes have tightened at the corners as his left shoulder pulls forward in the smallest way. A memory comes to mind of how my father's bad shoulder used to cramp up after a long day. It was much more noticeable than this, but is it the same for him? He did fight off a murk yesterday and has carried that pack for two days straight.

"Your shoulder bad?"

"It's fine." His voice is flat.

"My father's shoulder would cramp up when he'd use it too much, an old injury acting up." I continue talking about my father and his injury and about some of the healers I worked with to fill the silence. He simply listens, and I end up feeling like I shared too much.

A minute later, Ikar speaks. "You talk about your father as if he no longer lives."

It's a statement, but I can sense the question within. For some reason, maybe because he's been tolerable and, you know, sort of saved my life, I decide to answer this time.

"He doesn't. Neither does my mother. They died when I was fourteen, and I spent the next four years with my fae aunt."

We're walking side-by-side now, the feeling between us very close to a comfortable camaraderie. My first instinct is to rush ahead and remind him I'm in charge and that we're not friends. But I don't, and don't try to ask me why because I won't be able to tell you.

"And after that?"

"After that, I left. Went off to make my own way."

I remember all the energetic zeal I'd had at eighteen, leaving my aunt's home of comfort and wealth with nothing but the small amount of money my parents left to me. That's when I got caught up in the trouble with that first contract with the Class A criminal where I almost died. Obviously, things haven't improved too much. I scoff as I look down at the pants that will hardly stay up, the boots that are a size or two too large with laces so worn I've had to attach other pieces of string to keep them tied up. I've intentionally dressed in men's clothing as a matter of self-preservation, and that part, I still don't mind. My whole goal in life is to not be noticed. But their condition has deteriorated, and I've been so focused on saving every bit of money, I haven't been willing to replace anything. I'd never really cared before, but I feel a twinge of something I can only label as self-consciousness for the first time in a long time.

"You see how that's gone." I laugh a little like it's a joke and then quickly redirect the conversation. I shouldn't have said that last sarcastic part. I really don't want a placating, obligatory compliment. I hurry to ask him something instead. "Tell me about your family." It sort of comes out commanding, so I add, "If you want," after a long second. Why do I have to be so awkward?

He gives me a sideways glance with a bit of a smile at my attempt at normal conversation, but I see a flicker of grief in his eyes. "My mother died eight years ago, my father five. I'm an only child."

A sudden fountain of questions begins pouring into my mind now that I've allowed myself to ask him something. But by now, we're climbing up a rather steep incline, and with his taller build and stronger arms, he's able to more quickly pull himself ahead while I slip and fall to my knees again and again in my overlarge boots—I couldn't ask questions if I tried. He reaches the top as I'm scrambling up behind him and offers a hand as soon as I'm within distance. I stare at it for a moment. Two days ago, I would have lobbed a big spit in it rather than take it, but after a slight hesitation, I place my small hand in his larger palm, and he easily helps me to the top. *Look at us, getting along.* I brush the dirt and forest debris from my clothes, even though it does no good. I'm filthy as an armored pig.

We continue on, navigating through darkening forest. Shadows lengthen, and I begin to think I'm seeing things in my peripheral. When we'd left the Black Canyon, I'd thought for sure I saw shadowed forms when we'd made camp, but nothing showed itself. Just now, I'm sure I caught a glimpse of tall shadows not just from the suns going down, but from tall figures in the forest. But when I turn my head to look, there's nothing there. Again.

"You see something?" Ikar asks, craning his neck to search where my eyes have lingered.

"Thought so. There's nothing, though." I shrug. But suddenly, I find I'm grateful for Ikar's steady, capable presence at my side all the same.

We find a place to make camp, and I begin to build a fire while Ikar rolls up his sleeves again and prepares a small, wild turkey to be cooked.

"This one about begged to be caught." He glances up at me beneath his brows as he works, "Trailed us for two miles this evening."

I paste an innocent expression that consists of wide eyes and a gentle shrug, but inside I'm a thread's width from cursing my friendly forest animals. They're going to give me away, and I feel horrible about eating them. My stomach growls loudly, oblivious to my guilt.

He shakes his head and mumbles, "Never seen anything like it."

We sleep soon after. Doesn't take me long to drift off anymore, with the long days of walking and climbing. Apparently, I'm more tired than I thought since I keep seeing things that aren't there. I drift for awhile in light sleep before I wake and lay there, wondering how late it is and seeing that Ikar still sits before the glowing embers of our fire. He has pulled something from his pack that looks like a round, flat badge of some sort, but I don't ask about it. I'm supposed to be asleep, and I shouldn't care anyway.

His shoulders are hunched forward, his forearms on his knees, and he holds it between his hands. Turning it between his fingers in a habitual, familiar motion as he gazes, unseeing, into the fire, lost in thoughts so intense I'm not sure I want to know what they are. I can't tug my gaze away, even though I feel like I'm infringing on a moment too personal. He's always so guarded and emotionally blocked off. All business, all the time. Smirking and leading and trying to order me around, and quiet when he's not. But if I didn't know him and I'd happened upon this scene, I'd think he held the weight of the world on his shoulders. I study his face, wondering at the emotion so openly displayed there. I struggle to define it. Sorrow, worry... maybe even guilt? Because of his assortment of violent crimes, probably. I shouldn't feel so bad for him. He's still a Class A criminal. Just apparently a very respectful, kind, and good one. I sigh in disgust. *How confusing.* My guilt finally wins over my curiosity and forces my gaze away, but it's awhile until I calm the questions in my thoughts so I can sleep.

Chapter 23

Vera

We rise early and continue our journey, and I admit that I'm proud for surviving my third night on my own as a true bounty hunter. My criminal didn't kill me yet. That's good. That emotional wall is back up around him, tall and thick as ever. His blue eyes are guarded but friendly enough. The longer we walk, the more my cheer fades, though, because I realized just hours ago that my magic, or me, or both, seems to be even *more* drawn to this man than on the first and second days. What does that say about me? Of course I'm drawn to a criminal. Typical. Doesn't matter if he's been on his best behavior these last few days to attempt to persuade me to uncuff him. I just *know* that's why he's been nice to me. There's no other explanation. I definitely can't trust him, and I need to distance myself to stay safe.

I don't have the best track record in the judgement or magical departments, and here is a prime example of *why*. Magic has caused a lot of trouble for me in my life, mostly because, as a Tulip, my magic is broken, weak, however you want to describe it. It's not *enough*. And on top of that, we're hated. But this time, I will make the right choice. I wind the unruly magic tendrils up as tight as the braid I'm currently weaving my messy hair into and glare at Ikar's very muscular back for good measure, effectively returning him to his place as my enemy. A Tulip killer, probably. Something is off with my magic, that is certain.

How did he take the lead again today without me noticing anyway? I blow a dirty strand of loose hair, that I apparently missed when rebraiding my hair this morning, from my face in exasperation. I assume it has something to do with the way magic is weakening, I don't have enough experience to figure out why these strange things happen, the only other person I'd felt this draw toward was an ex-boyfriend, Drade, from my teen years. It hadn't ended well. No one who isn't a king can return the bridge that my magic begs to create, even though I've been told it's not strong enough anyway. I've never felt that my magic is weak, but I'll trust Tatania on this one. I plan to someday marry a *regular* man, which is why I'd had to break things off with Drade. He had become the fae king through challenge, and I could *never* marry a king, as it would entail *bridging*. Even low kings can bridge. I shiver, glad that I'll never be part of such a dangerous connection.

I'm taken from my thoughts when I hear Rupi's happy chirp as she glides through the air and settles on my shoulder, shuffling her wings and side-stepping until she gets comfortable. She still isn't acting quite normal. Not once when Ikar has gotten close to her has she quilled up. I mean, she let him pet her yesterday three times, and that's just not like her. She's showing no symptoms of being sick, so I've reluctantly let her have her freedom today, but I watch her closely.

"Enjoy your morning fly?" I whisper, as I reach a finger up to stroke her small head.

Ikar glances at the two of us, and I see what looks like a flash of humor in his eyes. I know he thinks Rupi is a ridiculous pet.

"Do you have an animal?" I ask, truly curious. They say that people often choose animals that match their personality.

A wistful look touches his eyes. "Two. A hawk and a wolf-beast dog mix."

I instinctively place a protective hand over Rupi's soft back, hawks being one of her greatest predators—just as Ikar is to me.

"Fitting," I say, saucily.

He grins proudly.

I continue with spite in my voice, "Both powerful, violent, murderous types like their owner."

At that, he scowls, but it's more of an irritated-looking smolder, which annoys me because I like it.

For a moment, I feel a pang of regret over what I said, that bit of camaraderie I'd felt between us yesterday having lent itself to today, and I've just squashed it. Then I remember *again* that I don't need comfortable companionship with a criminal. I shouldn't have cared about his shoulder pains, or his family, or had friendly conversations with him over the past two days. Nor should I be enjoying his ornery, handsome scowls. I raise my chin, unwilling to take it back. Ikar is not my friend. He is *my* criminal, who *I* arrested and who has committed horrendous crimes to have a reward so large attached to his name. I'd do well to start remembering it.

We continue walking the rest of the day, mostly in silence after that. I've only pulled the map out three times so far today, and as far as I can tell, we make good time, I think. Since I stubbornly won't allow Ikar to look at the map again, I can't know for sure, but to offer the map would be an invitation for him to step closer to look at it 'cause I'm certainly not letting him have it. I certainly don't want him stepping closer, either.

We stop for water at a tiny stream. The small streams, creeks, and pools are the only safe water to drink nowadays. The Lucent River is never used for its water anymore since it's been overtaken by gloam. When I lift my waterskin to my lips, I pause. I push my magic out, searching. I take a quick drink before throwing it in my pack and scanning the forest around us. It's quiet, but not in a peaceful way. My magic tells me there is gloam—there's always gloam, small bits that haven't conglomerated and created a monster yet, but what I sense isn't gloam. It's also not friendly.

"Something follows us," I say quietly. Ikar frowns at the cuff on his wrist, and I'm sure he's cursing it. It makes me wonder what kind of magic he has. Mercenaries and soldiers are usually hunters, and hunter magic would have sensed it even before mine. I assume he's a hunter, then, based on his reaction.

"What is it?"

I shrug, and he frowns deeper. Another thing his possible hunter magic could have helped with. I resist the urge to apologize. Bounty hunters don't apologize to their bounties for blocking their magic. We continue on our way, but Ikar scans and listens, and we move much more quietly now. I catch a glimpse of its black, lithe body here and there, so quick it could be mistaken for a shadow. Ikar is the first to identify it.

"Bantha," he says under his breath.

"What does that mean?"

"You've never seen a bantha in all your extensive bounty hunts?" He raises an eyebrow, a sarcastic tone now underlying his words.

I don't like it, but what can I expect after the way I've treated him today? Anyway, it's good, right? *Distance.*

"Like I said last night, I'm not a *hunter*. I assist." And if I were to be completely honest, I'd tell him I usually choose jobs that are closer to home than this and there aren't banthas in those areas.

"It's a really big black cat with leathery wings, sharp claws, and teeth. And it's a relentless tracker."

"Is that all?" My voice is sarcastic, but my anxiety jumps up to the next level. I find I've suddenly had a change of heart, and I don't mind if he hangs a little closer. Maybe I should pull that map out and offer a look now. I settle for walking beside him instead of ahead as I scold myself for my fear and set myself right.

We continue to spot it as we walk, never close enough to attack, but never losing it, either. It's just always there, on the edge of our peripheral. Lingering and creepy and silent. Like the figures I keep seeing at random times.

I think for sure it will pounce or fly or whatever a bantha does to kill its prey. I try not to imagine what killing its prey looks like. I stop thinking about it since I'm sure that's the opposite of helpful, but hours later we are still waiting for it to make its move, and my nerves are fried. I'm used to traversing the woods during my hunting contracts, but I've never been tracked by a bantha. I won't deny that I sidle up a little closer to Ikar as the sunlight begins to fade and the shadows grow long beneath the tree tops. Close enough that my shoulder brushes his arm every so often. I have enough sense to maintain my dignity, and I refrain from wrapping my hand around it and clinging to his bicep, although I'll admit the idea is tempting for much more than just safety.

"Do you think it's still there?" I whisper, bumping my

shoulder into his bicep for the millionth time because I walk too close.

He lets out a sigh. "Yes. Until it attacks, it will be there. Banthas don't give up prey."

"You say that like you're familiar with them."

"I am," he says dryly.

"You've fought one?"

He ignores my question. "Do not let it stab or bite you. Both its claws and fangs contain venom and detach. Just, stay back," he orders in an exasperated tone.

Great. Venomous, detachable fangs and claws. Thick leather wings, and a huge cat. But the tiny part of me that's unrealistically optimistic is still hoping the bantha gets bored and leaves us alone. Most forest animals have a natural, friendly draw toward me, one of the benefits of Tulip magic that has been particularly difficult to hide from Ikar. Pretty sure that same squirrel Ikar spotted has been scurrying just out of sight since the Black Canyon. It better stay away, or it'll be dead and cooked over the fire like the rabbit. But that same magic doesn't apply to the gloam creatures, the ones that have seemingly multiplied in the last two years. In the past, enchanted weapons could easily kill them, and there weren't many. It was rare to happen across one then. Now, it's guaranteed you'll see one of them if you travel any distance. Which is why I usually don't.

I need a distraction. My eyes turn to Ikar, like the traitors they are. "Where is home for you?"

He seems to consider whether he'll answer my question for a moment, then he finally speaks. But there's none of the open friendliness I heard yesterday, today his voice is terse. "High Kingdom."

My brows raise in surprise. Not many criminals brave the High Kingdom, since it's heavily patrolled and safeguarded.

"What keeps you there? I ask, genuinely curious and very surprised.

"Work."

The conversation stops there, partly because it's pretty obvious he doesn't want to converse with me. *Still not apologizing.* I press my lips together. It's not just that, though. He's completely focused on listening and watching. And eventually, he stops.

"We can't out-travel it." He glances watchfully into the gathering darkness. "I prefer to fight it with some light left. We'll stop here and hope it attacks soon. But it'll probably wait until dark anyway."

I almost wheeze. *Hope it attacks soon?* Spoken like a true mercenary, or criminal, or whatever he is. Personally, I'm more in the *let's run for it* mood. I stare deep into the shadows of the forest. I don't like that I don't know what to believe about the man. He has defended himself from the start, and I would think by now he'd admit that he did *something*. Most criminals have an odd sense of pride about their criminal accomplishments, yet Ikar has mentioned nothing. I eye him as he removes his cloak, sets his pack down, and begins gathering wood and bunches of dry grass to build a fire. His leather armor is like a thick vest, he wears a shirt beneath that covers his arms, and bracers protect his forearms. He's certainly built like some sort of fighter. It's much too easy to appreciate the strong line of his broad shoulders, and the way his waist tapers hints at a muscled torso. I can easily see the strength of his arms move through the fabric of his shirt as he places the sticks and efficiently brings a flame to life.

I realize now, that never have I found fire building so enjoyable to watch. He glances up at me as he stands, brushing his hands off, and I look away, embarrassed for being caught staring. Then I catch a glimpse of the shadows around us again and remember we're being stalked by a creature of death and I shouldn't be getting distracted by the handsome criminal I've arrested. My traitorous gaze goes back to him anyway. I feel a niggle as my intuition persuades me to believe he's a just a regular guy. I mentally snort. This guy is far from regular. Maybe a soldier? Not sure that would be better. I don't work with anyone who works for the kings, even soldiers. Doesn't matter, though, I shouldn't want him to be a good person because I *need* the money I'll earn from the reward of his capture.

We sit by the fire after we finish our meal, him looking entirely too calm and relaxed. And me, wound up like an anxious spring. I'm almost afraid to talk, worried I'll miss the forest sounds that indicate the bantha is about to attack. Around us, though, I hear the titters and shuffles of nighttime creatures, most harmless, others apparently uninterested. I can only hope they stay that way. Rupi, unconcerned with the fact we will be attacked at any moment, hops around in the dirt and sparse grass, contentedly pecking for bugs and seeds.

"You need weapon training," Ikar says bluntly, pulling my gaze from Rupi, as he pokes around the fire and sparks shoot up into the air.

"Easier said than done." I shrug. I'm not offended, but it stings a bit. There are zero people who come to mind who could train me, and I can't afford that type of thing with my pay anyway. But I'm not going to tell him that.

"If you insist on withholding my magic, you need to be able to protect yourself. You knowing how to use a weapon could mean the difference between us surviving this journey and dying. We'll start tomorrow."

I think that's a bit dramatic, but I withhold the snort laugh that almost escapes my nose. From the look on his face, he's quite serious. Does he underestimate his own skill?

"Okay, but don't kill me," I say, then beneath my breath I mutter to myself, "Don't know what good a few days of training'll do anyway."

"You'd be surprised what I can teach you in a short amount of time." His eyes glint, and suddenly, I'm worried. Can't wait for that training. *Not.*

I leave my warm spot by the fire, unroll my bed, and warily take a seat. I'm scared of sleep and the vulnerability it brings, so I resist laying down, knowing my eyes will shut as soon as I do. The stress of the day has sapped my energy. Ikar notices.

"I'll keep watch," he says in a way that I think is meant to comfort me. It works, even though nothing he says or does should make me feel safe.

I nod. "Wake me when it's my turn."

"Go to sleep."

Him and his orders. If I weren't so scared, I'd tell him not to boss me around. Even though it doesn't look like it, I'm in charge here. I'll continue to attempt to convince myself.

He sits nearby, his arms braced on his strong thighs, his sword in hand, watching the fire that burns lower and lower, highlighting the angles of his face with the flickering movements of glowing light and deep shadows.

He makes it easy for me to forget that I've forced him to protect me, that he doesn't do it out of any kind of regard for me. The cuff on his wrist reminds him every day that if I die, his magic is gone—blocked forever. I want to punch my pack with frustration. I won't, because I don't need to look or feel any more ridiculous than I already have this entire arrest. Instead, I obediently lay down and pull my covers over half my face, just how I like it, and sulkily wonder why I had to arrest this tempting criminal of all criminals.

Just as I'm getting sleepy, he speaks again. "Feel inclined to remove this?"

I peek my head from beneath my blanket, and he lifts his left wrist where the charmed cuff sits. It slides down his arm a bit with the movement, "I could really use my magic right now."

"Nice try," I grumble, as I begin to burrow back beneath my blanket, but then I realize I don't even know what magic he has. I snap the blanket down once more. "What magic do you have, anyway?" I tilt my head and narrow my eyes as I consider him.

"Doesn't matter if you won't remove the cuff." He smirks because he assumes it will irritate me to high heaven now that I've asked and he won't tell. I refuse to play his game, and instead of replying, I burrow back beneath the blanket for the third time. Feeling irritated that I'm irritated that I don't know his magic. He's a rogue. I'll continue to assume he's a hunter.

Sometime later, I'm awoken by steps near my head. Or is it over me? The fuzziness of sleep hangs in my mind as I sort through the sound. Doesn't seem like something Ikar would do. An overly friendly animal offering me protection? It's happened before. My eyes fall sleepily closed again, peaceful and feeling safe. Then I hear the deep cat-like growl. My eyes jerk open. Growing realization has me trapping a scream in my throat as I attempt to lay still. Not a friendly forest animal, then—the bantha. *Over me?* My first inclination is to pull magic, since the dark creature should run from my magic if I pull enough, but there's not just myself to consider. If I pull magic and create an orb, I make Ikar the prey, just like what happened with the murk.

Instead, I very carefully scramble for my short sword within my blanket. Rupi shifts but seems to sense the need to stay quiet, because though she gets irritated when I disrupt her sleep, not a noise escapes her. She merely shuffles further into my bedroll when I pull the knife toward the opening, ever so slowly.

I hear a strange combination of leathery shifts and another, odd sort of growl. Worst-case scenario, *check*. I am currently beneath the paralyzing poison-fanged bantha, and I cannot use my usual defenses. Sweat begins to form along my body. My blankets now constricting and hot instead of cozy. Sword in hand, I attempt to tamp down the panic and slowly peek from the blanket. As expected, I get an eyeful of black fur. Dread curls in my stomach, and I die a little before my brain starts functioning. I slowly lower the blanket, hyperaware of the breathing belly a foot above my face.

"Don't move," Ikar states from somewhere. It sounds like he's barely moving his lips.

Like I'm going to allow this perfect kill position to disappear? I'll show him just how capable I am. I've got to redeem myself. But just as I'm about to force myself to slide the sword into its vulnerable underbelly, it powerfully pushes off its back legs and launches across the camp, straight toward Ikar.

I scream and scramble from my blanket as Ikar darts to the side, and the hideous bat-cat narrowly misses a large bite of his calf. Scrambling to my feet, I reposition my sword into a more comfortable grip and watch as they circle each other. Suddenly, the bantha growls and takes flight, disappearing into the night sky with a powerful beat of its large wings, which I find is even more disconcerting than watching it face off with Ikar. Now that it's above us, I have no idea what's next or what direction to expect it from. Ikar holds out a hand, gesturing for me to stay where I am as he turns slowly, watching and listening.

Half a second later, it comes barreling out of the sky—a black streak of spinning silent fury—and bowls Ikar over from the side, taking him to the ground. My eyes widen in horror as they tumble together and come to a stop, the cat atop Ikar's back. Almost faster than my eyes can track, a huge, clawed paw hooks into his upper back and drags down, and I watch in alarm as his armor parts easily with its force. At the same time, another claw hooks into the back of his thigh and Ikar yells out, thrusting an elbow back and catching the beast in the side of the head with the hilt of his sword, forcing it to release its hold. He rolls over, and with one expert swing of his sword, I watch with utter disgust as the head of the beast disconnects from its body, leaving a silvery, growing puddle of blood that soaks quickly into the earth.

I stand, jaw slack, at the fight I just witnessed. Shock fills my veins. I am honest with myself and readily acknowledge that my skills, size, and strength, are not in the same category as Ikar's, and I would have died if not for him. For the second time, or is this the third? And he doesn't even have access to magic. He's facing me now, breathing heavily, one hand loosely on the hilt of one of his sheathed weapons and the blood drenched enchanted sword in the other as he catches his breath.

"You may thank your so-called powerful, violent, murderous criminal now." A sardonic grin lifts one side of his lips.

He has a point, but I'm unwilling to admit it. "So you

finally admit you're a criminal?" I ask, as my eyes swiftly scan over him. I don't catch sight of any serious injury.

"I'm admitting nothing, only making a point." He notices my concern and frowns, then looks down his arms and legs while holding out his hands, sword included. "I'm fine."

Then he turns away to wipe the silvery blood off his sword, and my jaw drops when I see the damage that apparently he feels is *fine*. His armor is shredded, but it seems to have protected his skin. There's only a small tear where one of the claws reached through to the fabric of his shirt, not even any blood. But I'm not worried about that. My eyes focus on only one thing. I suck in a breath and hold back a retch. Amidst three other deep gashes, a long, disgusting, claw protrudes from the back of his thigh.

When he stands from wiping his sword, he stumbles. I almost miss it, it's so small, but it's not like him. Paralyzing venom at work, I'm sure. Well, that, and the claw imbedded in his muscle. He stands still for a moment, facing away from me still, then slowly limps to a nearby tree and braces an arm against its bark covered trunk, resting against it.

"Give me a minute, then we'll go so you don't have to sleep by the carcass," he says when he hears me come up behind him. His voice sounds strained.

"Stay still," I command in a firm tone, as I come up behind him.

I assume this won't hurt as bad as what's coming, so I kneel behind him, cringing as I wrap my fingers around the claw. He stiffens and jerks his head around to attempt to look over his shoulder.

"I said don't move."

"A claw?" He groans and rests his head against his forearm, then curses under his breath.

Look who's in charge now. But I find no joy in giving the orders in this situation—the man could die.

"Just do it," he growls.

Swallowing down my lunch from earlier, I grimace once more at the thought of what I'm holding, and then I pull. Harder than I thought I'd have to. A pained shout that turns to a growl comes from deep in his throat before he falls to a knee, one hand still pressed against the tree and a hand in the dirt to steady himself. He curses under his breath again and shakes his head like he's trying to physically shake it off. I'm impressed... until he collapses on the ground.

I flutter around him in a panic for a full thirty seconds, attempting to weave my scattered thoughts into a plan. Rupi lands atop his shoulder, then hops forward to peck at the exposed earlobe his turned face offers. He offers no reaction, and I'm too flustered to overthink her offered affection and concern.

I think my bounty might be dead. I don't even know if you still get paid for dead bounties. Then I feel a wallop of guilt for even thinking about pay and hastily press my fingers to his neck. He still has a pulse. I can heal him... but I can't. The rule book says no. I war with myself as the poison Ikar told me about seeps through his body. Rupi gives me an indignant look as I stand there, doing nothing. I have no idea how long it takes until it will kill him. I pull a hand roughly along my braid in frustration, tugging and pulling on the end. If I heal him, *he'll know*. No Originator is also a Healer. It's unheard of. Add to that, he's a mercenary. He can easily track me down after I hand him over to the authorities, but would he? I don't know. Think, think, think. I pace around, my gaze darting back to where Ikar lays unmoving beside the tree. Then a plan forms. It's not a very solid one, and it has more holes than a cracked strainer, but it's a plan, and right now I don't care how many holes it has.

I remember the vial of fae potion that rolled out of his pack two mornings ago, or three. Doesn't matter. I hurry to his pack and rip it open, tossing things out haphazardly and completely ignoring how neatly he likes his things kept. We can make it nice and tidy again if he survives.

"*If he survives?*" I squeak.

When did I start to care so much? What state am I in if I kinda like the guy who I also don't trust to not kill me next week? I shut the thoughts down. Now is not the time. I spot the vial in one of the pockets and snatch it out. I've never used a fae potion. I can't afford luxuries such as these. I assume you just pour it on. *Like water on a plant,* I encourage myself, *milk over oats.* I gulp when I look at his leg, I may have ruined oats for the rest of my life. I hold back a gag. Bloody wounds and I don't mesh. There's a reason I would never choose to be a Healer. I glance at the vial in my hand. He told me it was expired, but maybe, *hopefully,* he was mistaken. If it truly is expired, I move to plan B.

I'm about to uncork it, but then I decide to shake it, because it just seems like something you should do, but I have no idea if it's necessary. Though I've assisted fae potion makers by offering magic to *create* fae healing potions, I've never asked how to use one. I pop the cork off with my thumb nail and kneel in the dirt beside him. There's no way I'm taking his clothes off, so the trousers are staying put. I simply tear the remaining strands of fabric from around the claw marks, but doing so loosens the fabric and reveals a well-healed scar on the side of his leg. It leaves me wondering just how many scars he has. My face heats at the direction of my thoughts, and I quickly shut them down.

My hands shake as I tip the bottle and carefully drip the liquid over each long gash and the deeper wound where the claw had been. I watch closely as the liquid absorbs with a few sparks and a somewhat loud sizzling sound. That's odd. *Maybe this stuff does go bad.* I hold the bottle up for a closer inspection, sniff the opening, and then glance at Ikar's face in worry. What does expired fae potion even do? Doesn't matter. I toss the bottle to the side. If he finds out I'm a Tulip and comes after me, so be it. But something deep inside me cares, and I'm not letting him die. *I'm not a murderer.* Criminal or no. I pull cool, white magic through my veins and direct it toward his leg, watching as the flesh and muscle begin to knit back together and trying not to gag. As badly as I'd like to completely heal it, I know I can't. One bottle of *potent* fae potion wouldn't heal this severe of an injury. It would take more. I don't know how many, but several. So, I let it get to a point where I think he's going to be okay, hoping the poison is gone and he's able to travel. Then I pull the magic back, wrap the wound in clean bandages, and wait.

Chapter 24

Ikar

When I wake, I find my cloak folded beneath my face. The rest of me lays atop sparse grass and dirt. I feel as if I'm recovering from an illness that includes a heavy dose of brain fog. I groan and push myself up, wincing at the tug in my leg.

Painfully, slowly, I stand, gritting my teeth. Vera's taking a clean, dry shirt off a line, which has me wondering how long we've been here.

"What happened?" I ask, my voice rough and my throat dry as the dirt I was lying on.

Her brow pulls together with concern, and I don't like it. I feel vulnerable and uncomfortable, and I have no idea what happened after I killed the bantha. A cool breeze makes its way between the slashes of my ruined armor, but I'm relieved when I reach back and find my shirt still mostly intact. Mark entirely hidden. But my trousers are another story. Torn irreparably and baring my bandaged thigh. I touch the bandages, confused. I immediately head to my pack, but my body feels stiff and off, and my leg aches, causing a hitch in my stride that further irritates me. I resist the wince that tugs with every step.

"I had the great privilege of yanking a bantha claw from your leg yesterday," she says tartly from behind me.

I whip my head around too fast, and everything blurs together. Between the disbelief, dizziness, and the headache at the base of my skull, I find myself scowling at her. I remember the fight, but I know no possible way I'm still alive without a Healer nearby. My mood darkens further. If anyone has a reason not to trust, it's me. *What did she do?*

She picks an off-white, dirty, blood-covered object off the ground and holds it out to me between two pinched fingers, her nose wrinkled in disgust. "I thought you might want it as a trophy... of sorts. Seems like something a mercenary criminal would do." She shrugs.

This situation is so strange and unbelievable that I simply stare at it.

"I'm not a mercenary *or* a criminal," I growl. Though at this point, I probably look like both, and it's not helping.

"That's yet to be proven." She quirks a brow. A muscle ticks in my jaw as I return to the difficult job of reaching my pack. I rifle through it, further irritated at how messy it is, until I find what I'm looking for, then turn with clean trousers in hand toward the forest. From behind me, I hear the claw drop into my pack with a soft thud as she follows me.

"Do you need help?"

"No," I say curtly. "Unless I'm dead, I won't need help dressing."

"You make a very ornery patient," she mumbles under her breath, so low I know it wasn't intended for my ears. She doesn't realize how good my hearing is, even if she has blocked my magic.

I find a small creek nearby where she washed the clothes I saw drying. Questions tumble through my mind as I quickly wash the accumulation of dirt and sand from my body before donning the clean trousers, which takes a ridiculous amount of time in my injured state. While changing, I take a moment to inspect my leg, unwrapping the bandages that show no blood. Apparently, I was only asleep for a day. My logic tells me there's no way, but my eyes say opposite. I never saw the initial wound, but it's partially healed. Enough that I can walk without assistance, even though my muscles and skin feel tight and resistant to moving, and it aches and pulses uncomfortably. With movement, I hope it will loosen up. I take a moment to inspect my torn leather armor. It's definitely beyond repair, but some armor is better than none, so I put it back on.

When I get back to camp Vera is snacking on fresh berries, and Rupi has returned. She throws out some birdseed, and the puff ball bounces around, pecking happily. I sit a few feet away and consider her carefully.

"How'd you do it?" I ask, suspicion strong in my voice. This slip of a woman is more than she seems. I feel it like a pebble in my boot.

She chews for a moment. "I used that fae potion in your pack." She pops another berry into her mouth.

"It wasn't potent, and even if it was, one potion couldn't have done all of this," I say firmly.

She looks down at her hand and lets a few of the berries roll around her palm. "You must have acquired it more recently than you remembered, or maybe it came from a particularly potent batch." She shrugs. "I don't know. I just remembered you had it and used it, and you're part healed now."

I glance at the spot where I woke, uncomfortable with the fact that no one is here that I trust to support her account. I spot the empty bottle near the tree, make my way over, and gingerly bend to pick it up. I slip it in my pocket, then turn to find Vera watching me with a guarded look in her eyes.

"Can't leave glass in the forest. It could injure an animal," I say, matter of fact. I don't know why I feel the need to explain my actions to her, but I do.

She accepts that answer with a suspicious glint in her eye. Really, since she needs to visit the fae anyway, I plan to talk to one of them about this apparently *potent batch* of fae potion, but she doesn't need to know that.

My limp isn't so bad we lose too much time, more of an issue when we have to climb than anything. But the slower pace is irritating when I'm already in a rush, and the suns seem to make their way across the sky faster than ever. On top of that, the heat of the day has been brutal, mixing with the moist shadows of the forest and creating an insufferable humidity to trudge through. Then a heavy wind came out of nowhere midday, and even though it's gusty and hot, it cools the sweat, so I savor it while I can. Who knows what will come next, the weather patterns grow more unpredictable every year, and this year has been no exception.

We make camp just before the third sun sets, and even though my leg is still stiff, I follow through with Vera's weapon training. I don't know why I care so much if this bounty hunter assistant knows how to use a weapon, but I do. I pull my sword and begin some warm up movements, watching as she pulls her short sword and a knife from their sheaths at her hip. I notice the way her trousers crinkle at the waist, and her belt seems much too large. It's limp and worn with rough holes cut ever further from its end to better fit. I wonder at her choice of men's clothing and why she appears to be starving if she takes regular contracts as she implied. Where does all the money go if not clothes and food?

I'm pulled from my thoughts when she holds two weapons before her and asks, "Which one?"

"Sword."

She replaces the intricately carved dagger and holds the short sword out uncertainly. "Now what?"

I stalk toward her like a predator, and I see a flash of fear in her eyes as she begins to step back.

"Aren't you supposed to teach me *before* we fight?" She practically squeaks as she steps back faster at my approach.

"No time for that. I'll teach you *while* we fight. Sword up."

I know she doesn't trust me, has been around more than enough criminals to know that there are some crazy enough to kill her for their freedom, even though it would cost their magic. I've seen the way she watches me, trying to figure me out, unwilling to believe anything I say. So, I take advantage of it. Nothing quite like fear as a motivator.

Two hours later, Vera drops to her bedroll in exhaustion, taking a longer than normal drink of water before falling to her back somewhat dramatically. I hide a grin, remembering my own training when I was a young boy. Rhosse was never easy on me, and I often woke so sore the next morning I could hardly dress myself. A stab of worry shoots through me at the thought of my missing friends. Watching Darvy being dragged beneath the surface of the river, struggling with some unknown monster, then both of them gone in the blink of an eye, I painfully admit that it's not likely they survived. I take time to clean a few of my blades, the motions and sounds therapeutic to the sorrow and worry. I know it's unwise, but though I saw them disappear with my own eyes, I argue with myself that they are two of the most capable and expert warriors I know. I hold on to a bit of hope.

My thoughts gradually turn to Vera. She's surprisingly strong for being so small, and her blocks improved quickly today. I withheld my praise so she doesn't get lax. I have only days to teach her the fundamentals, and she has much to learn.

"You're scary with a sword, you know that? Kinda scary always, actually," she mumbles from several feet away, her voice tired and sleepy.

I grin in the shadows, knowing she can't see. "Go to sleep."

I hear her mumble something about me and my orders before she turns over, and her breaths fall into the even patterns of deep sleep.

The next morning, we start early again, hoping to reach the city before the Shift Forest by this evening. Even with our grueling pace, the suns seem to race us in their descent. It's another sweltering day, so hot that in the patches of bare field we see waves of heat drift off the ground, and it seems the vegetation wilts before our eyes as morning moves to afternoon. Today, there is no gusty wind to cool the sweat that slicks my clothes to my body. As closely as I'm tracking the suns to set our pace, I'm also tracking the sporadic weather patterns, even if it's useless. One moment, it's hot and sunny. The next, we could be blown into hiding by gale force winds and hail. These past two days, it's been hot, but generally calm. And while I enjoy the reprieve that comes with times like these, that usually means something violent will come next, and something inside me says it's soon. I find my eyes drifting to the sky often, every breeze that moves across my skin has my eyes scanning for a tree that might work as an anchor for us.

I've noticed that Rupi appears to sense it, too. She's stayed close to Vera these past few hours, as she usually does before the weather changes from what I've observed. Maybe the bird is more useful than it first appeared. I don't know how she knows, but she does.

We continue forward as I feel the breeze pick up, the air cooling considerably, but still, the few clouds in the sky are as white as Rupi and just as fluffy. Good, I don't want to stop earlier than we have to. We've had enough delays already.

"We need a place to wait out the coming storm," Vera calls.

"Soon," I reply, unwilling to stop before it's absolutely necessary. Besides that, I'm still scoping out a decent place. I'd spotted a mountain wall a few miles to the east and redirected our path there, hoping there would be somewhere for us to sleep out of the elements soon to come.

The weather cools drastically as the clouds gradually turn from fluffy white to dark gray. We stop for only a moment to put on our cloaks when chill rain begins to fall, slipping beneath the collar of my shirt and rinsing the sweat from my body and clothing in an uncomfortable way. Along with the clouds and rain, a heavy fog has rolled in, weaving eerily through the trees and covering the forest floor. Vera begins to walk more closely beside me.

"You got a plan?" she asks me, her teeth chattering a bit.

"We're almost to the mountainside. It'll be safer to be beside it than in the forest if high winds kick up."

She nods and pulls her cloak tighter. The chill makes my

injury ache, and I find the hitch in my stride worsening as the evening grows later.

Finally, with relief, I spot a place that might work—if we can get there. With Vera shivering hard beside me and even my own bones feeling chilled to the core, I point to a small, dark hole above us in the cliff wall. "There."

Vera eyes the rock face we'll have to climb uncertainly. "I don't know." She looks back at the fog infested forest almost longingly.

"We can't wait much longer. The wind is picking up, and the temperature is dropping." I have to raise my voice now to be heard, even though we stand close, as the winds howl and whip around us. I don't wait for her to over think it. Instead, I say, "You first," fairly pulling her to the wall and pointing out where to begin. "I'll be right behind you." That is, if my leg doesn't give out. I keep the concern to myself.

She begins climbing. And soon after, I follow, guiding her to next handholds with shouted instructions as well as I can, but I begin to question my decision when we are halfway up and her foot slips. I see her waver as she looks over her shoulder at the distance we've climbed. My leg aches furiously now, pulsing uncomfortably with overuse and fatigue.

"Keep going!" I shout.

My fingers feel as slick as the rock looks, but that hole in the cliff wall isn't so far now. I search for the next handhold, determined to reach safety.

Chapter 25

Vera

My numb fingers slip and scrape clumsily, looking for handholds in the freezing rock, but I bite my lip and force myself to keep going. Rupi rests somewhere beneath us in the cover of the trees, and I don't blame her. This storm is a bad one. My arms and legs burn, my nose is running from the cold, and I'm almost positive my face is frozen into the unattractive, somewhat distressed expression I adopted at the beginning of this horrid climb. I breathe a sigh of relief once I haul my tired body into the small opening and plant myself on the edge out of sheer exhaustion, my legs still hanging over the side. I sit for a moment to ground myself, pressing my right shoulder and hip up against the rock at my side so Ikar has room to climb in. Even injured, he's much faster than I am, but I vastly underestimated the breadth of him. When he seats himself, we find our shoulders pressed tightly together, and he hunches over a bit to avoid hitting his head on the ceiling.

Our legs hang over the edge while we look over the dreary, foggy view that spreads out before us. Dark clouds churn and hover on the tips of the deep green trees. It's eerily beautiful. I catch a tall shadow that doesn't quite match the rest near the edge of the trees where we were just moments ago in my peripheral, but when I shift my eyes to see what it is, there's nothing there. Again. It's easy enough to explain away this time. It's probably the combination of sore muscles, freezing cold conditions, and eerie forest playing tricks on my vision. Still, I won't deny that I'm glad Ikar is beside me, and I find I'm much more grateful for the height of our shelter than I was two minutes ago. I stare at the spot where I thought I saw the shadow for at least another minute. There's nothing there but wet soil, grass, and trees.

Ikar turns his head to look over his shoulder and takes in the tiny space, a hint of a dismayed frown pulling at his brows. I twist a bit so I can see, too. It can't quite be called a cave, the ceiling is so low we won't be able to stand, and it's very narrow. So narrow, in fact, that I'm not sure the two of us will be able to lay down to sleep in it. More like a hole in a wall than a cave. But all it takes is another quick glance at the ghostly forest to make our hole in the wall look very, very comfortable.

Ikar is the first to act, always decisive and matter-of-fact. I'm beginning to appreciate that my criminal harbors many helpful qualities. He begins moving and shifting to remove his pack and bring it in front of him. But in doing so, his arm and shoulder jostle against mine even more in the cramped space. I practically get mashed into the wall in the process as I try to press myself against my side of the rock to give him more space, but my efforts prove entirely unhelpful, and I find myself irritated by my awareness of him. Curse his broad, muscular shoulders.

He pulls out his bedroll and then we both move at the same time. I pull my legs up from their dangling position, against my chest almost, and try to gracefully turn toward the back of the cave without touching him. He seems to have the same unspoken idea, and our legs quickly tangle up awkwardly. My left shin is somehow against one of his calves, my right calf is tangled with his left thigh, and my back still pressed to the chilled rock behind me does nothing to cool the temperature of my burning face. I hear him mutter a string of grumbles and curses beneath his breath. I never thought I'd be grateful for wind-chapped cheeks, but at this moment, it's providing a perfect cover. We untangle ourselves eventually. Then he tosses out his bedroll on the right side of our shelter and does some sort of forearm crawl forward until he settles himself onto it.

I toss out my own bedroll with still-flaming cheeks and pretend like I don't see that the material of mine covers his by at least a few inches. I crawl onto it without making any sort of eye contact and sit down pressed against the cold rock. I wrap my arms around my knees, staring out the entrance and watching fat flakes of snow fly about in howling wind. The rock shelters us from much of the storm but not all, and I shiver in my still-wet clothing.

Rupi joins us a few minutes later, snow and ice coating her fluffy feathers so thick she looks more like a flying snowball than a bird. She barely makes the opening of the cave when a large gust of wind blows her too far, and she comes to a some-what rough landing. More of a tumble, really. I laugh a little and am promptly shot a grumpy, frazzled look as she rustles feathers partially turned to quill. I carefully scoop her up and begin brushing the snow off her before she quickly hops forward to warm herself by my neck. I cringe a little at the cold wetness, probably her revenge for my laughter, but I let her stay, and she dries quickly. She'll be all fluff within minutes. I notice then that Ikar has been watching as he rubs the back of his leg, a small grin lifts one side of his mouth. I look away, slightly embarrassed, and decide I need to redirect his focus.

"Is it worse?" I ask, trying not to be concerned about his injury. Even if it is, I can't risk helping him by healing it further.

He stares at the roof of the cave. "It'll be fine."

"You always say that."

"It will. I've had worse and survived," he says bluntly. It brings to mind the other scar I saw, and that summons the heat back to my cheeks. It feels like I've invaded his privacy. I'm also reminded that he lives a violent life by choice, and I shouldn't care about his injuries.

I busy myself digging dried meat and fruit from my pack and toss him some of what I find. Meanwhile, two suns have set, leaving us in near dark besides the glow of the heavy flakes that fall outside our cave as the third sun takes its light with it. I could create light using my magic, but it'll glow an unearthly white, and I don't want Ikar to see it for too long. Instead, the shadows grow deeper as the already dark sky grows darker.

After we've eaten, Ikar insists on perfecting my grip on my sword before we finally call it a night. After I struggle to follow the example he's mirroring with his own sword he moves closer and repositions my hand for me. I should pay attention to the change he made so he doesn't have to correct me again tomorrow, but he's so close, and the smell of leather and pine, and the sound of his low voice beside my ear, and his knee brushing my thigh has me struggling to breathe a little. His large hand is still over mine, and he appears to be waiting for a response to a question, but I have no idea what he asked. My cheeks redden.

"Does that make sense?" he asks, I'm pretty sure this isn't the first time he asked.

I simply nod since I know my voice will be shaky if I speak. I'll have to face the awkwardness of admitting I'll need a redo on this lesson tomorrow, but I'd get a lot more out of it if he'd keep his distance. Not that that's what I prefer right this moment. I brush a stray strand of my hair behind my ear, waiting for him to move back to his side of the cave, but my bracelet catches his eye. Instead of moving back, his finger catches the bracelet, and it sucks the air from my lungs as he lifts it from my wrist gently.

"No clasp," he observes, "You cuffed, same as I?" I can hear the joking tone of his voice, and I see that handsome half smile on his face, but the question hits me unexpectedly. I'd never considered myself cuffed, but I can't remove the bracelet. Something uncomfortable triggers at the realization. I look down at the purposefully nondescript and innocent-looking piece of jewelry. The higher class Tulips have a fancier style, one more fitting for their place in society. Renna's and mine, though woven with a delicate chain, are merely an unblemished silver. He drops it, leaving my wrist tingly where his finger brushed.

"It's a friendship bracelet." That's my memorized, automatic response to anyone who questions the bracelet that is constantly on my wrist, but I find it comes out a hint defensive this time.

"A friendship bracelet?" He seems genuinely curious. He's still too close. Intoxicating.

I twist it again, trying not to sound breathless. "Yeah, me and a group of friends have them. We're like sisters." I feel relieved I didn't really have to lie, but then I realize I may have said too much. I wait, a little scared to see what he says next.

"I know Originators are a close group." He says it like it makes sense that we'd have friendship bracelets. "But all the

Originators I've worked with dress in white and in styles that always show their mark. Why don't you?" He looks curious, glancing at my black cloak and the shirt that covers me from wrist to neck.

My heart feels like it's beating too fast. I'm grateful his hunter hearing is suppressed, otherwise it would surely give me away. I struggle to think of an acceptable response. "I've never felt comfortable with the showy stuff," I mumble, looking down and twisting my bracelet around a few more times as a distraction. It's not a lie, but also not the full truth.

He shrugs. "I can understand that."

He moves away after that, and while I miss the warmth his presence gave, I'm relieved I can breathe again and that he didn't ask more questions. We both quickly climb beneath our separate blankets. It's too cold to not.

We lay there in the dark, and I'm freezing. I removed my sopping jacket, and that helped for a few minutes, but my shirt refuses to dry in the bitter cold that has crept into our cave from the storm. My eyes and arms burn with fatigue, and my teeth ache from the constant chattering the last several hours. I cuddle in a tight ball against the wall of the cave and try to hide the sound beneath my blanket.

"Toss me your blanket, we'll layer up to share heat," Ikar says from a couple feet away. There is a distinct lack of emotion in his voice.

I freeze in a different way and hesitantly turn my head over my shoulder to look at him, desperate at this point for any warmth I can get. Is he being serious? Should I allow this?

He just looks at me, his outstretched hand waiting for my blanket.

Against my better judgement, I remove my blanket and toss it to him, watching as he doubles them up neatly and then lays them back down, but for me to share, I'll have to get closer. I scooch over, only as far as necessary to fit beneath my side of the blankets, eyeing the few inches between us. Then, I turn away from him and pull the blankets back up over my shoulders. He lays on his back, staring up at the uneven rock ceiling above us.

Everything I was told about Ikar seems wrong, and I feel confused. I feel safe with him, I even feel like we've developed a sort of friendship, which has never happened between myself and a bounty. Even Rupi, my trustworthy character judge, seems to have warmed to him. Do I trust my gut and my bird or trust whoever set the bounty? Guess it doesn't matter, no matter what I decide I won't be removing the cuff. I'm just as trapped as he is at this point. I feel like a criminal myself, considering breaking rules and handling this entire arrest the way I have. I've heard all sorts of sob stories, lies twisted and used to attempt to manipulate a release, but I always see through them. I keep up thick walls around myself as protection, which I've tried to do with Ikar, but he seems to have torn them down brick by brick in a matter of days. His strong, steady presence. That smirk that so often lifts his lips. Even the irritatingly confident way he forges through any situation. I usually go with my gut, but my attraction to him has me wondering if it's reliable in this case. I don't want to believe that this man, who I've come to respect and feel comfortable with, is a Tulip killer. But Rupi wouldn't peck at his earlobe like she does if he was a Tulip killer, right?

My eyes beg to close. I know I need rest, but before rest, I want answers. I decide to risk it for a short moment and pull magic. I hold a small ball of light in my hand, enough to dimly light our cave, but I keep it at my side and hidden from his direct sight. For a moment, I wish my magic was warm, like an

Originator's, but nothing I wish will change the fact that it will always be cold, bright, white. Rupi lifts her head from her wing and turns an eye toward me inquisitively. Even if she could ask what I plan to do, I couldn't answer because there is no plan. This is a desperate, spur-of-the-moment decision that I may regret. She re-tucks her head in sleep, and I drag my gaze toward Ikar, lying just inches away. His hands rest atop his chest as he stares at the pitch-dark ceiling, quiet. He doesn't look at me, but I can tell he's awake. I can practically feel his thoughts turning. Now, I find myself asking the burning question that has risen to the surface for the last few days.

My voice, though soft, seems loud in the quiet around us, and Rupi lifts her head again to give me a side eye of annoyance at the second interruption. "What were you doing with the mercenaries if you aren't one?"

My heart beats hard as I wait for his answer. I hope I hate his answer, that my lie alarm starts ringing and I can know he's just another bounty. Maybe Rupi's quills will even burst out. But the fear that resisted this conversation reminds me how dangerous it is if none of those things happen. Part of me still thinks I'm nuts for doubting the fact that he is a criminal when the largest bounty I've ever contracted for is on his head.

He turns his head to look at me, as if he's considering if he'll talk or not. My stomach twists in hope. For some reason, I so badly want to know him. It takes him a moment to respond as he seems to put the right words together. My heart beats a little faster as he begins to speak.

"I'm in search of something that will save a lot of people," he says carefully, "Two things, actually."

I stay silent and wait for him to continue. He knows I want more than that. I already know about the flower. I don't know what the second thing is, but I'm not concerned about that right now.

He turns his gaze back to the ceiling. "Believe it or not, I am not a criminal nor do I plan to become one."

For some wild reason, I truly do want to believe him. Nothing he will say changes the fact that I have to treat him as a criminal, but I'm relentless. "Why were you with the mercenaries?"

Was he searching out Tulips for money? We haven't talked about that list since I ruined it. I don't want to mention it again for fear it will remind him that he thought I knew something. He was suspicious enough that he followed me, or maybe he was out for revenge. But then why did he rescue me? I'll have to sort through that later, but the Tulips in general are not something I should know or even care about it if I'm an Originator.

I look back at him, but he still stares straight up at the rock ceiling, and the light in my hand is just enough to give shape to his face and expression. Is he waiting for me to get bored and go to sleep? I'll stubbornly stay awake until he talks. No handsome profile will distract me from my quest for answers. Mercenaries give me the shivers, and I never accept jobs to work with them. That is one of my biggest hold ups in believing his story. I just want to know, but if he tells me, will I even believe him?

Finally he speaks. "My First Co—" He clears his throat and corrects himself, "...close friends and I are on a mission for our kingdom. Darvy and Rhosse. I was never actually *with* the mercenaries. Merely fighting to gain information. We'd just left them when we... *met*." He smiles a little, and my heart pauses beating in my chest for a moment as I wonder if he considers our meeting with fondness as his smile implied. I force my thoughts away from that because he'd just dropped a hint. Before he corrected himself, I'm positive he was about to say his

First Commanders are his close friends, and I'm familiar enough with rank to know it indicates he may be a royal soldier for one of the kingdoms. Does that mean Darvy and Rhosse are his leaders? But why would he fight for a list of Tulips? I want so badly to blurt it out, but my anonymity depends on my avoiding that topic, and since he didn't bring it up, I can't, either.

"You are claiming to be a royal soldier, then?"

He sits up and pulls his pack closer. I increase the light in my hand to help him when I see that he's searching for something. Soon, he finds what he's looking for and tosses something small to me. I catch it and find a small circular patch in my hands, about the size of one of my palms. I don't know which kingdom it indicates, but it looks very similar to the one stamped on our currency. And, as far as my limited military knowledge goes, it appears legitimate.

I react on pure self-protective instinct. "So, you killed a soldier and lifted his patch? You've certainly built a decent cover, probably stole the poor man's identity, too." I narrow my eyes at him.

If a glare threw daggers, I'd be dead three times over.

I toss the patch back to him, feeling a little guilty at being the cause of the extinguished hope in his eyes that had flared for a moment.

"Don't ask questions if you're not ready to believe the answers." His tone is as icy as the chill winds outside, and I shutter my gaze so he doesn't see the guilt there. I should have just gone to sleep. It wouldn't matter if I believed him anyway, I wouldn't uncuff him. I'm grateful for the steadying support of my rules. Those rules are my backbone, and they say to never trust a bounty. I broke rules, and now look where I am. Breaking more rules will only make it worse.

He looks away as he places the patch back in his pack. "I know I'm asking a lot here, but I can promise if you release me, I won't hurt you. And you won't become a bounty."

He just can't help but push my limits. Who does he think he is? I pull my eyes from his and pick at the stitching along one of the blankets that cover us.

"So, you know that if I break the contract and don't deliver you to the authorities, I become a bounty as well. Interesting that you know that tidbit." I look at him suspiciously. How many arrests has he manipulated his way out of? "And promising that I won't become a bounty for breaking it? That is impossible. So, that'll be a hard no. But I do hope you're able to find what you're searching for." And I mean it. If he truly is a soldier on a mission to save his people, I hope he's successful. Until then, he's my bounty. A very dangerous one, at that.

I turn onto my side, facing the cave wall. I'm about to extinguish my light, prepared to fall asleep and forget that disappointed look on his face that will probably be seared onto the backs of my eyelids. I hear him shift, feeling the blankets pull and loosen while he gets comfortable. Then Rupi chirps contentedly, sounding further away than before, and I realize she's no longer by my side. I lift my head to look over my shoulder and scowl when I see that she's nestled herself in the warm crook between *Ikar's* neck and shoulder. I stare in shocked silence at my traitorous pet. Ikar doesn't acknowledge me, though I know he knows I'm looking in his direction. And maybe I imagine the smug quirk to his lips as Rupi practically coos as she tucks her head to sleep, but I don't think so. I purse my lips as I quickly lay back down and stare at the cave wall. He's so dangerously alluring even my loyal bird has left me for him. See if I ever buy that expensive birdseed again.

And then all is quiet. Tension from our conversation

lingers, but I refuse to turn and apologize. This softening heart of mine is growing dangerous. I stubbornly lay facing the wall, unwilling to move any closer to him, even though the warmth he emanates is tempting. But a different sort of tension joins the mix. Every breath and movement feels so close within the confines of these walls. I try to ignore our close proximity. He may be a dangerous, manipulative criminal, but so far, he's protected me and treated me well, and that only makes him more attractive.

I'd also like to point out that it's very different sharing a blanket than walking side by side—too intimate and warm. I shift as far as I can toward my side of the cave, which is maybe a hair's width more, while still ensuring the blankets are covering me. The chill in the cave is deepening, and I don't want to freeze in my sleep, but I also don't want to fall asleep beside the man that I feel guilt for calling a criminal even though he *is* one. I don't know if Ikar feels the same tension as me as we both lie beneath our doubled blankets, but I assume not, because, within moments, his breathing settles into the deep, rhythmic breaths of sleep. I don't know how to feel about that, wondering if my attraction is one sided, and then angry with myself for caring if a bounty is attracted to me or not. After fighting with myself for an undetermined amount of time, I also, finally, drift off to sleep.

I'm in that fuzzy state between waking and dreaming, wrapped in warmth so deep I never want to move. I sigh in comfort. I'm content to stay where I am as I enjoy the slow process of coming fully awake. My eyes open blearily, then I blink twice, and they open wide in a flash. Very, very wide. *The cave.* My body awareness slowly kicks in, and I realize my head rests in the soft spot between Ikar's shoulder and his chest, his strong arm wrapped around me. My eyes travel the length of my right arm laying across his broad chest and find my hand curled into the fabric of his shirt, his larger hand resting over mine, both of which rise and fall slowly, up and down with the movement of his chest.

I'm afraid to move my head to see what my legs have done, but I don't need to see to know that amidst the mess of blankets, one of mine is twined with one of his. We sleep as lovers, which we most definitely are not. *Don't cuddle with dangerous criminals. Make that any criminal,* I mentally scold myself. Then my eyes snag on a ball of white, still huddled beside Ikar's neck, near the steady beat of his strong pulse. Rupi's tiny body rises and falls, her head tucked beneath a small wing, soundly asleep. As content as I was just moments ago. My eyes narrow. *Traitor.* But if she's one, then I am too. I carefully gulp and look up just as he's slowly blinking away sleep himself.

"Storm's passed," he mumbles.

And then, for what seems a very long second, he realizes what I realized. We both move at the same time. Rupi flaps her wings ornerily at the disruption as I laugh awkwardly, and I mention in words that leave my lips too rapidly how bad the storm was while he quickly agrees, and I scooch back to my side of the cave feeling cold and something else I don't want to admit might very well be disappointment at the separation.

Morning light reaches into the space, and already the air is warm enough to begin to melt the icicles that formed from the storm like jagged teeth across the cave entrance. I know we need to leave soon. I sneakily glance across at Ikar again, who has rested his back against the cave wall, and find Rupi once again settled on his broad shoulder, right beside his neck, and frown. *Jealous of Rupi? Absolutely not.* My eyes don't linger long, but I notice that what was once a shadow of beard along his jawline when I first arrested him is now darkening, he looks more dangerous, and more handsome, as he sits looking like a pirate, inspecting and organizing his weapons. Though, the white fluff on his shoulder that has her tiny head cocked at an innocent angle is a far cry from a battle-hardened parrot.

Time to go. I swallow dryly.

We set off quickly after that, and the warmth of the morning soon has us removing our heavier layers and strapping them to our packs once again.

"We should be able to cross the Shift Forest in three days, maybe four." His eyes scan the map that I've given him, mentally calculating the distance and time. "Then we should reach the fae." I'm happy to let him guide. I've given up, as long as we really do stop at the fae. I've got dues to pay and Mama Tina is my messenger.

"One day there," he says.

I quickly curb his attempt at taking charge. "Two." I know he's in a hurry, but I only see Mama Tina twice per year.

He frowns. "Two days there, then we head to Moneyre. That means we should be there in less than a week, if all goes smoothly."

A week longer to resist the wiles of my criminal. A week until I get the reward I need. A week until I'm free. I can do this.

Chapter 26

Vera

We walk through the city before the Shift Forest. *The Gatekeepers,* they call themselves, according to a large sign that welcomed us when it came into our sights. It's a whimsical place, one I've never seen since I've never been this far west. I'd have almost thought we entered a garden instead of a city. After I'm able to pull my eyes from the life-size topiaries shaped into all varieties of animals, I begin to look past them and see homes, interspersed between quaint shops, almost built atop each other they are so close. One small house is the palest blue. Two large, round windows are set on either side of the door, and three more line the second floor. The door is a blue so dark it's almost black with a circular gold handle. Most cities I have visited have bland-colored buildings, with occasional pots of flowers to give color, but I find as I look around that the blue house fits in among the rest. Another is tall, painted a minty green, but its windows are long, narrow rectangles. Almost as if someone wants light, but not too much. Its door is also so narrow and tiny that it appears completely impractical, until I see a black salamander with green spots and gold eyes scamper out. The other houses are all unique, painted in colors from shades of pastel to bright pops taken straight from a field of moody flowers. I see windows of all shapes and doors from the tiniest to a double set so large I'm not sure I could pull them open by myself.

Animals and other humans fill the garden paths, and I notice quickly that most, whether in animal or human form, have gold eyes. A city of shifters. I begin to think the bit of gold on each of their buildings has something to do with that. The only commonality they all have is the gold door handle.

"This place a little creepy, or is it just me?" I whisper to Ikar, as we walk. Rupi must agree because she's been huddled on Ikar's shoulder since before we entered the city, her feathers halfway to quills, revealing her nervousness. I don't mind her choosing him over me this time. I can't blame her. If I could fit, I might jump on his shoulder, too.

"No. It's creepy," he mumbles, but his confidence never falters. There's hardly a hint of the limp in his step today, his stride long and sure as ever. I almost have to jog a bit to keep up.

Besides being one of the few humans amongst a population of potentially violent shifters, I can't pinpoint *why* it feels so creepy. Maybe it's too perfectly weird? Manicured grasses and enormous beds of oddly shaped, bright flowers lead through the city, intertwined with all sizes and varieties of animal topiaries, from small rabbits with horns to lions, banthas, and armored wolves. Fountains with statues of animals atop their burbling streams are artfully placed along the path. I spot several animals lapping water from their depths and birds perched on the edges and realize they were placed there for more than just viewing.

From what I can see, it seems a friendly, happy place,

except for the panther topiaries that remind me of the bantha Ikar killed just days ago. Admittedly, most of the shifters look very... predator-like, even in their human form. All stealthy with hungry eyes. A tall, gangly man sniffs me as I pass, and I cringe away, bumping into Ikar. No one has stopped us or spoken to us, though we do garner a few more sniffs. I make sure to keep up with Ikar, but I can't help but think that if the Shift Forest is as odd and weird and easy as this, it will be the most enjoyable part of our journey yet.

We finally approach a wood structure painted in deep burgundy with the words 'Shift Forest Authority' engraved across a metal plate and bolted to its exterior. A heavy gate blocks the entrance to a spindly-looking bridge that spans the length of a deep crevice, and my eyes widen as I see the length of it dance and quiver in the breeze that blows between the canyon walls with a high-pitched whistle. I look at Ikar uncertainly, but he sets his jaw determinedly and steps forward to rap on the door.

A handsome man opens the door, his hair is long and tied back low with a band. He's wearing a pair of snug-fitting trousers, and his shirt is half unbuttoned, not leaving much to the imagination in regard to his muscled chest. He looks like he belongs on a pirate ship with Ikar. My cheeks pink, and Ikar scowls as the man's golden gaze locks on mine.

"Welcome to my humble abode," he says charmingly, his hands spread in a gesture of welcome. His eyes catch on Rupi perched on Ikar's shoulder, and I see mocking laughter tug at his lips until they twist.

I ignore his antics and quirk an eyebrow, glancing around. Looks like a place of business rather than a house. "You live here?"

He laughs. "Only when on duty." He keeps his eyes on me

while he slowly grabs my left hand, then flips it over quickly. He glances at my wrist and then back to me with a look in his eyes I don't quite like. "In search of a mate, my lady?" Anywhere else and that question would be odd. How exactly can he tell I'm not mated simply by looking at my wrist?

Ikar clears his throat, but it sounds more like a growl. "She has one."

I don't know if it's the tone or the growl that surprises me more, but I think being amongst these shifters is bringing out his inner animal. I try not to think too hard about how it makes me feel to hear him say we're mates. I know it can't really be. *He's my criminal, not my boyfriend.* I repeat that five times to really cement it. Besides, we aren't even shifters.

The two men stare each other down, but finally the shifter smiles, a contrast to the simmering intensity in his eyes. "If you plan to *temporarily* mate, you can head to the office of licenses in town. "*Humans,*" he says, like we're a group beneath him, "can't gain entrance without it." Then he turns his gaze to me. "If you find you need something *more,*" he drawls, "I'm here. Shifters can mate with humans with no expiration." He winks for good measure.

Ikar's hand curls into a fist at his side, and Rupi's chirp sounds borderline indignant on his behalf. Her feathers have rustled and quilled, stabbing Ikar in the neck. To his credit, he doesn't even wince.

I quickly wrap my hands around his fist as I begin to pull him away, shaking my head at the fact that my bird has become protective of my criminal. Not sure how it's going to go when I drop him off with the officials. Will Rupi decide to stay locked up with him? I don't know anymore. Rupi's never acted this way, but he's certainly tempting enough that I begin to wonder if she might choose him over me.

"We'll be back soon," I say quickly, tugging Ikar back toward town. No way am I allowing that guy to be my no-expiration-date mate. The way he emphasizes every word like everything he says is as gold as his eyes is far too annoying.

Ikar gradually relaxes, and somewhere along the way I reluctantly release his hand and walk beside him like I know I should. Rupi's feathers slowly return to their familiar softness, and only then does Ikar reach up and wipe a bit of blood from his neck, looking at his fingers with a frown.

"She's more dangerous than she appears," he mutters.

I laugh at the bewildered look on his face. "Want me to take her?" I ask, as I begin to reach for her.

He steps away so I can't reach. "I actually think she likes me." He cranes his neck a bit to see her better where she perches on his shoulder, then pets her so carefully you'd think she was made of spun glass. Rupi practically croons beneath his attention.

I mutter beneath my breath and shake my head. What exactly am I supposed to do about my traitorous pet? Doesn't help that, apparently, we have the same taste in men. She's making it even more difficult to hate him.

The city isn't very big, consisting of the path we took here and a handful of other intersecting streets, more aptly described as garden paths. The walkways this time of day are teeming with people and animals. We pass a few shops that smell of meat and bread, and I'm tempted to try to tug Ikar into one, but as we pass, a cat lazily flicking its tail off the awning above hisses at me, and I find myself stepping away too quickly and bumping into Ikar again. Rupi gives a string of upset chirps as she shuffles down the length of Ikar's shoulder and back to his neck again, her feathers beginning to quill again with nerves at the sight of the predator. I glare into its golden cat eyes.

Rude. I highly doubt Ikar would set aside the mission for a bite of fresh food anyway.

We pass a family of rabbits, and my eyes are drawn to a baker shouting at a squirrel that apparently snitched something. I laugh until it turns to a yelp as Ikar pulls me quickly into his side in order to avoid my squashing a larger-than-normal scorpion beneath my boot.

"Watch your step. They don't allow killing in the city," he says sternly.

"I wasn't *trying.*"

He shrugs. "Doesn't matter. Don't kill anyone."

I'm ready to toss back a sarcastic comment, but it's swapped with a very pertinent question. "Wait. Does that mean they *do* allow killing in the forest?"

Ikar chuckles low and deep. "How else do you think they survive?"

My voice grows higher, "They hunt *each other?*"

"Not intentionally, probably. But they are part animal." He says it in that matter of fact way of his.

I have no response to that. With that knowledge, my dreams of a whimsical, safe Shift Forest journey have turned to dust. I purse my lips, but I keep my eyes on my feet more closely. Don't want to unintentionally kill a shifter on our way through town. I avoid bugs, too—just in case.

We turn down one street, and then another. I catch sight of a couple of wolves with their golden eyes stalking down the street, and even a few birds with eyes as golden as the wolves', indicating their shifter faction. With how busy it is, it's easy enough to find someone on the street to direct us to mate licensing, and we finally find ourselves standing before a small and ridiculously designed shop at 3rd and Main. A curly and dramatic sign hangs in front of a yard reading 'Mate Licenses' in bold font. Inside the small wrought iron fence is an untamed garden full of a variety of flowers of all colors and sizes, including a wall of robust roses that climbs the front of the building, almost hiding it beneath their heavy blooms. Two pane-glass windows peak out behind roses on either side of the narrow wooden front door with a window the shape of a heart in it.

I'd been looking for a more... official-looking office, but after double-checking the address and re-reading the sign three times, I'm positive we've found the right place. I shouldn't be too surprised. This building is much like the others in this odd city. I march, determined, up to the gate and pull it open, heading toward the front door in the midst of the heavy scent of the flowers around me. I look back to see Ikar, unmoved, outside the gate. *Look who's wasting time now.*

"Coming?" I call.

"This can't be the right place," he argues, as he steps somewhat hesitantly through the small gate. I hold back a snort, and look away to hide my grin. The man will fight vicious magical creatures without any wisp of magic, doesn't blink when stabbed with poisonous claws, willingly traverses dangerous mountains, and sneaks through goblin nests without a second thought, but hesitates at the gates of this tiny shop. How bad does he think this can be?

I open the shop door with the heart window and hear a dainty bell ring as I step inside. The scent is heady, a perfect combination of sweet and musky. To the right is a pretty, natural wood counter with flowers that match those in the front yard tumbling from a tall etched-glass vase atop it. The back of the shop contains an intricate wood arch with more flowers adorning the top in an artful design. To my left are built-in shelves that span the length and width of the wall, holding vials of all sorts of colors with tiny labels beneath each. Interesting.

"Oooooh! Delightful!" A round, kind-looking woman comes scurrying toward the door with her hands pressed together in front of her generous bosom. Her eyes seem to glow just a little brighter gold. "I just love to see such a charming couple."

Ikar steps in behind me, coughing slightly at the smell and appearing as if he's just stepped into a den of gloam snakes. I'm not sure someone could look more out of place in this shop with his thick leather armor and tall boots, but it's the weapons that fill his pockets and sheaths and the tears across the armor on his back that add an extra dollop to his already dangerous look. Not to mention the glower on his face, only enhanced by his unkempt beard. The woman's eyes widen as she takes in his appearance, lingering a moment too long on his accessories, but she quickly recovers her cheery and professional demeanor. She wraps her arm around my shoulders in a motherly way and guides us over to the shelves of tiny vials. Small description labels sit directly beneath each row of varying colors.

"Before we begin, please understand you aren't actually *mating*." Dread curls through my belly as I wait for her to jump into further, highly awkward details. Ikar's jaw is like granite, but she seems oblivious to our discomfort and continues into a memorized explanation. "This license will give you temporary use of a mate bond, which will protect you as you cross the Shift Forest. For non-shifters, a mate license is temporary and must be renewed every six weeks to be considered active. If one of you dies, the other will be vulnerable to a searching mate, so travel carefully and don't get bit." She smiles brightly.

Alright, then.

"Now for the fun!" She gestures to the vials. "Here are the mate bond types. Think of them as the *spice.*" She gives us a knowing look. "Do you have a preference?" She eyes the two of us, not waiting for a reply. "I'm thinking this one." She pulls a burgundy vial from the shelf. She looks between us with squinted eyes, thinking hard. "Or maybe this one." She grabs a gold vial and sets them both on the wood counter in front of the shelves.

"Isn't there just a *bond?*" Ikar asks, sounding grumpy.

She gestures to the vials, "*Those* are the bond, young sir. It's so much more fun with variety, don't you think?" She looks at me as she says the last part, and I smile uncomfortably. She winks. "When you've chosen, bring it to me, and we'll get you mate bonded in no time!" She giggles and scurries back to the other side of the room behind the wood counter, where she grabs a large piece of parchment and starts scrawling across its surface.

Ikar and I stand a bit awkwardly in front of the shelf, both unmoving for a long moment. I scratch my arm even though there's no itch, then check the tie at the base of my braid while I wait for him to make the first move. He doesn't. *Now* he decides he doesn't want to be in charge? I sigh. Fine. I lean in a little closer to read some of the descriptions.

Below a row of green, I read aloud, "Adventure." I look back at Ikar with a brow raised to gauge his reaction. "This is kinda fun, right?"

He mostly just looks bored and uncomfortable. I notice that the hand he rests on his sword pommel twitches like he might be in actual danger. So, the man *can* be dramatic. I would laugh, except I'm also quite nervous about this whole mate bond thing. Only one way forward.

I continue by dragging my finger to a row of light-blue vials next. "All Business," I say, louder this time, feeling more confident in our options.

Applicable, but boring.

My eyes slide to the next color, a row of bright pink vials, and read, "Romance." I don't look back at him this time. In order to diffuse the awkwardness of the last label, I move too quickly to a row of sunshine yellow vials and blurt out, "Reproduction," before I realize it's worse than the last. My cheeks are flaming. I'm pretty positive we aren't ready for that, and I thought these were temporary anyway. I have questions for Miss Mate License.

Ikar growls, "This is ridiculous."

He decisively reaches over my head and grabs one of the gold vials recommended by the shop lady without reading the label and walks toward the counter to pay for it.

"Wait! I didn't read the description on that one," I whisper-yell at his back. Besides, after seeing some of those vials, I don't trust this woman's recommendations.

"We know it's not *reproduction*," he mutters beneath his breath without slowing and slides it across the counter into the hands of the cheery lady. I'm just walking up to the counter when she smiles knowingly, "*Wonderful* choice, you two. It's worth the expense." She hands Ikar a receipt with a total so large at the bottom I choke a little.

I lean around his arm, worried and feeling a little panicky. "Maybe we should take a look at the others?"

He counts out the money and hands it to her. He seems out of his element in this odd little shop, his discomfort almost tangible. His face is unreadable. Is mate-bonding with me just to get across a forest so awful? I cringe at the thought. He just wants out. So, while paying that amount of money would make me cry, it's clear that he's earned so much from his violent escapades as a mercenary he gives no thought for expense.

The woman takes the money and then hands us each a charmed quill. "Sign here and here." She points to two lines at the bottom of the contract she's just written. Ikar's eyes skim the contract, but he keeps glancing outside, probably hoping we can get back to the gate before the suns go down and it's too late. I haven't read all the details about the binding, but before I can finish Ikar signs his name with a flourish and slides the paper to me. "Sign," he commands.

I carefully sign my name, and our names settle permanently into the parchment with a flourish of sparks. I gulp.

The woman quickly rolls it up, ties it with a wide, flashy red ribbon, and hands it to Ikar. "Now. The mate bond. Would you like to do that here or on your own?"

Without waiting for an answer, she eagerly leads us over to the back of the shop with the wood arch I spotted earlier. Roses trail down outside the window. It's a bit overdone for my tastes, but I smile anyway, trying not to think about if this were an actual marriage to Ikar and not just a temporary mate bond. She flings a startlingly bright white fur cloak around her shoulders and prepares to begin.

Ikar stops her. "We'll take care of this on our own, but thank you."

The woman's face falls a little. "I do love to do the bonds with the gold vial," she removes the cloak, "but I understand." She scurries back over to her desk and shuffles noisily through a drawer. Bits of ribbon fall, twirling to the floor, and papers in all shades of pink and red messily peek over the edge. She finds what she's looking for and heads back over to us with a piece of paper and a delicate gold chain in her hand. She neatly folds the chain up inside the envelope. "Here are the instructions, follow them *very* carefully to make sure it's done properly. You wouldn't want anyone else bonding with your lady." She winks at Ikar and leads us to the door. "I wish you every happiness."

I thank her, hoping the wariness doesn't show too much on my face. She sure acts like this is a big deal, when we just don't want to be forever bonded by wild shifters on our way through the forest.

We step outside with our flashy-wrapped parchment and crystal vial of gold liquid, both of which Ikar promptly shoves in his pack and away from outside eyes. I would laugh, but a rush of nerves flutters in my stomach, which is ridiculous. Nothing about this is meant to be romantic or meaningful in any way. I search Ikar's face. Yep, all business. Shoulda chosen the blue vial, or was it the green? Doesn't matter since Ikar panicked and grabbed gold before I could investigate. Though, maybe he isn't quite so unaffected. I see that telling muscle in his jaw clench, but that's usually a sign of irritation. Not quite what I'd like to see in my ideal mate bonding situation.

In search of a place to figure out this bond, I follow Ikar out of town a ways, until the manicured gardens and topiaries disappear and we find ourselves in natural forest. He stops after awhile and looks around. "This should work."

We stand in long, soft forest grass surrounded by saplings, their coin-shaped leaves fluttering lightly in the breeze. Light filters softly through their branches, and I can see dust particles float in the streaks of sunlight that make it through. He couldn't possibly have chosen a more romantic location. I peer at him carefully, wondering if it was intentional, but his face is emotionless. Rupi shows her approval by flitting amongst the thin branches, happy to have some freedom after being perched for so long.

He leans down and pulls the envelope and gold vial from

the pack. He stands once again and I take the gold vial while he opens the card and unfolds the instructions, the gold chain dangling from his hand. He starts reading to himself.

In the shop, the gold vial looked glittery, but as I hold it up to the sunlight to inspect it closer, I realize it isn't glitter, but miniscule flashes of light continually bursting. Curiosity pokes at me. I really wish we had read the description. Maybe I can go back to see what he's purchased later. If we don't already know by then. More butterflies flutter in my stomach. I watch Ikar as his eyes scan the page, focused. I step closer to him and angle myself so I can read the page, too.

The instructions are relatively simple. Stand close, place a very careful droplet on the inside of each of our wrists, then press them together and wrap the gold chain around both and secure it with a charm. Then it's done.

"Are you okay with this? We can always try to find a different way around," he says.

I look up into Ikar's blue eyes, shadowed with concern. "Another way around may not even be possible, and there's no time to search."

He nods firmly.

"Are *you* okay with this?"

He swallows and looks out into the woods, his body tense. I grow concerned when he doesn't say anything for a few moments.

I put a hand softly on his arm. "You don't have to be bound to me. I know we won't ever be... like that. There should be another way."

That muscle in his jaw clenches again, and he shakes his head. He takes the gold vial, muttering something bitterly under his breath that sounds a lot like, "special type of torture," as he pops the lid off.

With a gentleness that belies his anger a few moments ago, he steps closer to me, my shoulder against his upper arm, and takes my hand to turn it palm up in his larger one, the inside of my wrist facing the sky. I watch as ever so slowly he tips the vial, and a single drop clings to the rim until finally it lets go and falls to my wrist. It immediately soaks into my skin, forming a small, light-sparking circle. Before I have time to inspect it further, Ikar passes me the vial and turns his hand so his wrist is up. I cup my hand beneath his and tip the bottle, a single drop once again clings to the edge as if giving us one more moment to make sure this is what we want. I tip it a tiny bit further, and the drop falls, immediately melting into his skin the same as mine and leaving a matching sparking circle.

He takes the vial and pops the cap back on, dropping it in one of his many pockets before he once again takes my hand. We press our wrists together in a moment that is growing far too intimate for our spoken relationship status. *Criminal and bounty hunter,* I remind myself. The moment he secures the delicate gold chain around our wrists, it feels like the sparking circles meld together. The warmth grows between our wrists and spreads up our arms and through our bodies in a heady way, a rush of gold overwhelming my senses. Bright lights behind my eyes block me from my physical sight while our souls seem to connect in an impossible way. I feel complete. The feeling is beautiful, safe, warm. A high I didn't know if I'd ever feel again. I soak it in for as long as it lasts. Gradually, the sparks lighten behind my eyes, and my vision clears, the warmth retracting back to our wrists. I find myself wrapped in Ikar's free arm, pressed against his solid chest. *When had that happened?* We watch as the gold chain separates into two, and the ends meld together and seem to fizzle into our skin as if they never existed. We are left with small, glimmering dots, the only visible proof of the bond.

We pull our hands apart, and I look up at Ikar and meet his eyes. His guard is down and there is something deep and intense smoldering there.

My logic tells me to tread carefully—this unguarded and somewhat new behavior from Ikar could be a result of the new bond I know nothing about *thanks to him.* But the side of me that has been fighting my feelings for him jumps at the opportunity, slamming the door in logic's face. I only slightly lean toward him before he crosses the distance. I feel his lips a breath away, wanting. And then I hear a rustle and the quiet crack of brush nearby. We both snap out of whatever that moment almost was and stand straight, searching. I catch a tall shadow in my peripheral, but when I turn my head to get a better look, there's nothing there. I'm beginning to wonder if something is seriously wrong with my vision. The odd shadowy shapes that keep appearing at the sides are becoming regular enough to be concerning.

"Do you see anything?" I ask.

"No. Sounded like an animal of some sort." He leans down and grabs his pack. "We should go." He avoids my eyes, and just like that, the moment is over. Rupi flutters to my shoulder, weaving her way through my hair and settling in for the walk back to the Shift Authority.

Chapter 27

Vera

We waste no time making our way through the odd city, stopping only once to replenish our supply of food and get something to eat before we arrive back at the Shift Authority Office. I make sure we skip the ornery cat's place, and I'm hoping the pirate shifter's shift has ended, but no such luck. He steps out, a blindingly white smile on his face. Being bonded to Ikar, apparently, doesn't worry the man. He checks both our wrists.

"This is *temporary* and will wear off in about six weeks." He drops my hand. "Be out before then, or there's a likely chance you'll be forced to mate bond with a shifter and be stuck in that forest the rest of your lives. And most of 'em aren't as kind as I. Got it?"

I sure hope we aren't in that forest for six weeks. I have dues to pay and a friend to save. I gulp. *How horrible is it?* He stalks toward the gate and unlocks it using a large skeleton key. It swings open on silent hinges. Ikar steps forward first, seemingly unfazed by the decrepit old bridge as he walks past the gate. He must sense my hesitation because he reaches a hand back for mine and looks at me with an *are you coming* sort of look. I slip my hand into his strong grasp and step through the gate. It swings shut behind us and locks.

There's this tiny part of me that instinctively wants to turn and grasp the solid iron bars of that gate and scream for someone to let me back out, but I throw water on that emotional fire and squeeze Ikar's hand a little tighter. I keep it to myself, but I'd choose sticking with Ikar even traversing a creepy shifter forest over staying behind without him. The bridge is only wide enough for us to walk one at a time. I fully expect Ikar to continue this thing where he voluntarily goes first and leads the way, but this time he steps back and motions me forward.

"You first."

I narrow my eyes at him, "You want me to see if it's safe? Fine," I say with teasing in my voice to keep the throat-tightening fear from crawling out in a wild scream, but I know he does it to make sure I get across.

All he does is give me an encouraging look with a lift of his eyebrows.

With a deep breath, I grasp both sides of the bridge. Before I take a step, Rupi takes flight, her tiny wings flapping furiously and I watch nervously as she bounces around with the gusts of wind, fighting and struggling her way across. She makes it, and now it's my turn.

The sides are made of a thick, twisted rope that's rough against my hands. It feels so worn and spiky that I'm worried I'll end the crossing with rope slivers galore, but I'd rather that than fall... down there. My gaze drops to a deeply shadowed, foggy crevice. An especially forceful gust of wind blows through, violently shaking the bridge and forcibly lightening the fog for a small moment, revealing a muddy river far, far below. Then the fog recovers its density, and all I can hear is the distant rush of the water. I feel dizzy, and my hands are white from gripping so hard, and I haven't even stepped on the bridge yet. I stretch my fingers out, then grasp it again and take a cautious step forward.

I'm three steps in, and the worn planks feel thinner the further I go. This was a horrible idea. How can a city that seems so well-kept, whose citizens apparently use this bridge often to cross to the forest named after their kind, have a bridge as neglected and worn as this? It's absurd. The prickly rope continues to poke at my hands as I slide them across, and I wonder how they test the safety of this thing—or if they even do.

"You think they've got regulations for things like this?" I call over my shoulder, trying to keep my voice light, masking the fact that I'm scared out of my blazing mind.

I hear Ikar laugh a little, and it lightens my anxiety a smidge. "Doubt it."

He mutters something I can't hear over the wind in my ears, then steps on, and I feel the bridge bounce a little beneath me with his weight. I wait until it settles again, as much as it does with the wind blowing through it, then I step ever so carefully, one foot after another. I try to go faster, and I think I'm doing really great until I chance a look behind me to search for Ikar and the vertigo attacks. I'm left spinning and nauseous with my eyes shut, pretending I'm *anywhere* else. The wind picks up the further out we get, and near the middle, it feels like a hurricane. And then I slip because the holey, warped planks turn damp and slippery toward the middle, too. Don't know how they stay wet with these kind of winds keeping them company, but they are. Strings of loose, weakened rope whip in the wind, along with my hair. The bridge creaks and sways, and

I see another tiny piece of rope break. I start walking faster, but the bridge shakes so hard with another gust that when I take a step too large, I'm knocked to a knee and feel like I'm about to slide through the gaping sides.

"Hold on!" Ikar shouts. The wind blows so hard it's difficult to even control the expression on my face, and I'm sure I look like a dog happily riding in a speeding wagon, tongue hanging out and all. But that doesn't matter when the bridge begins to tilt.

"Both hands on one side!" he yells again. I wouldn't be able to hear him if he didn't. But I quickly obey, even though it's terrifying to let go of one side for even a second. The bridge flips and sways roughly, and I scream as my arms jerk against my tightly gripped hands around the rope. Ikar and I dangle above the muddy abyss, and I freeze.

Chapter 28

Ikar

"Hand over hand," I yell when she doesn't move. We have a ways to go, and I don't know how long she can hold on with this wind.

She finally starts moving, sliding her hands rather than releasing one, but I don't care, as long as we're making progress. We're currently hanging from the most violently swinging portion of the bridge—its center. The sooner we move toward the other end, the better. It's a good thing the shifter is behind a locked gate and a flipped bridge, or I'd be on my way back to finish whatever game he plays. There'll be time for that later, after I've restored my kingdom. Also, this bridge will be covered at the next King's Council.

We are three fourths of the way across when Vera stops again.

"Keep going!" I shout through the wind.

She shouts something, but I hardly hear her words. I can see the way her hands are beginning to slip and tire.

"We aren't dying in this muddy canyon today. Move!" I yell harshly.

I treat her as one of my soldiers, but it seems to work, and she begins moving once again. Even *my* arms begin to burn, so I can't imagine how hers feel. We finally reach the edge, and I continue to coach her through the tricky process of half-climbing, half-pulling herself up onto solid ground. Once there, she falls back with gasping breaths, clutching the short grass beneath her. Rupi darts from the trees and barrels into Vera, hopping over her chest and chirping until Vera lifts a hand to calm her. I make my way up, arms on fire, and feel as if my hearing is permanently muted from the intense volume of the howling wind in my ears as I crossed. When I look back along the length of the trembling bridge, I see the guard walk through the gate and proceed to work with the wind to restore the bridge to its upright and functional position. When he finishes, he gives me a mock salute, then exits through the gate once more.

Anger has me fixing my grasp around the hilt of my sword, but I know I can't go after him right now. I reach a hand down to Vera, unwilling to let her wallow in her panic. "Let's go."

I want to pick her up and grasp her tight to my chest with relief that she didn't let go, but I don't want her to see how shaken I am. Or how much I care when I really shouldn't. She knows I need her alive to get my magic back, but she doesn't know I want her alive because I care. As she looks at my hand and then back at the bridge, then back to my hand, I see the resolve steel her eyes. She's stronger than she thinks she is, and I'll keep showing her until she believes it. She takes my hand, and I pull her to my side.

We find ourselves facing a rustic sign attached to a thick wood post with 'Welcome to the Shift Forest' scrawled across its front in a thin script. It sits a bit crookedly, but oddly, it does lighten the atmosphere after that cursed death trap behind us. I stretch my neck side to side, not liking the way our trip has begun, but I know we have no other option now that we're here. Besides, this is still the fastest route—we just have to survive it.

"What do you think this mate bond does?" Vera asks, as we begin walking, holding up her arm and tilting her wrist this way and that to inspect the glowing dot.

"All that matters is that it will protect both of us from being tricked or forced into a mate bond with a shifter as we cross the forest," I say, though I do wonder if I should have read the label first. *But that mate bond licensing office...* I cringe. My throat goes tight just thinking about it again. Stuffy, pink, uncomfortable. Vera's face when she was reading the vials and blurted out *reproduction.* I stopped thinking and impulsively snatched the gold one just to escape the confines and awkwardness of the overbearing place.

Vera lips curl in amusement at my expression. "Thinking of that shop again?"

I give her a flat look, and she laughs, but my mood lightens. If my discomfort can make her laugh, I'll do it over and over again—it's like the warm rays of sunshine after a freezing rain. She's a confusing one. Captor of my magic, and potentially my heart, if I don't protect it better.

Chapter 29

Vera

I started out through the Shift Forest jumpy and anxious. The woods here are different. All curly twisted branches, thicker than normal tree trunks, and dark, but after a day walking through, nothing has happened. Rupi has become comfortable enough to flit from tree to tree, no longer huddling beside my neck like she was after she flew across the windy crevice. Besides the bridge, the trip has been surprisingly uneventful, which is scary in itself, but it has also made it really difficult to keep my mind from revisiting that almost kiss. I've had strange scenarios skittering through my mind, crazy ones, like what if I really *were* to date my criminal? What if he reformed and left his criminal life? He seems normal enough. I'm confident he could be successful in a career other than violent mercenary. I mean, I'd for sure be willing to wait for him to finish his jail time. The quiet burst of laughter that escapes me at the thought catches Ikar's attention, but I shake my head, not willing to offer an explanation.

According to the map and Ikar's guesstimates, along with the pace we've kept so far, we just might arrive at the kingdom of the Fae earlier than expected. We've left a deeper part of the forest where the shade and shadows created by the thick canopy above forced me to use my cloak, but now the sunlight streaming in magical shafts through the trees warms my skin.

I stop and take in the mountain peaks in the distance capped with white snow, misty fog clinging around them. Then, I take a moment to absorb the magical simplicity before me. Here in this valley surrounded by gentle hills, the sun is warm and soothing. A clear, burbling stream weaves through wavy grasses and in between the trees, tiny lavender flowers spread out before us, growing as one with the grass. Their light scent calls to me, and I want to lay down, close my eyes, and revel in the perfect calmness of this little valley in our huge kingdom. Birds call happily in the trees, and I spot a rabbit dart away from us, hidden beneath the bed of purple. Ikar didn't stop and is nearly to a stand of trees a distance away, following the curve of the stream. I am in no rush to leave this place, so I slow my pace and let the grass and flowers slip lightly beneath my fingers as I walk. When I reach the shady stand of trees that Ikar entered, I see silky white flowers, their centers lightly glowing. I want to reach down and investigate, but Ikar calls me over. He stands before a pool of water surrounded with beautiful greenery and bushes, a small waterfall gushing from above causing ripples and waves to spread outward. The tiny lights of the flowers glow around us in the shadows, creating an almost romantic atmosphere. I mean, if you're thinking about romantic things. Which I'm not.

"Are we going to stop here for the night?" I ask hopefully. I'm loving the ambience. I want to build a cottage and live the rest of my life here. I already decided. I scoop Rupi from my shoulder, and a few flaps later, she's hopping around in the flowers, searching out bugs and spiders to eat.

"We still have half a day's light, but I thought we could wash here. Looks like as safe a place as any." He turns and glances around, confirming his observation.

I head straight for the pool of water, Ikar following in my wake. He pauses before he touches the water, and his head angles in thought, as if he's thinking it over. I almost laugh, wondering at his hesitation. It seems like he waits for something to rise from its surface, but I'm so filthy that I'd bathe with a blackipor if I had to. I imagine the creature rising from the depths of this small pool and grin. It just doesn't fit in this lovely place. The black reptilian skin over the huge body of a water-dwelling mammal with black tusks and a gaping, strong jaw. I know they dwell in the Lucent River, but here? No way. I crouch down and swirl my hand in the water, creating a tiny whirlpool to entertain myself while Ikar sits on his haunches and studies the pool. I've found he is one of those hyperalert and ready-for-anything types, and I can appreciate that, so I wait.

"Are we good?" I ask, beginning to be concerned with his hesitation but getting impatient. I glance around, wondering what exactly it is that has triggered his hesitation. Does he sense something I can't? I'm probably too distracted by the fifteen layers of sweat and dirt in every crevice of my body to really be aware at this point.

"I don't know." He frowns and slips his hand beneath the surface, testing. "Something feels off. I think we'll try another spot." He begins to pull his hand from the water, but I feel the sharp tug the same time he does. In the next half second, I see a chilling face just beneath the water. Before I can even scream, we are pulled in by our fingertips. The depths of the pool are freezing cold and pitch black, a direct contrast to the beautiful, warm image presented at its surface. But whatever the creepy creature is, it continues dragging us down. Further and further into black, cold water. My oxygen is nearly gone, and I feel like I'm about to pass out. Just as lights begin to herald in the darkness that comes with lack of needed breath, we fall in a heap on a soft, almost cushy surface.

"Vera?" Ikar asks from somewhere near me, he's breathing in great gulps of air, same as I.

"I'm okay." I press against the softness and find it's very moist moss. Probably grows like a wildfire in the warm, humid environment we've been dragged into. I blink to clear my stinging vision, then I realize then that there should be a large puddle of water around me, my clothes should be sopping wet, my hair drenched. But there's no water, and I'm *clean*. I don't know if we're about to die or not, but the fact that I'm clean lifts my spirits, and I laugh out loud, which draws a concerned look from Ikar. I don't blame him. I figure whatever dragged us down here didn't do it to offer us a cup of tea and send us on our way, though we appear to have been dropped in a garden fit for the fanciest of parties. An odd, filtered, watery-like light bounces off the garden scene we've been dropped in and draws my eyes upward. The pool is a sphere of water above us. Cover for a well-disguised trap. Clever.

That knowledge leaves me with a cave-like feeling about the place, but there is no evidence of it beside the lack of direct sunlight. I realize that aside from the dim light that barely reaches through the pool, the only other light comes from the same variety of white flowers with glowing centers that we saw above. The entire place is almost fae-like in its extravagance, only missing the jewel-toned flowers. Vines drip in large, tangled clusters from somewhere I can't see, tiny white buds of growing flowers along their length. There isn't a space that's not covered in the soft, fuzzy moss. I'm not sure how a place beneath a freezing pool of water can be so *green*. Or hot. It won't be long before I'm drenched in sweat in this garden sauna.

"Where the blazes are we?" I whisper beneath my breath.

I glance at Ikar, who is focused on something ahead as he moves into a defensive crouch. My gaze follows his as tinkling laughs raise the hair on my arms. Four bobbing lights, similar in color to the glowing centers of the flowers in the shady wood and those in this cave garden, lengthen and transform into four beautiful women before us. Everwisps. Silk dresses that match the velvety white of the petals I'd admired less than an hour ago flow over their feminine curves artfully, accentuating all their best parts. A dip in fabric here, a slit to reveal a shapely upper thigh there. I'm not sure I've ever seen women as beautiful as these. I'm currently feeling as pretty as the blackipor I was willing to swim with earlier, but my comparison switches to a strange sort of jealous possessiveness when their eyes literally glow with delight as they move their gazes slowly over Ikar, drinking him in like they're desperate for water on a sweltering day. I am completely ignored by the shifters. Apparently, I do not merit even a glance of their golden eyes. I want to be offended, but I stay quiet, observing. Best to keep the *not dangerous* label I've been afforded, so I stand but don't pull a weapon.

Their hair is entwined with the white flowers. Two have silky-looking brown hair, one has shiny black hair straighter than I've ever seen, and the last has hair the color of red and gold autumn leaves that falls down her back in tumbling curls. I grudgingly admit that each of them appears to be a work of art.

One of the brown-haired women walks with a sultry air toward Ikar. I notice his grip on the sword handle tightens.

"Stop," he commands.

She continues toward him, hips swaying. "If you comply, your lady friend will be safe." She speaks smoothly, never taking her eyes from his form.

Still, I'm not enough of a threat to warrant a look.

"If you hurt me, she dies." She says it so sweetly and with an air of flippancy that you'd never expect she was speaking of murder.

The other three women surround me. Their nails lengthening into razor-sharp claws, though they don't touch me.

His face is expressionless, and he doesn't move. The woman laughs that tinkling, irritating laugh again, and I watch as she stops right before him, pushes his blade to the side with her hand, and steps a hand's width from his chest. I begin to worry that she's entrapped his mind somehow—why did he let her so close? Did we miss a step with the mate bond? My heart begins to beat erratically.

"We don't often get such a... handsome package." She's practically purring. She steps closer, inhaling and running a caressing hand from his left shoulder down to his chest. I see a muscle in his jaw tick. She leans in close, and I barely hear her whisper. "You know you never needed that mate bond?"

I don't have time to think about why that might be and what her words mean, so I tuck it away for later.

A long, graceful finger continues its way down, tracing down his shirt, over his muscled chest and torso. "We've been waiting for centuries for the right man to father our children, but having *you* here is above my every expectation," she whispers again, her words only for him, as her finger drops lower and slides slowly along the top edge of his leather belt.

Rage ignites inside me. If Ikar is feeling hesitant to use that sword, I'll do it for him—with pleasure.

Ikar slowly goes from expressionless to smiling in that charming way of his as he deftly scoops her hand away from his belt and into his and brings it to his perfect lips for a sultry kiss. My heart drops. This is just fantastic. We've been entrapped by lusty flower women bent on killing me and stealing my criminal, and apparently, they've overtaken his reason.

"You are a vision, my lady." He looks into her eyes. What kind of power do these everwisps have? What was the mate bond for if not for this? A scream is waiting to erupt from my throat.

She smiles, her golden eyes glowing warmly at his appreciation, and she steps in a little closer.

Then his expression drops to a soft look of apology. "I apologize for the inconvenience, but you will need to find another..." he clears his throat, "donor... for your offspring."

The golden glow in her eyes flickers darkly, and the smile drops from her lips, but he continues.

"I am honored by your invitation, but, unfortunately, I cannot father children." A sadness darkens his eyes, and I wonder if he is for real. If not, he's good. *Really* good, because I feel actual sorrow at his statement. And relief. A lot of relief. He's not wrapped in whatever spell their presence apparently weaves.

A feral smile lights her lips, the hiss that escapes her mouth could rival a cat's. "That's a lie. I picked up the scent of your virility a mile away." She laughs again. "Most men are more than pleased with *my* beauty, but perhaps you have different tastes?" Her golden eyes give me a once over, and her lips purse like she sucks on something sour as she thinks about what she'll have to do next.

Ikar begins to speak, "It's reall—"

Two vines shoot out of somewhere in this creepy garden cave, faster than I can track, one wraps around Ikar's sword, and it's yanked from his grasp and rolled up against the ceiling. The other whips in my direction, and hot pain slices through my forearm. I cry out in surprise as blood spreads across a clean cut that reaches three inches down my arm, soaks through the sleeve of my shirt, and begins dribbling down my fingers. I watch as drops begin to hit the moss at my feet and soak into it like it's dropped onto a wet sponge. My ears buzz with pain and shock, so I don't hear what Ikar shouts at the everwisp. I'm too busy wondering what the blazes I did to deserve being attacked.

I look up with fiery words to say, but I forget it all when my eyes meet my own face. I do a double take and shake my head in denial, then step back, forgetting, until I bump into the ever-wisp behind me. She hisses in my ear and I remember I'm still surrounded. The one before me, who stole *me*, wears the same white dress... but the body, the light spatter of freckles across her nose, the flyaway hair. It's all *me*. For a moment, I appreciate how I could look if I felt the urge to update my wardrobe, but then I realize that, apparently, this mossy substance is somehow *her,* and she literally took my blood to copy me. I'm standing on it and getting more grossed out by the second. While I'm battling a combination of disgust at that realization, along with a bout of dizziness, she turns with a commanding look over her shoulder at Ikar and heads toward the inky blackness of the garden tunnel ahead of us. Hips swinging like mine never have. It's odd, feeling jealous of yourself.

Ikar stands for a moment. I can't call it indecision on his face, he's too decisive for that. Calculated choosing is what it is —which is sometimes scarier. His enchanted weapon is still wrapped up in vines, and he glances at me surrounded by the other three everwisps. I realize the situation isn't great. They've got me surrounded to force him to do their bidding, and he knows if I die, his magic is gone. But there's no way he'll go with her, right? He has other weapons. I know it, I've seen him remove them, though never all at once, of course. And none of those other weapons will kill an everwisp as quickly as an enchanted one, but still. I look at him with a question in my eyes. He takes a step forward. Whether he's stepping forward to follow or fight her, I don't know. But I do know there is no way I'm letting him go without a fight. *Because I like him.* No. Because I need the money. And I want that vile woman's hands away from him. Forever. I ever so slowly slip my knife from my right hand to my now weakened left hand, forcing my grip to hold even while it's slick with blood.

Our eyes hold for a second, then we move at the same time. I lose sight of him when, with all the strength I can muster, I wrench my elbow up and back—fast and hard—into the throat of the unsuspecting everwisp hovering behind me, while thrusting my knife through the everwisp that stands at my right side. The stabbed one collapses to the ground, and the rosy color of her skin and rich color of her hair leech out, leaving her with a bruised tinge. I grimace as I step forward and pull my knife from her, then she bursts with light and is gone. I don't have time to see if she actually died or just disappeared because the nails of the one I throat punched are apparently stuck in the back of my jacket, and she pulls me back as she stumbles, coughing and hacking in way that doesn't match her unearthly beauty from my throat hit. I switch my knife to my stronger hand. I could definitely overthink this moment, but I can't. So, while I have the chance, I thrust it into her, too. She screams out in rage before all the color in her hair and skin drains out in a horrifying way that matches her sister, her face slack and lifeless as she falls to the ground before glowing brightly and disappearing. A wilted gray flower lies in her place. I hope that means she's dead.

I look over my shoulder as I grab my sword off the weird moss floor to see Ikar standing off with the brown haired leader. She flashes away in a snarl and whirl of skirts, revealing a bit more of my skin than I'm comfortable with. Curse her. At her retreat, the other everwisp takes her place. She flickers in and out of sight, glowing extra bright in surges that burn my eyes, then darkening and leaving me blind. Appearing and disappearing in different parts of the garden, she messes with my vision, leaving bright imprints that are difficult to see through when they intentionally darken the room. Ikar appears unfazed and watches closely. He pauses a moment when one flickers out, like a pinched flame. Then she appears to his left, her razor nails at the ready. She's just out of reach, so he expertly spins the knife in his hand and throws it. It lands in her chest right as she begins to flicker again, but instead of disappearing, she falls to the ground in solid form with a spongey thud. Her form glows brightly like the ones I witnessed just before, then disappears, and the knife lays on the ground again. I watch him unsheathe another when I begin to feel movement beneath my feet. Vines circle around me, and the moss seems to have grown spongier. I quick step and begin to scramble with a yelp, trying to avoid the vines but they continue their circling until both my feet and lower legs are caught up in their ever-tightening grip.

I forgot for a moment that she wants him alive—it's me they don't care about.

I look down at my own feet. My vision begins to blur a bit, and I almost fall over. I notice there's blood staining the moss all around me now, and the vines are climbing higher, already up to my mid-thighs. They're probably the reason I haven't toppled over from blood loss, but I'd still prefer they get off me. I begin chopping at them with my sword, careful to avoid my legs, but it seems as soon as I get a cut in, another vine sprouts from the opening and makes it worse. They travel up, wrapping around my hips now, and I begin breathing too fast. The last everwisp, dressed in my body and face, her swaying hips and dangerous golden eyes, makes her way toward Ikar.

I see his shoulders bunch as he readies for the fight and stalks forward to meet her. Gone is the well-mannered gentleman with the handsome, charming smiles. Now he is darkness and power and predator. Very much like the man who almost strangled me that night by the river when I arrested him. Glad I'm not on the receiving end of his anger this time.

"Ah-ah-ah," the demon woman says with a smile.

Before he gets too close, a vine snakes around his wrists, around and around and around. They wrap so tight that his hands smash together, and his knife clatters to the ground. The vines wrap around my midsection, and I begin to see spots. The everwisp, somewhere between wisp and solid form, flies around him and appears again in front of him.

"You are immune to my draw." She chuckles and leans in to his ear. "I know what you are, and it only makes me want you more," she whispers to him, her finger now trailing up over the shoulder that pains him sometimes and down the back of his shoulder blade again. That mask of ice forms over his face. Her words carry and seem to slam into the solid stone walls of our prison, falling heavily around us. *She knows what he is? A criminal? Something else?*

"Should I tell her, or is it our little secret?" She laughs.

"There is no secret," he says flatly, but I can see the small tick in his jaw. There is most definitely a secret.

Chapter 30

Ikar

"**E**nough of these games. I don't care what secrets you do or don't share, but you will give me a child, or she dies." The devastatingly beautiful woman who wears Vera's face before me hisses.

I clench my jaw and work to tamp down the concern that she knows what, or rather *who*, I am. I can only hope Vera doesn't bring this up again later.

The woman smells like flowers, heady and strong, and I assume that's supposed to draw men to her. But I am immune, apparently because I can only be drawn toward a Tulip, and the mate bond is supposed to help with situations like this, but, according to the everwisp, I didn't need it in the first place. What normally would have been a benefit in this forest has also almost given away my identity. I need to end this. My hands are bloodless and limp, my wrists throbbing. It feels like they are being forcibly separated from my arms at the joint.

"All I want is *one*, and then the two of you can live your life as you like." She eyes Vera with disgust. She drags her gaze back to mine and once again grabs my belt. "*If* you keep your end of the bargain."

Even if I were a regular citizen, there would be no child making between myself and this crazy wisp. But I'm a king, and it's even more important that I not spread seed around the five kingdoms and have long-lost children coming to challenge my future heir for the throne. Vera unexpectedly throws her sword toward the woman, but the everwisp stands too far and too easily turns to wisp. The sword only runs through her dress and scratches a thigh before she flickers away and is back again. She stares at Vera with hatred and darkness, and I hear Vera begin to struggle to breathe as the vines forcefully tighten under the everwisp's gaze.

I dive to the ground, toward the knife I left lying there, to slice through the vines. Like Vera's vines, they seem to grow more appendages from the cut parts, entangling my knees now that I've touched the ground, but I free one hand, and that's enough. I awkwardly turn and throw the knife, watching as it pierces her back. Vera's body and face seem to melt away from her as she weakens, and gratefully, so do the vines. Her beauty and color seeps from her body, and she crumples with a flash.

And then we're left in almost complete darkness, and I hear Vera sucking in deep breaths. I stand before my eyes have completely adjusted, ripping the lifeless vines away from me and grabbing my enchanted sword from where it's fallen onto the mossy ground, free of the vines that held it fast. I make my way quickly to Vera. I find her on the ground, bracing herself on her hands while still kneeling and breathing too heavily. I lower to a knee beside her and place a hand on her back and rub in slow circles until she's calm. When she finally sits back on her heels, I gingerly pick up her left arm, the one where the vine cut. I'm surprised she lets me. I move the fabric to see it better and frown at the deep cut.

"It's not that bad." She pulls it away. "How do we get out of here?"

"It needs to be bandaged, at least." I watch as blood still drips from her hand.

With effort, she stands, then takes a moment to stop swaying once she's there. She holds out her arm. "Just bind it. I want to leave this creepy place."

I carefully, but firmly tie a bandage around it, hoping it'll be enough for now.

The filtered water light casts odd, moving shadows around us. It's disconcerting that we are still surrounded by white, slightly glowing flowers. The silence is thick and broken only by our own movements. The white flowers continue to provide just enough light as we make our way deeper into the cave, and I find myself hoping there actually *is* an end. There is no map for this, and I've never found myself caught in an everwisp trap.

"It appears you don't like the pushy types." Vera attempts a teasing tone, but she looks too tired and pained for it to ring true. That, and I saw the way her eyes lit with anger when the woman came close and made her demand.

I give her a dry look. Obviously, I don't want to be with a murderous everwisp. "You did good back there." And I mean it. I saw the throat punch and the quick stab, even being injured.

"It pains me to say that your lessons may have helped," she says wryly.

"You're welcome."

"I never said thank you." She narrows her eyes a bit.

I simply toss her a knowing grin that I know drives her nuts and continue forward.

Chapter 31

Vera

We wander through the cave for what seems at least a mile, and we finally find an exit that spits us out onto a grass-covered hill that's so steep I almost roll down. We only spot a white flower here and there after that, but I no longer want to stop and admire any. I'm jumpy and worry with every one we see that the light that rests inside it will spring out and explode into another sultry-looking woman who wants Ikar's children.

By now, we've lost hours of precious daylight. The second sun is already about to set, but neither of us want to make camp anywhere near that awful little valley. Soon, though, I start slowing. My bandage soaked through long ago, and I'm feeling weak and tired. And Rupi hasn't appeared again yet. She found me before, so all I can do is hope she does again. When Ikar finally chooses a spot, I simply want to lay down and sleep.

He seems to sense my fatigue and grabs my bedroll from my pack. I'm about to gratefully thank him until he speaks.

"Lay down, and I'll see to your arm. Then you can sleep."

I've been going between nausea and dizziness, add to that a

splitting headache triggered by the near suffocation earlier and my arm spilling my life blood down my fingertips all day, and I'm in no mood for further pain. I'm done. I'd rather wait. And who is he to have that sort of commanding tone with me?

"It'll keep until we reach the fae. I'll clean it when we find more water," I say, as I take a shaky seat down on an uncomfortable boulder and let my shoulders hunch over. I've never wished that I could use my own healing magic on myself more than this moment. My heavy eyes readily take me toward sleep as soon as I relax. He takes a moment to toss out my bedroll, and I'm about to sleepily thank him before I fall onto it and pass out for the night. Instead, he takes a step toward me, and I tense up, feeling the command in his words.

"You can get there on your own, or I can tend it where you sit. You're not dying on my watch." Then he adds, "But it'll be easier by the fire."

I scowl at him because I know he'll actually do what he says he'll do. Him and his orders. In my exhaustion and pain, I want to lash out at him. The angry part of me thinks he only cares because he wants to be free of that cuff. But another, smaller, part of me brings up that near-kiss, and I wonder if maybe he's been feeling some of the same things I have. Maybe even remembering that night in the cave. My cheeks heat, and I'm even more unwilling to go now.

He comes toward me with his long strides, and I carefully stand before he reaches me, breathing deep to keep my senses about me. Then he's at my side, and with a gentle hand, he grips my good arm and helps me to my bedroll where I lay down and try not to show how much I needed the warmth of the fire.

He kneels beside me, his jaw set in that down-to-business way he gets, but I catch a hint of concern before he masks even that. He remains expressionless as he unties the blood-soaked bandage he tied earlier and removes it. I stifle a sound of pain from fully escaping when he pours heated water over it to loosen the torn fabric of my sleeve.

"Do you know what you're doing?" I ask through gritted teeth.

He stays focused, offering no response.

"You learn this skill from the mercenaries?" It's low of me, but I want a response, and I know I'll get one if I use the mercenary card.

"Told you I'm not a mercenary." He smoothly threads a needle.

After that, the pain's too much, so I keep my jaw clenched shut and turn my head to stare into the flames instead of his handsome face as he starts talking. I'm proud when, even as he begins to stitch it closed, I make no sound, only a couple of instinctive twitches of my arm give away any indication I feel it at all. I can't take all the credit, though. I'll never admit it aloud, but his ongoing one-sided conversation has been more comforting than I expected. He's been talking the entire time in that deep, steady voice of his. Something about a shard beast battle that I missed most of after a particularly tender needle tug, another part about an archery contest when he was a kid, and an extra long bit about his hawk named Simon and his beast dog named Arrow. After he's finished and his talking has stopped, and the only sound between us is the crackle and pop of the fire, I find I wish I'd been able to pay a little better attention.

I realize as he carefully wraps my arm and sets it lightly across my stomach, and my eyes open and shut tiredly, that he's never shared anything like that before—the personal things that seem unimportant but make a person real. I want to know more. How could this man be a Tulip killer? A mercenary, even. It just doesn't *fit*.

My eyes feel heavier than they've ever felt, burning and dry. Closing them has never felt so good. But as I enjoy the sweet relief of darkness and almost-sleep, my thoughts begin to free themselves from the confines of my mind and come out mumbled and nearly indecipherable through my lips.

"You don't really seem like a mercenary... don't think you kill Tulips."

My sentence drifts off, and I open my eyes once more to drink in the sight of him before I sleep. I notice he appears to have frozen as he was inspecting one of his many knives, looking at me with an intensity that almost wakes me up. But nothing can wake me up now. My eyes close, and I reach sleep.

Chapter 32

Ikar

I stay awake long into the night, my thoughts keeping me company as I guard our small camp. The magic that increases my hearing ability may be blocked, but I'm gifted with excellent abilities even without it, and I know I heard what I heard. She's doubting that I'm a mercenary, she even said something about Tulips, and that topic hasn't been spoken of since the night she arrested me.

I've been waiting to get more information from her, but I've resisted the urge to ask since she believes I'm out to kill them. Any curiosity from me will only reinforce her wrong belief about me, so I've kept my questions to myself, but as we near the end of our journey, I find myself feeling antsy. If she really does drop me off in the hands of the officials like a common criminal and disappears, I will be at square one. I'll have to track her down again or find information somewhere else—so much time wasted.

On the other hand, maybe I shouldn't worry over it yet. If she's beginning to believe I'm not a mercenary, or a killer, the odds are swinging in my favor that I can convince her to let me go before we get to Moneyre. Maybe she'll even work with me long before then and all of this will be resolved, but that seems a lot to hope for when I'm still cuffed.

Vera shifts in her sleep and draws my gaze. My eyes freely trace the curve of her nose and pause on her lips, lingering on how her bottom lip is a bit fuller than the top. She's so different than any woman I've been around before, especially Nadiette. At first, I considered her somewhat of a scrawny tomboy, dressed in her overlarge men's clothing and her face framed with flyaway hair. She comes with enough attitude to make up for the fact she had no idea how to wield a weapon. In fact, she seems almost the complete opposite of Nadiette in every way I can think of, which is why I'm surprised that I find myself more attracted to Vera than I have ever been to any other woman. I drag my gaze away and run a hand through my hair. This can't happen. This attraction. The almost-kiss. None of it. Not when I am looking for a Tulip to be my future wife. Guilt swarms my chest.

I sheathe my weapons and force myself to shut down my thoughts for the night. Never before in my life have I been blocked from my magic, been forced to fight without it, and it's more physically draining that I would have thought. I lay down, knowing I need sleep more than ever if we're to make it through this journey alive, but I lay there for a long time before sleep comes.

When I wake, my eyes burn, but we waste no time preparing to set off in the morning. Rupi returned sometime in the night, and Vera woke up overjoyed to have her nestled against her chest. I admit I am relieved as well—the small bird has grown on me.

"How's your arm?" I ask, sinking to my haunches near where Vera sits as she struggles to braid her hair with her injured arm. If I knew how, I'd help.

"It's fine," she says, finally tying the end off with a wince.

"That's my line." My lips twist wryly.

My words have their desired effect, bringing a small smile to her face and easing the tension at the corners of her eyes. I snag her hand in mine and turn it over, revealing the side of her arm that I stitched last night. She doesn't say anything as I remove the bloodied bandage. Being this close, I can feel her light breath on my neck as I work, and she smells good. It makes it difficult to focus. The stitched wound is swollen, and it looks painful. I can't hide a frown at the sight of it, but it's normal for this stage of the healing process.

"You stitch as neatly as any Healer," she says with appreciation in her voice, as I begin to wrap a clean bandage around it.

"A necessary skill on the battlefield," I mutter.

I chance a look at her eyes and see that my comment has triggered that fearful glint again. Probably for the best.

I stand and step away, needing distance. I busy myself by opening the map and scanning it, estimating where we are before we set off. "I think we can make it out of this forest in two days, maybe less. Then we'll be on fae land. If we make good time, we should be to Moneyre in five days."

Vera merely nods as if she barely heard me, trusting me to navigate as she croons to Rupi. My, how things have changed—she's beginning to trust me whether she recognizes it or not. I refold the map and pocket it once more, feeling renewed motivation to quicken my pace today. Vera keeps up, even as she's busy with Rupi for the next while, until finally Rupi swoops into the air and disappears into the trees.

The silence is comfortable between us until Vera snort-laughs through her nose, and I throw her a questioning frown.

"What?" I ask, not sure if I truly want to know.

She bites her lip in an attempt to stop a grin from turning into a full-blown smile, but it doesn't help. "Nothing... just thinking about yesterday." She giggles again.

"I don't recall anything particularly humorous about yesterday." My frown deepens as I think about the everwisps again, trying to figure out what she's talking about.

She laughs out loud this time. It's genuine and light, and I think I'd like to hear that sound every day of the rest of my life.

"Just say it."

She takes a moment to press her lips together and steady her laughter before she says, "Pretty impressive that she was able to pick up the scent of your... virility..." she snorts again, "over a mile away." Then her restraints fail, and she ends up in a fit of laughter.

I rub a hand over the back of my neck, shaking my head a little, unsure how to respond. I found that more terrifying than funny, but her laughter is so natural and warm that I can't help but smile because of it.

She continues, seeming encouraged by my embarrassment. "That's got to boost your confidence a bit, right? Attracting all the ladies without even trying."

And then she slams her mouth shut as if she knows she's gone too far, and I can't help but take advantage of the moment.

"*All* the ladies?" I ask in a drawn out voice.

Now it's her turn to be embarrassed—her cheeks pink in a flattering way.

"Well, I don't know." She stumbles over her words, looking everywhere but at me. "I mean, I assume... you know, that ladies like—you know..." Her eyes drag from my boots up to my face, and the pink deepens to red in her cheeks.

I smile, amused at how flustered she's become.

She abruptly stops walking and whips her pack off her back as fast as she can with her injured arm. "Hungry? I've got some jerky left in here," she mumbles, as she digs through for an extra long time, long enough for her blush to fade, I assume. She hands me some without meeting my eyes again and acts as if I burn her when our fingers graze, the way she yanks her hand back toward her. Then she hefts her pack back on and takes a bite big enough that she couldn't converse if she tried.

My smile grows wider, but I duck my head to hide it, aware that I've pushed her enough already. I feel the attraction between Vera and me. I've seen the battle of her will in her eyes as she thinks herself attracted to a criminal she's arrested. Sometimes I can see she's afraid of me—of what she doesn't know—and she should be. It's times like this, when she has practically admitted that she's attracted to me, that worry me because I have been fighting the attraction as well. I've noticed too many feelings toward her that lean toward affection, and that isn't acceptable—I can offer her nothing in regard to a relationship.

We walk in silence a little longer. I still feel frustrated that we fell into that everwisp trap in the first place, but I had no idea everwisps could *sense* virility. Since that is the case, they probably would have caught us somehow, even if I knew to watch for them, but the truth is, without my magic, my senses are as dull as a flat quill. It's frustrating beyond belief. As far as I know, everwisps only live in the Shift Forest, which is why I haven't had a lot of experience with them. I've seen some scary creatures in my life, but those ones top my personal list—never has a creature been after my manhood. A shiver creeps up my spine, and I shake my head to clear my mind. I'm left wondering—what else do I not know about in the Shift Forest?

Chapter 33

Vera

I f I ever get out of this cursed forest, I will never return. My arm aches and throbs, but I make sure not to show it. My criminal has already been acting overly protective today, offering me a hand over even the smallest of obstacles, wordlessly watching for blood on the bandage, and glancing at my face for signs of illness or pain like a hawk. He acts as if I almost died, and while his concern is sort of adorable, we don't have time to linger in these woods until he deems me ready to travel again. We lost half a day yesterday in our battle with the everwisps, and today we need to make up for it. Ikar and I are both fatigued and injured, and it's showing. Even though we push ourselves, we are slower than we should be. The weather is mild today, but the last three days it's been mild, and I expect a show of force from the atmosphere soon. I'm too tired to stress too much over it, Rupi always sticks close before a weather change, and she's currently nowhere to be seen. I shrug. She'll return by tonight, I'm sure.

Releasing my stress about the weather gives me space to think over what happened with the everwisps. I have a lot of questions now. And suspicions. That brown-haired vixen said she *knew what he was*. Pretty sure she wouldn't say that about him being a mercenary. Mercenaries aren't anything special unless a person is looking for a violent, honorless, weapon wielder to get a job done. When I think about it that way, though... yeah, maybe everwisps *are* attracted to mercenaries. But what if that's not what she meant? What if he's really not a mercenary... like he's said over and over again? If he's not, what *is* he? Assassin? Soldier? A famed hunter I've never heard of before? Women often love the hunter and soldier types. I'm ashamed of myself for falling into the stigma I've always mocked.

Ikar navigates a boulder-strewn portion of the trail before he reaches back with his hand extended to help me. While I usually wouldn't need help to traverse a path like this, without both arms at full capacity, it makes it difficult to climb. I place my hand in his larger one without hesitation.

Whatever he is, I no longer fear him, and it worries me—a lot. That healthy dose of fear kept my heart hard and safe, and now that it's gone, it's worrisome. I *have* to keep my end of this bounty contract. Renna is depending on me, and so is my future. I have to complete this job. For a second, I imagine the impending moment where I drop him off with the officials in exchange for a large sack of money. But even imagining the weight of the money in my hand is nothing compared to the feeling I imagine I'll have when I walk away from him. I swallow tightly, uncomfortable.

We begin our way up another rocky incline and finally emerge onto a wide path that appears to cater to wagons. Deep ruts eat into the earth on either side. I'm not sure what city comes next, but maybe we can find somewhere to clean up and possibly even hire a healer to fix my arm. With that thought, I quicken my pace, sufficiently motivated. Wagons mean civilization, right?

Apparently, Ikar doesn't agree. He pulls me back toward the side of the road, his eyes alert and his shoulders tense. I know he prefers the off-the-path routes, but this one is much easier to walk with injuries. I don't argue about it yet.

Instead, I decide this is the perfect moment for a distraction. "What did the everwisp mean when she said you are immune to her?"

Ikar hyperfocuses on a point ahead of us, rather than look at me. "That's the first I've heard of such a thing." His voice is terse.

"What about the part where she said she knows what you are?" I cock my head, waiting.

He finally looks at me, exasperation on his face. "Any other questions?"

I shrug with a guilty smile. "I'm bored." And I want to know. Badly.

"You don't believe me when I answer your questions anyway."

I regret the way I treated him in the cave. I know that's what he's talking about, but I still don't apologize. I can't, or it shows how far I've softened toward him. I walk close enough that I can bump him with my shoulder. "Come on, tell me. If she gets to know your secret, I should, too." I smile. How bad can it be? "You truly are a criminal and don't want to admit it, is that it?"

"What? No. I told you I'm not a criminal." His gaze scans the woods around us.

"But you are—"

He puts his hand over my mouth and listens as I continue to speak through his hand. "Sh!"

I stop and listen. The loud rumble of a wagon on this bumpy road is distant but growing closer. I almost bounce with joy and peel his hand from my face.

"Maybe we can hitch a ride," I whisper with excitement. I already feel the steamy bath, warm soup, soft bed.

Ikar grabs my upper arm and hauls me into the woods to our right, but there's not much space to hide before the trees drop away and we're left beside a steep hill. Steep enough that if we fall, we won't be able to stop. He shushes me with his blue eyes and keeps moving forward, completely silent. My own steps seem to magnify. No matter how I step, I find myself cringing with every crack and crunch of forest below my feet. How is a man his size so quiet?

But as the wagon grows closer, I hear sounds of crashing and movement through the forest behind us, it makes me want to forgo all my failing efforts at stealth and charge recklessly away. The only things that would be making sounds such as these are large, dangerous animals, and I don't want to meet them. Ikar was right. *Like he always is.* I purse my lips.

The sounds grow closer, but even though Ikar could probably run and maybe get ahead, I can't. *Dratted everwisp and her nasty vines.* When my instinct says to hide, to imagine myself as the smallest fern amidst this forest of towering trees, I fight it. Ikar doesn't stop, and there's no way I'm choosing to pretend to be a fern over following my criminal. He's proven over and over that he's my safest bet. He starts running, and I force myself to keep up. Leaves and branches slap my arms and face, bushes clawing at my clothing like they're trying to hold me back.

The mixture of growls that surround us, ahead and behind, tells me we've been caught, but we keep running. A great, hulking beast of an animal sends some sort of yipping signal to his friends, and within moments, we're surrounded by a group of shifters, some in animal form, some in human form. Either way, it's intimidating.

They don't wait long to demand our weapons. And when we refuse, an arm wraps around my neck and squeezes.

"Drop them," the voice says behind me.

"We mean no harm," Ikar says placatingly. "Just trying to cross the forest." He carefully lays down his sword and two other knives, along with his bow and several arrows. The enchanted sword lies among the assortment innocently. I can only hope these shifters won't know what it is, and we can somehow get it all back.

"Trespasser is what you are." The weapons are snatched up, and my neck is released. Someone roughly jerks my arms behind my back and forces me toward the road. I don't try to fight, even when my forearm burns with pain. The shifters in animal form have their teeth bared threateningly, and growls come from deep in their throats as they surround us. It feels like they wait for an excuse to rip our throats out. Ikar must sense it too, because he is surprisingly compliant.

Everyone kept warning about mate bond this and mate bond that. So far, the mate bond has been the least of our worries. The group of shifters tosses us in the back of some sort of low-level prison wagon, stripped of all our weapons. Our packs, everything except the clothes on our backs, have been stolen.

The wagon is like a large, rectangular, filthy coffin. Low and flat, I doubt the sides are more than two feet tall. I cringe as a heavy board is lifted up and slammed over the top, effectively cutting off all sunlight, and possibly even oxygen. My nose is inches from the top. It smells dusty, and I sneeze twice, my forehead almost hitting the board above us with the motion. A unique way to make sure prisoners can't escape since I can't even bend my legs enough to use any strength to push against it. I hear what sounds like someone latching the sides and then the creaking weight of someone taking a seat on top. The cracks that had been showing, letting in the tiniest bit of light and air, are gone. Never mind about the sunlight and oxygen. My chest grows tight, claustrophobia settling in.

"Now would be an excellent time to remove the cuff," Ikar suggests simply in the darkness. His voice low and smooth.

"Don't take advantage of the situation." I gasp between quick breaths. I'm on the verge of hyperventilation.

"I'm definitely going to take advantage of the situation."

I don't know if he's joking or not, but likely not, with the present circumstances. I don't know what to say. I finally decide on a simple, but wise, response. "No."

"Fine. We'll probably suffocate within the hour, but it's up to you," he says, like it'll be all my fault. I think I feel his shoulder shrug carelessly.

"It's up to *me*?" My voice is a rising whisper.

"I can get us out of here in five minutes, tops, with my magic freed."

Ikar is naturally confident, but this is over-the-top cocky.

Now I'm just getting mad. "You tell me you're not a criminal, but you sure lie like one."

This is not the time to play these games.

"Why won't you trust me?" He sounds angry now, but he keeps his voice low.

"Because you're a criminal."

He growls in frustration, and I turn my head in his direction, ready to scold him into silence. "Why can't you just beha—

My words are cut off when he looks at me at the same time, and we find our faces mere inches apart. The frustrated pull of his brow softens in the dim light, and I forget what I was trying to say. The claustrophobic feeling fades, the dirty prison wagon fades, and Ikar and I both move to close the small gap.

Then we hear a muffled yell with a snap of reins, and the wagon lurches forward. I yank my gaze back to the board above us as awkwardness fills every dirty crevice of the wagon. Is it shrinking in here, or is it just me?

I just almost kissed my criminal. Again. Hold up, *my* criminal? How long have I been calling him that? I start panicking. He's not mine. He's a bounty. I've never kissed any bounties. That's definitely on the *never do* list. Tatania would be so disappointed. And I *almost* just kissed him a second time. If anyone ever finds out about this arrest, I'm going to have a lot of explaining to do.

The wheels turning over dirt, roots, and rocks are noisy and awfully jostling, and we must have gone over some sort of slanted hill because I slide into Ikar, and my head hits the front of the wagon simultaneously. I do my best to wiggle back to my side. Once I'm situated again, I let out a long sigh, probably using up precious, limited oxygen by doing so.

What if he was being honest? What if he *could* get us out in five minutes? It's hot in here, I'm sweating, and it seems like it's harder to breathe by the minute, but I acknowledge that that could just be my anxiety. I bite my lower lip indecisively. I'm not sure where these people are taking us. Maybe they're going to deliver us to the nearest law office, and it'll all be sorted out without violence, but I doubt it.

"Ask me anything, and I'll answer truthfully, and in return, you remove the cuff."

Ikar and his bargains. I roll my eyes. "I don't need to know anything more about you." Doesn't mean I don't *want* to, but I force myself to stay professional.

"You asked me what type of magic I have. I'll tell you."

"I already know. You're a Hunter." Did he forget I've spent most of my last several years with Hunters? I guessed from the start.

"You've noticed the scar through my eyebrow, I'll tell you how I got it," he continues. "I'll get you out of here. Isn't that what you want?"

I give a sharp laugh. I *have* wondered about that scar. I wonder more about the large one on his thigh, but there's no way in blazes I'm asking about that one.

"The scar, right. Let me guess. You were fighting a death-stalker, and right before you delivered the killing blow it took one last swipe with one of its venomous claws and forever marked the handsome face of Ikar the criminal?"

"That's the second time you've said I'm handsome."

There's no way to come back from twice admitting my attraction. "Don't overthink it." My cheeks heat, and I find I'm actually grateful for the darkness provided by the prison coffin. I can practically *feel* his satisfied smirk. He's insufferable. An arrest has never gone so wrong as this.

"You don't want to know more about me. Fine. But my initial offer still stands."

But he doesn't know how wrong he is. I care much more than I should about him, and I want to know everything he will tell me. And I know exactly what offer he's talking about. The one where I remove a cuff from a Class A criminal, then start working *for him* instead of the law. It's never seemed as enticing as it does now. I feel my firm grip on the rule book weaken, an obvious sign I shouldn't make any sort of deal with him. Maybe I shouldn't blame it on the situation, but the heat in this wagon is unbearable. My clothing is plastered to my body, my hair a damp mess. I'm dirty, and maybe I'm over-thinking it, but it seems like it's getting even harder to breathe.

"Promise me you won't take off," I say, a flash of guilt is followed by hope that maybe he really can break us out. Even if it takes him thirty minutes, I'll be happy. I can have reasonable expectations.

His voice is deep and low and completely serious. "I promise."

"Are you going to kill me?"

"I could never kill you." I hear a smile in his voice, as if he thinks it's ridiculous that I would ask. Is there deeper meaning here? My heart patters giddily before I shush it. I must be pretty desperate if I think someone saying they won't kill me is flirting.

Then, he adds, "Besides, I need your help."

I can almost tangibly feel his urgency to move, but as I reach for his wrist, the cart stops, the lid to our coffin is wrenched off, and the men step away from the wagon and into the shadows, leaving us alone. Maybe they left. We seem to be in a dark cave, but I have full confidence we can find our way out.

"Well, that was just too easy," I say, sitting up with relief and wiping sweaty strands of hair from my face.

Then a voice echoes from behind us. "Welcome to my kingdom, trespassers. I am Silas, king of the shifters."

Ikar scoffs beside me, and I slap his arm and frown. We don't need more trouble.

But he ignores my warning and then he speaks in that commanding voice he sometimes uses, the one that's deep and solid and confident and practically forces you to obey. "There is no shift king. This land falls under the rule of the High King and is free for all to cross."

A wicked-looking knife appears suddenly beneath Ikar's chin, pressed to his throat. A drop of blood gathers and leaves a deep red trail to the collar of his shirt, but he doesn't flinch. Apparently, that commanding voice doesn't work here. A man with sun-bronzed skin speaks close to his ear.

"The High King?" he whispers with a deadly, deep, and decidedly cat-like tone to his voice. And by the looks of the hair on his head that can only be described as a very large, knot-infested mane, he's a big cat. I gulp. His shifter eyes glow eerily in the darkness of the cave.

"The High Kings who, one after the other, have failed to protect this kingdom? I have claimed this land, this forest, and it is mine. If ever I hear of a king here, high or low, I will hunt him down, and after a slow, torturous death, I will add his molars to my necklace." He lifts something, and I hear bits of bone clacking together. My face scrunches in disgust.

"And if you even so much as mention the *High King* once more, I'll add one of yours."

Ikar's jaw ticks, but I let out a breath of relief when he stays silent. Silas removes his knife and stands tall.

Another shifter closes in, swinging a sword artfully around as if he can't wait to strike us. Ikar growls, and I realize that swinging weapon is, in fact, his enchanted sword. The shift king turns and makes his way out of the cave, calling over his shoulder.

"Don't kill them now. I've been waiting for another competitor. This one appears worthy." And then he growls in a way that somehow sounds very much like laughter.

Chapter 34

Vera

We are roughly bound, led out of the cave, and separated. I have no idea where Ikar is taken, but I'm tossed into a large tent. A musty-smelling carpet of animal skins softens my fall, and though it's relatively normal for people to have rugs such as these, I find it creepy that shifters have animal pelts in their tents. I shiver and pick myself up awkwardly with my hands still tied behind my back, and stumble to standing. The thick tent walls block all the breeze and contain all the heat, and I immediately begin to sweat again. A wad of fabric comes flying through the tent flap and lands at my feet, then the guard unbinds my hands.

In a slithery sort of voice, he threatens, "You try to take off, and your boyfriend is dead. Got it? Put the dress on. You have three minutes before I open this flap again."

I purse my lips and glare at the shifter guard as he steps out. I bet he's a snake in his animal form from the sound of his voice and his beady eyes, but what do I know about shifters? I lift the hulking mess of material between two fingers and wrinkle my nose. The dress is an atrocious creation. I cringe harder and lean away. Are those tiny animal heads adorning the fabric? I hesitantly reach out to touch the whiskers of a small fox face about the size of my fist, almost expecting it to snap at me. I pull my hand back in disgust. I quickly avert my gaze after I catch a glimpse of a tiny squirrel head and a rabbit head with velvety ears waving limply about.

"One minute," calls the guard. I frown, pretty sure he's counting twice as fast as me. I hold back a strong gag and refuse to think about what is touching my skin as I pull it on.

The dress may be creepy as heck, but I have a feeling that if I choose not to put it on myself, someone else will ensure I do. I find that, gratefully, the back rises all the way to my hairline with a stiff sort of collar that comes forward in pointy angles. But apparently, all that fabric that makes up the back was stolen from the front. My bust is covered on either side, sort of. My cheeks redden as I look down at the nonexistent neckline that dips so low I'm sure I get a peek of my belly button.

I have no longer to worry about it. I quickly pull my braid free and pull every bit of hair that I can over my shoulders to cover what any decent dress already should before the tent flap flies open, and my hands are bound once more before me. Except now, if I let them rest against me, the very dead and dry nose of a raccoon face rubs my fists.

I'm led through the gates of a thick, smooth wall and up to a platform. Silas eyes my gown with pleasure.

"You've met my friends." His smile reveals large canines.

I'm not sure how to respond, so I don't. The man is strange. His half-open shirt flaps in the cool breeze, revealing a hardened chest beneath a smattering of golden hair. He places his hands on his hips and surveys the land before us.

"My arena." An eagerness lights his eyes as he thrusts his tanned chest out with pride. "This wall extends twenty miles square. A charm above and around to prevent any of my precious competitors from escaping. Perfect for our games." A glint of that animal inside of him shows in his eyes, and I instinctively step away.

I'm quickly yanked forward to stand beside a roughly constructed throne. And as soon as I'm in my place, Ikar and two other men are led before the platform, standing below us in the dirt. My eyes drink him in, flitting over his strong frame, his handsome face, his stormy eyes. I'm relieved to see no further injuries. Then, I remember the dress I wear. Not only is it as ugly as a decomposing deathstalker, but the boning along the torso is pokey and tight. And I can only hope the dead animal heads sewn at random draw the eye more than the amount of décolletage I currently bare. I have aptly named it the dress of death. I'm grateful I thought to intentionally leave my hair down, and I appreciate the cover, but then a cool breeze picks up, and my attempt at modesty is quickly defeated. I refuse to act like I care, lifting my chin in the air. Ikar smirks at me from where he's been placed in a row with the two other supposed criminals, and I narrow my eyes at him.

Beside me, the shift king takes a seat, sliding down into an easy slouch, one leg casually thrown over an arm of his rough wooden throne. The necklace of molars and other shapes and sizes of teeth around his neck makes me want to gag. I hear them click together as he shifts to get comfortable. His wild mane waves slightly in the breeze, and his gold eyes shine brightly with excitement. Another button or two of his shirt have come undone, leaving almost his entire torso bared. I wonder how long it will take before he sheds the shirt entirely.

My eyes drift back to the competitors. Ikar stands tall and broad, but the other two are formidable in their own right. I watch with fading hope as two shifters pat each competitor down, stripping them of any possible remaining weapons. All the same, I admit that if I were a betting woman, my money would still be on Ikar. I don't know the rules of this game yet, but I eye the cuff on his wrist. If ever there was a time I should have removed it, it was in that wagon. I swallow tightly with regret.

"Welcome, competitors," the king says loudly, and the crowd of spectators in the stands above us begin to shout and roar.

"Before us, we have the trespasser human, Ikar, and his lovely lady," he gestures from Ikar to me, then moves on to the second man. "One of our own, the traitor, Jyson! A bantha shifter."

The crowd boos and shouts, and then the shift king moves to the third man.

"Last, Enzyr of the fae, the murderer!"

The crowd shouts angrily in response.

"The winner will gain their freedom, and, in Ikar's case, the freedom of his lady as well. If there is no winner, she will be forfeit. To me." A pleasurable growl comes from deep in his chest as he sends a sultry smile my way. This is the first I'm hearing about this. I fix my gaze on Ikar with a silent command to win, but he keeps his face expressionless, his eyes on Silas. His hands are grasped behind his back, his natural confidence so obvious in his stance. I glance at the other two, who seem worthy competitors.

"I declare a hunt!" the shift king roars, two hands punching into the air. His voice sounds more animal than human now, as if he himself wants to leap to the ground and join the hunt. The bystanders cheer raucously. My hands are slick with sweat. A hunt won't be so bad, right? Ikar has proven himself by providing every meal of our trip so far. I've been fed better than ever. It'll likely be a fox, maybe even a deer or a moose. He can do that, even without weapons, I'm sure. I hope. Still, my heart races.

And then it screeches to a complete stop. A large animal is led into the space, two thick horns protrude from a brown face covered in fur, its snout ending with a black nose and its mouth full of sharp teeth that it is currently baring, though its mouth is forced closed with some sort of harness. It stands as tall as a horse, but its legs are thick and strong. Hard, reptilian-like interlocking plates cover its body. Its paws are as long as my foot and just as wide with long, wicked claws. My jaw drops. My criminal is going to be killed, and I'm going to be stuck with these crude shifters. And if I'm honest, I kinda like him and don't want him to die.

I throw my panicked gaze to Ikar and gesture to my wrist, hoping he gets the message. I have to release the cuff *now*, or I'll have murder on my hands. Without thinking of the consequences, I run and jump from the platform, my legs tangle in the dratted death dress. He's still several feet away, but if I can just touch the cuff—

Thick arms grab me from behind. I struggle in their grasp, animal heads knocking together on my dress. "This isn't a fair fight!" I shout. "He has a cuff." But my mouth is quickly wrapped with a filthy piece of fabric that's knotted behind my head and tangled in my hair painfully. I'm yanked back up to the platform roughly once again, and this time my hand is tied to the shift king's throne so I'm forced to lean down at an awkward angle. I hadn't realized how much more uncomfortable this day could get.

The shift king strokes a large hand over my fingers. "I see the animal in you. You'll fit in just fine," he purrs.

I meet Ikar's gaze again, and I see barely-concealed rage. If

I didn't know him better, I'd be afraid of him. I'm not sure if he's angry about the rough way I was treated and tied, or the creepy flirt from Silas, but he stares daggers at the shift king, unmoving aside from the muscle that's clenched in his jaw.

Silas continues. "The armored bear. Return with it dead, and you win your freedom." He smiles smugly, knowing as well as I that the chances are slim that any of them return without the help of weapons. The two shifters who led the armored bear into the space lead it to the edge of the forest, and very carefully, weapons at the ready, release it. With a huff so loud I hear it from where I stand, it's off and running, its deep grunts fading with my sight of it.

"Let the hunt begin." Silas raises his hands in a dramatic flair again, and the crowd roars with approval. With one last look, Ikar disappears into the forest beyond.

Chapter 35

Ikar

The man they called a traitor, Jyson, sprints ahead and mid-air shifts into his bantha form. Completely ignoring both myself and the fae, he runs ahead and disappears into the shadows. Eager to earn his way back into shift society, I suppose. I have no other form to shift into, no magic to use, so I begin to run at a slow jog, observing my surroundings and gaining my bearings. I watch the fae disappear ahead with a look over his shoulder and force myself to stay calm. I've worked with the best of the best when it comes to trackers, and I know what to look for.

I keep a steady pace and watch carefully, redirecting my course to keep the trail of the bear. But even with my extensive training, I know my chances aren't good. No weapons, no magic, and an armored bear to kill and somehow return to the Silas without the benefit of the extra strength my magic gives me. And, to top it all off, I have to be first. I hear Rhosse's rough voice in my head telling me to focus, and a grim smile crosses my lips. I hope he and Darvy made it.

I'm left in the quiet darkness of the forest. Birds begin to chirp, and the gentle rustle of bushes indicates small animals are once again active and no longer scared. I calm the stress rising inside me. The only way I can win this is with focus and wit, and I remind myself that fastest isn't always best during a hunt. I watch for anything I can form a weapon from, snagging a branch that feels solid enough and has somewhat of a broken point on the end. Though it's not much, and will probably snap in half on my first strike, having something in my hands helps ease the ache for my enchanted sword. I'd take even my smallest knife at this point.

I slow as I hear the unmistakable screech of the bantha shifter ahead and some distance to my right. It sounds as if a battle has already begun, and the hunt only started an hour ago. I curse beneath my breath. Warily, I move forward, and within several minutes, I'm crouching behind a tight bunch of large bushes, watching the scene unfold before me.

Jyson strikes at the bear, coming from above, slamming a venomous claw into its plated shoulder. It seems like a logical way to defeat it, and I warily wait for the bear to begin to stumble from the poison of his claw. But it doesn't. Jyson underestimates its swift reaction. With a lightning-quick swipe, the stocky bear's paw connects with his leathery bat-like wing, and I inwardly wince at the gruesome tearing sound. Jyson drops to the ground with a shriek and a sickening thud as he struggles to gain his balance with an unusable wing and missing claw. But the bear doesn't hesitate, barreling toward the downed bantha and ramming its horns into the weakened shifter's underbelly. In moments, Jyson is dead.

I could jump out right now with my stick and charge the bear, but that ensures a speedy death, if the bantha's fight was any indication. I eye the stick in my hand with disgust. As I deliberate over whether I should attack or go in search of a better weapon, a flash of color catches my eye and comes soaring out of the forest from my right, careening into the bear's side. The force of the hit slams the bear violently into a nearby tree, and I hear the crack of wood along the hefty trunk. While the bear struggles to gain its balance, the fae grips the edge of an armored plate and climbs astride. No one can say these criminals aren't brave.

With an ear-shattering roar, the armored bear regains its feet and recovers from its temporary stun. Enzyr quickly throws his arms around the bear's neck and tightens his grip with all of his fae strength. I've seen fae crush human bones in their fist, and it seems as if the fae's approach may get him the win. I'm about to jump up to battle the fae for the bear's last breath. I stand as it struggles, weaving and stumbling from side to side. One moment. Two. Three. I begin to make my way forward when it lurches to the side and slams its body against a tree, its neck connecting against solid wood. I don't want to consider whether the snap I heard was wood again or the fae's arm, but I see the panic on the fae's face as his arm is rendered useless. I step back and crouch down a bit since it appears the fae isn't giving up yet. He grabs the same plate of armor and holds on, attempting to get a better position to squeeze the life from the animal with just one arm, but in the next moment the armored bear effortlessly tosses the fae from its back, then charges with teeth bared. I look away, and when I look back, Enzyr is dead, too.

Just the bear and me now. In minutes, it has killed the other two competitors. No wonder Silas has difficulty coming up with competitors when he spends them like a reckless gambler at a game of cards.

The armored bear's sides heave, the plate the fae used is lifted and loose, and a bantha claw sticks out of another piece of its armor awkwardly. But it otherwise appears unharmed, as if it wasn't just attacked by two worthy enemies. The bear sniffs at the carcasses at its feet before it lifts its nose and sniffs the air. I wait, worried it'll sniff me out when I have no sound plan, but finally, it turns and lumbers off deeper into the forest.

After witnessing the gruesome destruction of the shifter and fae, I take a second look at my crude spear and slam the end of it into the ground in frustration, surprised that alone doesn't break it in half. Practicality, reality, whatever you want to call it seems to shout that all is lost. Vera, my magic, my life, my kingdom. As I sit here, cuffed as a common criminal, my kingdom continues its slow march toward death. There's a good chance my closest friends are dead, and I'm further from a solution to restoring magic than I was before I started this journey. I've been so busy keeping Vera and I alive the past few days that it was easy to push away the thoughts that failure was my destiny. But here, I'm reminded of all of it. It seems as if whispers of demons fill my ears. *Unworthy. Weak. Failure. Murderer.* I almost expect to feel the burn furthering its blackening journey across my mark. Magic's tangible reminder that I am failing. It doesn't come, but it will. It always does.

I grip my spear tighter. I may not be able to save the kingdom before it's consumed with gloam, but I can do my best to save Vera from mating with the insane shifter. I haven't failed until I die, and I don't plan on doing so today. I box the disaster of my life up and shove it in a corner of my mind, quieting my thoughts. I stalk from my place of cover, standing amidst the carnage as I consider my next move. I have no doubt I can track the beast, but I know before I do, I need a plan.

The fae, attempting brute force, failed. The bantha shifter, attempting to poison through armor, failed. I eye the stick in my hand, then the bantha claws still attached to Jyson's large paws. I recall the weakened armor and quickly get to work.

A short time later, I finish securing three claws to the tip of my spear, if you can call it that. I twist it back and forth, examining my work and frown. Rather than looking like a deadly weapon it resembles a crudely built, three-pronged garden rake. It will have to do. If Darvy saw me now, he'd be rolling with laughter. I grin sadly.

I take a moment to find the trail and set off with my poison rake in hand. It doesn't take long before I come upon the bear near a creek, sniffing out berries. I wonder if the red around its mouth is berries or blood from the dead fae. I eye the loose armor plate and readjust my rake. The bear lifts its head and sniffs, searching. I remain crouched, taking slow, silent breaths. My chances of success drop significantly if it charges me. I notice as the bear wanders closer that a few of the armor plates have been damaged, I assume due to other violent battles. This one is a seasoned fighter.

I wait as it wanders closer, mere feet from my position, before I launch myself forward, and my fingers clamber for the jagged edges of the imperfect plates to pull myself atop its back. I feel as the bear begins to react, raising up on its hind legs to attempt to toss me from its back. A flashback of the bear slamming Enzyr against the tree briefly flits through my mind. I hurriedly grab the loose armor and thrust my poison rake claws into the soft, vulnerable tissue beneath before it can do something similar to me. The bear roars again, shakes its heavy, armored coat, and swipes back with an enormous paw. Its claws catch my armor, and it easily throws me through the air. I land with a bruising thud several feet away, flat on my back.

My breath won't come, but the bear is. I'm like a gasping fish as I try to call back necessary breath. Dread pools when I realize that the bantha poison, my stick spear, wasn't enough. My worst fears come to pass. *Failure.* Dead before I can help my people. Vera stuck with Silas. I hope with my last thought that the magic goddess, Lucentia, will have mercy on my people with my death. That a new, more worthy king than I will be chosen to save them.

Already on its hind legs, I watch as it rises above me, its shadow covers my body, and I prepare myself mentally for its death blow. Its roar sounds muffled to my ears mixed with ringing and spots in my vision. It lifts a clawed paw and swings toward me as it falls and lands in a dusty heap beside me, a heavy, lifeless arm falls over my torso.

I lay there in silent disbelief, sucking in lungfuls of air. I stare at the gaping mouth inches from my face until I can breathe again. Then I pull myself from beneath its weight, lifting its massive arm off my torso and wincing at the pain in my back. It seems my already shredded armor couldn't protect me fully this time, but there's no time to worry about it. At this point, I hardly feel it as it's masked by amazement that the bear lies dead beside me. Maybe Lucentia can use me yet, a light sense of hope accompanies the thought.

Next step, bring the bear back. This has to be some sort of joke for Silas. I eye the bear. If I could pull magic, *maybe* I could haul it back, but that day is not this day. It has to be hundreds of pounds, maybe thousands, much heavier than me. My gaze catches on the mouthful of teeth again. Silas seems to like jokes. We'll see if he can take a joke as well as he can play one. I hope what I'm about to do is enough.

Awhile later, I haul my aching body from the forest, forcing my back tall and my shoulders straight as I once again enter the open space before the platform. The sun is setting now, and the smooth walls of the arena reflect its orange glow, as though everything is on fire. Before anything else, I search out Vera, and though her mouth is no longer tied, I find her still bound and tied to the king's throne. She no longer stands, but kneels. Hot anger bunches in my muscles at their treatment of her, but I won. Soon. Soon this will be done.

My eyes then shift to Silas, but as soon as he spots me, he raises his brows, and I know he questions my return without the prize. I stalk forward until I'm at the edge of the platform. I know I'm taking a very big gamble, and I can only hope it'll work in my favor.

"A tooth for your necklace, *shift king.*" I can't help the emphasis on his self-proclaimed title as I place the bear's tooth on the platform in front of him.

The lion considers the tooth with a growing grin on his face. Another shifter quickly scoops the tooth up and drops it in the king's hand, where Silas tosses it up in the air and catches it again in a practiced way.

"You return without the prize, trespasser."

"You didn't specify how much of the prize was to be returned." I shrug nonchalantly.

Vera's eyes are wide with fear and concern, but I resist looking at her. I don't want to fuel Silas any further.

The spectators watch the two of us in near silence. The guards around us seem wary, and I don't blame them. Silas is unpredictable. Even now, instead of anger, I see his considering eyes gleam with something that looks like glee.

He looks closely at the tooth for a moment, then tosses it back to me. "You have earned your *own* freedom. Not that of your lady. It's a generous offer when all you've returned with is a single tooth." His smile turns to a smug sneer, and he runs his tongue across his elongated canines as he looks down at Vera.

My chest tightens with rage. If my magic was uncuffed,

there would be a severe amount of damage. This entire thing is fraudulent, and I can stand here and do nothing but fist my hands. Vera's gray eyes are wide, shocked, panicked. A light breeze blows strands of hair across her face, and I'm taken aback how even clothed as she is in a dress of animal heads and horrific ruffles, she's achingly beautiful. I swallow hard.

A gate to my left is pulled open by three shifter guards.

"Leave, or I'll kill her," Silas commands, as he holds a gleaming knife to Vera's throat.

I shove the tooth in my pocket and glance once more at Vera, then stalk out of the arena without looking back as guilt churns in my gut. *Failure.*

Chapter 36

Vera

I watch as the large gate closes behind Ikar with dread settling in my stomach. *He didn't really leave me here. He's cuffed, and he was forced. He'll be back... right?* I can't name the look in his eyes before he turned and left, but it's not the sort of look I imagine someone having before they leave someone behind. Even with that intense look he gave me, I can't help but wonder as I'm roughly pulled by my tied wrists back to the musty smelling tent if maybe I'm so much trouble that he's decided he will be better off without magic the rest of his life. Wouldn't blame him for it. I never intended for this arrest to go this way. Never before, in all the contracts I've accepted with bounty hunters, has one ever been so wrought with wretched obstacles. And never before has a criminal drawn me in like Ikar. It's probably for the best he's gone free. If we did happen to stay together, it seems as if our lives would be destined for danger and forbidden love.

As we leave the arena, I hear Silas roar to the crowd, "In two days, another wedding!" The response from the crowd is so loud my ears ring.

Another wedding? How many has he had? Just as I thought I'd avoided a romantic entanglement with one criminal, which I actually feel sad about, I find out I'll be forcibly married to another—who's much less desirable—all in less than ten minutes.

I'm delivered back to the tent full of dusty animal pelts, my hands tied tightly together at the wrists to wait for my impending wedding. The ropes are so tight I'm sure there'll be red welts. My forearm throbs. I sit there in shock for a long time. This is the closest I've ever come to wallowing in self-pity before. Worse even than when I was lost for a month on that first Class A criminal contract I accepted—at least then I was free. A few tears begin to drip into the matted fur of a rabbit, making it smell even mustier and gross, so I stop them pretty quick. It's difficult to be appropriately emotional while smelling that.

Even as I dry my tears with my shoulder and try to quit sniffling, I consider my situation. Is this it, then? The rest of my life, I'll be one of a number of wives to an eccentric, self-declared shift king who kills people for entertainment? The charmed bracelet on my wrist unfortunately doesn't protect me from anyone but a king. I should clarify, a *true* king. And that's only if he tries to find or bridge with me. As Ikar so bluntly stated when we first met Silas, the shift king is not recognized by law—my bracelet does nothing against him. I can only hope the mate bond I have with Ikar will keep Silas from trying to bond with me so I can eventually escape. What did Miss Mate License say? The bonds last for six weeks? I think that's right. I have six weeks to escape, minus the couple of days we spent traveling already.

If I don't escape, what will Mama Tina do when I never return for a visit? What will the Tulips do... and Renna? I feel a wave of guilt for not thinking about Renna more these past few days, I hope she's found another contract since it's not looking like I'll make it back to help her. My eyes begin to well up with tears that I have to work to stifle before they hit the furs again.

When the day passes into night, and then into morning of the next day, and I haven't heard or seen any sign of Ikar, I come to the painful realization he may have truly left me here. Or died—but that's not likely. I thought I noticed the mate bond dot on my wrist glow a little brighter in the night, but it appears normal in the morning, and I think I just wanted to hope for something. For Ikar to be close. For Rupi to show up. Anything.

My animal heads have stared at me for the last day and a half and kept me company during the night—even if it was forced—so I consider us acquaintances by now. They seem a little friendlier after all this time. It only makes sense to name them, so I do. When I get done with that, it's noon, and the guard comes in to spill water into my mouth and leaves a large piece of crumbly bread on a horribly dented tin plate before he leaves once again. I refuse to think about where my food has been as I choke it down. Then in my panic and stress, I'm talking to Darla, the fox with the cute tiny whiskers, and nothing against my new silent companions, but that's when I realize that this will be my life if I don't do something more.

Instead of talking, I busy my mouth by tearing at the ropes with my teeth. I figure if I'm doing this, I won't find myself accidentally having one-sided conversations with the animal heads attached to my dress. I don't know if I'll have teeth left after, and I don't know how I'll get out of this forest without Ikar, wherever he is, but I'm getting out. Don't know if I'll ever even see him again, but one thing he's taught me is to fight. I continue to pull and wiggle and tear against the ropes around my wrists. Hours pass, the suns set, and eventually, the only light comes from a lamp outside the tent door where the guard sits. And finally, I'm left with a mouthful of filthy rope fibers, aching teeth, raw lips, and close-to-bleeding wrists, but I'm loose.

One benefit of a floor covering of animal furs? It's quiet. Don't want the snake guard hearing me. I think he's a snake, at least. His S's sound sort of hissy like that. I silently creep along the perimeter of the interior of my tent, silently shushing my animal heads as they knock together while I search the edges of the tent for anywhere I may be able to squeeze through. On hands and knees, I finally find a place where I can slip my hand beneath. I kneel there on the filthy pelts, listening. I've heard sounds of some sort of celebration with tribal drums and shouting all evening, a distance away. All I can hope is that most everyone is busy there. My heart beats almost in my throat as I shove my head beneath and begin to try to wiggle my shoulders through. It's tight, and my arms are still stuck beneath the tent at my sides. I can't see anything but dirt and grass, so when a hand covers my mouth, I begin to struggle in panic, sure that snake shifter found me.

"It's me. Quiet."

Ikar. I try not to be so excited. I really shouldn't depend on him so much, but I admit that if I was free, I would have launched myself into his arms in relief. I was doing just fine on my own, wasn't I? But it feels much better to have a friend by my side. If only I considered him just a friend.

"You came back," I whisper after he removes his hand with a little too much surprise in my voice.

"Of course I did," he whispers back like he's offended I said that while he grabs beneath my shoulders and pulls as I continue to wiggle through. Pretty sure I'm going to have a dress full of dirt by the time I'm free due to the nonexistent neckline of this frock, but I'll take it if it means I get free. We get my arms loose, and he continues to pull while I wiggle harder, trying to get my hips through. I've never felt more ridiculous in my life.

"My dress is stuck," I whisper, panicked. This is taking too long.

Ikar curses and kneels by the tent to tug the animal heads through. I almost tell him to be careful with Collette when I see how he pulls on one of her delicate rabbit ears, but I catch myself and press my lips together. I don't want to see the look he would have given me had I said that out loud.

And then the guard comes trotting around the corner with a raspy growl. My eyes meet his glowing ones. A wolf, then. Hm. Definitely not a snake guard. It appears I do not have a talent for guessing a shifter's form. Ikar jumps to his feet and launches toward the wolf before its teeth can catch onto my shoulder. While they battle it out, I continue to wiggle through, talking my animal heads into submission until I pull myself free and come to standing. A few minutes later, Ikar drags the lifeless wolf into the tent, leaving me a moment to hurriedly pull my hair forward to cover up what the dress doesn't.

When he returns a few seconds later, his warm grip finds mine, and he tugs me behind him and into the shadows at the outside of the large shift camp. If we get caught, I don't think Silas will allow Ikar another chance to fight for our freedom. My palms begin to sweat within Ikar's grasp.

We sneak past an unmoving guard. I don't know what Ikar did to him, and I don't ask. He leads me carefully around the shift camp, and I don't see any other dead guards, but I'm sure there are more. He pauses here and there to wait for guard rotations. I don't ask how he knows, I just follow. We finally dart into thick forest after we watch two guards head to our right, conversing quietly as they make their rounds. The sounds of the tribal celebration have faded into the night now, and all around us are the normal sounds of the forest.

We creep through dirt, shrubs, and low-hanging tree branches in the darkness. Ikar stops suddenly, and I squint to see into the darkness. The moons light a wide open field with dim whiteness, revealing what looks like a pack of some sort of flying animals. All I see are large wings glinting in the moonlight.

"What are those?" I whisper.

"Sharp flyers."

I can't see much. The forest is dark and gloam magic lurks, increasing the shadows, but it's obvious the creatures are huge. Other than their size, I can make out no details no matter how I strain my vision.

"On the count of three, run."

"Do you know how to ride one of these?" I whisper warily. "What exactly is it?"

"Best if you don't know. One, two, three." He jumps up, pulling me with him. I gather a wad of the dress in my hand to clear the way for my feet, and we charge across the field, but as we near, I tug back instinctively. The beasts were huge from a distance, and now they are enormous. My eyes are drawn first to the long, curving neck that ends with a flat-shaped, wide head. A horrifying mix of dragon and scorpion. And to my horror, I hear the click of pincers that I can barely see in the darkness. I step back, my eyes trailing down the reptilian neck, the insect-like jointed six legs. I see the smoothness of the creature's skin reflect the small bit of moonlight and then there's a huge saddle in front of my face. Behind the saddle, on either side, stretch long, translucent, razor-edged wings. We stop beside it, and I'm not sure what I expect to smell, but I find I'm strangely comforted when it's simply leather. The one we stop beside towers over Ikar by at least three feet. I see the foot grip of a saddle dangling at the height of his shoulder, and wonder how people even get on.

"I think this is a bad idea," I whisper, my eyes still focused on that odd, flat head and the pincers. *Gag.* But Ikar ignores me, his hands busy running over the saddle. He finally finds what he's looking for. His hands grip what appear to be handles built into the thick leather, and he jumps and pulls himself up, high enough now to force his left foot into the foot grip and swing his right leg over the other side. The beast shifts two steps to the side, and I jump back in fear. This is a terrible, terrible idea. I just know it's going to buck him off and come after me. But Ikar rubs its long neck and murmurs something I can't decipher to it, like it's his favorite horse. I hold my breath, but it seems to work, and the beast stills. Ikar leans over with a hand out, and I have a decision to make.

"I'll sit behind," I say firmly, best to keep some distance from my handsome criminal. I am entirely too happy he returned for me, and I might actually kiss him for it if I get the chance. So, backseat it is. And also to avoid that disgusting head. I shiver a bit.

"You sure about that?" Ikar looks over his shoulder, and I follow his gaze. In our rush to escape, to steal one of these creatures I have never seen before in my life, my focus on its head, I haven't taken the time to truly see what it is. Why it's called a sharp flyer. I thought it was the pincers, the sharp-edged wings. Now, I see. A deadly, sharp stinger, like that of a scorpion, and nearly the full height of me, hangs from the end of a large, curved tail. Dangling just above where I planned to seat myself. *No. Just, no.*

Though I can't see his face well, I can sense the smirk that he surely wears, and I eye his outstretched hand. But I can't do it. I can't ride this monster.

"Plan B, Ikar," I whisper yell, aware that there could be guards around, but unable to force myself to grab his hand.

I hear sounds then from behind me.

"This is the only plan. Now, Vera," he says firmly.

I hear running. And then, one-by-one, huge magic-fueled lights begin to spark on around the field, illuminating everything and waking the rest of the sharp flyers. This is not good. The beast begins to side step nervously, one of its six jointed legs almost bowling me over before I jump out of the way with a yelp. I look over my shoulder and see a large group of guards spilling onto the field. I cringe, grit my teeth, and grab Ikar's hand. He pulls me up like I'm a sack of feathers and plants me in front of him. I hurriedly settle myself as far ahead of him as I can. The dress is forced up to accommodate my position on the saddle, revealing my knees and lower thighs. I gasp in horror— I'm not one for revealing attire. I'm the girl that dresses like a man and is mistaken for a boy, not an everwisp sister. I tug at it while Ikar nudges the sides of the sharp flyer with his heels like he would a horse, and I prepare myself to take off into the air. But there's no wind in my face. It doesn't move. He tries again, slapping the reins. Still, nothing.

"You've flown one of these before, right?" Every time I tug on one side of the horrendous dress, it reveals more of the opposite thigh. On one side, Darla stares at me, the other, Collette, the rabbit. I forget the dress—it's covering the most important parts. Barely. I blow a piece of hair from my face and grab the saddle with both hands.

"This'll be a first," he grunts, as he continues to try different things to get it moving. He clicks his tongue, pulls the reins in different ways, everything. I pretend like he didn't say that. I pretend like he said he has one of his own that he rides for fun on the weekends, and he knows exactly what he's doing. I look back at the guards, completely illuminated in the bright lights. One of them shouts something at us, and others are already running our way. A few have nocked arrows, others have swords drawn. They can see us just as clearly as we can see them. A distant roar that sounds much like Silas meets our ears, and I gulp. It sounds as if he just found out his newest fiancée escaped.

"Your magic. Try it," he practically shouts in my ear.

My hands fumble around in the air like an idiot as my thoughts scatter like fall leaves in a chill breeze. I have no idea what he's asking me to do. I pull lucent into my hands, it webs across my skin this time, and I place both my hands on the creature's neck, sending magic to it. But still, nothing. I look over my shoulder, panic making my magic flicker.

"Focus." Ikar pulls his sword, prepared to fight if I can't get this monster moving.

If I can talk to dead animal heads and make friends, I can talk to this big guy. I close my eyes and send more magic, speaking like I saw Ikar do to calm it. "Fly, Sharp Flyer."

It begins to move with a strange, skittering gate. We start out slow, and then the ground begins to blur beneath us, and before I can scream, we're in the air. I dare not remove my hands or my magic, worried I'll lose the connection and we'll tumble from the sky. It climbs at a steady pace, and I refuse to look to one side or the other. I clutch its disgusting, reptilian-like neck as hard as I can, my back ramrod straight and my thighs already burning from my attempt to keep my seat atop this odd, horrifying creature. Tears stream from the corners of my eyes from the force of the wind, but I don't lift a hand to wipe them away, even as my dress blows up and billows around me. Good thing Ikar is behind me.

I take a deep breath and let it out. *We did it.* I'm about to smile when Ikar wraps his arm around me and slams me back against his hard chest as the creature takes a sharp right, and we dive. I lift off the seat with the force of our plunge, and my stomach rises and falls again, my dress following the same motions as the yards of fabric blow up in front of me. I think I'm going to be sick. I swallow it down and try not to fight the motion of movement. I use Jasper, the raccoon, and Greta, the squirrel head, to tuck the dress and hold it beneath my thighs. I try to tuck my long hair into the back of the dress, since someone forgot to finish the front, but the wind is too much, and it pulls free and fans out wildly, slapping and stinging my face. I hear Ikar growl irritably behind me, and with it, the creature wobbles and turns like it doesn't know where to go.

Even for a beginner, Ikar is doing horribly. "You need practice," I call over my shoulder, grinning as I imagine the frown he'll surely make.

An arrow shoots past, I hear the whistle and cringe away out of instinct. So, maybe he's doing better than I thought. I didn't realize we had attackers behind us.

"Your hair!" he shouts over the wind as he lifts his chin high to avoid it and still see. And I realize that if it's in my face it's most definitely in his.

Another arrow flies behind us, this one catching Ikar's coat and leaving a flapping tear in the arm. He pulls back on the reins, his arm gripping me against his chest still as we take another sharp turn. I don't want to free my death grip to gather it, but when I do, I'm horrified to realize I've been gripping Ikar's thighs and not the saddle. My face burns, and I'm grateful he can't see it while I grapple wildly to pull my hair in while he's straining to see through it. I see another flyer come up to our left, its rider nocking another arrow just as I get my hair under control.

"Take the reins." Ikar shoves the thick leather straps into my one free hand.

I try to tell him I can't steer this creature with just one hand, but my words are lost to the wind.

He grabs an arrow and nocks it, then takes aim. "Power this." He keeps his eyes focused on the shifter flying across from us.

I've never done something like this, but I quickly pull a little lucent and direct it into the enchanted arrow by releasing my fisted hair and touching it with my hand, Ikar's magic is still blocked, and he can't do it himself. That cuff is becoming more and more inconvenient. It doesn't take much before the arrow glows and he immediately lets it fly. It finds its mark, sending the rider soaring to the world beneath us.

The riderless sharp flyer immediately pulls back, the slack reins signaling its freedom. I hope Ikar doesn't notice how white my magic is. I bite my lip even as I adjust the reins in my hands and try to gather my hair with one hand. The next one is above us, and I see the arrow aimed at Ikar just before he releases it. With one hand still on the reins, I pull the sharp flyer hard to the right, watching as the arrow barely misses as we cross beneath the other and end up on its left.

"A little warning next time," Ikar grunts, as he climbs back on to the saddle from the side where he slipped off from the sudden movement.

I nod, more scared than I'd like to admit that he'd almost fallen.

"Magic," he calls again as he stretches the bow tightly, once again aiming carefully. I give up on holding my hair, pray to

Lucentia that he's too busy aiming at the enemy to notice the color of my magic, and quickly touch the arrow. It glows, and he immediately sets it free, but the other flyer dodges, his flyer spinning to the side, and I have no idea how he hasn't fallen off. It makes me wonder if I have more influence over this creature than I realize. Strands of my hair rebelliously whip around my head, making me feel like some sort of sharp flyer goddess.

My hands still glow with lucent, and I press one to its neck. I'm not sure if I have to touch the beast now that I've established a connection, but better safe than sorry. I speak to it again as I tentatively pull back on the reins, thanking it, even as another arrow whizzes by.

I glance above us and find the flyer still there, and an idea comes to mind. I don't know if it will work, but these stingers have got to be useful for something. Another arrow comes at us, and I press myself against the flyer to avoid being hit. While I'm there, I speak to it again, this time with my thoughts as lucent sparks between it and I. *Slow down, and quickly rise behind the other.* I visualize it as I speak to the creature, and I don't know if it senses my plan or knows my words, but surprisingly, it obeys.

"Brace yourself!" I shout, but it wasn't enough warning, and Ikar falls against my back with a grunt as I slide forward against the pommel of the saddle with how quickly it slows, then just as quickly, it's rushing forward again, but this time directly behind the other flyer. *Use that stinger.* It seems to greedily eat up the air between the flyer ahead of us, and with deadly accuracy, the stinger raises, and Ikar and I slide forward as its body moves up almost completely horizontal with its attack. I tumble forward onto its neck, my face almost on top of its flat head, and then it lashes out with its stinger, and the rider is ripped from his seat and tossed out into the open air with a scream that fades as he falls. The stinger falls back to its normal position and then it turns to avoid crashing into the other flyer that, without the guidance of its rider, has slowed its pace. Its turn has me slipping around its smooth neck, and I scream, finding myself dangling above open sky from beneath it, grasping with both arms. Sheer terror overtakes me.

"I've got you! Let go!" Ikar shouts, as he grabs my upper arm tightly.

I shake my head, my eyes squeezed shut.

"Let go! Now!" he shouts again.

I release my grip, knowing that if he fails, I die. With a hard yank, Ikar pulls me back up and into his arms. I shake with nerves and shiver from sweat that has cooled from the high atmosphere and its cooler air. My body feels numb all over. My dress blows up in the front like an enormous balloon again, animal heads flapping around me. I shove it down with a growl, using Jasper and Greta to once again tuck it beneath my legs to maintain some semblance of modesty.

Wordlessly, Ikar wraps a strong arm around my waist and pulls me close against his chest, placing me snuggly between his strong thighs and opening his coat wider to share his warmth. I should argue and push his arm away. I know we can't be together like that, but I realize how close to dying I just was, how tired my muscles are, how warm he really is now that I'm here. And I revel in the fact that he came back for me. Admittedly, though, a lot rides on my safe arrival to the city so he can have his magic back. Some of the joy sucks out at that thought.

I'm stuck on top of a terrifying monster, wearing the dress of my nightmares, higher in the sky than I've ever wanted to be. I've just helped kill two people who were trying to murder us, and I'm still low on money and in over my head with a criminal I never should have arrested, who doesn't really seem like a criminal at all. It feels good to let everything go for a moment. I breathe in the cold, fresh air. *Just a moment.* Then I'll be back to sitting on the neck of the monster, trying to tuck dead animal heads beneath me so they don't hit me in the face, and will be distant once again from this very warm and handsome bounty, ready to finish the journey to get the bounty reward, save Renna, and free myself from this job.

I finally stop shaking and relax bit by bit, my body and muscles exhausted from stress and nerves, and finally settle my back against his chest. But with every bit of my body that relaxes against him, a different sort of warmth ignites. I'm hyperaware of each strong breath his chest moves with, the way the stubble of his beard catches in my hair. The way the muscles in his arms and legs tighten and move on either side of me as he takes over leading the sharp flyer. This is what I was afraid of, why I sat practically on the creature's neck to keep my distance. I'm content. Where moments ago I was terrified to be flying so high, now it is a haven, and I never want to land. I lay my head back and revel in the warmth of his coat around me, the smell of leather and a musky scent that's *him*. He's capable and strong, and I feel brave and safe with him. He seems just as comfortable as I.

A thought wiggles its way through my mental wall. Could this criminal be reformed? I've heard of it before. I bet he wouldn't care about my mark, about what I am. With his history, he probably wouldn't even blink. Maybe, if he chose to live on the right side of the law, we could—

No. I give myself a mental shake. There is no more than this moment. *Enjoy it while it lasts.* I gather my wandering, impossible thoughts, tuck them away, and relax a little deeper against him.

Chapter 37

Ikar

We've been flying for several hours now, and the first sun has almost set, taking its light with it. After seeing Vera almost slip from the monster, I instinctively pulled her to me and held her close in relief. But instead of putting the usual distance between us right after, this time she relaxed. Her small frame in front of me, safely tucked into my coat and sharing my warmth, feels too right for a man destined to marry another woman. I swallow tightly. To her, I am a criminal, a bounty. And sometimes I wish that's all I were because then I could choose to be with her, and I would.

I gave her a mocking smile when I saw her stand on that platform so proudly in this strange dress, but the mocking was to hide my awe at her beauty. Even wearing animal heads and ruffles that most women would die before wearing, she draws me. Now, the fabric is all tucked around her, revealing shapely, creamy legs, and with the wind, her hair no longer covers what she attempted to cover on the platform. I keep my eyes safely on the horizon and distract myself with questions. Unlike most Originators, Vera does not dress to show her mark. Now that I think about it, usually every inch of her, from ankle to wrist, is covered in clothing no matter the heat, and I wonder why. There are many things I don't understand about her. I sense the secrets she holds so close, I don't completely trust her because of it, but I'm drawn to her anyway.

I'm not sure how far this creature will take us, but I know that it has saved us many days of travel through a forest that turned out to be much more trouble than we ever expected. Our last stop is the Fae Kingdom, as Vera has so stubbornly required, before I can get to an authority to get the bounty situation cleared up. I feel torn between my rush to get to Moneyre to, hopefully, meet up with Darvy and Rhosse to continue my mission and lingering and spending more time with Vera. I remind myself that these moments are all we have, and then we're done. It'll do no good to develop further feelings for a woman I can't be with.

An hour later, as the second sun begins to set and we are left with the little light given off by the third, the sharp flyer begins to descend. It was not at my guidance, so I assume we've gone the distance it will take us. Vera shifts and wakes before me with the change in speed and direction. She tilts her head up with a smile, warm from sleep to meet my eyes, and she pauses there. Time stops. Her mouth is mere inches from mine. If I lower my head, my lips will meet hers, and I imagine she tastes like the warm glowing sunshine that is drawing out the gold in her hair and reflecting a hint of orange in the gray of her eyes. Her lips part like her thoughts are one with mine, and I nearly groan. With torturous restraint I didn't realize I had, I pull my eyes from her lips back to her eyes and then out to the sky ahead of us.

"We're about to land. Our sharp flyer has taken us as far as he can go." My voice is rough with want of her. I swallow it down.

She straightens wordlessly and once again shifts forward in the saddle, and I feel cool air where moments ago there was warmth. *Necessary distance.* The creature circles and slowly brings us back to the ground, landing gracefully even with its odd, insect-like legs. I watch as Vera leans forward, presses her hands to its neck once again and seems to thank it. In the meantime, I dismount and scan the field where we've landed. It looks safe enough, no immediate danger. The flora and trees seem more fae than shift forest to me now.

After determining which direction to head, I turn to reach for Vera, but instead of accepting my help, she hops to the ground beside me. Back to the usual then.

"You can remove the cuff now." I offer my wrist to her. I've more than earned my freedom at this point.

She pushes my hand away, rolling her eyes. "If you're so capable you can kill an armored bear without any of your weapons or magic, you'll be fine until you can prove your innocence."

I'll take that as an odd sort of compliment.

"I just saved you from marriage to a shifter," I argue, dropping my arm heavily.

"Thank you." She smiles too sweetly, then grabs the fabric of her dress and hitches it to her knees before making her way forward.

I shrug, less disappointed than I should be that I'm still her bounty, and quickly catch up to her.

Chapter 38

Vera

I may have grown fond of these animal heads, but I miss my trousers, boots, and my loose shirt. I used to be mistaken for a boy, but I wonder now what I would be mistaken for. A creature risen from the depths of the Shift Forest is what I look like. My hair is a mess of snarls from the windy ride, and it adds the perfect touch of 'mussed underworld goddess' to my outfit. The dress snags and catches on every branch I pass, and I jerk so hard once that I hear a loud rip. Ikar muffles what suspiciously sounds like a snort, and I whip my head around to glare at him. He looks at me with complete innocence, acting as if nothing happened. I'd like to see him traverse these woods in a dress such as this. Who knows what's crawling around in the layers of this dratted outfit? I'm forced to hike it up to scramble over downed trees and rocks that block our way, baring more skin than I ever have in my life. Ikar respectfully keeps his eyes averted, but I feel like my cheeks are one never-ending fire.

While I carry my fisted dress in my hands, I hear familiar birdsong. I glance around, searching eagerly. I've been worrying for Rupi for over two days, and my heartbeat picks up in pace. I don't hear it anymore, and I wonder if I imagined it, but I grin widely when a moment later I see her bobbing through the air. I stop and angle my shoulder out for her to land, but when she sees me, she quickly changes direction and aims for Ikar instead. I frown as she flutters to his shoulder, and he greets her with a stroke of his knuckle. I haven't seen her since two days ago, or was it three? I admit that I'm a little hurt she chose Ikar over me.

Ikar chuckles at the expression on my face. "It's not you. It's the dress."

My dress? I look down, spreading the fabric wide and revealing four animal heads from the folds. Rupi gives a trilling chirp and hops closer to Ikar's neck, her feathers knife-like quills as she eyes Jasper, Collette, and friends. Ikar winces when she attempts to nestle up. I don't envy him there. I've felt the pricks of her feathers, and it burns.

"Can you put the heads away?" He winces again and tilts his head as Rupi trembles in all her sharp glory against his neck.

I sigh and let the fabric drop. He's right. It appears I'll have to choose between the animal heads and Rupi when we reach civilization.

I step away, and Rupi calms, but even when I try to get her attention by waving a hand full of her favorite birdseed, she won't look at me. She acts as if she's been betrayed. Ikar takes the seeds, and I watch, slack-jawed, as Rupi hops to his palm and begins cracking the seeds happily, acting as if I'm not there. Moody bird. But the scene holds my gaze for a long moment. Seeing my tiny fluff of a bird hopping around in Ikar's large, calloused hand isn't something I'll be forgetting anytime soon. My mood softens toward both of them. It's not their fault I was forced to don this dress.

After Rupi's reaction to my frock, I'm even less inclined to wear it, so after it snags once more, my patience snaps. I stop with a huff, but when I reach for my knife, I remember it's not there. *None* of my stuff is here. I sigh heavily. It's going to cost me to replace it all. I curse Silas.

"I need a knife." I place a waiting hand out in the air. Ikar slowly slips one from his collection and places the handle in my hand.

I immediately set to work, jaggedly sawing away the lower length of ruffles, careful to avoid any of my friendly animal heads. They don't deserve to be cut off, even if Rupi hates them. It now stops at my knees, the front a little shorter than the back with my hasty tearing. Without the added length and weight of the ruffles, it poofs out slightly, resembling a party dress. A very creepy party dress. I worry I've made a huge mistake when a breeze blows by, and I quickly press the fabric down with my hands, but I find I don't need to—the animal heads will weigh it down sufficiently. I pat Jasper, the raccoon head over my left thigh in thanks before I hand the knife back, and we continue.

"Did you just pet one of those heads?" Ikar appears genuinely concerned for me. Rupi quirks her head on his shoulder, and I get the feeling she is, too.

"You would too if you spent a night alone with them," I respond with a little spice in my voice. "You know, if you would have returned sooner, I wouldn't have had to become friends with them in the first place. What took you so long anyway?"

His mouth opens, but I get the feeling he doesn't know where to start with what I just said. Ikar is often quiet and broody, but this is the first time I've seen him speechless. He rubs a hand across the back of his neck and shakes his head.

He's still shaking his head. "No. You cannot be friends with dead animals," he says firmly.

I respond quickly with some attitude. I've been waiting for an explanation. "Too late. You were going to tell me what took you so long?"

He eyes the animals on the dress again in exasperation. "If I'd known you made friends with dead animals, I would have left you," he mutters.

My jaw drops with a sharp laugh. "You didn't just say that." I punch him in the arm, and he laughs, stepping away with his hands up in a placating gesture.

He's still laughing when he begins again. "You know I'll always come back for you." There's a look in his eyes that I really like. While a warm, happy feeling curls in my chest, he continues, his voice more firm and his jaw set in that down-to-business way again. "But I had to get my weapons back first."

That cools the warm feeling real quick.

"You rescued your weapons *first*?" Maybe I don't have a crush on him anymore.

"You sure appreciated them when I killed the guards to get us out of there."

I can't argue with that. "Fine. But next time, be faster. I thought I was going to have to marry Silas."

He laughs under his breath, and I revel in the light feeling that lingers between us.

We journey through forest so deep sunlight no longer shines down through the needles of the fir trees above us. But in the sun's absence, the beauty of the fae arises around us. Tiny beads of water cling to plants, grass, and leaves like the tiniest of sparkling crystals. The colors of the flora around us have deepened considerably, and everything seems of a jewel hue, rich and deep. We come to a bridge that is obviously fae, built by the best, and it shows. Beautiful bits and pieces of the highest-quality wood are fit perfectly together in intricate designs and dramatic pictures, guiding travelers across. As a teen, I'd thought it was so romantic. The fae and their potions, their criminal minds, fancy clothing, and their crafting of picturesque villages high in the trees. I'd even had a fae boyfriend here years ago, who, I'm sure, has moved on by now.

"Let's just stick to our original," I say decisively, preparing myself for the coming introductions.

"That I'm a criminal? Or mercenary?"

I smirk and lift an eyebrow. "So many options."

He gives me a dry look, absent a smile, and I almost laugh out loud.

"Let's go with criminal," I say. "That way we're not lying."

"It's a complete lie," he deadpans.

I stop walking and turn toward him. "Look. My aunt can read me like a book, so our best bet to keep you safe is to go with what we are already familiar with. Which is you being a criminal. Besides, it hasn't been proven otherwise."

"Fine." He starts walking again, but I see his jaw tick.

"You don't like playing the criminal?" I almost laugh.

"I hunt criminals."

"You do?" My eyes light up with interest. "Tell me more. My bounty hunter skills could use some improvement."

Ikar chuckles deliciously. "Some?"

I toss a narrow-eyed glare at him.

"You almost got me killed. Several times."

He's making some excellent points this afternoon, and I don't like it.

"No need to bring up the past," I say tartly, "but I should mention that my aunt and her friends won't like you, so be prepared for that." I shoot a warning glance at him. The fae have some of the strictest border crossing laws, and they don't like visitors who hang around too long. On top of that, Mama Tina is very protective of me, her only niece.

"I'm not concerned about whether your family likes me or not."

"That's rude to say." I try not to be disappointed by his practical response.

"It's not rude. It's a matter of fact and circumstance."

"Well, it'll probably be best for both of us if you just stick to your room and be quiet until we leave." It's true that it doesn't matter. We aren't together like that, but it's easy to pretend he's mine with this mate bond glowing on my wrist and catching the sunlight. I twist my wrist so the small dot catches a bit of sunlight that appears through the trees.

"You ever figure out what flavor of bond you bought?"

He glances at my shining wrist. "It's how I found you."

I twist my wrist back and forth a few more times, enjoying the sunburst-like sparkles before the shade blocks out the light again. "It's a good thing we had one then, even though apparently you never needed one." I remember the everwisp commenting on that, I'd forgotten I'd never really gotten an explanation for that.

His eyes quickly dart to mine, and I find them guarded. The corners of his eyes are even creased a little in worry. He's not usually so reactive, which is interesting. I meet his eyes thoughtfully, deciding whether I should press it or not.

"Want to tell me why that is?"

"Not particularly." He stares straight ahead now, and I feel a bit of tension settle between us.

I shrug, willing to let it go. Doesn't apply to him being my bounty, so I figure if he doesn't want to share, I shouldn't push it.

The tension fades as I begin to tell him about Renna and my frustration with her boyfriend, which somehow leads into some of my more interesting bounty contracts. He listens, and we laugh off and on as I share some of the odd and humorous things I've experienced. I get too comfortable and don't see that the conversation naturally leads to his next question.

"How did you get started with bounty hunting anyway?"

That's a loaded question if there ever was one, but I decide it won't hurt to share the short version.

"Soon after I turned nineteen, I broke up with a boyfriend and needed space." I shrug. "It wasn't just that, though. My mother's sister, who everyone calls Mama Tina, took me in after my parents died, and I truly loved living with her, but I felt like I needed to make my own way. Ya know?"

"And you caught on to it, just like that?" he asks, surprised.

I give a derisive laugh. "Unfortunately, no. I was overconfident and needed money. The first contract I took was for a Class A criminal, and it didn't go well."

Memories of that day still rise up in my nightmares sometimes, and now that we're talking about it, the images begin filtering through my mind. I keep talking without thinking.

"The criminal killed the hunter, then almost got me, too. I ran but ended up lost for a month before I found my way back. I told myself I'd never take a Class A criminal contract again." It wasn't until I said it that I realized I shouldn't have.

"I'm considered a Class A criminal."

I sense the question behind the statement, and he looks at me closely.

My mouth is very dry. How do I explain the urgency of Renna's need for money without giving away who we are? "Renna ran into some serious financial problems and needed help. I did this for her."

He nods with understanding. "I would do almost anything for my closest friends, as well." I sense the sorrow in his words. He's not spoken of Darvy and Rhosse, and I feel guilty that I haven't thought to care until now.

I surprise myself by slipping my hand into his, and I hear a quiet chirp from Rupi. "We won't know until we get to the High Kingdom. Don't lose hope." I feel him grip my hand a little tighter for a moment. I expect him to drop it afterward, but he doesn't, so we walk through the forest hand-in-hand the rest of the way, and our conversation moves to lighter topics.

I find that he shares freely when I ask about Simon and Arrow, the hawk and dog he mentioned while stitching me up. The guardedness leaves his eyes, and he launches into details about their training and hunting expeditions. Most include Darvy and Rhosse as well, but the sorrow doesn't touch his eyes like it did before. I smile a little as I listen, enjoying the sound of his voice and hearing about his life. For days, all I've wanted is to reach Mama Tina and be done with this trip. But now, walking hand in hand and talking about life, I find I'd rather stay here with Ikar. The thought tries to make me uncomfortable until I smother it. Not now.

Chapter 39

Vera

J ust before the suns set, signaling the end of the day, we reach one of the entrances to the fae. This one's more commonly used by only fae, but there are other more easily found and recognizable entrances for visitors. This one is a tiny door that sits between two enormous boulders, and since I'm half fae and lived there for a time, I can use it.

"Here it is." I hope the charm word is the same and speak it quietly. Immediately, either the door grows larger or we shrink, I've never figured out which, and we easily walk through. It slams shut behind us, and we are left standing before a circular set of stairs that winds up and around the inside wall of the tree as far above as we can see.

I regretfully pull my hand from his and begin to lead the way up the stairs. Rupi flies ahead almost eagerly, disappearing above us around the circular staircase. I assume we'll find her at Mama Tina's.

The burn in my thighs is forgotten in my eagerness to experience the beauty of the fae again. Their attention to detail, even on these hidden-away stairs, is easily the most beautiful artwork I've seen in my lifetime. Each stair is engraved with small pictures that cover the surface, probably charmed, since they look no more worn now than they were ten years ago. I hate to step on them, they are so beautiful. I pause for a moment, my eyes begging to linger on some of the engravings, but I continue up.

When we reach the top, we step out onto a balcony, a wall of greenery the height of my hips surrounding the edge, a protective barrier, of sorts. We are so high in the trees that the ground is no longer visible when I look over the edge. Before us, a single path leads off the balcony and into the city. From that one path, several paths join and spread, connecting tree to tree in a seeming maze of fae-crafted walkways, similar to the first one we crossed to get over the canyon. Small multi-faceted crystal orbs sit in ornate wooden posts standing at calculated intervals, lighting the paths before us with warm, golden light. Greenery grows artfully between the crevices of the paths and around the waist-high rails on either side, vining leaves drip off the edges and down toward the ground below, so long they disappear into the black below us. We step onto the first path, and I breathe in the scent of pine, fresh earth, and a light flowery scent with a hint of honey.

I lead Ikar over one path, then another, and more until we reach a set of stairs that winds around an enormous tree, this time around the outside of the trunk. The stairs stop at a small, but ornate door built into the trunk. I knock softly, and a moment later, it swings open.

"Mama Tina!" I greet the aged woman before me with a grin.

A broad smile lifts the deep wrinkles of her face. "Come

here, my girl." She opens her arms wide and wraps them tightly around me when I step forward. Tears prick my eyes. I've missed her more than I thought. I'm glad all over again that I'm not stuck with Silas. After a moment, I push myself back, deciding it's time I introduce Ikar.

I gesture toward him. "This is Ikar, a Class A criminal I'm taking back to Moneyre."

Mama Tina's eyebrows rise high as she looks him up and down, sizing him up with pursed lips. His armor and coat are the worse for wear, torn up at the back and sleeves, add to that the dried blood on his shirt in various places. His beard is no longer a shadow, but a full week's growth, his hair mussed, and anywhere you look on his person, there's a weapon sheathed. Mama Tina for sure won't like him—he's delightfully dangerous looking. I stuff a laugh back down my throat at his expression. That dark and broody look, the one he always wears that makes my breath a little tight, adds to our cover—and his intrigue—though I know he's not trying.

I tried to warn him that Mama Tina wouldn't like him, so he shouldn't appear so grumpy about it. But after eyeing him closely, Mama Tina leans in close to my ear, speaking loud and clear. "I'll take him."

I choke on my spit a little. "Mama Tina." I only half-jokingly scold her with my voice, but my eyes are bright with censure. She ignores me and slips her hand around Ikar's bicep and proceeds to pull him into her house. Rupi chirps with approval from her perch in the sitting room to the left, and I frown. What is happening?

Mama Tina is so old no one ever gets upset at her often highly inappropriate comments, or her clothing for that matter. My cheeks are hot, and I can't look at Ikar. Instead, I eye her dress as I follow along behind them. It looks like a repurposed drape. Most fae wear beautiful clothing, I know from experience. When I turned sixteen, Mama Tina gifted me a spider-silk dress that was so delicate I'd been afraid it would fall off me if I sneezed. I'd only worn it once, but I knew it had cost a fortune. I know her tastes are nice, even elegant and expensive, but she persists in wearing bold colors and awkward fabrics. Even with all that, she's the most elegant and beautiful woman I've met.

She shifts her attention to my dress over her shoulder, arm still tightly wrapped around Ikar's. "I like the high-low design of the cut, but the animal heads are a bit much, my dear."

If even Mama Tina thinks that's the case, this dress is even worse than I thought. An exasperated sigh escapes, which is promptly ignored as Mama Tina smiles up at Ikar, who returns it with one of his dangerous half smiles.

She has eyes only for Ikar as she says, "I'll show you to your rooms. Come along, Vera."

I'm left to trail behind the two of them, who continue arm in arm. I quickly swing by Rupi's perch to urge her on to my finger. She knows there's another one in my room, but she side-eyes my dress with disdain before reluctantly hopping onto my finger. We start up the stairs, and I catch sight of Mama Tina laughing with Ikar, almost to the second floor. I purse my lips. Mama Tina is entirely too approving of the criminal I brought home. This is unacceptable. I march up the stairs behind them, not able to hear what Mama Tina is whispering to him as they lead the way. It's not that I thought she'd be concerned about his criminal status, but concerned that I was alone with a criminal of his caliber. Apparently, she doesn't care who I spend my time with as long as they look like Ikar. Good to know. I huff out a breath as we reach the landing at the top of the stairs. It's circular with plush carpet and five doors evenly spaced around the wall in a semi-circle.

The fae look like the most delicate of creatures, but they are strong. So strong that, if they aren't careful, their grip can shatter human bones. Along with that, they are magically-gifted with the ability to glamour their looks. Only enough that they can mask the color of their hair, eyes, clothing, and other surface layer things. I didn't inherit those gifts, being only half fae. I also didn't inherit the tendency toward criminal activities like the rest of them. I should have figured that Mama Tina wouldn't mind me bringing a bounty home. He'll fit right in.

I don't need her to show me to my room. I know exactly which one it is, so I squeeze around them and hurry to the door as she leads Ikar to the next room over to the right.

"There is food in the kitchen, if you're hungry." She eyes both our overall appearances with a raised brow, "And I'll send up a bit of healing potion." She turns then, and the light catches her dangling peridot earings—her fae artifact. While she often glamours them to match whatever peculiar outfit she's chosen to wear out, at home she rarely does so.

Mama Tina says over her shoulder, "Oh, and Renna arrived three days ago. I'm sure she'll be happy to see you in the morning."

I breathe out a sigh of relief. Renna is safe. One worry down, innumerable more to go.

After a quick glance at Ikar, I quickly slip into my room and close the door behind me. Rupi immediately distances herself, flying to the gold perch complete with a small rope, a bell, small mirror, and a fancy birdseed tray. She lands on the rope that stretches from one side of the perch to the other and promptly begins to drag her small beak through her feathers, cleaning them in small motions.

I step a little further in. My room looks much the same as it did the last time I was here six months ago, but mostly, it's how it feels. Like home. I embrace the familiarity, especially after the week I've had. After my parents died and Mama Tina took me in, I felt like too much of an outsider to fit in with the exclusive fae. But with Mama Tina heading the way for me, I soon became comfortable here. Along with introducing me to fae society and helping me build a life as a teen here, she'd helped me design my room, and I'll never change it. The wood of my bed and dresser are light and elegant, all straight lines with beautiful, natural texture. Two large, floor length windows let in warm light in the mornings, and both are framed by floor length drapes that puddle on the ground elegantly. My bedspread is soft as spider silk and piled artfully with an assortment of pillows and a deep green, thick rug lies beneath my bed. I'd leap onto that tempting pile of pillows, but being within Mama Tina's clean home, I find I can now smell my dress. I wrinkle my nose and rush into the bathroom.

Somehow, a hot bath has already been drawn. I wince as I unwind the bloodied bandage around my arm, the injury a puffy hot mess. Hopefully, with a bath and a few healing potions, it'll be healed in no time. I strip the dress off next, making sure to arrange it in such a way that I can bathe without the animal heads staring at me and spend the next hour soaking in perfectly lovely steamy water with my favorite scented soap to wash my hair. As I dip my shoulders beneath the water, I think how tempting it is to just stay here. I never really *had* to leave. Mama Tina actually encouraged me to stay with her. But from the moment she learned I paid dues to the Tulips, she never seemed to approve, no matter how I tried to explain it, and I never felt right about using her generosity to pay them. Instead, I made my own way, and I paid my own dues, as it should be. She still sends my payments, though it's with pursed lips and disapproving eyes, but I don't complain. Admittedly, it wasn't just my independence I was seeking when I left. There was also Drade.

I still remember when he'd returned triumphant from the challenge to be low king. The fae are the only ones who determine their low king based on pure strength and intelligence. The other kingdoms' kings are born to their positions. We'd been courting for over a year, and he'd never told me he planned to do it. It should have been a time we celebrated together, but it was the opposite. Because he'd become a low king, he unknowingly made himself unavailable to me. I had to leave the people I'd tried so hard to become part of.

A piece of my heart still feels cracked. That was the moment I realized I didn't truly belong anywhere. I'm not full fae, and I'm not full human. I'm a Tulip who doesn't even quite fit in with her own magical kind, and my parents had died. I broke up with Drade on the spot, and ever since, I've been on the run. I'm not friends with kings. I don't date them, and I don't marry them. I'm a Tulip, and that would never be okay. I donned men's clothing for protection and gave up on romance. That was years ago now, but I still wish I'd handled the situation better. I know I'd hurt both him and Mama Tina in my rush to leave. While I've made things right with Mama Tina, I don't plan to have that chat with Drade.

When the water cools, I step out and wrap myself in a fluffy robe. It appears that during my bath, a silver tray with three bottles of healing potion was delivered and sits, waiting, on my dresser. I rush toward it, prying open the cork of the first one with my teeth, holding out my arm, and carefully dousing the injury with it. It sizzles and pops, but there's no pain, merely a fuzzy, warm feeling. It smells like vanilla and warm berries. I sigh in relief as Ikar's careful stitches are closed and the thread loosened by the liquid until I can pull it away painlessly. I use up the other two bottles to get it completely healed, but when I'm finished, only the smallest hint of a thin scar remains. I press my lips together, not sure how I feel about a permanent reminder of that night. My cheeks warm at the thought of it.

I pull the robe sleeve down my arm to cover it and head to a tall wardrobe that sits in the corner of the room, opening the long doors which swing out to either side and revealing several evening gowns. Along the bottom, beneath the dresses, is a large drawer. I pull it open, and my eyes track across the unique assortment of items I've gathered to stock the shelves of the shop I hope to open. This is only a portion, the rest stored in a room here in Mama Tina's house. I frown, thinking of the beautiful comb nestled safely inside my pack. The pack that is currently lost somewhere in the shift forest, along with my only weapons. I sigh. No clothes, no pack, and no weapons. My stomach turns, thinking of asking Mama Tina for a loan. I groan, almost shoving the drawer shut, but my eyes catch on my mother's journal and the book that she used to read to me set inside a couple of nested fancy painted bowls at the bottom of the drawer. I grab the books, then close the drawer and turn to sit on the wood floor with the wardrobe against my back.

Rupi flutters from her perch by the window and hops into the folds of my robe as I open the journal to a page in the middle where a bookmark of pressed flowers is still where my mother left it and smile. She was known for her green thumb. Around our home, the plants grew lush and abundant, the trees wide and tall, nearly engulfing our small house. I wonder what she would tell me about Ikar. Would I find advice about how to manage wayward feelings in these pages? I read small parts here and there, some about plants, some about healing. Most of which she had already taught me. It's all very practical, nothing about feelings or dating or what to do when you find yourself crushing on a criminal. I sigh and flip to the beginning where she'd written the stories that she'd told me at night.

One was a powerful story of Lucentia, the goddess of lucent magic. It was the kind of story that every young girl loves to hear. Lucentia was a revered woman, said to be the embodiment of magic. The image on the left side of the page catches my eye. Lucentia, the woman the Black Tulips are named for. At least, that's the way my mother portrayed her in an intricate sketch, using the description that was passed down through the ages. A woman in a beautiful black dress faces the side of the page, her golden hair tumbling down a shoulder to reveal the black tulip mark at the base of her neck. Black tulips and the whitest of small, fluffy birds fill the rest of the page around her, a woven crown of black tulips around her head and a white lucent orb in her hand.

Rupi hops onto the page and attempts to gently peck at the woman. She's always loved this story. I trace a finger over one of the birds. They look so similar to Rupi, but I've never seen another one like her with my own eyes. My gaze then moves to the woman's profile. I tilt my head in thought. It seems I have nothing in common with this legend. The woman in this picture appears elegant, the set of her shoulders sure and confident. I practically feel her power emanate from the page. I twist my lips to the side, feeling small. Definitely not how I'd describe myself.

Lucentia made a deal with the kings, but no details were ever written in this book, and I wonder what they could have been. Nothing good, I assume, since Tulips are now a hated bunch. We are the pigeons among doves. Whatever she'd done must have been horrible.

I wait until Rupi hops away from the page and shut the journal, then pick up the bound book that I'd been given as a Black Tulip. I open to the middle of the book, and my chest tightens at the black and white picture. A terrifyingly beautiful woman with a black tulip proudly displayed on her neck is depicted with her foot atop her king's head as a numberless crowd of his people bow to her. At her side is a tall figure cloaked in black and smoky wisps and clouds of magic waft around their forms. It really is creepy. Rupi pecks aggressively at the page, ripping a corner away.

"We don't peck books, Rupi," I scold. She knows better, so I frown at her for good measure.

I scoop her up and set her on the floor. I'd read the story before and chose not to revisit it. That's the story the Originators used to turn the kings against us. The vision the supposed seer saw. I don't know if it's true or not, but it's generally accepted as such. I flip to another page. This one has a picture of a frail looking Black Tulip engulfed in a plant prison, her face gaunt and hollow, a symbolic bridge of flowers connecting her and the king, who turns a key in a lock, sucking the life from her. Rupi chirps angrily and flaps her wings until she's back on my lap and pecks again at the page, making small indentations even with her stubby beak, then her feathers burst into sharp quills, sticking into the page. When she won't stop, I finally lift it away and slam it shut.

"Fine. I won't read it."

Her feathers return to normal, and she takes a moment to fluff them indignantly, then she flies back to her perch to shuffle across the gold bar and stare at herself in the mirror. I shake my head at her antics. Moody, like I said.

I move to my knees and place the books back in the trunk and close the latch. But though I shut the books and put them away, the reminder is still there. I climb into bed and pull the covers up to my chin. This is why we don't trust kings and why I can't wait until I don't call myself an Originator any longer.

Chapter 40

Vera

I spend the next afternoon chatting with Mama Tina and Renna. We sit in a beautiful, circular sitting room with windows lining the entire back to look out into the deep woods. It's cozy and comfortable, and I never want to leave—it's my favorite room in the house. Rupi has joined us, perched on a tall, elegant bird stand Mama Tina had custom made just for her. She rings the gold bell with the tap of her tiny beak, and a maid slips in to place a small pile of cut fruit and chopped nuts in her tray. This is exactly why Rupi *loves* to be at Mama Tina's. I smile a little as she dives into her feast.

I sip a cup of hot tea with honey and a hint of lavender and fiddle with pieces of my squeaky clean hair as I listen to Mama Tina update me on the current fae happenings and gossip. She makes sure to add in a large piece about Drade and his success, which I promptly ignore. I'm relieved when she moves on to other topics, but the one we settle on has me tense once again.

"So, Ikar." Mama Tina tips her cup and takes a delicate sip as she stares at me over the rim of her fragile cup. I know that stare. Rupi stops crunching the tiniest piece of chopped nut I've ever seen and looks up, too.

"What about him?" I frown, feeling my defenses rise. There's no way I can keep my feelings a secret if Mama Tina decides she wants to pry.

"You like him."

Renna chimes in, too. "Yep."

I swallow in a strangled sort of way and look down at the blanket that I've curled up beneath. I twist a loose thread around one of my fingers. I could go off about how he's my bounty, simply a criminal I'll promptly be dropping off to officials as soon as we get to Moneyre. But I know if I choose that route, it'll just drag the conversation on longer.

"A little." I don't look up, but I hear a contented, short trill of song from Rupi. "It can't work, though. If he's truly not a criminal, he's a soldier, which is worse. Too close to a king," I almost whisper. Saying it out loud hurts and makes me face reality. I finally look up and see understanding on their faces. Mama Tina is the only non-Tulip, besides Lillath, who knows what Renna and I are. And suddenly, I want to share more.

"He offered me a contract." I laugh like it's ridiculous, but Mama Tina's next words cut it off.

"Why not take it?"

"He's likely a criminal. That should bother you," I say with accusatory eyes.

"His heart is good. I sense it." She glances at Rupi on her golden perch where she pauses her cracking once more at the attention. "And so does Rupi."

She chirps in the affirmative.

I simply stare at her, frowning. Then I look at Renna, and she simply shrugs as if saying, *"Why not?"*

I drain the rest of my cup, unsure what to do with Mama

Tina, Renna, my feelings, Rupi, or my criminal. How did life get so complicated?

"I've planned a small get together tonight. I've already sent for dresses to be delivered to your room and a suit for Ikar." She stands and brushes out the wrinkles of a dress with so many pleats I can hardly tell the pattern of the fabric, but I think I see frogs and bright pink flowers, and lots of light blue.

I pull my gaze from her distracting attire. "You're inviting my bounty?" I ask with humor in my voice.

"For purely selfish reasons, of course. He will look absolutely dashing in the suit I've chosen." Her eyes glitter with excitement. "I need to speak with the chef about tonight." She gestures toward a nondescript, folded parchment on a side table nearby. "That arrived just a few days ago, and thank goodness I didn't forward it right away since you've come for a visit. Until tonight, girls." She smiles, and with a whisk of pleated dress, she's out the door.

I set my teacup down and stretch over the side of the couch to reach for the parchment. My stomach tightens with anxiety as I rip it open; communication outside the annual meetings is rare and unusual.

I motion Renna over. "It's from the Tulips." She sets her cup down and scoots closer, until we share the page.

My eyes quickly scan the message.

Dearest Queens of the Night,

Tulip dues have been the same amount for over thirty years, and to keep up with increased costs, it is my duty to inform you that we can wait no longer to raise them. Our bracelet charmer will no longer work with us if we do not agree to the increased costs, and we all know we can't have that. If any of you are in need of help to pay, please contact me right away, and we will figure this

*out together as the sisters we are. See you in one week's time, my
flowers.*

At the bottom is the total amount due in one week. I curse
out loud, and Renna gasps quietly. My heart is a frozen chunk
of ice in my chest. The amount is large, a third more than we
were asked to pay before. A third I don't have for myself or
Renna. I will have to give my own dues, all the funds I make on
this job, and all my savings to cover both mine and Renna's
dues. Everything I have. All my work to save over the last years
to open my own shop, to not call myself an Originator... It's all
gone, sucked into the never-ending abyss of Tulip dues. Anger
streaks from my heart, pulsing through every vein in my body
as I crinkle the parchment in my fist. I'm done.

Anger hardens my voice. "What kind of life is this? To live
behind the mask of an Originator, hiding, living in fear, and
destitute. I just took one of the most dangerous contracts I've
ever seen offered to make enough money to protect myself from
the *kings*." The irony hits hard. "I am much more likely to die
on one of these reckless, money-making contracts than if I let
the dues default and lose the protection of the bracelet. I'm
certain that no king is going to start sniffing me out. Tulips are
nobodies. Obsolete. Weak. Originators are all the rage right
now."

"Don't say that—any of it," Renna says quietly. "You're just
upset right now." I see the concern and stress in her eyes, along
with guilt. I feel bad for speaking my thoughts aloud without
thinking, but all of it's true.

Immediately, all the opportunities begin to filter into my
brain as I consider how much money I could save and what I
could do with it if I no longer pay the dues. Am I brave enough
to cut my link with the Tulips? To live on my own? Tears burn

behind my eyes, and a scoffing, sharp laugh erupts from my throat. I don't need to be afraid to live on my own, to support and protect myself. I've been doing it for years while simultaneously supporting another penniless Tulip.

With every rip of paper, I feel more free. Soon, the parchment is in shreds in my lap, I gather it into my hands and toss it into the nearby crackling fire with finality.

Renna is pale, watching the pieces burn. "What will we do?"

I don't answer right away. As I watch the shreds turn to ashes, Ikar's offer comes to mind. He's proven over and over again to be honorable this past week. I admit that's not a very long time, but I trust him. He even said he could get me out of becoming a bounty myself when I let him go—I didn't even know that was possible. Do I trust him *enough*? He offered double the reward money. I'd have more than enough to get my shop off the ground, be able to rent that beautiful, perfect space, and still help Renna, too. It would be the perfect way to show myself how strong I truly am. If I can survive a trip with my criminal such as the one we've had, I can be an Originator for a group trying to find a simple plant. A trip into the Lucent Mountains may be dangerous, but at least there would be purpose behind it, and I *need* purpose right now. Part of me screams in terror and panic that I'm making this decision, the other wants to run and sign the contract with Ikar immediately.

"We don't pay the dues. At least, I won't," I say bluntly.

"What?" I hear the panic in her voice.

"I'd rather be found by a king than continue to live the way I have." A small bit of regret for my impulsive words grows in my chest, but the guilt doesn't smother the bitterness that rises. "I love my Tulip sisters, but the organization of the Tulips has offered me nothing. I don't see the value. I promised you I'd help you, and I will if you want to pay the dues. I don't leave for another day or two, so you have some time to think about it."

Renna nods and looks down at her hands. A maid enters the room just then, pulling me from my thoughts. "I've been sent to assist you."

The party. I almost forgot. I look toward Renna. "Are you joining us tonight?"

She nods. "I'll be there."

"Good, you can help me reign Mama Tina in." I say lightly over my shoulder as I leave the room while both of us know that *no one* can reign Mama Tina in.

She smirks and wiggles her fingers in a silly wave, but I see the tension in her eyes. She's worried for me, and I get it, but I'll show her that it'll be okay. I have a plan.

I follow the maid back to my room, tucking my newfound decision away. I'll inform Ikar later and hope that the terrified side of me doesn't win out. I feel like a rebel—it's foreign and uncomfortable and terribly exciting. If I don't pay the dues or show up for the meeting, it will be the first time in my life that I've gone against the rules of the Tulips. I twist the bracelet around on my wrist. The first time I will be vulnerable to being found by a king.

Chapter 41

Vera

The maid who curled and styled my hair into a half-up half-down masterpiece left the room a few minutes ago. I know I should go meet Ikar, make sure he doesn't walk into the party alone, but I check my appearance one more time in the floor length mirror in my room. I turn one way and then the other, surprised at how feminine I look, which brings mixed feelings. I've missed feeling like a woman. The men's clothing serves an important purpose, mainly helping me stay safe and unnoticed, but I find it's nice to wear something that makes me feel beautiful again. Rupi seems to agree as she gently taps at the fabric on my sleeve and chirps.

"I'm glad this dress meets with your approval," I say, stroking her small head. She merely ruffles her feathers in response. I carry her back to her perch for the night and make sure she has fresh seed in her tray before I stand before the mirror again.

The dress has small cap sleeves and a sweetheart neckline, and I find I appreciate how much it covers after the last couple days. The spider silk has been dyed the deepest blue I've ever seen, like a night sky. It hugs my hips and puddles on the floor. It looks perfect, but when I turn, I see how low it dips in the back, and I purse my lips. I'll be having a chat with Mama Tina about that. She knows I like to keep my mark covered. I ensure that the half of my hair left down and curled covers it sufficiently.

Butterflies flutter in my stomach when I hear a soft knock. I open the door to find Ikar dressed in deep blue fitted trousers and shiny leather boots. He wears a matching jacket that emphasizes his muscular build, and beneath that is a fine, creamy shirt that reveals a spectacular bit of chest and completes the ensemble. It appears Mama Tina enjoys playing dress up with the two of us. My eyes return to his face. Even the day I met him, he had a couple days' beard growth, and I thought him handsome then. Now, his strong jawline is clean-shaven and free for my eyes to trace. Naturally, my gaze drops to the corded muscles of his neck which lead my eyes back to that bit of chest—

I feel the blush in my cheeks when I yank my eyes up to his. The gentle smirk on his lips doesn't match the intensity in his eyes. I offer no compliment, assuming my blush speaks for me. Instead, I quickly walk toward the stairs attempting to gather enough moisture to wet my dry mouth. This feels too much like a date. It's not a date. Neither of us speaks as we make our way down the stairs, but goosebumps spread across my skin when Ikar's fingers graze my back as I make my way unsteadily down, darn these heels. The awareness between us as we make our way is heady and distracting, and it doesn't help my balance. And what is that incredible smell on him? Mama Tina must have given him some type of fae cologne. She plays dirty.

I'm not surprised when we enter the party to see the room almost filled with fae. I don't think Mama Tina knows what a *small* get together actually looks like. With effort, I create a little distance between us, resisting winding my arm through his. I shouldn't act like he's mine, but I stay near him as we mingle with other guests amidst the low thrum of conversation and clinking glasses. It only makes sense with the whole *he's a criminal* story. Can't very well leave him wandering alone to be accosted by the like-minded fae. Mama Tina's silent approval has spread to the rest of her guests. I can tell by the smiles and greetings we receive, but rather than put me at ease, it puts me on edge.

We wander our way through the room. Here and there, I'm greeted by familiar friends and people I know from my teen years, and Ikar politely smiles, perfectly mannered. Then I see Drade across the room, and I pause. His dark eyes meet mine in a magnetic lock and practically sizzle as he heads in my direction. I bite my lip. It has been years since I've seen him, since I broke things off. He's still as darkly handsome as ever. A genuine smile graces my face as he approaches. Even though it hadn't felt right to stay in a relationship with him, I still love him, in a platonic way. Behind all the broody orneriness, that is. He smoothly grabs my hand and brings it to his lips as he looks into my eyes, and it feels like we step into the past.

"You are the image of everlasting beauty this evening, Vera."

A hot blush heats my cheeks. I feel, rather than see, Ikar stiffen beside me, which slams my very high heels back to reality. He snorts and then weakly attempts to cover it with a cough. I've had about enough of his half-laughs. What happened to his very respectable and perfect manners? I give him a *what the blazes* look, then look back at Drade. The two men have some sort of silent challenge right in front of me, and the tension winds so tight I think we might burst into flames here in the room. I pull my hand from Drade's and step back to form more of a circle between the three of us.

Drade directs his gaze to Ikar. "To what do we owe the *pleasure* of your company?" His tone is bored, but I see venom in his eyes as he gauges the possessive way Ikar steps closer to my right shoulder.

I immediately jump in. "I've arrested him. I had to stop here on an errand, and he has been forced to tag along."

"A bounty?" Drade's smirk grows as Ikar's eyes turn dark as a midnight pool of water.

My gaze jumps between them, confused by the growing tension.

I can see mocking entertainment in Drade's eyes. Ikar's eyes stay dark, and he is still as stone.

I finally speak up, not liking the way I have been reduced to a third wheel in some type of confusing, unspoken argument between two men who have just met each other. The drama. I roll my eyes.

"Looks like it's time to take our seats for dinner." I smile and grab Ikar's bicep, hoping he'll budge when I pull, since I know if he doesn't want to move, there is no way I can make him. I breathe in relief as he and Drade break their silent glare war, and he walks beside me to the dining room. His hand, simultaneously respectful and possessive, hovers just above the bare skin of my back. I can't handle his nearness without melting into a puddle of navy dress, so I take a step away, though I can't stop myself from quickly glancing his way. A knowing look at how he affects me touches his eyes, and the hint of a pleased smile twitches about his lips, but he drops his hand and makes no move to step closer.

"What was that all about?" I hiss, looking over his shoulder in Drade's direction. "Do you realize he's the low king of the fae?" I want to punch him in the arm, but it won't hurt him. I've tried it before.

"What's he going to do? *Arrest me?*" The cocky grin on his lips has me swinging between flustered and irritated.

"Yes. Behave yourself." It's all I have to time to spit out before we've arrived at the table, and I plaster a pleasant smile back onto my face. I'm left wondering what has gotten into him.

We find our places clearly marked, and I'm happy to find that Renna's placecard is directly across from mine. Now is as good a time as any to introduce my best friend to my criminal.

"Ikar, this is Renna, my closest friend. Basically my sister."

Ikar inclines his head and offers a dashing smile. "It's a pleasure to finally meet you."

Renna blushes prettily, and I rush ahead. "Renna, this is Ikar. My—er, the criminal I arrested."

Her eyes look between us knowingly, but she merely smiles and offers a perfectly polite reply. "Nice to meet you. I'm glad you both made it here safely."

Mama Tina raises a glass to call the rest of the guests to the table, and people begin to fill the seats around us. Ikar pulls out my chair, his respectable and perfect manners back in place, and helps me scoot closer to the table before taking his own seat beside me. Drade sits silently beside Renna and watches us from his seat across the table moodily while Renna appears somewhat apprehensive about her broody dinner companion.

Dinner is served, some type of bird, insects I don't know the name of, and a plant of some sort. One thing I don't miss—fae food. I gulp. It is the height of rudeness to leave food on your plate in this kingdom, so this entire thing is going down tonight.

I glance up to find Renna looking a little green and I give her an encouraging smile. She's not used to the fae food like I am.

Ikar acts like it's a regular mouth-watering feast. He snaps his napkin out and lays it across his lap, practiced. He smiles handsomely at Mama Tina and one of her friends who chats with him across the table, eating ever so properly and without gagging even once. Impressive.

I watch him, fascinated by this side of him I've never observed. I've grown used to my criminal wearing a growing beard, clothing fit for a journey such as ours. Now, he becomes intimidating to me. His clean shaven face reveals his strong jaw, the cut of his suit seems tailor made to emphasize his muscular physique. His movements are smooth, confident, controlled. His hair has grown longer, but his perfectly mussed style has only improved, a light curl broken free at the front, lending the perfect touch of imperfection to his appearance. He smiles handsomely, his blue eyes deep and mysterious. Honest and true soldier, lying criminal, violent mercenary, or a dangerously seductive combination of all three?

Mama Tina is enjoying him entirely too much, as am I. I'm startled when my gaze catches on Drade. He looks intensely into my eyes, tilting his head to the side, a touch too intent. Questioning, even. He speaks up, his voice deep and rich. "What were you arrested for?"

The table goes silent, but Mama Tina leans forward almost eagerly, her hands clasped beneath her chin. "Yes, do share."

My eyes dart to Ikar. We haven't discussed this. I hadn't expected the topic to come up at a *dinner party*.

He wipes his mouth carefully with a napkin before he leans back, grabs his wine glass, and swishes the liquid inside. He takes a slow drink and sets it down but doesn't release the stem. "Magic siphoning."

Everyone gasps. Admiration shines brightly in Mama Tina's eyes. "I'll pay three times as much as the person awarding the bounty."

I barely hold back an eye roll. This is getting out of hand.

Why hadn't he chosen something less *bad*, like, I don't know, smuggling or theft or something? Now all the fae women are infatuated, and the men look eager to talk business. If they find out we're lying, we're as good as dead. Well, I'm safe. But Ikar would be dead. Fae don't forgive.

I stand abruptly, attempting to pull him up by the elbow. "Time to go."

He just sits and gives me a lazy smile that steals all the breath from my lungs. He is a scoundrel. And playing the part of criminal a bit *too* well this evening.

Mama Tina rises, comes up beside me, and leans in, saying in her not-so-quiet-voice, "You've always had a thing for the bad boys, just like your Mama Tina." She pushes my shoulders gently down, and I sit. She winks before she walks toward the kitchen, calling over her shoulder, "I'll send dessert for everyone but Vera... since she already has some." She laughs as she turns the corner, and Ikar grins. My face grows hot. I am positive that the situation can't get any worse. Then Drade stands and rests fisted knuckles on the table, towering over us. Renna warily shrinks back in her chair beside him.

"I call your bluff." His deadly glare is centered on Ikar. Once again, the table goes silent.

"Go ahead." Ikar smirks.

My eyes jump between them, and I put a hand on Ikar's shoulder in warning, which he seems to promptly ignore. What has gotten into him?

"You're no criminal. And how do I know?"

"I'm sure you'll tell us," Ikar says lazily, but I can see his shoulders stiffen and a glint of warning cross his eyes.

"You *bonded* with her." He speaks through his teeth, anger forcing the glamour hiding his fangs to disappear. He looks ready to jump the table and tackle Ikar.

"What about it?"

"Vera would never allow herself to be bonded, especially by a criminal."

My heart pangs a bit, seeing the hurt behind his anger. But it never would have worked between us, I told him as much the last time I was here. Wait, did he say Ikar bonded with me? I lift my wrist with the glowing mate bond circle.

"Drade, it's just a temporary mate bond." I stand and attempt to show him my wrist and then realize I just admitted at a table full of fae that I mate bonded with my criminal. Whispers rush across the table like a wave, and my cheeks burn. And why does Mama Tina look so *proud*? I huff out a breath.

"I'm easy to love." Ikar shrugs, too carelessly. I glimpse a hint of challenge in his eyes right before Drade jumps the table and tackles him. His delicate chair shatters with their combined weight, and they both land on the floor, Ikar pinned beneath Drade's hands.

Drade grips Ikar's forearm, tighter and tighter, expecting a shatter. Ikar jumps on the moment, head slamming Drade's forehead, dazing him enough that Ikar is able to gain the upper hand, pulling him up and over and slamming him into the floor above him. He rolls and comes to standing as Drade does the same. They take defensive positions before they lunge at the same time, struggling between each other's weight for a moment, then crash out the window beside them.

I gasp in horror and run to the now shattered stained glass.

Mama Tina re-enters the room, hips swaying. "What excitement we have tonight."

"Do something please," I practically beg.

"They're two jealous, virile young men. Drade has challenged him. Let them fight it out. Whoever wins will be your match."

No. No, no, no. "Those are fae rules, not *my* rules. And what about my say in the matter?" In reality, I can have neither of them. I head toward the door, but Mama Tina firmly wraps her wing around me, guiding me back in the direction of the banquet room and the guests still seated there.

"You are on *fae* land and will obey *fae* rules, just as you always have."

I sit like a frustrated child.

"We are going to sit and enjoy our meal, m'dear. They'll probably be just fine." She sweeps gracefully into her seat.

"Probably?" My voice has a high-pitched, panicked quality to it. My criminal just somehow entered a match challenge with a very past ex fae boyfriend, who happens to also be one of the low kings. I kinda like Ikar, even if he is unavailable to me, and I don't want Drade hurt either. He may look moody and dark, but he has a kind heart.

I tap a finger against the table as I gag a few bites of the spongey plant down my throat, waiting.

Hours pass, and guests leave until Mama Tina's house grows quiet. Neither Ikar nor Drade return. Renna smothers a yawn, she's the only one who remains at the table with me now. I have wound and unwound my hair around my finger so many times it's halfway to a dreadlock. Finally, after attempting to convince me to head to bed and me refusing, even Renna leaves, giving my shoulder a gently squeeze and bidding me a quiet *goodnight*.

In the early morning hours, I finally climb the stairs wearily to my bedroom. Ikar is the most resourceful, resilient person I know. Drade is, or at least *was,* the strongest. But Ikar's magic is blocked. My nerves feel like sparking wires along my spine. *They wouldn't kill each other.* I hope.

Chapter 42

Ikar

I'd felt Drade's stare on me all night. Like a predator. I had no idea I'd meet him here, but the glamour worked because I saw no sign of recognition when he first saw me. And though I fear some of the low kings may mutiny, I'm sure he never would have acted toward me the way he had tonight if he knew I am his High King. But my hackles went up when he set eyes on Vera. It's obvious they have history, and the possessive way he took her hand almost had me reaching for my nonexistent sword. Good thing no weapons were allowed, or our battle may have begun before the meal was served.

I wasn't at all surprised that when we'd sat down for dinner, he'd caused a confrontation. His longing for Vera was obvious, and though I know I can't have her, I feel a possessiveness that I can't explain. I want her. It's torturous to be around her but never call her mine. He'd challenged me. I'd seen it in his eyes, I felt it to my core in his tone, and I'd accepted. Ready to show him that Vera is mine. Though, she isn't. Two kings, men powerful enough to have almost anything they want, can't have *her* and fought over it.

We crash from the window in a shower of stained fae glass. We hit an innumerable number of hefty branches on our way to the forest floor, but neither of us relinquish our hold on the other.

"I can't... believe... you *mate-bonded* with her!" Drade pants when we slam into the very hard ground. I shove him off me and stand. He comes right back at me, barreling into my midsection with a shoulder and slamming me back to the ground. I throw my arm around his neck and hold strong until he punches me in the side, and a searing pain forces a growl from my throat. He's broken a rib, maybe more than one. I can't pull magic to protect myself, and if I don't do something soon, he really will kill me. He's a formidable opponent, even when I have magic. There's a reason Drade is king of the fae.

I'd lost my hold and now brace my forearms beside my head to block the worst of the beating. I am strong without magic, but the fae are naturally stronger, and if he gets his hands around my neck, I'm a dead man. I simply endure, waiting for the right moment. When it comes, I throw him to my left and stand, my hands up in a peace-offering gesture.

I breathe hard, out of breath, my side refusing to allow my lungs to breathe as deep as I need. I grasp my side as I inhale and feel what seems like shards of glass slipping between my ribs with each breath. I grimace.

"It's me," I rasp. "King of Moneyre. Ikar."

Drade lets slip a sound that's as close to a laugh as I think I've ever heard from him, but he pauses in his advance. How to convince him?

"Last council I suggested finding the Tulips."

I see the moment he believes me, and his shoulders relax a bit.

"A glamour." He narrows his eyes at me, but he's immediately more guarded and formal. "What are you doing as Vera's *bounty*?" He asks it in an overly controlled manner. He may believe me, but I can still feel the challenge for Vera beneath his understanding. No matter who I am, I'm involved with the woman he still apparently harbors feelings for.

"It's a long story, a big misunderstanding."

"Why haven't you told her who you are?" Drade asks, staring me down. A trail of blood runs off his forehead and into the neck of his dress shirt. His perfectly pressed suit now looks no better than mine.

"I showed her my seal. She thought I murdered someone and took it. But it's better if she doesn't know who I am, I think. Seems she strongly despises kings. But I need her help to find a Tulip."

At that, Drade scoffs. "I could've told you that. About her hating kings."

"You two were... something?"

"Until I challenged the fae king. She left the night I won."

"You love her, don't you?"

He looks away and shakes his head, a muscle in his jaw jerking. A couple of fools in love with a woman we can't have. "She thinks you're a criminal, and she still mate-bonded with you?" His face is etched with disbelief and even a hint of pain.

For a vulnerable emotion like that to show before another king means it runs deep. Especially for Drade.

I don't know their history, but I'm not cruel enough to continue the charade, even if Drade is one of the low kings and the urge to irritate and annoy any one of them runs strong in my veins. I remind myself I'm meant to unify them, bring the kingdoms together. Here's a chance to start.

"Only one kingdom recognizes the bond as a commitment, and if it's not kept up, it fades after six weeks until it's gone.

That was always our plan. It was a means to an end. Feel better?"

The truth jabs me in the heart, even as the relief of it shows on his face. I swallow the uncomfortable realization and hope it will digest and disappear. I am supposed to be searching for a Tulip to bridge with me, which makes me completely unavailable to any other woman. My kingdom is depending on me, and duty has to come before my heart, but I'm too selfish to tell Drade she's fair game. I turn and walk away, holding my aching side. I know we need to talk, but it'll have to be later, when I've set my mind and ribs right.

Chapter 43

Vera

I step inside my room and gently kick the silvery heels off, leaning back against the door. That's when I hear footsteps in the hall. *Ikar.* I wrench open the door and step out to find his hand on the doorknob of his door.

I fling my arms around him in relief, and after a surprised moment, he slips his around my waist.

"Missed me?" he asks with teasing in his voice and a wry smile on his lips, but I can hear exhaustion in his voice.

I step back with a blush on my cheeks, which quickly cools when I take in his disheveled appearance. The beautiful navy clothing Mama Tina gave him is completely destroyed. The sleeve on his right side is half ripped away at the seam, two of the four buttons are missing, and there are tears and dirt everywhere. Blood soaks the collar of the once cream colored shirt he wears underneath, the culprits a cut on his cheek and two slices across his neck that appear to be healing. Looks like someone stopped for some healing potion, or it was offered by a much-too-approving Mama Tina.

"If you could quit acting like a criminal, it would be much easier to believe that you aren't." I fold my arms and step back.

"That's why I fit in so well with your *criminal* family." His eyebrow raises in half-joking accusation. "Makes me wonder what activities you're involved in that I don't know about yet."

"You'll have to stick around to find out." There's borderline too much want in my voice along with a hint of challenge. The late hour and whatever was in that fae drink tonight have loosened my tongue. Or it's his lethal half-smile. I don't know what to blame, but I feel another blush coming on at my forwardness. Time to get down to business before I say or *do* anything else that will further reveal feelings I'm not allowed to have. But based on his behavior tonight, I'm a hair's width from backing out of my already questionable decision to leave the Tulips and work with him. Am I sure I can trust him? Or will he take off as soon as I've removed the cuff and leave me to become a bounty myself?

He leans a shoulder against the door frame, one hand in one of his suit pant pockets that's still intact, relaxed and comfortable. Not only has he survived the fae fight, which is unheard of for humans, but he stands there looking like a model street fighter.

No, I'm not sure I can trust him. Too handsome, too capable, too smart, too everything. Trying to keep myself from grabbing the lapels of his jacket and yanking him toward me, I step back again, creating needed distance to switch this from a romantic midnight rendezvous to a professional contract acceptance.

"There's something I need to tell you." I reverse my distance decision and step closer, grabbing his hand with the wrist that's cuffed, all the while hoping I'm not making the biggest mistake of my life.

He nods, curiosity in his eyes mingled with a bit of something warm I can't think about right now.

I raise my chin, shoulders straight and strong, all business now. "I want to formally accept your contract." I touch the cuff on his wrist, mutter the charm word, and it slithers off and returns to the tiny ball lying in my hand.

His brows raise in surprise, and a pleased grin pulls his lips into a smile that has me, once again, feeling everything but professional toward him. I can tell he pulls magic, getting reacquainted with it right there in the hall in front of me, in his own world for a few prolonged seconds. It seems too intimate a moment to share with him, since I'm the one who blocked it in the first place.

He looks at me hard. "You trust me, then? You no longer believe I'm a criminal?" He searches my eyes, and a bit of fear shoots through me. I can sense the immense power at his fingertips, magic pulling from around me.

But I nod firmly. "I trust you enough. We'll sign the contract tomorrow."

That hope in his eyes dims a little bit at my answer, but I refuse to lie to him.

"What changed your mind?" he asks, his voice low and rough.

The depth of his gaze has me looking away. My decision is too new, too fresh, and he can't know the details anyway. I look down at the plush carpet beneath my bare feet and rub an invisible spot with my toe while I think about what to say instead.

I stick with the surface level of truth, shrugging. "Circumstances in my personal life have changed rather suddenly. I think it's time for me to do something different. Truthfully, I've begun to doubt that you are a criminal. But after tonight—" My eyes narrow suspiciously.

"I'm not," he says darkly.

"Great," I say with exaggerated cheerfulness. "We've got a deal, then."

I look up at him and practically challenge him to ask me more. I know my response was more than cryptic, one that will have him coming back for answers eventually, but for now, it will have to be enough.

After he looks at me for so long I begin to grow uncomfortable, he finally nods. "Tomorrow."

The moment turns warm, the two of us standing there in the quiet hall in the middle of the night. Without the cuff—the physical barrier between us that labeled him my criminal— we are on equal grounds. My flight response engages, and I turn to escape to my room, not able to function properly with how distractingly handsome he is.

"Well, goodn—"

I stop with my hand on the knob and then spin around. I need to know the outcome of the challenge. I'd been so distracted by the contract I hadn't even thought about the consequences of their fight this evening. In the deep recesses of my mind, I wonder how it couldn't have been Drade. I've never seen anyone beat him. Ever. But I've underestimated Ikar in the past, in pretty much every situation, and he's proven himself every time.

Straight to the point, I blurt, "If Drade won the challenge, I have to match with him."

His eyes turn intense, heat simmering beneath their surface as he steps away from the doorframe and comes closer. "And if I won?"

My mouth goes dry, and I swallow. I try the logical approach. "Well, according to fae law..."

He brings his hands up and slowly slides them along my jaw, then into my hair, and we lean into each other, our lips a breath away.

A door handle clicks, and Mama Tina pokes her head out. "Are two bedrooms not enough?" she calls, tossing ice water on our moment.

Ikar immediately drops his hands and steps back to a respectable distance, turning slowly with one of those handsome smiles. "Our rooms are more than perfect. We were just saying goodnight."

He gives a perfect, gentlemanly bow to Mama Tina, then to me, and enters his room, closing the door with a click behind him.

I attempt to toss a fiery glare at Mama Tina, but her door clicks shut right after his. It was probably for the best since we can't have each other anyway.

Chapter 44

Ikar

I've never reveled in the feel of my magic as I do now. It's powerful warmth fills my body, my senses attune to every smell, noise, and sight around me. Details in the woodwork come to life that I hadn't been able to see before. I simply let a low level of magic flow through me, feeling restored and more like myself than I have since I was cuffed. And Vera trusts me. Maybe not fully, but enough to uncuff me and accept the contract. I didn't realize at the beginning how much that trust would come to mean to me. She trusts me enough to risk becoming a bounty herself, something I will quickly take care of. But, quite frankly, I'm surprised, and curious, about what prompted this change when she was so close to claiming the reward for my arrest. She's agreed to work as my Originator for the coming journey, which means I'll have plenty of time to find out.

For the first time in several weeks I feel tentative hope. All I need to do now is get to Moneyre and meet up with Rhosse and Darvy, if they're alive, then we can head into the Lucent Mountains. I'll probably need to spend a few days in the High

Kingdom to attend to business, but I haven't worried too much, knowing that although Jethonan is eccentric, he's trustworthy and the kingdom is in good hands while I'm away. It feels good to finally be moving forward with enormous tasks before me. I let the magic go, and sleep better than I have in weeks.

The next day Vera and I head to the nearest legal office to have a contract written. Rupi has been acting more energetic than usual all morning, flitting around our heads, pecking at our earlobes, and when she has perched for a moment, she trembles until she takes off again. The man writing the contract seems to be growing irritated with her behavior and the bits of feather that flutter to his desk, so I finally catch her between two hands and clasp her gently, feeling her excited trembling. I look at Vera with my brows raised, and she simply shrugs. I return my attention to the contract that is swiftly being written before us. After the obstacles and difficulties of the past week, the moment where she signs my contract passes almost too easily to believe. Within the hour, I officially have an Originator. Rupi sings happily within my grasp as we leave, and when I finally open my hands, she bursts out like a tiny arrow. I chuckle at her unpredictable behavior. It seems she more than approves of Vera working for me.

The next stop is a shop filled with displays of a variety of clothing where I promptly leave Vera busy with Renna and Mama Tina. I bid them goodbye, remind Vera I'll be back to meet her, and leave to meet Drade. I'm grateful she's distracted, or I'm not sure how I would explain my need to meet with him when our last meeting ended in a challenge battle.

I make my way to the official quarters of the low king for

the fae. It's an interesting thing to walk around as a regular citizen, when usually my arrival is met with fanfare, crowds, and formal ceremony.

Having visited many times before, I am prepared to send a message with the guards that wait outside the hallway that leads to his office. Within minutes, I'm standing before his door with a guard at my side who knocks once and swings it open. I find Drade seated behind his desk, his back facing the door as he stares out the wall of windows that look over fae land. The natural wood walls, floor, and ceiling are as minimalistic as he's always kept them. A single plant with a burgundy colored flower and deep green leaves is about to bloom on his desk, but aside from that, the only other variation in colors comes from the deep blue suit he wears, the black chair he sits in, and a neat pile of cream colored parchment. There is nothing personal in the room, nothing that would allow anyone to know anything about him.

He turns toward me, his brows raising when he sees who has entered his office. He stands and bows stiffly. "Your Majesty."

I try to ignore the slight smugness that accompanies his words.

"Or shall I say, *criminal?*"

I know he's trying to raise my ire, so I simply lift my wrist. "I'm a free man." I resist a grin as the humor on his face slips. "Please, sit." I gesture back to his chair and take a seat in one that sits before his desk. He eyes my free wrist with suspicion. I'm sure he assumes something has changed between Vera and I, and he's correct. He probably thinks it's romantic, and I would assume the same, but he won't be getting an explanation from me.

I waste no time in pulling the small bottle from my coat

pocket. "Can you tell me what was in this bottle?" I slide it across the desk and lean back in my chair.

Drade frowns at me like I'm insane, but takes the bottle and briefly waves it beneath his nose. He hands it back. "A standard fae healing potion."

"You sure?"

He looks at me with an eyebrow lifted in obvious irritation at my doubt of his expertise.

"I am positive," he drawls. "Why are you asking?"

"A severe injury was healed using this potion."

He scoffs, and I feel like an absolute nutcase because I know about as well as he the improbability of what I am suggesting.

"It's not possible. Even in the good days, our potions expired after two months. Now, it's not even a day. Unless this was bought and used fairly quickly on fae land, it wouldn't have done anything. It has gotten worse."

"There has to be an explanation," I growl. I refuse to let this go.

"I agree, but the explanation does not lie with the expired fae potion that was inside this bottle."

I grip the bottle tightly before I place it back in my pocket. Until I figure this out, it will stay with me. I think of Vera, the only one who truly knows. The answer *has* to lie with her, but she has repeated over and over that the fae potion had done it. Drade accurately guesses the direction of my thoughts and narrows his eyes at me.

"Pardon me, *Your Majesty,* but I don't like the way you look at her."

I smirk, but it's only to hide the pain I shoved down from last night. I can't have her. "I'm destined for someone else," I say with a hard glint in my eyes.

"About that," Drade pauses, picks up a quill, and taps it like something bothers him. "There have been whispers of unrest among the kings. Do you really think you should be searching out a Tulip if it will cause a war for the High Throne?" His face is still hard and emotionless, but there's genuine question in his eyes.

"It'll be worth it." I say it as much for me as for him. "Do I have your loyalty?"

"As much as ever, my king."

As intended, I feel no reassurance from his response.

I scribble out a quick message to Jethonan with an update on my mission and leave it in the care of Drade's secretary. Then I leave Drade's office and head back to the seamstress where I left Vera. I'm about to open the door when Mama Tina and Renna exit with laughter and goodbyes to Vera, who steps out last, Rupi perched proudly on her shoulder.

I halt too quickly. Gone are the loose trousers and man's shirt that engulfed her frame, gone are the raggedy, too-large boots. Now, she wears a closer fitting, creamy shirt with blousy sleeves beneath a fitted vest with a square neckline made of sturdy, navy fabric that laces up the front and accentuates her narrow waist. My gaze tracks lower. Fitted, fine leather pants end with a pair of boots that hug her narrow calves. She carries a deep green long coat over one arm. A sheath intended for a knife is wrapped around one thigh, and a low-slung belt holds a scabbard for a short sword. Both are empty—a result of her pack and weapons being stolen by the shifters. That won't do. I make a mental note to do something about it.

"Better than the dress of death?" She holds her arms out and turns from side to side.

My mouth is dry as sand, but I force an easy grin. "You named the dress?"

"It seemed appropriate at the time." She shrugs.

"You look like a true adventuress." And more, a tempting siren, but I keep that to myself. She smiles brightly, seeming happy with my compliment. I notice Mama Tina watching the exchange between us with a wide, satisfied smile.

I direct my gaze forward as we make our way back to Mama Tina's for our final night with the fae. Vera is happy to chat with Renna and Mama Tina while my thoughts turn. I can't help but consider Drade's question. *Should* I be searching for a Tulip when my own kings may very well aim for my throne in my absence? This is messy work, finding a Tulip. If I don't marry a Tulip, Vera and I could be together, too. It's a tempting thought since it seems like a win in two ways. Too tempting. But with those two wins brings the greater loss. Lucent magic will continue to weaken, and my people will continue to die. I would be returning with no solution for the gloam that is literally destroying my kingdom.

My will hardens as I rebuild my confidence in my decision. No matter how deranged the low kings may think I am, the weight of duty is mine to bear, and that means restoring magic for my people. Hopefully before a war is started that will kill even more people and my throne is stolen from beneath me. Not only that, what is the explanation for the fae potion that healed me from the bantha claw? I trust Vera, but I acknowledge that she still holds much back from me—as I do from her. I can only hope our secrets don't end up destroying our mission.

Chapter 45

Nadiette

King's Council

The four low kings sit around the table, all with various expressions, most displaying frowns bordering on confusion on why they were called to a King's Council, and their High King isn't at the head of the table. Strange how an empty chair can have as much presence as a filled one.

I stand. "I am here on behalf of the High King—"

Drade speaks up, not attempting to hide his irritation. "This is unheard of, an abuse of the council." His voice is like ice.

He's joined by other mumbles of assent. I hurriedly continue, aware that I'm close to losing control of the room.

"The High King has gone in search of a Queen of the Night, and he must be stopped from this foolishness." I state firmly. "I have attempted to delay him in his efforts, but I'm not sure it will be enough."

"What I find odd is that you still expect him to marry you after what you've done." Drade lifts a brow derisively. Humor laces his dark expression at my expense and I hear a muffled chuckle from someone else in the room.

My eyes flash with anger. "How do *you* know what I've done? Have you seen hi—"

Waylon intervenes, waving a hand through the air. "Enough. This is not a time for silly quarrels."

Drade's lips twist in a smirk while I merely nod and force myself to primly sit back in my chair to listen.

"I have employed the help of an experienced mercenary." Waylon pauses to shuffle a few papers and brings one to the front, then lifts it a bit closer to his face and reads, "Ah, yes, Renton is his name." He looks up and lays the papers flat on the ancient table. "He approached me, asking about the Black Tulips—I must say his timing was impeccable. He has agreed to track our wayward king and deliver him to the High Kingdom safely, and in exchange, he has asked that we don't interfere with the Black Tulips. I agreed on the council's behalf." He looks my way. "And that includes you, as well. No more interference, m'dear."

I nod slowly, fisting my skirt in my hand beneath the table.

Rhomi leans back in his chair. "This Renton, is he trustworthy?"

Everyone looks toward Waylon.

With a confident voice and relaxing into the arm of his chair, Waylon says, "He has the same goal—to prevent any Black Tulip from bridging with our king. He has agreed to find King Ikar and return him to the kingdom, while also taking care of any possible Black Tulip *problems* that may arise. Tell, do any of you have any other, better, ideas?"

The room is deathly silent. Drade appears annoyed, a slight sneer twisting his lips. Rhomi shifts uncomfortably in his seat. Waylon and Adrian looked between each other with an indecipherable look.

Drade speaks again, this time a sarcastic note in his voice.

"Have we considered simply *trusting* the man who was raised to be High King and getting back to the business of ruling our own low kingdoms?"

My voice hardens toward Drade, irritated. "Sometimes the weight of responsibility, when carried alone, causes people to act in a way that isn't normal for them. This isn't who Ikar *is*."

"You just want to be queen," Drade says with acid in his voice.

I hate that I sputter a bit, my cheeks red. "I want the best for our kingdom. And the best for our kingdom is Ikar and I. Not a dangerous Queen of the Night."

Waylon speaks up with a calming voice, attempting to lower the growing tension. "The king is in danger. His heart is good, but he takes a great risk in bringing the Tulips back into power, blatantly ignoring the advice of the council. We must remember the danger they present."

The table is once again silent.

"I'm asking for each of you to help me."

Rhomi speaks next. "If we do, what happens next?"

Adrian lifts his chin from his chest and growls, "Nadiette will marry Ikar, and Renton will take care of the Tulips. Listen up, boy."

Waylon nods. "Nadiette's loyalty is proven by her many years as the royal Head Originator. She can be trusted to do everything in her power to protect the people. She deserves to be queen."

Drade scoffs beneath his breath.

Adrian lifts his stocky arm. "You have my support."

Waylon smiles like a cat. "That's not all, though. I will continue to lend my support and stay in contact with Renton," he looks at me, "but if the marriage falls through, we will take the High Kingdom, and it will be split equally between the low kings. King Ikar has shown he may not be fit to lead any longer. If he refuses you, he is ours."

The reek of mutiny fills the silence.

My smile turns stiff, sweat breaking out across my brow. "Then, I must ensure we marry." My eyebrow cocks at my uncle in challenge.

"Don't worry, my dear, whether you marry him or not, you'll have a high place with the kings."

Chapter 46

Vera

We stop outside the doors to our rooms after another unique fae supper—this one a much smaller affair which, mercifully, hadn't included a round of fights or any challenges. I'm wondering if he's going to try to kiss me again and what I should do if he does. He seemed preoccupied most of the evening, broody even. I'm working for him now, and my rule book is screaming that I should keep a professional relationship. I decide it's best if I head straight to my room and not leave any opportunities for this forbidden relationship to develop further.

Once we reach the top of the staircase, I keep my focus on the fancy curved handle of my door instead of the expensive fae scent Mama Tina gave him. It's had me distracted all night. My hand closes over the chilled metal, and I throw a quick, "goodnight," over my shoulder.

"One thing, Vera."

When I look over my shoulder and up into his dark blue eyes, I see something I can't name, but oddly, there are bells of warning clanging in my head. It's foreign when I've always felt solid safety with Ikar. I tentatively turn around, but confusingly, I would rather dart into my room than linger here with him because, somehow, I am sure the intensity there has nothing to do with the physical. I shift backward and turn the knob behind my back again, intending to tell him that I'm too tired and we'll talk tomorrow, but he steps forward, matching my retreat with his advance.

"I learned something today." His voice is deep and smooth. Pensive.

"Hmmm? That's interesting. You'll have to share it with me tomorrow." Or not. Because something about the look in his eyes says that maybe I don't want to know. I smile and start to turn toward my door, but he steps closer again, and there's nowhere for me to go but against the wall. He braces a hand beside my head and leans in, almost as if he intends to kiss me. I don't know whether to feel like a lover or prey right now. But instead of my lips, his five o'clock shadow brushes my cheek gently, and I feel his lips nearly graze my ear. The hint of expensive, masculine scent lingers, and my breath hitches as skittering chills race across my skin. This is torture.

"The fae potion didn't heal me," he whispers beside my ear.

I stop breathing. His proximity causes tingles to run down my body, or maybe it's fear. What exactly is he implying?

"Care to explain? Or shall I do it for you?" Delightful shivers run through my body, though the words should have me running.

I swallow. He waits.

How does he know? My brain screams to run, but my body wants to stay right where it is. Body wins.

"It did." My voice is too breathless.

He chuckles deliciously, brushes his lips against my neck once, and then pulls away and looks straight into my eyes. The shadows of the hallway have him looking dark and dangerous and much too attractive.

"You want to do it this way?" He waits patiently for a moment, but I don't reply. "Okay." He continues in that deep, silky, dangerous voice that I'm finding I really like. "You're a Healer." His eyes search mine, waiting for confirmation, but I mask everything.

I breathe a premature sigh of relief. He doesn't realize that healing goes with Tulips. But then dread sinks like a rock in my stomach because it's only a matter of time before he realizes that Originators are never Healers, and my secret will be out.

"Who told you this? They're crazy." I laugh lightly.

With his free hand, he pulls something from his pocket and holds it up between two fingers for me to see—the fae potion bottle. My hands shake, and I press them against my clothing so he doesn't notice. I should have buried it when I had the chance.

"The fae king was kind enough to give me a little lesson on fae potions." He drops the bottle back in his pocket and steps back. "He confirmed that not *one* potion has stayed potent when taken out of this realm recently." He raises an eyebrow at me, waiting for an explanation, but he's not getting one from me. Also, I thought they hated each other, and now he tells me he had a civil conversation with the fae king? I'm all sorts of confused.

"Sounds like something you need to discuss further with the fae, I have nothing to do with the potency of their potions, but I did pour it on your leg, and it helped." *Not a lot, but maybe a bit.* Is that still a lie? It's certainly not an answer to his question. My brain is misfiring and tired, and I know I can't handle much more of this before all my secrets gush out into the open. I can't have that.

An intensity simmers in his eyes, maybe even a hint of desperation. "You're a Healer, just tell me yes or no."

"Okay, fine, yes. I'm a Healer." *Sort of.* I add in my mind so it doesn't feel like so much of a lie. I smile in a somewhat normal way as I push a finger lightly against the muscles of his chest, and he respectfully steps back, but there's a knowing, confident sort of smirk on his face. I worry that I have, indeed, made myself prey. What began as a seemingly straightforward arrest-turned-business-deal has become even more tangled and confusing. I don't want to lie more than I already have, but I can't tell him the rest. Ever. Especially now that it sounds like he's friends with one of the low kings somehow. For being so serious and overconfident, he makes friends easier than I do. I'd sulk about that for a moment, but I need to escape from this dangerous, and somehow very heady, conversation.

As I'm about to attempt another exit, he leans in again, his nose practically nuzzled into my neck, and then ever so slowly leaves a scorching trail of the lightest, heat-inducing kisses I've ever experienced up to my jaw. I don't know what his plan is, but I will not be seduced. In the next moment, my breath is shaky, and all I know is that, criminal or not, soldier, whatever he is—I want him. I try to resist and fail miserably.

I turn my head, and my lips find his, a perfect balance of warm, soft, and firm as he leads us into a realm all our own. I slide my hands around his sides and pull myself closer as his gently slide across my jawline and back into my hair, tilting my head for a better angle to deepen our kiss. That fae scent mixes perfect with the leather and musk that always clings to him, the hardness of the strength beneath my hands, his lips against mine, the light scratch of a day's whiskers against my skin. Him. He's intoxicating. He pulls back and presses his forehead to mine, and I notice with wicked delight that his breathing is nearly as heavy as my own. I want to grab the lapels of his jacket and drag him into my room, tell him every secret I've ever had, wake up beside him in the morning, revel in the safety of his presence that I've gotten so attached to.

But I don't. I've completely forgotten why I'm out here, and now all I want is him.

He steps back, eyes still matching the desire I feel and whispers a rough goodnight. He enters his room without a backward glance.

I'm thoroughly dazed and somehow stumble my way into my room, slip out of my dress and heels, and lay in bed. I replay the evening, wondering who he really is. He seemed to have enjoyed our kiss as much as I had, but he seemed like he *needed* to know if I was a Healer. Is he playing me? Why does it matter if I am or not? I wonder if he has fae blood. He's too good at these games. I flip over in frustration.

———

The next morning, I don my new clothing and take a moment to inspect it in the mirror. It's been a very long time since I've worn something as feminine and form-fitting as this for work. It feels good. It helps that Mama Tina bought it for me since I'm too cheap to spend anything on decent clothing myself. Besides, I couldn't afford these on my own right now. If my clothes hadn't been stolen by the shifters, I may have just stuck with those, dirty and ripped as they were. For so long, I've hidden beneath men's clothing. Trying to be small, unnoticed, and to be honest, uncaring about my appearance. Being mistaken for a boy at times has its benefits in my line of work. But something has changed. When Mama Tina joined me to buy clothes, I expected to hate it. It's been years since I've let her buy me anything. This time, I was immediately drooling over this outfit. Now that it's on, I feel more like myself than I have in years, and I find I don't miss my over-large clothing anymore. Not only that, I have two more outfits already folded neatly in my pack.

I head down the stairs. We have our things packed and ready to leave by the door. Neither of us mentions the kiss from the night before, but I can hardly look at him without blushing. If I don't pull it together pretty quick, Mama Tina is going to end up in the know, and that's the last thing I want.

Ikar and I end up at the door for one more round of good-byes. Mama Tina leans forward to hug me, and I wrap my arms tight around her, her light floral scent surrounding me. I inhale deeply and squeeze her a little tighter before I let go, savoring her familiarity and motherly sort of love. When we finally step apart, she turns to Ikar with a sparkle in her eye and hugs him, whispering something in his ear that has him chuckling and nodding.

Mama Tina turns back toward me and lifts a questioning arched brow. I realize she's waiting for the money to send to the Tulips. I never told her my decision.

I lean toward her, give her one more quick hug, and whisper, "Use the money I left to pay for Renna's dues. I won't be paying them any longer for myself."

I can tell she wants to know more, to ask questions, but she smiles widely. I try not to let that approval buoy me so much. I made this decision for me and me alone. And though I don't need her approval, it's nice to see that she's pleased with my decision.

I glance at Ikar and see questions in his gaze. I forget he has his magic back, and he may have heard, but I act as if nothing out of the normal has happened.

Renna steps forward next and I squeeze her hard. "I left the money. Use it for your bracelet, okay?" I whisper.

She nods. "Be careful, Vera." She eyes Ikar for a moment over my shoulder and then returns her attention to me. "And thank you. You've given me more than I can ever hope to return."

"Sisters by magic," I whisper with a grin, as I hug her again before I step back and grab my new pack.

We throw out a few more goodbyes, and I quickly wipe away a few stray tears. It's always difficult to be away. And then we're off. Only another two days to the High Kingdom, and hopefully Rhosse and Darvy are waiting for us, alive and well.

Rupi finishes devouring the pile of seeds, tiny worms, and nuts a maid has left on her fancy perch in the sitting room, then she swoops to land on my shoulder as we walk out the door.

Usually, she acts a little down when we leave Mama Tina's. She is never better fed than when we're there, but this time, she seems happy to be on our way, chirping cheerfully as we stroll through the complex and beautiful fae city. I soak up the depth of color and smell here. Colors appear deeper, beautiful aromas clearer, and sounds of the forest as a true symphony. As soon as we step through the realm door, the world will seem muted, as if the fae stole half the world's beauty and doubled their own.

Ikar pulls me from my thoughts. "I think meeting your family was a complete success," he says with a confident grin and a swagger in his step. We've left the fae now and are entering forests shared between kingdoms. We see occasional travelers and fully expect the rest of our trip to be uneventful. I appreciate the reprieve before we enter the Lucent Mountains for the job I accepted.

I look at him, attempting to gauge if he is joking or not.

"Which part was the most successful?" I hold up my fingers

one by one as I list off. "Getting into a fight with my ex-boyfriend at the dinner party? Getting caught about to kiss by Mama Tina? Or, lying to the fae about being a criminal so you'll never be welcome there as anything else?" I wait for his reply.

"All of the above." He grins proudly. "I've only had a chance to fight a fae once before, so this one went better than expected." He rolls his shoulders like he's anticipating another challenge in the near future. "I'm sure they'll welcome me again." He's never sounded more confident.

I saw the way he was so readily accepted, so this time I don't argue with him.

While we walk, I let the reality of my decision sink in. I'm leaving with half the savings I had, as I left the rest with Mama Tina to pay Renna's dues. At least Renna will be safe with the fae, and happy. She deserves it.

And while I feel a new sense of freedom, I also feel terrified that I messed up. My parents sacrificed so much to keep me safe and keep the dues paid. They, and the Tulips, have stressed the importance of that protection since I can remember. And now I have simply decided to set aside years of warnings and sacrifice. Apart from that, I never considered when the protection of the bracelet will lapse. One month? Two? A few days? Yesterday? I've never been able to remove the bracelet, its charm ensuring it won't fall off or be removed. Now that I haven't paid, I test it with a strong pull. It holds, so I suppose it's still working. It'll probably fall off when the money should have arrived to Tatania and it doesn't, but how should I know? I have the strongest urge to turn back and shove the money into Mama Tina's hands and go back to living my life the way I always have. I don't realize how fast I'm walking, how my fists are clenched, or how fast my breathing has become until Ikar speaks up.

"What is it?" Ikar asks, looking concerned.

I hesitate, not sure how much to share. "Have you ever done something that seems like the right thing, but most would say is wrong?"

Ikar looks at me intently, that guardedness fills his eyes again. "Yes, many times."

"Did it turn out okay?"

"Most of the time, yes." He speaks slowly now. "My current situation, I have yet to know."

"What is your situation? I know you're searching for a flower. Then what?"

"Then I have to find a person." I can practically see his strong shoulders sag beneath the weight of it as the words leave his mouth.

He's not being evasive at all, and he's no longer smiling. It's duty I see in the set of his face and shoulders. What does that mean? I'm not sure if I want to know more, but the decision is out of my hands when Ikar jumps into talking about maps and how many days we have left to get to Moneyre, where instead of him being dropped off with the officials, we will be searching for Darvy and Rhosse. My mind still spins thinking of how plans have changed. I can no longer claim Ikar as *my criminal*. It's almost become a term of endearment, and I snicker to myself, considering if I should continue to use it. But then I stop laughing as I realize I still don't even know what Ikar *is*. I feel as if I know him so well when I hardly know him at all. And here I've contracted to work with him.

Not all mercenaries are criminals. *Just most of them.* Is that what he is? I've already decided he's not one of the Tulip killers, so while I worry for the safety of my sisters, I know no harm will come from him. What is he, then?

"What exactly is your profession if you're not a Class A criminal?" I ask, almost afraid to hear the answer.

He considers for a long moment. "Are you sure you want me to tell you?" he asks with a questioning brow. "Because we can complete this mission without you ever knowing."

He's being quite serious, and now I'm even more scared. But what could be worse than a Class A criminal?

I nod.

"I'm a high-ranking officer in the High King's army."

I swallow tightly, trying to school my features. Worse. Definitely worse.

To be continued in The Black Tulip Chronicles Book Two: Queen of the Night

Coming in 2025

Continue reading for a sneak peek of the first chapter...

*Author reserves the right to make any necessary changes to the first chapter prior to publishing "Queen of the Night."

Vera

I've heard Moneyre is a beautiful city—too bad it's the home of the High King and I'll be stuck there for the next two days.

I'll admit it. I messed up.

I cringe thinking about attempting to explain my recent choices to Tatania, the leader of the Black Tulips, also known as the Queens of the Night. But if things go well from here on out I won't have to. I still won't need the dratted bracelet that costs an exorbitant amount of money to keep me anonymous, and no one will know that I took a very lucrative contract offered by a man that I was eighty-five percent sure wasn't a criminal before I found out that he's actually a high-ranking officer of the High King. While that would make most women feel safe, for me, I would have preferred he admitted he actually *was* the Class A criminal I believed he was.

And see, this is where it gets tricky. I've been told, and I've spoken oaths with the Black Tulips, to never work for the High King, his officers, or anyone close to him because of the danger it presents to the Black Tulips who are still in hiding after being hunted down and killed by the High King and his Originators over two hundred years ago. Now, we're mostly forgotten, and we'd like to keep it that way. I've never heard anyone mention our name aside from stories people tell children to scare them. That is, until a little over a week ago when Ikar handed me a list of the Black Tulips with seven of our names on it, including mine. I promptly doused it in hot tea, and I hope it's gone forever. He asked me about it once, but I expertly dodged his questions. I can only hope he doesn't bring it up again.

We left Mama Tina's two days ago and should reach Moneyre late tonight or early tomorrow. The shock of Ikar's revelation has worn off a bit—numbed would be a better description. I was angry with him at first, but it only makes me look more suspicious, and I've already signed the contract. I decided two hours into my anger that it would be better for me to focus on being as normal as possible rather than throwing a fit about his status.

So, here we are. Friends again. Friends that shared a spectacular kiss the night before leaving Mama Tina's and haven't spoken of it once. I won't be the one to bring it up now that I know for sure we can't ever be together like that. The thought saddens me more than I care to admit. I've grown so fond of Ikar these past days that I can say for certain I've never felt anything stronger for another man, but I refuse to look closer on those feelings when they are forbidden. I must not be the only one who knows distance between us is necessary... Ikar has kept a polite and gentlemanly distance since that night. My cheeks flush at the thought, I hope he's not regretful, at least.

I'm pulled from my thoughts when Ikar tugs the hood of his cloak over his head, draping his handsome features in shadows. Rupi peeks from within, huddled near his neck, and I purse my lips as she turns her head and one sassy black eye meets mine.

She still favors him even after he admitted that he's a high officer, and I can't quite forgive her for that yet.

I watch him with a raised brow. "What are you doing?" We're still at least three hours from the city, and we've passed maybe two other travelers.

"Attempting to enter the city without recognition," he says as we begin walking again and he makes further, careful adjustments to his hood.

"For a supposed law-abiding citizen you're acting blazing suspicious." I lift a brow.

"I'd prefer to reach the castle without being stopped. I'm well known in this city, and the charm I used to hide my identity has likely worn off."

Well known for magic-siphoning and other under-handed deals with the fae like he pretended at Mama Tina's? Or a high officer like he said he was?

"You really are a criminal aren't you?" Better that than an officer for the High King. A girl can hope.

"I'm sorry to disappoint you, but for the thousandth time, *no*. I am not a criminal." He says it in that matter-of-fact deep voice of his, and I have to believe he's being truthful. He continues to adjust the hood until it shadows his face to his liking.

When he's finished, all I can see is his strong jaw covered in a day's growth of beard. But I think that even if I saw him covered in his cloak, I'd recognize his confident stride, broad shoulders, and height. He's not one to be easily disguised, the way his confident presence nearly radiates off him, but I don't share my thoughts.

"So you admit to using a charm all this time."

His hood shifts and I know he looks my way, likely gauging if I'm upset with him again.

"They don't work on me, you know." I divulge the secret. I'd bet all the money I make on this contract that no one knows that small, almost useless, detail about the Black Tulips.

I sense his surprise. "...and you didn't recognize me?" His tone is very careful.

"Should I?" I laugh. "You're just a high officer, not the *king*. Even then, I've never seen him, so I guess I wouldn't know." I shrug with a laugh.

I can't see much of anything beneath his cloak, but I can definitely see the muscles of his jaw clench—a sign I've hit a nerve. Does he really think he's so important that commoners such as myself would recognize one of the High King's glorified soldiers? He needs to leave Moneyre more.

The closer we get to the High Kingdom, the busier the road becomes, and few words are exchanged between Ikar and I. Then, the well-traveled path becomes neatly laid cobblestones and is teeming with people. My nerves begin to tingle with anxiety the closer we get, knowing Tatania would choke if she could see me now. It feels so rebellious.

Then the forbidden city is before us, and I see tall, gilded iron gates that stand open with guards in pristine uniforms watching carefully as crowds of people come and go in a constant rush. Ikar leans close to me, and his hand suddenly finds mine. I feel him press a folded parchment in my palm. "Go there and give them this. I'll send word."

I look down, still getting jostled by the movement around me and open it. All that's written is, "The Dapper Canary" in fine penmanship, with "on the royal tab" written beneath, followed by Ikar's signature. And since we don't have access to parchment or quill and ink, I assume this was written while we were still at Mama Tina's. When I look up to ask what this is about Ikar is gone. With my only weapon. Well, besides Rupi and her quill feathers, which are currently stabbing into the tender skin of my neck. I'll admit I feel a little prickly myself at his behavior.

I look all around, turning in a full circle and bumping into other travelers, stumbling when a man with a cart loaded with summer vegetables pushes past, as I try to find him. No way could he have disappeared so quickly, and not only that, why would he? I don't know what I thought, but I certainly didn't plan on being separated at the beginning of this contract.

I quickly find my confused behavior has drawn the attention of a few of the guards, so I stuff the paper in my pocket and quickly continue through the gates and into the city. Don't need trouble with the High King's law enforcement today.

I still feel miffed that Ikar deserted me, but I'm distracted soon enough. I try to keep my mouth from hanging open in awe as I walk through the large city. Shops of various heights line the winding streets in an orderly fashion. Flowers and vines fill flower boxes and large, decorative pots outside shop doors. Ladies in elegant dresses perch on fancy benches, talking and eating pastries purchased from a nearby bakery that emits smells so delectable my mouth waters. I pass a shop with a swinging wooden sign that has a spool of thread pictured, and two dresses hanging in the large window. Another shop catches my eye, this one with a sword on its sign and its front window featuring an impressive assortment of enchanted weapons. Out of habit, I wonder if their weapon enchanter is in need of an Originator, but within moments I catch myself. I don't need to keep searching out contracts any longer, this is my last job as an Originator. I mean it this time. Besides, no one will find me working in Moneyre.

I see a group of Originators coming my way on the already crowded sidewalk and instinctively pull my jacket a little tighter around me, protecting the secrecy of the mark at the base of my neck. Rupi offers a disgruntled hum and a slight poke in the neck with her quill feathers before she settles again on my shoulder beside my braid. The Originators pass, one of their stark white skirts brushing against my tall leather boots. While I hire myself out as an Originator, no one would know it since I dress in mostly dark greens, browns, and black. Working under the facade of being an Originator has been necessary for me to survive, but while the lie has helped me find work, the Originators are the ones who started the rumors about Black Tulips years ago that got them hunted down and killed. I've never loved what I've had to do to survive.

I may not be planning to pay the Black Tulips any longer, but I still need money, and Ikar offered a contract so enticing I couldn't resist taking him up on the offer.

And that brings me to *why* I'm poor as dirt and in this city that is somewhat dangerous for me to linger in. My best friend and fellow Black Tulip, Renna, ran into money trouble and couldn't pay the dues required by the Black Tulips to keep her bracelet active. I ended up taking a risky, dangerous job, which I didn't end up getting paid for since I didn't deliver the criminal. Instead, I'm working for the man I arrested, Ikar, who I was told was a Class A criminal, but be assured, he's not. Instead, he insists he's a high-ranking officer in the High King's army. Which, in my opinion, is infinitely worse. But my traitorous heart likes him, enough to wish that the incredible kiss we shared wouldn't be the last. But people like him don't court people like me. Apparently, though, I enjoy torturing myself because I went ahead and signed a contract to work for him.

I gave Renna my savings to offer her the protection of the Black Tulips that means so much to her... and decided I don't need the bracelet or anonymity it offers any longer for myself.

Especially while I'm on a remote mission in the dangerous and gloam-infested Lucent Mountains. What are the chances I'll meet the High King? I nearly snort right there on the street. It's ridiculous the way Tatania and the other Black Tulips have scared us all these years, and I'm over it. The money was due by today, so I expect something to happen to my bracelet soon. Maybe it'll break, or maybe it'll just stop working. Maybe it'll rust and fall off my wrist in dry, brown ashes. I have yet to find out, since not one of the current Tulips has dared allow their bracelets to lapse.

My contract with Ikar will bring in more money than I've made in the last two years combined. Our job, to find a simple magical flower for the High King. The drawback... it's in the Lucent Mountains, a place overrun and occupied by gloam. Not gonna lie, I'm a little nervous. But if I survive, I don't have to pretend to be an Originator anymore. I'd say that's a pretty good deal.

Instinct urges me to hurry and find The Dapper Canary, which I assume is an inn or tavern. But another window full of an assortment of items catches my eye, and I backstep until it's in full view. I hurry and enter the shop, gazing all around. *This. This is what I want.* I've just entered the shop of my dreams. I walk down one of five rows of tall, wooden shelves. I stop part way down and, with an eye of appreciation, pick up a finely engraved compass, turning and opening it before placing it back gently. Then I find a set of dice encased in glass, and gasp when I see they're made of dragon horn and priced to match. I pass a multitude of other items before I come upon a dainty solid-wood box with the most detailed, tiny bird perched on the edge of its lid. I pick it up and open it, the small hinges moving effortlessly. I don't think, I simply take it to the counter where a kind young woman wraps it in several layers of paper and ties it up while I count out the last of my money to pay for it. Should I be purchasing things for my future shop? No. Do I have room in my pack? No. Am I still buying the box? I slap the money on the counter. This will be perfect to add to the other things I've collected over the years and extra motivation to keep my head on straight during this contract so I can toss off the mask of Originator and open the shop I've always dreamed of. And best of all, be *free.*

The Black Tulip Chronicles Book Two:
Queen of the Night

...Coming in 2025

Keep reading for links to my newsletter and social media pages to stay in the know with sneak peeks, updates, and more!

SIGN UP FOR MY AUTHOR NEWSLETTER

Be the first to learn about Kaylee Jarvis's new releases and receive exclusive content for both readers and writers!

https://www.kayleejarvis.com/newsletter

Acknowledgments

My first and biggest thank you goes to my husband.

When I started this book I never intended to share it. In fact, I was terrified at the thought, but I *needed* to finish it. For me. My husband understood that and never pushed me to share it with him before I was ready, but he would listen to me talk about the plot at all hours of the day and night, help me fix issues that came up, brainstorm ideas, write battle scenes—all before he'd read even one word of my story. It was several months before I worked up the courage to share a scene with him, and when I did... he loved it. After that, he started encouraging me to publish it and continually boosted my confidence when I doubted myself. Without his never-ending support and confidence in me and my abilities this story would simply be a file saved on my computer, only ever read by me. His support changed everything.

Next, I want to thank my kids for putting up with their extra busy mom and always being supportive of my passion to write and tell stories. My family are my first and biggest fans.

Along with my husband and kids, I want to give a special thank you to my mom. Not only has she encouraged me and read my book over and over to help me, she's always ready to listen about what I'm working on.

Special thanks to my dad, other family members, and the

best friends a girl could ask for, who offered immediate and whole-hearted support as soon as they found out I was a writer.

I love you all.

I want to give a huge thank you to the professionals who were a vital part of preparing my book to be published. Whitney, my editor, was incredible. She helped me polish and bring my work to the next level. And Dragana, my brilliant designer, who was ever-patient with a brand new author. She brought my book to life with a gorgeous cover, fantasy map, and more.

About the Author

Kaylee Jarvis loves telling stories filled with fantasy, romance, adventure, and humor. She enjoys writing no-spice, sizzling romantic chemistry, creating complex and relatable characters, and bringing it all to life in unique worlds.

She is originally from Southern Utah. Now, as an active duty military spouse, she makes home wherever the military takes her—and as a bonus, she gets to see her handsome husband in uniform almost every day of the week. She's mom to four rowdy boys and one sweet girl who is the caboose of their family, and pet mom to their much-loved family dog. When she's not writing or reading, you'll find her buying more plants, lifting weights at the gym, and eating dark chocolate (which she believes is its own sort of magic).

www.kayleejarvis.com

Find her on Instagram, Facebook, and TikTok
@kayleejarvis.author

Made in United States
Troutdale, OR
11/15/2024